Trophy Kill

Book One in the Sidney Reed Mystery Series

by

R.J. Norgard

"[*Trophy Kill*] is classic, old-school detective fiction. A beautiful woman. Murder and mystery. Lots of booze and hangovers. Wonderful descriptions of the Alaskan countryside and weather and an array of fascinating people who populate this wilderness. It's a page-turner . . ."
— *Pudding Magazine*

"Norgard does a solid job of making genre conventions feel fresh. A sympathetic lead and nuanced characterizations bode well for future series entries."
— *Publisher's Weekly*

"In this accomplished novel, Norgard brings his own experience as a local newspaper reporter and a private investigator to bear on a mystery that he imbues with a palpable sense of place . . . An offbeat mystery story that builds a strong stage for future whodunits." — *Kirkus Reviews*

"Just as Stieg Larsson's Millennium series is enriched by its Swedish backdrop, R.J. Norgard uses the stark, extreme setting of Alaska to set the tone for his taut thriller. Fans of Larsson's Mikael Blomkvist will make fast friends with P.I. Sidney Reed, the novel's damaged, witty protagonist." — Julia Watts, author of *Quiver*

"*Trophy Kill* goes well beyond offering the ingredients that fans of this genre expect. It is exciting, well-paced, and sprinkled with that special surly humor characteristic of a hard-boiled detective telling us his story . . . I highly recommend it."
— Patrick Lawrence O'Keeffe, author of *Cold Air Return*

Also by R.J. Norgard

Road Kill

A SIDNEY REED NOVEL

R.J. NORGARD

Bird Dog Publishing
Huron, Ohio

Bird Dog Publishing
An imprint of Bottom Dog Press, Inc.
P.O. Box 425
Huron, Ohio/44839
http://smithdocs.net/bird_dog_books

Publisher's Note: This is a work of fiction. Names, characters, places, and incidents are a product of the author's imagination or are used fictitiously. Locales and public names are sometimes used for atmospheric purposes. Any resemblance to actual people, living or dead, or to businesses, companies, events, institutions, or locales is completely coincidental.

Cover photo: Abode Stock 221468174, licensed.

ISBN 978-1-9475-0430-1

Printed in the United States of America

This novel is for the men and women of the Alaska Innocence Project, and for all public defenders and defense investigators who are fighting the good fight.

The truth is never pure and rarely simple.

—Oscar Wilde

Prologue

Snowflakes danced across the bleak and barren highway to the frightful howl of the wind. Willie Olson tugged at the lapels of his tattered wool coat and turned his gaze toward the slate gray building barely visible fifty yards away. The hammering beat of "Highway to Hell" bled from a ground-floor window. He poked gingerly at the bruise on his cheek, cursed under his breath, and kicked angrily at the loose powder swirling around his feet.

A truck thundered past, engulfing him in a roiling white cloud. He spat and crossed over to the westbound lane where, on wobbly legs, he began the long trek toward downtown Anchorage and the comfort of the Brother Francis Shelter.

With an ear-splitting headache and the taste of vomit ringing his mouth, Willie struggled to recall the events of that Friday evening: dinner at the Bean's Café homeless shelter, then smokes and a drink out back with some friends. One of them, Donnie, mentioned a party somewhere on O'Malley Road and a hint of free liquor and pot. Willie had hesitated leaving the familiar surroundings of downtown, but Donnie had assured him *everyone* was invited, so he'd hopped a cab, using what little remained of his Alaska Native corporation dividend money.

The party house was right where Donnie had said it would be. Rock music thumped inside, beckoning him to enter. His spirits lifted. He pressed the doorbell, anticipating a good time.

Willie was unprepared for the sight that greeted him as the door swung open: A dozen white college boys glaring menacingly, as if the Grim Reaper had come calling. He'd seen those same stares—so searing in their condescension—his entire life.

A big man with a fat moustache, muscled arms folded across an expansive chest, spoke first. "You wandered into the wrong party, friend."

Willie silently acknowledged the truth of that statement. He was turning to go when a tall slim guy wearing a wife beater and a crewcut came up to him and, beneath a thin veneer of sarcasm, said, "Don't mind him. We love our Alaska Native friends, don't we, fellas?"

"Sure do," a voice chimed in. Another asked him his name. He mumbled, "Willie."

There were chuckles. Crewcut wrapped a muscular arm around Willie's shoulders and led him to a white plastic chair set against one wall and handed him a drink that had the rusty color of whiskey. He smiled and thanked the man.

Maybe this won't be so bad after all, he thought.

Willie scanned the faces of the young college men as they laughed and talked. Sipping whiskey contentedly, he had begun to mellow. The acrid aroma of weed hung in the air as a blunt made its way from one partygoer to the next. When it was Willie's turn, he took a long drag and dutifully passed it along. It was good, strong weed. One of the group said it was Matanuska Thunderfuck, a local favorite produced in the Mat-Su Valley.

Sweet home Alabama . . .

The white-boy rock music was deafening, but after ten or fifteen minutes he'd managed to tune it out. Everyone was acting like he was one of them, except for the dude with the fat moustache, whose unrelenting stare made him uncomfortable.

He was well into his second cupful of whiskey when the big man's voice boomed above the din of the music. "Hey you! Eskimo Boy!"

Willie's head jerked in the man's direction.

The murmur of voices ceased.

"Haven't you drunk enough of our liquor yet?"

Bleary-eyed, Willie studied the man. He'd taken shit from white assholes his entire life, but he was too mellow from the weed and whiskey to take offense. The music sucked but, hey, at least he wasn't huddling beneath a wooden pallet in a patch of woods in Mountain View. Life was good. He lifted his cup, as if offering a toast, and smiled impishly.

The big man's scowl deepened. "I asked you a question, Cochise."

All eyes were now on Willie, who reached over to set his half-filled cup near the edge of the low glass table in front of him. His aim was poor and the cup spilled its contents on the pale white carpet. Someone chuckled boozily. Someone else cranked up the stereo.

The boys are back in town, the boys are back in town . . .

Crewcut guy sprang from his seat, glaring at Willie. "What the fuck?"

Willie snatched up a napkin from the table and dropped to one knee to clean up the spill, but, before he could, he felt his body being yanked backwards. Meaty hands spun him around until he stood facing a solid wall of angry muscle—the big man from the divan.

"What are you doing here?" the man screamed over the music. "You don't belong here!"

Willie opened his mouth to speak, but the man cut him off. "I don't want to hear a goddam word, capiche?"

Muscled arms spun him in the opposite direction, and he found himself facing Crewcut, who grabbed Willie by the lapels and shook him. "You ruined my fucking carpet, asshole!"

Though the guy was easily a head taller than Willie, a nauseating blend of whiskey and weed assaulted Willie's nostrils as the man spoke. Willie's stomach churned like a washing machine. Without warning, he vomited on Crewcut's gray sleeveless SEAWOLVES t-shirt, hitting the green team logo like a bullseye.

Afterwards, he remembered only flashes: a fist slamming into the left side of his face, rough hands dragging him out into the snow. He'd asked someone to call him a cab. The question had elicited laughter. He was told to call his own fucking cab. He remembered, too, the sight of his own blood in the snow, black as ink under the dim porch light. He staggered to his feet and stumbled toward the highway.

The wind howled with a force that seemed to penetrate deep into his bones. He squinted into the darkness for a glimpse of the Seward Highway intersection—he thought he must be close by now—but saw only a white wall of snow.

A sudden gust of arctic air struck him like a giant fist and he pitched forward into the icy pavement. He rose shivering to his knees, anger boiling up inside him. They wouldn't dare treat him like this in his village, not when his father was a big muckety-muck in the native corporation. In Anchorage he may be just another Street Indian, but in the village, he was somebody.

Fuck 'em, he thought. *Fuck 'em all.*

Willie rose to his full height, spat, and kicked at the snow. He thought about turning around and going back there and kicking all those white boys' asses, and in his rage and the howling wind he didn't hear the truck roaring up behind him until, with a twist of his head, a flash of light caught his eye. He turned and they were almost on top of him—two orbs of blinding white light, racing toward him like craven monsters. He opened his mouth to scream, but his desperate cry was swept away by the wailing wind.

Ten months later

One

Maria said, "Would you mind slowing down?"

"Seriously?" I replied. "I'm doing forty in a forty-five."

"Whatever. You're going too fast."

I glanced to my right and smiled. I may have been driving the car, but my date, Maria Maldonado, was driving me crazy.

It was a Saturday night in late November in Anchorage, Alaska. Conditions had deteriorated rapidly since I'd picked her up at her condominium, but I was determined to press on.

It wasn't easy keeping my eyes on the road with Maria sitting next to me. She wore a black satin evening dress that caressed her delicate curves down to mid-thigh. With each passing streetlight, I caught a tantalizing glimpse of nylon-wrapped leg. Her chestnut hair shone black in the Subaru's shadowy interior.

In a mellifluous voice she said, "Where did you say we're going?"

"I didn't say," I said with a smile she could not see.

"Uh huh," came her unsmiling reply.

It was our first date. A prior attempt at dinner had ended when someone broke into my apartment, rearranged both my furniture and my anatomy. But that's another story.

My name is Sidney Reed. I was a successful private investigator—some say Alaska's best—until life dealt me a shitty hand. Since then I've been living in a dingy apartment above a downtown Anchorage coffee shop. Six weeks ago, out of financial necessity, I'd taken on what I thought would be a simple surveillance assignment. Turns out, it wasn't all that simple. In the process, I met Maria. That's another story, too.

I turned my head and marveled at how lovely she looked in the shadowy light. I said, "Are you working on anything interesting at the moment?"

Maria was a reporter for the *Anchorage Daily News*. She'd migrated to The Last Frontier from Texas a few years back after some kind of trouble down there. In the short time I'd known her, she hadn't been forthcoming about that.

"I'm covering the Rudy Skinner murder trial this week."

The Skinner case was the talk of the town, notable because the victim, Willie Olson, was the son of a prominent Native leader. Maria's assignment to such a high-profile case told me my would-be girlfriend was a rising star at the paper.

"Congratulations. I'm sure you'll do a fine job."

"Thank you, Sidney. This is a big step for me."

I squinted at the flickering lights ahead. Snowflakes the size of golf balls pelted the Subaru's windshield. A slash of stray light revealed the worry in her eyes.

"Maybe we should do this some other time. It's getting worse by the minute." The stress in her voice was palpable.

"We'll be there soon," I assured her.

I eased up on the gas pedal and leaned over the wheel. Eerie strands of light darted between the wiper blades. As the car passed under a sodium vapor lamp, I half-turned toward Maria, her black coat splayed open and her long hair, almost as black, draped over the collar. Her nose and cheekbones cast long shadows across her face, and her eyes were dark and limitless. The light quickly passed, her image fading to black.

I had longed for this night. For the chance to move on, to explore something new and exciting. The words of my psychiatrist, Dr. Rundle, still rang in my head: *What are you waiting for? Call her.*

"Sidney?" Maria's voice was clipped and edgy. "Did you hear me?"

I twisted my head to the right. "What did you say?"

A roving shaft of light brushed her lightly parted lips and then evaporated. Her voice poured out of the shadows.

"I said, watch the—rooooooaaaaaad!"

As her cry filled the space between us, a stray band of light exposed her terror-filled eyes, now fixed on some horror to her front. The instant I pivoted left, a hulking black shape appeared, like a ghostly apparition, in the white-hot glare of the Subaru's headlights.

What I saw in those few nanoseconds before impact—what I will never forget—were two huge lifeless eyes staring down at me. With that image burned into my brain, the car struck the animal's front legs at the knees, snapping them like twigs. Too late, I mashed the brake pedal to the floor as the head and torso of an enormous bull moose sailed over the windshield and crashed down onto the Subaru's roof amid a sickening crunch of metal.

An ear-splitting explosion shoved me back against the seat, launching tentacles of pain through my chest.

Everything stopped.

I sat in stunned silence, chest heaving, a bolt of pale white fabric in my lap and a strange acrid smell assaulting my nostrils. My eyes roamed the dim interior, illuminated eerily by the diffused glow of streetlights and the sweep of headlights as they passed. A powdery white mist hung in the air.

Why is it snowing in the car?

The fabric in my hands provided the answer: the airbags had deployed. A faint moan pulled my gaze to the right, where Maria was shaking her head from side to side. She didn't answer when I asked if she was all right. Her face seemed frozen in an odd, dazed expression. Was it shock?

"Maria!"

Her eyes drifted upward. I followed them and gasped—the roof of the car bulged grotesquely inward, the ominous crunch of twisting metal filling the air.

The roof of the Subaru was buckling under the weight of the dead moose like a beer can in the grip of a wrestler's beefy fist.

"Maria, honey. We have to get out of here—right now."

She mumbled something unintelligible just as an ominous rumbling shook the car's frame.

I reached over and squeezed her arm. "Maria!"

That did it. She swept the air bag aside and swiveled to her right. Seizing hold of the door handle, she shoved with all her might.

It didn't budge.

"It's stuck!" she wailed, her voice laced with fear.

"Try again!" I shouted.

With an anguished grunt she threw her shoulder against the door. It yielded, and she tumbled out onto the snow-covered street.

I unsnapped my seatbelt and reached for the door handle to my left.

Jammed!

I gritted my teeth and pushed, to no effect. Another ominous crunch of metal told me I'd better hurry, so I was marshalled all my strength for one final attempt. It was then that I heard something thump dully against the window. I peered curiously through the glass, but a vague presense, dark and formless, now obscured the window. I couldn't quite make it out . . .

What IS that?

And then I saw it all too clearly: the dangling head of the dead moose draped over the driver's side door, its eyes, bulging dark and vacant, staring eerily back at me. Blood dripped from its gaping maw.

Fuck ME.

I swiveled to my right, scrambling over the center console. My knee slammed painfully against the shifter knob. I grunted and, like a blind contortionist, twisted and rolled into the passenger seat. My body pumping adrenalin, I lunged head-first through the open door, but my left foot became entangled in the deflated air bag and I landed hard on the icy pavement.

With my last ounce of strength, I low-crawled away from the Subaru and callapsed. Exhausted, I sucked in great gulps of air, the fall having knocked the air out of my lungs and sent a fresh wave of pain shooting through my chest. Then a sickening crunch of metal drew my gaze upward, in time to see the Subaru's roof collapsed under the weight of three-quarters of a ton of big, hairy beast, his body filling the interior where we had sat moments before. I gave a shudder.

Fifteen seconds sooner and . . .

I shook off the image and rose shakily to my feet, glanced around and spotted Maria on the side of the road some forty feet away. I made my way to her, my legs unsteady on the slick road.

"Are you all right?" she said as I approached.

I nodded, still huffing from the exertion.

She had her coat pulled tight around her. Flecks of snow roosted atop her head. Her checks were red as fresh apples.

I studied her closely. "Are *you* all right?"

"I'm fine," she snapped.

"That was a close call. We might have been—"

"Dammit, Sidney! I told you to slow down!"

I didn't argue the point. I was glad we were alive.

I turned toward the Subaru, now dead in the middle of the south-bound lane. It had struck the moose's long bony legs and driven underneath its torso like a wedge, so that the roof had absorbed most of the beast's weight. We'd been lucky.

"We'll have to wait for the police," I said. "After they take my statement, I'll call us a cab."

"If you don't mind, I'll find my own way home."

She was trembling from the cold, or from the adrenalin, or both. She'd just been through something deeply traumatic. Some weeks ago, shortly after I'd first met her, she'd revealed to me that her mother had been murdered. I'd tried to get her to open up about it, but she couldn't bring herself to do it. I very much wanted to comfort her now, so I put my hand on her arm. "I'm sorry about this, Maria. I can see that you're upset."

"You're damn right I'm upset. We might have been killed!"

"Yeah, well we weren't."

"No thanks to you!"

Despite myself, I felt my anger rise. "You blame me for this?"

"Yes, I do. You were driving irresponsibly."

Before I could reply, a black three-quarter-ton Chevy, a row of custom spotlights mounted on the cab, pulled up to the curb. Its driver-side window lowered and a young square-jawed man sporting a big white cowboy hat and big white cowboy teeth stuck his head through the window. "Tough break. You folks okay?"

I told him we were. He asked if there was anything he could do.

"If you don't mind," I said, "you could call the police."

"Already done it. They're on the way."

"Thank you. I appreciate you—"

Suddenly Maria rushed toward the truck.

"Sir? Can I get a lift home? This man will wait for the police."

From Sidney to "this man" in just a few short minutes. That's quick work, Sid.

"Glad to, ma'am," he said, touching the brim of his hat.

She turned to me, eyes clouded in anger. "Goodnight, Sidney."

I raised my arm in a wave. "Call you later?"

"Don't bother," she snapped. She climbed in the cab and they sped off into the gloom.

With flying snow whapping my face, I trudged to the far side of the car—what was left of it—and stuck my hand through the passenger side window and pried open the glove box. I wrapped my hand around the Ruger .357 magnum revolver resting inside, and stuffed the gun in my coat pocket. Then I went around to the trunk and took out a reflective red warning triangle and a couple of road flares. I paced off a hundred feet behind the Subaru and I set out the triangle and flares. Three lanes coalesced into two.

Five minutes later an Anchorage Police Department cruiser, its overhead lights flashing, rolled up. I brushed snow from my coat and loped over to it.

A tall, board-straight officer exited the cruiser. His nametag said MILLER. I recognized him from cases I'd worked on. He'd seemed on those occasions to be a straight shooter.

Together we surveyed the damage. He shook his head. "Second one of these tonight."

"You guys ought to make these moose wear reflective tape."

"We would if we could get them to stand still long enough."

After a pause he said, "You look familiar. Aren't you Eddie Baker's investigator?"

"Guilty as charged." I shook his hand. "Sidney Reed."

"Greg Miller. Let's get the ball rolling so you can get out of here, Sidney."

As he reached into his patrol car for his clipboard, I stared mournfully at the remnants of my beloved Subaru, now bedecked with one very dead moose. My first attempt at a date with Maria never happened. Instead, I'd spent the night in the hospital after being assaulted in my apartment. Now this.

In baseball, I believe they call that *Strike Two.*

TWO

I pushed open the door to my apartment at a quarter to midnight and switched on the light. A black ball of fur rushed up to greet me. Wearily, I bent down and scratched her on the head.

"Hey," I said. "Sorry I'm late." She danced concentric circles around my legs, cooing.

Priscilla had been Molly's cat. In a strange way, it felt like a part of Molly still lived inside of her. Sappy, I know, but I missed her that much.

I hung my coat on a hook by the door and headed for the kitchen, grabbed a Corona from the fridge, and returned to the living room. I eased into my cozy old sofa, twisted off the cap, gulped beer, and thought about Maria. Damn moose had put the kibosh on our second attempt at a date. I raised the bottle to my lips. I felt numb, overcome with the mental image of that hairy beast splayed out on the roof of my Subaru. I loved that car.

Damn moose.

I hit my mental delete button, gulped some more beer, and cocked my head toward the corner of the room where Priscilla had claimed her prized spot on the beat-up old rocking chair sitting there. It had been Molly's favorite piece of furniture, a gift from her beloved grandmother. The cat, the rocking chair, and a diary were pretty much all I had left of Molly now. The chair had been all but destroyed a month earlier when an intruder broke in and smashed it over my head. It had cost me a pretty penny to get it repaired, but it had been worth it.

Priscilla needed a place to sleep.

* * *

I woke Sunday morning sweating like a long-distance runner, my heart pounding in my chest. The clock radio beside the bed read 9:37 a.m.

The nightmares went something like this: Molly are walking together in some idyllic setting—often a field of flowers. She is dressed in white and, in fact, everything in the dream is tinted a soft white, like a photograph taken with a diffusion filter attached to the lens. Soon I am lulled into a state of euphoria. Suddenly—inexplicably—she's holding a gun. She presses the barrel against the side of her head. The blast that follows shocks me awake.

I shook off the grotesque image, stepped into the shower, and twisted the handle labeled "C." Frigid water hit me like a punch in the gut. I reveled in it, letting the icy liquid pour over me for a full minute. My fingers traced the outline of the scar on my chest and I winced—my three fractured ribs were healing well enough but still tender to the touch.

I shut off the water and reached for a towel. The soothing voice of James Taylor singing "You've Got a Friend" seeped through the floor from the Mighty Moose Café and into my consciousness and the part of me that still felt normal revealed itself.

I dressed in a hurry, craving caffeine.

"You don't say?" Rachel Saint George slid a steaming mug of black coffee across the counter, eyes aglow as I regaled her with a riveting account of the previous night's moose and Subaru mash-up. I'd gotten to the part where Maria climbed into the pickup truck with the cowboy-hatted Good Samaritan.

"Too bad," she said. "I was starting to like her."

"Me too." I reached for the mug.

"What happened to the moose?"

"Get this," I began. "The cop made a phone call and thirty minutes later a guy in a big flatbed pulls up, winches the carcass onto the bed, and hauls it away."

Rachel sipped coffee and stared. I had her full attention.

"He was from something called the Alaska Moose Federation, a group that distributes roadkill moose to the needy. The cops keep a list of people who want one. Who knew?"

Rachel shook her head in amazement, her wild blaze of red hair swinging around. "I'll be damned." She sipped from her cup. "Too bad about your car. I guess you'll be hoofing it for a while."

"Guess so."

"Call your insurance company yet?"

"Last night. They're taking care of it." I held out a five-dollar bill. She waved it away. "This one's on me."

"Thanks, Rach." Mug in hand, I headed for my favorite table near the window. Despite last night's blizzard, pedestrians were traipsing up and down H Street as though nothing had happened, snow being a common occurrence in Anchorage. The municipality's efficient snow-removal crew had already cleared the streets and the shopkeepers had done the same with the sidewalks. The only hints of last night's maelstrom were the vaguely artsy ten-inch-tall columns of newly fallen snow resting atop the parking meters and in the few spots untouched by shovel or plow.

There were two other customers in the Moose, but that changed when a lanky man in a floppy black coat breezed through the door. I felt a twinge in my gut. Eddie Baker was Alaska's best known and most colorful criminal defense attorney. Over the years we'd worked on many cases together. He glanced around, saw me, and did a double take. After telling Rachel he wanted his usual, he came to my table.

"Hey Sid," he said excitedly. "I've been trying to reach you."

"Sorry about that, Eddie. I've had a rough weekend." I gave him the short version of the previous night's moose encounter. He listened in silence, shaking his head.

"Tough luck, Sid. Thank God you're okay."

I nodded.

He glanced around, fidgeting. "Listen, I'm in a bind. I know you're going through a rough patch, but I'm hoping you can help me out. It's nothing too intense, I promise."

"Why don't you call Dena? She's always looking for work." The moment I said it I realized I sounded like the whiney brother trying to get out of mowing the lawn. *Why don't you ask Billy? He's not doing anything.*

"I tried," he said. "She's visiting relatives outside all this month."

"Outside" is a term Alaskans use to describe anyplace outside the state. A part of me bristled knowing I no longer made Eddie's A list, even though another part of me dreaded what was coming.

"I'll be in my office the rest of the day," he said, interrupting my thoughts. "Come by and hear me out. That's all I ask."

With that, he turned toward the counter, picked up the tall cup waiting for him, laid down a greenback, and practically flew out the door.

Eddie Baker was always in motion.

I stepped outside into the crisp morning air as the sun rose over the Chugach Mountains. Exhaling a shroud of ice crystals, I mounted the shaky iron stairway leading up to my second-floor apartment. Priscilla remained coiled comfortably on the rocker as I came through the door, her head swiveling like an owl's in my direction. I shed my coat, fetched a beer from the fridge, and flopped onto the couch. It was threadbare but comfy, the centerpiece of a non-matching furniture set I liked to call The Sidney Collection. I'd furnished the apartment with a discerning eye, having made the rounds of Anchorage's finest thrift shops and second-hand stores.

Reaching for the remote, I switched on the television and channel surfed until I found a National Geographic special about Polar Bears, but the sight of all that snow reminded me of my disemboweled Subaru. I turned off the set after five minutes.

I sipped beer and thought about Eddie Baker's offer. Why was I so resistant to helping him? After all, it had felt pretty damn good taking on that job a few weeks earlier, despite having ended up in the hospital with three cracked ribs. The money had been good, too. It wouldn't hurt to have more of the green stuff coming through the door.

Of course, I knew the reason why. Molly's death still haunted me. Though almost a year had passed since that fateful day, the nightmares had never stopped. I wanted answers, but there were none to be had. It's not like I hadn't tried. Despite my natural resistance to therapy—real men don't see shrinks—I'd sought the help of Dr. Eliot Rundle, a respected Anchorage psychiatrist. After two sessions, though, I remained pessimistic.

I glanced over at Molly's photo sitting atop the bookcase and smiled. As much as she disliked my chosen profession, she would tell me to take the job and get back to work. *It's what you love, Sidney,* she'd say. And she was right. She was always right.

I lurched out of the sofa, reached for my coat, and headed out the door.

Three

E ddie Baker's office digs were located on the top floor of a five-story office building opposite the main courthouse and a short two blocks from my apartment. The walk was pleasant, the Alaskan sun a welcoming presence after the previous night's storm. I guessed the temperature to be somewhere in the mid-twenties—mild by Alaskan standards. Thanks to the wonders of de-icing technology, my boots touched only wet pavement on the walk to his office. I passed up the elevator for the stairs. It being Sunday, and knowing Eddie as I did, I entered without knocking.

The place was modest enough, with the usual collection of office furniture, bookcases, and filing cabinets. The only item arguably not modest was his desk, which was oak and comparable in size to both his fee and his ego. Atop it were three stacks of file folders, one of which reminded me of the Leaning Tower of Pisa, its ability to remain standing defying all known laws of physics. Nor was the mess confined to his desk. It spilled onto a nearby chair as well as behind his desk, where a credenza bore the weight of several Bankers Boxes with case names scribbled on them.

Eddie stood facing a window that ran the length of one wall and offered a commanding view of Cook Inlet and the mountains beyond. His gaunt frame thus silhouetted, he reminded me of a life-size paper cutout. He was too lost in thought to notice my arrival, so I cleared my throat.

He turned. "Ah, Sidney. Thank you for coming." He crossed the room and shook my hand, his ungainliness and shock of coal-black hair, which appeared not to have experienced a combing in recent memory, belying a keen intellect and a gift for oratory.

"Let's get to it, shall we?" He moved a stack of folders from the chair beside his desk to the floor—his idiosyncratic way of offering me a seat—and I took it. He settled into his, one of those round-backed swivel numbers made of solid cherry, and opened a two-inch-thick file folder.

I looked him over and grinned. He wore a barn-colored wool turtleneck sweater whose neck had stretched beyond all societal norms so that it more closely resembled a fire pit ring. His unkempt hair and days' worth of stubble told me he was in serious pretrial mode. But then, pretrial mode seemed to be his default. Anyone who'd ever worked with him knew all too well his penchant for intense negotiation right up to the start of trial, followed by intense last-minute trial prep. He was quite possibly manic-depressive and most probably obsessive-compulsive, qualities that vexed his courtroom opponents and frustrated his colleagues and staff. Over the years I had come to tolerate his eccentricities as much as I admired his intellect.

He looked up from the beefy file. "Have you been following the Willie Olson case?"

I had—sort of. There was a spare copy of the *Daily News* lying around the Mighty Moose most mornings, and recent editions had devoted copious amounts of copy to the hit-and-run death of Olson almost a year ago. His death had become something of a cause célébre in the Alaska Native community and in the press, given that his father was a prominent Native leader and corporate executive. I predicted front-page copy for at least the next week or so.

Nor had I forgotten Maria's comment that was she'd been assigned to cover the trial for the *News*, yet another painful reminder of last night's close call.

"I know the basics," I said. "Hit and run that went unsolved for months until your client—forget his name—blabbed to a cellmate that he'd hit Olson. APD charged him with murder."

"That sums it up pretty well. My client is Rudy Skinner."

"Who snitched him out?"

"A con named Borman. The guy's doing a nickel at Hiland for

robbery. Rudy was there serving time for possession. They ended up cellmates. You know how it goes."

I did. Getting out of jail was the dream of every inmate. The old hands liked to tell the younger ones the quickest way to an early release was to keep your mouth shut, your ears open, and become a jailhouse snitch. This guy Borman had no doubt seen Rudy as his chance to earn a get-out-of-jail-free card.

Eddie continued: "Borman told the cops Rudy had mentioned hitting a guy with his snowplow. When the cops interviewed Rudy, he confessed to hitting Olson . . . sort of."

"What do you mean, sort of?"

"The confession has problems. Rudy was pretty sketchy on the details. I suspect years of drug abuse have turned his brain into egg salad. The detective led him where they wanted him to go."

"I assume you tried to get his statement thrown out."

He leaned back in his chair and clasped his hands behind his head. "Of course. That went nowhere, so I had an expert look it over. He found problems with the interrogation, places to attack it, but nothing that rises to the level of a false confession."

"What about Skinner?"

"Long rap sheet, drug stuff mostly. I can't help feeling sorry for the guy. I've been talking to the D.A. for the past six months trying to craft a deal, but he's under pressure from Native community leaders to make an example of Rudy. It doesn't help that Fellows has his eye on the governor's mansion and needs the Native vote. To get it, he intends to serve up Rudy's head on a platter." Eddie's eyes narrowed. "They're not offering a deal, Sid. They want him put away."

I nodded. Justice may be blind, but it's not immune to politics. Eddie is as skilled a negotiator as he is a trial lawyer. If there was a deal to be had, he wouldn't have been so desperate to hire me. Most people don't realize the vast majority of criminal cases never go to trial. If they did, our court system would grind to a screeching halt faster than a carload of tourists in New York traffic. Despite the courtroom theatrics featured on television, the real battles are fought over the phone and in attorney's offices. Most end in plea deals. It saves money and time, as well as heartache for the parties who would otherwise have to sit through a grueling trial. Eddie had hoped for a settlement. What he hadn't counted on was the press making a martyr out of Willie Olson.

"I know this isn't your kind of case, Sid. It's more about dotting the i's than finding a smoking gun. I'll need you to interview a few witnesses, babysit my expert, serve a subpoena or two. That's it. How about it?"

He made it sound easy enough, but as I well knew, even the most mundane case can get messy. This one had mess written all over it. On the walk over, I'd decided I would politely hear him out and then explain that I wasn't ready to take on a major case. But Eddie is a hard guy to say no to. I could feel his steely blue eyes drill into me.

"I don't know, Eddie," I began. "I'm still working through some things . . ."

His eyes bore down on me. "Working through some things? Oh, really? I've got a client who's looking at ninety-nine years for second-degree murder. Try working through that."

No one lays on a guilt trip like Eddie Baker. The woe-is-me card didn't work, so I tried a different tack. "There's also the matter of transportation. You may recall I totaled my car."

He eased his chair back and scratched his head. "Tell you what. I'll give you a thousand-dollar advance to work on the case. I'll just subtract it from your fee on the back end. You can use the money to rent yourself a car, okay?"

I'd stepped into Eddie's trap with both feet. So much for telling him no.

Good job, dickhead.

I sat in silence as Eddie reached in his desk, scribbled out a check, and handed it to me. I stuffed it into my shirt pocket and said, "Thanks."

Eddie placed his palm atop a ream-sized stack of paper wrapped with an oversized rubber band. "Here's your copy of the discovery.

After you read it, go see Rudy at the Anchorage Jail. He'll need court clothes and a bit of handholding." He handed me the thick stack of documents. "I took the liberty of preparing a letter of authorization so you'll have jail access."

The bastard knew I'd take the case.

"Oh, one more thing. We've got an evidence viewing at APD tomorrow afternoon. Meet me there at two. You still own a camera?"

"I've got one."

He held my gaze. "Thank you for doing this on such short notice. I owe you one."

"Just one?"

He ignored that. "Rudy's a real burnout. You know . . ."

"Yeah, Eddie. I know."

I came out of my chair, discovery bundled under one arm, and stared out at the cold blue waters of Cook Inlet sparking in the morning sun. The opposite shore rose and morphed into the Alaska Range. To the north, rising above the flatlands, Sleeping Lady Mountain stood stark and frosty white, and on the distant horizon, North America's highest peak, Denali, lay hidden by clouds, unseen but ever-present. On those rare days when Molly pried me away from my work, we would go on hikes and watch nature's grand display from a grassy hillside. Oh, how she loved that view.

Eddie's voice broke through my thoughts. "Not to be rude, Sid, but I've got work to do."

I walked silently out of the room.

Four

I twisted the top off a bottle of Corona, eased myself into the sofa, and stared at the four-inch-thick stack of paper resting on my coffee table.

Damn that Eddie Baker.

I gulped beer and glanced at my watch: 12:45 p.m. I wrote down the time on a yellow legal pad. In order to get paid, I had to keep track of my billable hours and give them to Eddie at the end of the case. It was time to start the clock.

I leafed through the thick stack of material, known as "discovery" in the esoteric parlance of the legal profession. According to the Alaska Rules of Court, a phonebook-thick volume laying out the ground rules for the court system, the state is required to "discover"—turn over—all relevant materials in its possession to the defense. The D.A.'s office stamps each page with a sequential number, thus providing an efficient means of tracking and referencing every document disclosed to the various parties in the case.

The first document in the pile, the indictment, described the charges against Rudy and how the state believed the crime had been committed. Next came the APD's Report of Investigation, comprising the lead detective's summary, and the individual reports of every officer who worked the case. Each contained a narrative of what the officer had seen or done, and included a list of any evidence collected, identifying data on everyone they had interviewed, transcripts of those interviews, and photo logs. Taken together, you got a pretty good idea of everything the cops had done, and why and how they did it.

I grabbed another legal pad from under the coffee table and wrote "Timeline" across the top of the first page. Each time I came across an event, be it a phone call, interview, whatever, I added it to the timeline. Next, I assigned a notebook page for each officer, noting what that officer did and when, and cross-referenced it to my timeline. I also used these pages to record any follow-up questions I had for the officer. Once those preliminaries were out of the way, I read the individual reports, coming away with a pretty clear picture of what happened.

A grade school teacher named Sarah Adams was driving her son home from a basketball game in near-whiteout conditions when she spotted a dark shape lying in the road. She pulled over, thinking someone had hit a dog, activated her emergency hazard lights, and stepped out into the blizzard for a closer look. To her horror, it was the body of a man. She called 9-1-1 on her cell.

When APD officers arrived on the scene, they soon realized they had a hit-and-run on their hands. The victim, a young native male, had been nearly eviscerated by what detectives deduced had been a snowplow blade. They followed a barely visible trail of footprints to an apartment building a quarter mile away, where five college students were having a party.

Interviewed individually—standard police practice—they all said, more or less, that a young native male had knocked at their door around 11 p.m., eager to join in the merriment. They'd asked him "politely" to leave. Later, when the officers compared notes, they noticed discrepancies in the men's stories. With some added persuasion, the men finally admitted "roughing up the Indian" before sending him on his way.

This revelation, though, had brought the officers no closer to establishing who killed Willie Olson. Detectives canvassed the area and came up empty. They examined municipal maintenance records to determine who was on duty that night, then questioned the operators and inspected their trucks. They set up a Confidential Tip Line, hoping someone would come forward. All of their efforts were in vain.

So much for the officers' reports. I fetched another beer and turned my attention to the lab reports produced by technicians at the

Alaska State Criminal Detection Laboratory and the autopsy report filed by the State Medical Examiner's office. The forensics were not helpful. There were no useful tire marks at the scene, and, although the lab boys confirmed Olson had been struck by a snowplow, they could discern little more than the approximate height of the blade.

Southcentral Alaska's heavy snowfalls have spawned a lucrative cottage industry such that snowplow blades adorn countless pickup trucks in the greater metropolitan area. Even if the cops managed to find the right truck, there was a good chance it no longer bore trace evidence of the crime. I realized, as had the detectives involved, that the case would remain unsolved unless someone with knowledge of the crime came forward. No one did, and so the case grew cold and stayed that way for months.

I stood and stretched my legs. It was almost 4 p.m. with a third of the discovery left to read. Rummaging through the fridge, I found a package of sliced ham and half a loaf of rye bread. I made a sandwich and ate it hurriedly, washing the remnants down with my last beer, eager to dive back into the case.

Maybe I miss this after all.

I swung by the rocking chair to scratch Priscilla on the chin, then dug into the next batch of reports.

David Borman was a three-time loser whose conviction for possession with intent to sell had landed him in Hiland Mountain Correctional Center in Eagle River for a five-year stretch. For all his many negative attributes, Borman was an affable fellow, so when they put him in a cell with Rudy Skinner, he made it his mission in life to strike up a friendship. Soon Rudy was regaling Borman with his adventures as a snow removal entrepreneur. At one point in their conversations, Rudy mentioned that on one snowy night he'd hit a dog—at least he thought it was a dog.

Not long after, Borman happened upon a story in the paper about the unsolved hit-and-run death of Willie Olson, and the kernel of an idea was born. I imagined him passing the lonely hours in his cell thinking about his next move. Decision made, he placed a call to homicide detective Mike Banner, telling Banner he thought his cellmate had killed Olson. Skinner was talking a lot ... saying things. Was the detective interested?

Banner was skeptical, but willing to listen. After consulting with the D.A., he told Borman that if he could get Rudy to confess, the state would knock two years off his sentence, contingent upon Skinner's conviction. Banner wanted Borman to wear a wire and get Rudy talking. Borman agreed.

It takes a little finesse and more than a little moxie to be a snitch. You can't just come out and ask the suspect if they did it. You have to gain their trust, then keep them talking. And Borman was good. Very good. Rudy never questioned his cellmate's sudden frequent visits to his "counselor."

The transcripts of the wire recordings told the story. I had to wade through pages of innocuous conversation to get to the good stuff. One particular passage caught my attention.

Borman: Remember telling me you hit a dog?
Skinner: Well yeah, I...I hit a dog but I'm not sure where that...
Borman: You sure it was a dog you hit, Rudy?
Skinner: Well...I think so, you know, it was dark and...
Borman: Yeah, dark. Could've been anything. A moose even.
Skinner: (laughs) Yeah right, a moose. Wasn't anything that big.
Borman: Yeah, smaller though. Maybe even a man, eh Rudy?
Skinner: ...(unintelligible)...dog. A big old dog.
Borman: I know how it is driving in winter. It's so fuckin' dark you can't see shit. And if it's snowin' heavy, forget about it. If I was to hit somebody I don't know I'd even see 'em.
Skinner: ...couldn't see nothin'.
Borman: That native kid that got hit walkin' along the road, I bet he was hard to see.
Skinner: Who?
Borman: The Olson boy. Walkin' down O'Malley Road late at night. Snow plow killed him. It was a sad thing.

Skinner: Yeah, I heard about it. (unintelligible)...a sad thing. You
think?
Borman: Well, you don't even know what you...
Skinner: Did I...(unintelligible)...
Borman: Well, it seems kinda...
Skinner: ...(unintelligible)...it was goddam dark out there.
Borman: You know it was...who's gonna blame you for...
Skinner: ...(sobbing)...I thought I hit a dog...(sobbing)...it was so
fuckin' dark, man.

It went on like that for several pages, but I was getting the drift
of it. Rudy had wandered into a manure patch wearing his Sunday
best. When Banner thought he'd heard enough, he brought Rudy in
for an interview. I propped my feet up on the couch, transcript in one
hand, a beer in the other. I had the next best thing to a front-row seat.
Six pages in, it began to get interesting.

Banner: Do you know why you're here, Rudy?
Skinner: Ah, it's about that kid, isn't it? The one that was killed.
Banner: The Olson boy. That's right, Rudy. We're here because of
what happened to Willie.
Skinner: That was a terrible thing.
Banner: Yes, Rudy. Let me show you just how terrible it was. I'm not
supposed to do this, but I want to show you some photographs.

I imagined Banner opening a folder containing a stack of color
photos taken at the scene—pre-selected by Banner for their visual
impact and clarity—and showing them to Rudy.

Banner: Go ahead, Rudy. Take a real good look.
Skinner: No...That's not...
Banner: Come on, Rudy. Look at them. This is what it looks like
when you hit someone.
Skinner: ...(unintelligible)...That's not...I hit a dog...

Banner: A dog? Does that look like a dog to you, Rudy?

Skinner: No. Well, yes, but...

Banner: That's Willie lying there. Look at him! He had a father and a mother. And two brothers. How do you think they would feel if they saw these?

Skinner: (voice almost a whisper) It's...horrible...

Banner: Yes, it's horrible. We have to find justice for his family. Don't we, Rudy?

Skinner: Yes, of course, justice.

Banner: We have to make this right. For everyone.

Skinner: Yes...Make it right.

Banner had Rudy right where he wanted him. Now it was time to close the deal.

Banner: How fast would you say you were going that night?

Skinner: How fast? I don't...

Banner: In all that snow. Practically no visibility that night.

Skinner: I think, you know, thirty, forty...but I hit a dog and...

Banner: Come on, Rudy, does this look like a dog to you?

Skinner: No, of course not, but...

Banner: Maybe you thought you hit a dog. I can see, if you're going fast, fifty or sixty, you hit something and you can't tell.

Skinner: Well, forty or fifty maybe. And I hit...

Banner: You hit him, right? I get it. You were going fast and you hit him but you don't...

Skinner: It was snowing hard and I hit something.

Banner: The kid, right? You hit the kid?

Skinner: Well, maybe it's possible, I suppose...I don't think...

Banner: Come on, Rudy. It's dark. Snowing like crazy. You're tired...

Skinner: So tired.

Banner: ...and suddenly he's there in the road and you can't stop.

Skinner: Well, I suppose...yeah.

Banner: You didn't want to hit anybody.

It went on like that for another dozen pages. By the end, Banner had him. For the boys in the Major Crimes Unit it meant another case closed, and for the family and friends of Willie Olson it meant closure of a different sort. The only thing missing was a pretty pink bow to wrap it all up with.

At 6:30 I turned over the last page of discovery and set the whole pile off to the side. It had taken me almost six hours to work my way through nine hundred pages and a six-pack. I leaned and took a deep breath, shrugging off the urge to pop over to Annie's for more beer.

I rested my eyes on the stack of paper. It made a neat little package. I've never cared much for neat little packages. The sight of them makes me want to turn over rocks to see what's under them.

Five

From the outside, the Anchorage Jail—or "AJ," as we in the defense community liked to call it—looked like your typical American high school. Squarish and slate gray, the Department of Corrections had built it several years before to replace two older facilities deemed too costly to repair.

The moment I stepped from the car, an icy wind barreling in off Cook Inlet slapped me in the face. I was glad I'd sweet-talked Rachel into giving me a lift. I yanked on my coat flap and hurried inside, where a sign beckoned me to place my valuables on a whirring conveyor belt that passed through an X-ray machine being operated by a bored security guard. I made it through without so much as a buzz or ping and proceeded to a registration station surrounded by a chest-high counter and manned by an attractive woman in her forties. Making no effort to smile, she eyed me sternly. "May I help you?"

I saw no point in small talk. I wouldn't want to be sitting there on a Sunday night either. I said, "I'm here to see Rudy Skinner," and handed her the authorization letter Eddie had given me.

She gave it a cursory glance and shoved a thin black three-ring binder across the counter. "Complete and sign the register. I need a photo I.D. You'll get it back after your visit."

I dug out my driver's license and handed it to her. She snatched a numbered badge from a slotted metal holder and set it on the counter. I clipped it to my shirt lapel.

"Have a seat," she said in an unwavering monotone. "I'll get an officer to escort you in."

I ambled over to a backless metal bench set against the wall and sat down. The bench was gray and cold and perfectly matched the tone this facility was designed to convey, which was: YOU DON'T WANT TO BE HERE. Sometimes I'll hear someone talk about how good inmates have it—three squares a day, television in their room, free medical—and then I remember the countless times I'd been inside correctional facilities and how lucky I was to be able to walk back out.

A sharp clang and echo of metal drew my attention to my left, where a fiercely tall and broad-shouldered officer with rusty close-cropped hair was stepping through a doorway. He strode to the registration station, exchanged a few words with the officer there, then walked over to me. His name tag read BURGESS. He keyed a small black microphone clipped to his lapel. "Central."

The response was immediate. "Central here."

"I need Skinner brought to Visiting Room One," Burgess said.

"Roger," came the reply.

He motioned for me to follow and led me to the door he had just come through. He spoke into his radio. "Cor one." From my many visits here, I knew he was telling Central to open the door designated Corridor One.

The door sang out a loud metallic click. Burgess followed me through the door and into a sally port—a narrow hallway some fifteen feet long, with a door at each end and walls of glass on either side. At the far end he again keyed his mic. "Cor two."

We came out the other side into a long hallway, the far end of which must have been half a football field away. Burgess led me to a series of doors lining the wall to our left. He stopped in front of one labeled VISITING ROOM 1 and spoke into his radio. "Victor one."

Click.

Burgess stood by passively as I opened the door and stepped inside. It clanked shut behind me.

The visiting room was about twelve feet square and bare except for a small metal table with attached benches on each side, not unlike a small picnic table. A narrow window beside the door looked back into the main hallway and an identical window peered into the adjacent visiting room. There was an intercom mounted on the wall near the door. I took a seat and waited.

Roughly five minutes later, the sharp report of the lock announced the arrival of Rudy Skinner. The door closed behind him with that obnoxious noise that was so much a part of this place and he sat down on the cold metal.

He was a short, squat man, about five-eight and slightly stooped. He wore "prison blues"—consisting of loose-fitting trousers and shirt—which reminded me vaguely of pajamas, except these pj's had his prison number stenciled across the front. What little hair he had was silver gray. He wasn't fat but his potbelly made him seem that way. His weathered face, pockmarked cheeks, and sunken eyes all spoke of long-time drug use. His hazel eyes were bloodshot and seemed unable to hold a single point of focus for more than a few seconds. I guessed his drug habit of choice was cocaine or methamphetamine. My money was on meth.

He eyed me warily. "Who the fuck are you?"

"The name is Sidney Reed. I'm Eddie Baker's investigator."

With a vacant look he said, "Baker doesn't return my calls."

"He's preparing for trial. If you have a question, ask me."

"Trial?"

"Your trial starts this week. He picks your jury tomorrow."

His feet drummed on the floor. "I gotta talk to him."

"You can talk to me."

His eyes darted to and fro. "I don't know you."

Eddie was right, this guy was a burn-out. I said, "Look at me, Rudy."

Hands twitching, he glanced up, his eyes two red lumps rimmed with scaly white skin.

"Do you know why you're here?"

He blinked. "Yeah. I'm here for killing that boy."

"Do you remember what happened?"

Like all good defense attorneys, Eddie never asks his clients if they "did it," as doing so is apt to place both him and his client in an uncomfortable position should the client decide to testify. The legal canon of ethics does not permit an attorney to put his client on the stand if he believes the resulting testimony will be a lie, which is why they tend not to ask them a lot of questions. I, on the other hand, want to know everything my client knows. I don't like finding things out the hard way.

Rudy's raw red eyes arced upward, searching his memory. "I was coming back from a job up on the Hillside. Big black dog came out of the dark. I couldn't stop. Couldn't—" Rudy paused, feet tapping the floor, hands twisting as if he were kneading dough. "Knocked him down." He shook his head slowly. "I used to have a lab named Peetie. He looked just like Peetie."

"No, Rudy." I let my voice rise in volume, made him look. "We're not talking about a dog. We're talking about Willie Olson."

His eyes widened into saucers. "Did I?"

"The state of Alaska thinks you did."

"I never . . ."

"The detective said you did and you agreed with him."

"I don't remember nothin' like that, but I musta done it. They said it was a truck like mine that done it. My red Chevy."

"There's lots of trucks like yours, Rudy."

His feet beat a steady cadence. "But I told him I did it."

"You told him you hit a dog. *He* told you it was Olson you hit."

Rudy shook his head and tapped away like a street performer. He folded his arms and hugged his chest, as if trying to squeeze the air from his lungs. "Never saw him. Never . . ."

There was nothing more to be gained from this first meeting, so I gave him one of my old business cards. I'd kept them after all this time.

"Okay, Rudy, I'll be back. Call me if you need to talk." I reached over and pushed the button on the intercom. A few moments later a voice said, "Yeah?"

"I'm done here."

Rudy looked up from the card. "You're Sidney?"

"Sidney Reed. You can call me Sid."

Without blinking he said, "Baker never calls me."

I ignored him. "What size are you?"

"Huh?"

"Pants and shirt size. What are they?"

His shoulders drooped. "I dunno."

I looked him over. "I'm guessing you're a thirty-four waist and thirty length, shirt size large."

"I suppose. What's this about?"

"You'll need clothes for court."

"Oh." His eyes darted back and forth. "Did I kill that boy, Sid?"

"It's not my job to know that, Rudy. It's my job to make the state prove it."

He stared up at me, saying nothing. I shifted on my feet and glanced at my watch. It had been a long day. I wanted to go home and take a hot shower.

Without warning, Rudy lunged from his seat and grabbed the lapels of my coat, jerking me forward, our noses almost touching. He opened his mouth to speak, displaying a cavern of yellowed and rotting teeth. I winced at the stench.

I could have put him on the floor, but sensed he meant me no harm. What he wanted was to get my attention. He definitely had it.

In a dry, throaty voice, he said, "Did I kill that boy?"

Before I could reply, the door clanked and screamed. Rudy eased his grip. Eyes fixed on mine, he slowly backed away as the door swung open. Burgess poked his head in and motioned for me to come out.

Rudy blinked. "That's it?"

"For now," I said. "Don't talk to anyone. I'll be back."

Rudy watched in somber silence as I passed through the door.

"I'll come back for you in a minute, Rudy," Burgess said, and slammed the door, the dull, lifeless sound echoing down the long hallway. He led me back through the sally port to the security station, where I exchanged the badge for my driver's license. The clock on the wall said 8:39.

I could have waited twenty minutes in that cold, gray foyer until

Rachel came for me, but I had to get the hell out of there. I pushed open the door and my lungs devoured the frosty night air. These past dozen years I'd spent more time inside prison walls than I cared to recall, but now I was never so glad to be gone from it. Maybe I was just getting old.

I thought about how Molly must have felt about my late-night trips to the jail. More often than not, she'd already be in bed when I got home. Not wanting to wake her, I'd meander into the study with a cold beer. But there was one time she'd waited up for me. I'll never forget the look on her face—a strange mix of disappointment and anger. We threw words back and forth, but one thing she said stayed with me: "You care more about your clients than you do me."

Her words still haunted me.

Rudy was wasted and pathetic. Reasonable people, if you asked them, would say he wasn't worth the effort. His self-destructive life had brought him to this. But then I thought about his statements to the police and his broken memories and all the roads that led him to this place, and I realized Rudy Skinner was probably an innocent man.

No way could I walk away from that.

Six

At 8:30 Monday morning I was sitting at my favorite table in the Mighty Moose with a mocha and a blueberry muffin. Behind the counter, Rachel Saint George handed a to-go cup of something to a middle-aged man in a dark suit and wandered over to my table.

"So, mister detective," she began, easing into the chair opposite, "what are you going to do about transportation now that your spy mobile is permanently out of commission? I can't afford to keep hauling your sorry ass all over town."

"Spy mobile," I repeated. "That's cute. Actually, I'm renting a car this morning."

Her eyes widened. "Really? No offense, but it costs money to rent a car. How—?"

A raised palm stopped her. "Eddie Baker gave me an advance."

"That was nice of him. Not a permanent solution, though."

"Once I settle with the insurance company, my dear, I'll purchase a replacement."

"Good luck with that," she replied with a grin. We sipped in silence for several moments. "When do you see your shrink again?"

I glanced up from my muffin. At that point in my life, Rachel was the only person allowed to make such an inquiry. Even so, her words evoked a visceral reaction. Was it anger? Shame? I wasn't sure, but I held it at bay. "Later this week. We'll see how it goes."

"That's good, Sid." She looked like she wanted to say more, but didn't.

I washed down the last bite of muffin and stood up. "I better get a move on. I want to be there when the rental place opens at nine."

"Need a lift?"

"No, thanks. The walk will do me good."

"The weatherman says three inches of snow today, so be careful. I couldn't handle the financial burden of losing my only renter."

"Don't worry," I said. "This is the only place I can afford to live."

Rachel's forecast was spot on. By the time I arrived at my destination twenty minutes later, fresh snow had dusted everything in sight. An unimposing sign that read LAST FRONTIER CAR RENTAL hung from an even less imposing one-story building with a dingy yellow exterior that had probably not seen a coat of paint in decades. Slogging up to the front door, I stomped the snow off my feet and went inside.

To my left, a long counter stood between a small waiting area and a larger office area with a desk and an array of office equipment. In the back, a single door bore a sign reading MANAGER in small black letters. A young woman sat at the desk with her legs crossed, filing her nails with one of those flat boards that resemble a popsicle stick. She glanced up, smiled, and rose from her chair. She wore black yoga pants that fit her like a second skin and a light blue blouse with white stripes. We met at opposite sides of the counter.

She was in her mid-twenties, attractive, and she knew it. Her eyes were hazel, just short of pea green, and her lips were full and pouty, like a French actress. Her nose turned slightly upwards, though not too much. Her strawberry blond hair was cut short and freshly washed. She was sexy without meaning to be. Or maybe she did.

"How may I help you?" she said in a soft and velvety voice.

"I need a car."

"You're in the right place. We have lots of cars." She said it sassy-like.

"Well, I just need one. Something in an earth tone. Tinted windows, if possible. All-wheel drive. Perhaps a Subaru?"

"Hmm . . . such specificity. I don't have a Subaru but, I'm sure I can find something for you. Compact or mid-size?"

"Size isn't important. What I need is something with muscle."

"Muscle, eh?" She winked.

"Yes, ma'am."

"I'm too young to be a ma'am. Call me Andrea."

"I'm too old to be anything. Call me Sidney."

"You're cute, Sidney. Maybe we could go out sometime."

I grinned at her cheekiness. "I'm too old for you."

Her pouty lips got a little poutier. "I'm old enough. Besides, I'm mature beyond my years."

"Let's start with a car, okay?"

"Sure thing." Her fingers reached for the keyboard next to her and began tapping. "Guys my age are dumb. Their idea of a good time is getting drunk and stumbling around in a mosh pit."

"You're right, that *is* dumb."

She glanced up while continuing to type. "So . . . go out with me."

"I'd love to, but I'm sort of spoken for."

Her keyboard stopped clicking. "Why didn't you say so?" She tapped some more until an old dot matrix printer—I didn't think anyone used them anymore—began to buzz like a table saw at the back of the room. As the machine spat out paper, she walked over to get it, employing considerably more hip action than the mechanical act of walking required. She tore a sheet off the roll and returned to the front desk. "You're not wearing a wedding band, Sidney. How spoken for are you, exactly?"

Sure enough, I'd removed the silver band prior to my anticipated date with Maria and failed to return it to my finger.

She laid the printout in front of me and planted her elbows on the counter. We were practically nose-to-nose when she said, "Well?"

She was looking for someone more mature than what she'd been accustomed to. I couldn't blame her. Before Molly, I probably would have jumped into bed with her in a heartbeat, but things were different now. Molly's presence—her very essence, it seemed—followed me wherever I went. Then there was the matter of Maria. Would I be seeing her again? Despite the false starts, I wasn't prepared to throw in the towel just yet.

"I'm not in a good place to be seeing anyone right now, Andrea. My wife died not long ago."

"You poor man," she said, frowning. "Sidney, I get it. You've got to listen to that inner voice." Without missing a beat, she slid the printout across the counter and drew circles on it with a pen. "Initial here, here, and here, and sign here please."

I followed her instructions without bothering to read it.

"All set," she said. "I'll make you a copy and get your keys." Strolling to the back of the room, she made no sound, though her body was talking plenty. She arrived at a printer—not the dot matrix, but a big boxy thing that was twenty years old if it was a day. It whirred and coughed up a single white copy, which she swooped up before it stopped moving and then glided over to a big wooden board with rows of pegs, each supporting a set of keys. She found the set she wanted and brought them to the counter. "Burgundy Jeep Cherokee. Runs like a pissed-off grizzly. Give me a few minutes and I'll have it out front, gassed and ready. If you bring it back that way, I won't charge you for gas."

I watched as she laid the photocopy on the counter and wrote something across the top of the page and handed it to me. She winked and said, "My cell number—just in case."

Seven

Minutes later I was following the Seward Highway south, the Jeep nosing its way through a worsening snowfall. A slight tap on the Jeep's gas petal producing a muscled response. Andrea wasn't kidding—the car was a beast. I wasn't expecting to do any surveillance work, but if I did, this car would get the job done. Still, I missed my Subaru. I felt like I'd lost an old friend.

At the O'Malley Road exit I turned eastward toward the mountains. My thoughts drifted to Maria and our interrupted date. It irked me she'd been so quick to anger because of something beyond my control. I wondered if I should call her.

No, I thought. *Let her call me.*

As I neared the crime scene, I kept my eyes peeled for landmarks. Soon enough, I found one: a two-story home I recognized from one of the police photos. I pulled to the side of the road, engaged my hazard lights, and reached for the bundle of photos Eddie had given me. I leafed through them until I located the packet labeled "Scene Photos."

The APD detective who'd taken them had adhered to the golden rule of crime scene photography, first shooting a series of wide shots for context, then medium shots showing the body and the ground surrounding it, and finally, closeups of the deceased, paying particular attention to the wounds and anything else of evidentiary value.

Taken at night with a flash unit, the images were stark and visceral: the ugly scrape bisecting the cheek and nose where his face had struck the pavement, left arm broken and distended, and the fatal wound itself—a fearsome-looking gash where the plow blade struck Olson's body at mid thorax. The camera lens had captured every detail in living color. I've known first-year attorneys to lose their lunch after viewing photos like these, but they become numb to it soon enough. I've seen more than my share over the years.

I climbed out of the car, flying snow pelting my face. I crossed over to the westbound lane and squinted at one of the scene photos, comparing it against my surroundings. Using a telephone pole with a metal plate nailed to it as a reference point, I located the spot where the teacher first saw Olson's body.

I dug out another photo, this one showing Olson's head and torso at the edge of the curb, his legs extending out into the lane of traffic. I glanced around. Sarah Adams, the grade school teacher, had been driving east on O'Malley. I pictured her hugging the road in all that blowing snow, spotting the dark shape, pulling over, no doubt fearful of someone coming up behind her in the storm. She approached the shapeless blob, stooped down, and . . .

A three-quarter ton pickup roared past, leaving an impenetrable haze of drifting snow swirling around me. For a several seconds I couldn't see anything but white. Then it cleared and once again I focused on the scene.

APD detectives never established the precise point of impact due to the absence of skid marks and heavy snowfall that night. The killer had no doubt been traveling at a high rate of speed. There was no evidence he—if it was a he—had made any effort to slow down or stop to render assistance. One thing was clear, though: Olson had been facing the vehicle when it struck him. In all probability the last thing he saw in this world were two headlights bearing down on him.

I shuddered in the stiff wind.

Turning up my collar, I walked along the side of the road for a while, getting the feel of the place. O'Malley Road rose gradually in elevation as it flowed east toward the Chugach Mountains, meaning Olson's killer had been traveling downhill in the dark at a high rate of speed on a slick road.

As I often did in cases like this, I imagined myself as the perp. I'm driving along, it's snowing like crazy, I'm going a bit too fast, when suddenly I hit a guy standing in the road. Why not call the police and tell them some guy darted out in front of me, that I had no time to react? True or not, it was both plausible and forgivable. Unless, of course, I was intoxicated. Or had warrants. Or was coming from or going to some place I had no business being.

Or I *wanted* to kill him.

From my read of the file, the police had considered that last possibility and dismissed it. Willie's friend Donnie knew he would be at the party, but detectives were able to verify Donnie had been at the shelter all night. One of the partygoers might have been pissed off enough to chase him down, but none of them owned a truck with a plow on it. The detectives crossed that theory off their list.

I kept walking. Single-family homes and small two- and four-plex apartments lined the road on both sides. Detectives had gone door to door looking for witnesses, but had come up empty. I took a small digital camera out of my coat pocket and snapped a series of photos of the scene.

Satisfied I could do nothing more here, I returned to the Cherokee and drove slowly east, looking for the apartment where Olson had gone to party. I found it a quarter mile up the hill: a modest four-plex, painted white with green trim. I pushed the buzzer on Number Four while stomping my feet and rubbing my palms together for warmth.

I heard shuffling noises inside. The door was drawn inward by a young man in his mid-twenties with tousled wet hair, like he'd just run a towel through it. I made him out to be six-two, one eighty-five, give or take. The crew neck t-shirt did little to hide his muscled torso. Oatmeal gray sweats completed his ensemble. He had a self-confident swagger that screamed jock. Somewhere inside a stereo played "Smells Like Team Spirit" by Nirvana. I hated that song.

He eyed me suspiciously. "Can I help you?"

"Sidney Reed. I'm a private investigator. And you are?"

"Bill Stansfield." He didn't offer to shake hands. "What's all this about?"

"I'm investigating the death of Willie Olson, the young man—"

"Yeah, I know," he said with unconcealed irritation. "The Indian kid that got killed out here last winter. One of you guys just gave me a subpoena. What do you want now?"

"I represent the defendant, Rudy Skinner."

"I already told the cops everything I know. Go talk to them."

"I like to hear things for myself. May I come in?"

He paused, shrugged his broad shoulders, lacing it with a smirk. "Yeah, sure."

I followed him inside. It was a typical bachelor pad, with clothes and books and other stuff stacked in piles around a small living room. He waved me into a second-hand lounger covered over with a bed sheet. "Excuse the mess. It's finals week."

I waited for him to lower the volume on Kurt Cobain and settle into a chair, then I said, "What's your major?" A good detective always establishes rapport.

"Physical education. I got into UAA on a hockey scholarship." He shifted in his seat. "Can we hurry this along? I've got a date tonight and I need to get ready." He flashed another smirk. "You know how it is."

I hate arrogant jocks. Who was he kidding with the I-have-a-date excuse? It was barely noon. Given my two-smirk limit, I tried really hard not to look annoyed. You know, the rapport thing. "I'll try to make this brief. Tell me what happened the night Olson came over."

He exhaled a bored sigh. "Me and some friends were having a party. You know how these things go. Once word gets out, every-body and his brother are knocking at the door. I didn't know half the people there."

"Including Olson?"

His face darkened. "The dude didn't belong here."

When I was a much younger man, guys like this would piss me off so badly, I couldn't see straight. Then I met Molly. She introduced me to yoga and tai chi and all that new-age stuff. It got so I let most things roll off my back like spring rain. But now Molly was gone and the old Sidney was rearing his misshapen head.

"What's the matter, Bill? Wasn't he white enough for you?"

Forgive me, Molly.

He jumped to his feet and his arm shot straight out, the index finger pointed at me like the tip of a spear. "Hey, fuck you, man! It was supposed to be a party for my school friends. The guy obviously didn't belong here, so we . . . we told him to leave."

"How did you do that, exactly?"

He stared at the pile of dirty clothes at his feet as though he'd like to use it for cover—or pick it up and fling it at me.

"Like I told the cops, we got a little rough with him, okay? We tolerated him for a while, but he was loud and obnoxious. He spilled whiskey on my carpet. It cost me a hundred bucks to get it steam cleaned. Like I said, he didn't belong here."

"Yeah, you made that abundantly clear to Willie."

"We were pretty toasted that night, okay? Anyway, what does any of this have to do with that kid getting killed?"

Nothing. I just like seeing your arrogant ass squirm a little.

"Relax, Bill. I'm just doing my job. How long was he here?"

"Fifteen, twenty minutes."

"What time did he leave?"

"Why don't you look in the police report?"

"I'm asking you."

He smirked for a third time. "You sure don't act like a detective."

"I'm self-employed. Now let's try again. What time did he leave?"

He balled his fists. He wanted very badly to leap over that pile of skid-marked underwear and rearrange my jaw. Part of me wished he would try.

"Somewhere between eleven and eleven-thirty." He rose up out of his chair. "I think we're done. I've got things to do." He glanced across the room and the beginnings of smirk number four appeared on the corner of his mouth like warm spittle. "There's the door, Sidney."

I had no trouble finding it.

I had almost an hour until the evidence viewing at APD, so I swung by Grizzly Burger in Midtown and grabbed a Big Grizzly with cheese and a Pepsi from the drive-up window. I sat in the parking lot, eating my burger and listening to NPR as snow fell gently on the windshield. I conjured up an image of Willie Olson leaving Stansfield's apartment, beat up and pissed off, stumbling along the road in all that blowing snow, the truck barreling down . . .

I devoured a sizeable chunk of burger and washed it down with soda, still thinking. Willie's killer ran him over and kept on going, hoping like hell he never got found out. He couldn't afford to be. He was probably wanted. If he wasn't then, he would be now. Men like that are desperate.

Somewhere in the recesses of my brain, the kernel of an idea sprouted. I swiped my mouth with a napkin and smiled. I balled up the paper bag, stuffed it under the seat, and pulled out onto Benson Boulevard.

The *Anchorage Daily News* occupied a modern two-story building, like so many others built after the '64 quake. I entered the lobby and strolled over to the reception area where a twentysomething gal with bouncy blond hair, a killer smile, and twinkling green eyes greeted me. She wore a nametag that said LADONNA.

"May I help you?"

"Hi, LaDonna. I need to place an ad."

"Classified or display?"

"Classified."

She reached to her right, snatched up a half-sheet sized form, and slid it across the counter. Grabbing a pen from a mug, she pointed it like a wand at the form. "Write your name, address, and phone number here at the top and compose your ad copy in the space below. We charge by the word. You'll find the rates at the lower right."

She handed me the pen, and I stepped to the right while she waited on another customer. I filled in my identifying information and thought about what I wanted to say. Two minutes later I surveyed my handiwork: *Information wanted on a hit-and-run accident on O'Malley Road last January resulting in the death of Willie Olson. All information will be kept strictly confidential.*

Satisfied, I stepped up to the counter and handed LaDonna the form. She read what I had written. "Interesting. Are you some kind of detective, Sidney?"

I half smiled. "Private."

"I'm impressed. So, the way it works is, I assign a box number to your ad. If anyone wishes to respond, all they have to do is call our classified response line and punch in the box number listed in the ad. The call will automatically forward to your phone. Will that work for you?"

"No one will know I placed the ad?"

"That's correct."

"Sounds good," I said. "How soon will it be in the paper?"

"Tomorrow, if you like. How long would you like it to run?"

"A week should do it," I said, and paid for the ad in cash. I wasn't expecting a response, but you never know. A lot of detective work is throwing shit against the wall and seeing if it sticks.

"Will there be anything else, Sidney?"

"Yes," I said hesitantly. "I'd like to speak to one of your reporters. Maria Maldonado."

Her eyebrows lifted ever so slightly at the mention of Maria's name. She gestured across the lobby toward a black phone mounted on the wall. "You can use that phone over there. Punch in the three-digit code next to her name."

I thanked her and went over to the phone. To the left, a framed blackboard contained a list of names in alphabetical order. I found Maria's name and punched 3-5-7 into the black handset. After the first ring, Maria's recorded voice came on. The sound was pure honey to my ears: *You have reached the desk of Maria Maldonado. I am currently out of the office or away from my desk, but if you leave your name and number, I will return your call as soon as possible.*

After the requisite beep, I hesitated, then hung up the phone.

So cool, Sidney. So cool.

Eight

I strolled into the APD Headquarters lobby fifteen minutes later, at 1:56 p.m. Eddie Baker had not yet arrived, though I wasn't surprised. The man would no doubt arrive late for his own funeral. To kill time, I ambled into the APD Museum with its collection of old photographs, badges, patches and uniforms. Memories of my days as an army cop with the CID—the Army's Criminal Investigation Division—came in loose strands.

I emerged into the lobby just as Eddie was coming through the entrance in his trademark quick and nervous gate, navy blue overcoat trailing nearly to the floor. I intercepted his flight path and said, "Hi, Eddie." He wasn't smiling.

"Good. You're here." There was a growl in his tone.

"What's wrong, Eddie? Was there a problem with jury selection?"

"*Voir dire* went well enough." He hesitated. "I just got off the phone with the D.A. He received a complaint from one of his witnesses."

Stansfield. Figures.

"Goddammit, Sid. You can't go around talking to witnesses that way. When you're working on a case, you not only represent the client, you represent me and, for that matter, the entire criminal defense bar. You've been doing this kind of work long enough to know that."

I wanted to tell him Stansfield was an arrogant asshole who deserved it, but my time in the army had taught me a valuable lesson: When you're getting an ass chewing, stand there and take it, then move on.

"Of course," Eddie continued, "I assured him you're a consumate professional who would never badger a witness. He let it drop there."

He stared at me for a moment, waiting for a reply. I didn't

disappoint. "I've been called lots of things, but never consummate. Thanks, Eddie."

"I'm not joking around, Sid. Don't let it happen again. Perhaps I made a mistake bringing you back so soon after Molly's death."

"I'm fine, Eddie—really." I briefed him on my visit to the scene and interview of Stansfield.

He nodded. "Okay, let's get this done."

We approached a series of windows at the far end of the lobby where a young, officious looking cop looked up from a ledger. "May I help you?"

I said, "Eddie Baker and Sidney Reed to see Detective Banner."

He nodded. "Have a seat while I page him."

Eddie and I milled around the lobby. I was about to ask him a question when a door to our right clanked open and the familiar face of Mike Banner appeared. "Gentlemen, come on back."

I followed Eddie through the door and the three of us stood in a narrow hallway with gray-lined walls. After the two of them shook hands, Banner and I eyed each other warily. He hadn't changed in ten months: around thirty-two years old, with boyish good looks that made him appear younger, an oval face that was clean shaven and lightly tanned, with fine features and intelligent blue eyes. His short-cropped hair and trim blue suit completed the picture of a competent and confident detective. He had a reputation to match—the proverbial "straight shooter." Although as a defense investigator I'd worked on the other side of the aisle from him, our interactions had always been pleasant—until one horrific day ten months ago.

We were standing nose-to-nose in my living room at two in the morning, and I was screaming at him incoherently about not knowing his ass from an electric blanket. He stood there, arms folded, taking it all in with saintly patience, knowing that an hour earlier I had walked into my house and found my wife lying next to our bed in a pool of blood.

A swirl of emotions engulfed me. Not only was I embarrassed knowing I'd made a fool of myself in front of a man I respected, but the mere sight of Banner brought back memories of that night with a vividness I hadn't anticipated.

Banner broke the silence. "You're looking well, Sidney." His tone was icy. I managed a nod in reply.

Eddie glanced from Banner to me. "I suspect this has been a long day for all of us. Let's get this over with, shall we?"

The detective nodded and led us down a long hall and into a room lined with metal shelves, at the center of which stood a large stainless-steel table. He told us to wait while he disappeared through a side door, returning a moment later with a gray plastic cart, upon which stood a dozen or so packages of varying sizes, wrapped in plain brown paper and sealed with red evidence tape. Banner placed a large package emblazoned with a red BIOHAZARD label on the steel table.

That could only mean one thing: there would be blood.

Eddie and I watched impassively as he peeled away the evidence tape and gently pulled back the paper like he was peeling open a baked potato. I leaned forward and a foul odor invaded my nostrils. The same smell you get when you take damp clothing, splatter it with blood and vomit and urine, wrap it in brown paper, and keep it in a metal storage cabinet for nine months.

I glanced at Banner and raised my hands. "Gloves?"

"Right." He stepped over to a side table and snatched up a greenish-white box containing clear latex gloves and placed them in front of us. "Help yourself." I plucked two gloves out of the box and yanked the thin, stretchy latex awkwardly into place over my fingers. Eddie did the same.

"Read me the tag number," I said.

Squinting at the tag, Banner read off the number, adding, "Clothing worn by the victim."

I found the corresponding number on my copy of the police report and made a checkmark next to the entry. I set the report aside and stared at the pile of clothing Willie Olson had worn the night he was killed. Breathing through my mouth, I lifted a pair of jeans from the stack and laid them face up on the table. They were flecked with dried mud near the ankles and, higher up, with blood. Someone not accustomed to the sight might have mistaken the blood for black paint or ink or oil, but I knew what it was. There was a thick oily blotch of it near the crotch, and just below the knee there was a dark horizontal line where the material had almost torn through, and I realized that must have been where the lower edge of the snowplow blade caught him.

I took a series of photographs from various angles, then flipped the pants over. The backside held some dirt stains, but that was it. He'd ended up face down and died that way. I shot another series of photos and was about to place the jeans aside when Eddie spoke up.

"Don't forget the pockets."

"Right," I said, stuffing my hand inside both rear pockets and finding nothing. Same with the left front. Then I reached into the right front pocket and pulled out a crumpled up five-dollar bill and a quarter. That was all. I stuffed the money back in the pocket.

Returning the Levi's to the pile, I reached for a green flannel shirt. As with the jeans, I inspected and photographed it front and back. So it went with the rest of the pile: winter coat, socks, boxer briefs, boots. I found some loose change and a liquor store receipt in one of Olson's coat pockets. I photographed the receipt and put it back.

That left only the business records the cops seized when they searched the Muldoon trailer where Rudy lived with his girlfriend, Evelyn Waters. The D.A. would no doubt use them to show the jury that Rudy had operated a snowplow business at the time of Olson's death. We spent the better part of an hour combing through two stain-mottled Bankers Boxes stuffed with musty manila folders.

One box was labeled "Tax & Payroll Records" and contained seven thick manila envelopes, one for each of the last seven years. Each of these contained a stack of ledgers, with numbers written in them in a neat feminine hand. It had been a modest business, configured as a sole proprietorship, with Evelyn Waters its sole employee. She'd kept the books, answered calls, and billed the clients while Rudy pushed the snow. Clearly, Evelyn had kept that business running.

As I sifted through hundreds of sheets of paper, I tried to recon-
cile the diligent, hard-working man reflected in the records with the
drug-addled train wreck sitting in jail. Meth had no doubt taken its
toll on the man.

I set the box aside and turned to its mate, labeled "Business
Records." The various jobs were organized chronologically, each
consisting of two pieces of paper stapled together: a "Call Sheet"—
containing the name, phone number, and location of the customer,
date and time dispatched, and the time the job was finished—and an
invoice. Most customers paid by cash, although a few paid by check.

I zeroed in on the folder for the previous January. It was a hefty
one—January, I recalled, had seen record snowfalls. Eddie hovered
over my shoulder as I thumbed anxiously through the thick packet
of documents, beginning with January first. I noted that, although
there were as many as seven or eight jobs each night, none were out of
order. Soon I came to January Fifteenth—the day Willie Olson died.
There were no call sheets or invoices for that day. Not one.

That's odd.

To make sure, I checked forward and backward, but found nothing for January Fifteenth. In fact, I couldn't find a single misfiled
record—Evelyn Waters had been a diligent bookkeeper.

I whispered, "The January Fifteenth snowstorm was one of the
worst on record. His phone should have been ringing off the hook."

"I couldn't help overhearing," Banner spoke up. "I have a theory
about that. Those records tied your client to Olson's death, so either
he or his girlfriend destroyed them."

Eddie frowned but said nothing.

I glanced at Banner. "What about phone records?"

"They evidently did all their business via landline," the detective
said. "The phone company doesn't keep records of local calls."

Eddie and I exchanged glances.

"Well," Banner sighed. "That about does it."

"Not quite," Eddie said. "We're going to need copies of these."

"You should have requested copies before trial, counselor. I'm not about to ask one of my people to sit on their ass for half a day making copies."

"Sidney can do it. Just give him access to a machine."

I stared at the attorney.

Is there anything else I can do for you, like shovel your driveway?

"Okay by me." Banner said. "Now, will there be anything else?"

"Yes," I said. "We need to see Rudy's truck."

Eddie nodded. "Of course. The truck."

The APD had seized the pickup truck Rudy used in his snowplow business and, although the lab boys had found nothing linking it to Olson's death, we expected the state to claim any physical evidence would have been destroyed by now. We needed to see for ourselves.

Banner glanced at this watch. "It's almost four thirty. I've got reports to finish up. We'll have to reschedule the truck for another time."

"How about tomorrow at three?" Eddie said.

Banner agreed. They both turned to me and I nodded my assent.

While Eddie and I collected our things, I told Banner I'd hook up with him later about the photocopies. He followed us out of the room, locked the door, and escorted us back to the lobby.

The moment we left the building, I turned to Eddie. "No record of any call-outs that night. I don't like it."

"I don't like it either," he said. "It makes my client look guilty."

"Not necessarily. Maybe Rudy was sick that night."

"What difference does it make?" he grumbled. "Rudy can't remember what he was doing yesterday, let alone last January."

"We need to find Evelyn Waters," I said.

The icy wind whipped at his coat flap. "Add it to your to-do list."

"Should I add that before or after my photocopy assignment?"

"Would you rather I did it? Jeez, put your big boy pants on and get it done."

"My point is, the cops should do it, not us."

"It doesn't hurt to meet them halfway."

I kept further comment to myself as we strolled to Eddie's car.

He slid behind the wheel and looked up at me. "Will you be there for my opening tomorrow morning?"

"Probably."

"You don't sound all that enthusiastic. I hope your heart's in it."

I remembered what Molly used to say when she saw my anger was about to erupt like a pot of boiling water. *Take a deep breath, Sidney. Count to ten.*

Heeding her sage advice, I waited until my blood pressure dropped to a safe level and said, "Sure, Eddie. My heart's in it."

He displayed his signature self-assured grin. "Good. I'll see you first thing in the morning." With that, he revved up his Lexus and roared away, the car fishtailing on the icy pavement.

I watched his taillights fade down the street.

Nine

The Jeep kicked up a halo of powdered snow as I sped down Tudor Road, thoughts of the day's events churning around in my head like cow patties in a blender. I needed a drink—a stiff one—but first I had some errands to take care of.

I cut over to Northern Lights Boulevard and pulled into my favorite thrift store. Twenty minutes later I came out with a sports jacket, three long-sleeve shirts, two pairs of trousers, a leather belt, and five pairs of socks. Fifteen minutes after that I walked into the Anchorage Jail lobby, a bundle of clothes under my arm. A tall, thin corrections officer who reminded me of the Barney Fife character from *The Andy Griffith Show* eyed me impassively. "May I help you?"

"I have court clothes for Skinner. He'll need them tomorrow for trial."

He stared at the bundle like it was radioactive. "Are they clean?"

"They should be. I just bought them."

He made a show of exhaling carbon dioxide. "All right then, leave them on the counter."

I did as he asked and trudged out the door. That drink was sounding better all the time. I drove east on Third, then south on Gambell and pulled up to Annie's, a corner market I liked to go to when I needed to stock up on beer and other sundries. Annie, a short, squat Athabascan woman who'd moved to Anchorage from Fairbanks to look after her uncle's store after he passed away, was sitting behind the counter.

"Hello, Annie."

"We're out of Corona, Sid. My supplier didn't make it today. Sorry."

"What *have* you got?"

"Most everything else. Miller, Heine, Amber, Mick."

"I'll take a twelve pack of Amber and a package of hot dogs and buns."

She sped off to collect the items. The way it worked was, you told Annie what you wanted and she brought it to the counter—she didn't like the customers rearranging things on the shelves. She made a profit, though I could never figure out how.

"Ribs on the mend?" she asked from somewhere near the back, referring to my recent injuries.

"The bandages came off several weeks ago. I'm still a bit sore. Not bad, though."

Her tanned face peeked around an aisle. "You want the bun-length hot dogs or regular?"

I leaned over the counter. "Say, what's the deal with bun-length hot dogs, anyway?"

"You say something?" I could hear her rummaging in the back.

"The dog came first, right? I mean, it would have to, wouldn't it?"

"If you say so."

"There's no point in a bun without a hot dog."

"I suppose," a distant voice said.

"So, then why a bun-length hot dog? Shouldn't they be making hot dog length buns instead?"

Annie reappeared, plopped a brown sack on the counter, and stared at me. "Regular it is."

I handed her a twenty-dollar bill. "I think I made my point."

At just after 6 p.m. I pulled into the parking garage downtown where I rented space. Five minutes later Priscilla greeted me with a sweep of her bushy tail. Without taking off my coat I packed the beer and hot dogs in the fridge, said goodbye to Priscilla, clomped down the stairs to the windy street below, and hooked a right on Fourth Avenue. After a brisk two-minute walk, I left the bone-chilling cold of Anchorage's street for the smoky warmth of the Prospector Bar, a favorite with the downtown crowd and the criminal defense community's preferred watering hole.

The place was dark as a cave and smoke-filled, and I loved it. Sixties rock blared from a pair of small black speakers flanking the bar. I paused long enough to allow my eyes to adjust to the dim light. I was settling onto a shaky, upholstery-challenged barstool when a familiar voice said, "Hey, Sid!"

A lanky man with a full black beard that seemed to cover every discernible facial feature except his mouth and eyes came over and leaned on the bar in front of me. It was Daniel "Happy Dan" Dooley, bartender and part owner. I don't know how Dan earned his moniker. I'd always assumed it was his unfailingly rosy disposition. If it was something else, I didn't want to know.

"Second time I've seen you in the space of a month. To what do I owe the privilege?"

"Think of it as a pilgrimage."

"Does that mean you're ready to be counted among the living?"

"Better ask my psychiatrist."

"I'll do that. So, what'll it be? Regular or octane?"

"Octane. I've had a bad day."

"Scotch on the rocks it is," he said, then walked away.

I glanced to my left where, three stools away, a sixtyish man in a leather bomber jacket, gray-streaked black hair swept back in a ponytail, was cajoling a pretty blonde barely half his age. Her fingers were long and delicate, and when she wrapped them around her glass and lifted it to her lips, the silver band on her ring finger reflected light from a lamp behind the bar. She sipped delicately and feigned a smile while he regaled her with tales of his life as a fearless bush pilot. I had an overpowering urge to tell him to hit on someone his own age, and to tell her to go home to her husband.

Happy Dan's return interrupted my thoughts. He set my drink in front of me and leaned on the bar. "Another slower-than-molasses Monday, but who am I to complain? I think I'll spend a few minutes with my favorite private investigator."

I grinned faintly and lifted my glass. The scotch was smooth. I smacked my lips and nodded toward the couple. "Who's the guy?"

He glanced their way. "Rusty Gibbons. Works at Merrill Field."

"What is he, a pilot?"

"Maintenance supervisor. Flew for Mark Air back in the day. Lost one of their planes, or so I hear." The music stopped and he lowered his voice. "Comes in every couple of weeks, usually with a girl." He tilted an eyebrow. "A different girl."

Paul McCartney broke into "Hey Jude" and I half-turned in time to see Rusty brush his date's right cheek with his hand. She smiled shyly and glanced away. It seemed Rusty wasn't so rusty when it came to the ladies.

Dan said, "You're dating now, aren't you, Sid?"

"If you can call it that." I recapped my two attempts to have dinner with Maria, both of which had ended badly. I finished by saying, "Guess I'm unlucky in love."

"You must like her."

I lifted my glass and paused. "I guess I do."

"So call her up."

I conjured up an image of Maria sitting beside me in the Subaru, looking sultry in that black dress. "I'll think about it." I drank scotch and listened to McCartney's frantic wail fade away. I lowered my glass and stared into the amber fluid.

"Sid?" Dan was speaking. "Are you listening?"

"I'm sorry . . . what did you say?"

"I asked if you were working on anything."

I considered the question. "I have a trial starting in the morning."

"No kidding?"

I gave a nod. "Bring me another and I'll tell you all about it."

I staggered the two blocks to the Mighty Moose, staggered up the rickety metal stairs to my apartment, and staggered some more before collapsing on the couch. Priscilla appeared out of nowhere and settled into my lap. I tilted my head back, the previous two hours a blur. I had a vague memory of Rusty the daring bush pilot swaggering out of the Prospector, sultry blonde in tow. A while after that—God knows how long—Dan had told me, "That's it for you, buddy."

I looked at my watch: 10:05 p.m. I thought about calling Maria, but what would I say exactly? The moose was asking for it? No, thanks. I was in no mood for rejection. Truth be told, I was in no condition to speak at all, so I lay there, drifting in and out of sleep, wondering if I should open the package of hotdogs I had purchased earlier in the evening.

At some point, I clicked on the remote and was suddenly wide awake. One of the local stations was interviewing the district attorney about the Skinner trial. "Mr. Fellows," the female reporter was saying, "does your decision to try the Rudy Skinner case yourself have anything to do with your rumored candidacy for governor?"

Fellows put on a show of being offended. "Lucinda, I resent the implication that politics played any part in my decision to try this case. As you know, I have made no formal announcement in that regard. The fact of the matter is, I intend to see that justice is served in the death of Willie Olson. That is my only agenda."

"What an ass," I said, clicking off the set. I sank back into the couch and drifted off to sleep.

Ten

The dream de jour rattled me awake at 5 a.m. like a 6.2 earthquake. I sat on the edge of the bed, chest heaving, sweat rolling off my body.

Too . . . fucking . . . real.

The nightmares that began with Molly's death were visiting me with increasing frequency, and I didn't know how to make them stop.

Naked as a newborn, I liberated a bottle of Amber from the fridge and shuffled off to the living room where random streaks of light drifted in from E Street. I fell onto the couch, twisted off the cap, and swallowed. Then I wiped the cold sweat off the bottle with the opposite hand and smeared it over my face and swore out loud.

Each dream seemed to be a carbon copy of the one before it, right down to the white dress Molly was wearing, the eerie softness of her voice, and the same deafening roar of gunfire. What did it all mean? My next appointment with Doc Rundle was two days away. Although our sessions hadn't produced anything resembling a breakthrough so far, they were all I had.

Talk to me, Molly. What's this all about?

I sipped beer and glanced at her rocker. In the predawn gloom, I discerned Priscilla's vague outline and a memory slid into view. It was a Sunday morning three years ago. I was sitting on the couch in our West Anchorage home, morning paper in hand, immersed in coverage of my latest murder trial. My client's wife and daughter had been shot while they slept and now he was looking at two counts of first-degree murder. I'd been working nonstop for two weeks—interviewing witnesses, serving subpoenas, preparing court exhibits, and a dozen other things. I couldn't afford to think about the victims.

The state was marshaling its considerable resources to put my client away for a very long time. We had to put on a defense.

Molly sat in her beloved rocker, Priscilla burrowed in her lap. She hadn't said a word. Then she shot me a disapproving glance.

"What is it?" I said.

"Sidney, honey . . . how . . ."

I'd been married to her long enough to know that when she uttered the words "Sidney" and "honey" in close proximity, a reproach was soon to follow. I braced myself.

". . . how can you defend those people?"

All defense attorneys and investigators get asked that question, but this was the first time Molly had asked *me*.

"What do you mean, *those* people?" I said.

"People who do awful things."

I set the paper aside. "Everyone is entitled to a defense. What if it were me on trial?"

"You would never kill anyone."

"Okay, what if they have the wrong guy? The system isn't perfect."

Her lustrous green eyes looked right through me. "Is he?"

"Is he what?"

"Innocent."

I thought about how I should answer that. I could have told her it didn't really matter, or that it wasn't for me to judge, or that I was bound by attorney/client privilege, but I couldn't. Not to her.

"No," I said, "he's not."

The look on her face said it all. I might as well have told her I had drowned a puppy. "I love you, Sidney, but I'll never understand how you do what you do." She got up from her rocker, went to the bedroom, and closed the door.

I lifted the bottle to my lips and drained the last of it.

God, I miss her.

Had Molly asked that question about Rudy Skinner, I could honestly say he was innocent.

If only she were here.

I forced myself to think about Rudy's trial. This morning the lawyers would present their opening statements to the jury, District Attorney Grant Fellows arguing that Rudy deserved to spend the rest of his life in prison. Did he do it? Most assuredly not. Could the state prove he did it? That was another question entirely. The thing about criminal defense work is, the defendant's guilt or innocence often doesn't enter into the equation. Not exactly my idea of justice.

At least Alaska didn't have the death penalty. That's one sentence you can't take back.

Somewhere between my second and third cool one, I fell asleep on the couch. When I woke it was 8:10, barely enough time to shower and dress and get to the courthouse, which meant I had to forego a stop at the Mighty Moose for my daily caffeine fix.

And my head hurt like hell.

It was a five-minute walk to the Nesbett Courthouse—plenty of time for the near-zero windchill to numb and redden my cheeks. As I neared the entrance, I caught sight of a cluster of people waving signs and chanting, "Justice for Willie!" Off to one side, a tall, thin native man was speaking to a television news crew. Elderly and distinguished-looking, a thatch of gray hair peeked out from beneath the ruff-lined hood of his tan parka. I recognized him from pictures I'd seen in the media as Leonard Olson, Willie Olson's father. I sidled up close enough to hear the reporter ask, "What impact are you hoping this trial will have on the Alaska Native community?"

Olson squinted into the harsh white light spraying from an attachment atop a video camera. His tanned and leathery face was resolute. "This tragedy has united our community like no other. For too long, the indigenous men and women of Alaska have been marginalized and forgotten. What happened to my . . . my son should never happen to any of our sons and daughters. We will continue to—" Something seemed to catch in his throat. "I'm sorry . . . I can't . . ." Olson turned away from the blaring light and drifted into the crowd.

The reporter turned toward the camera. "There you have it. Native community leader and activist Leonard Olson speaking with us on this bitterly cold Tuesday morning about his fight to improve conditions for Native Alaskans. For him, the struggle is all too personal. We will bring you live coverage, as it unfolds, of the murder trial of Rudy Skinner, the alleged killer of Willie Olson, who was struck down on a South Anchorage street almost one year ago. This is Lucinda Farley reporting. Back to you, Jim." She handed the mic to the cameraman. "Carl, I'm freezing my toosh off out here. What do you say we take it inside?"

I glanced at my watch: 8:47 a.m.

That's not a bad idea, Lucinda.

I made my way upstairs to Courtroom 204. Two heavy double doors led to two more heavy double doors, which opened into a large room. Immediately to my left, a half dozen rows of pew-like seats were already filling up with spectators, many of whom appeared to be Alaska Natives.

A thigh-high wooden partition separated spectator seating from the courtroom proper, access to which was by way of a swinging door on the right side of the room, directly in front of me. To my right, a tall skinny kid was checking the connections to a television camera bearing the call letters of a local television station.

On the opposite side of the partition, two long narrow tables—one for the defense, one for prosecution—were set parallel to it, facing the front of the room. Abutting the wall on the right side of the courtroom was a large, raised gallery, partitioned on all sides and containing three rows of seats each—the jury box.

In the center of the room, elevated above everything else, stood The Bench. From this lofty perch, the judge presided with an all-seeing eye over the legal affairs of men.

Immediately to the left of and below the judge was the witness box, where I'd spent many an hour giving testimony. On the left side of the room, next to the judge's bench, a table held a computer screen, keyboard, telephone, and controls for the electronic recording system used in the courtroom. From here, the court clerk kept the trial flowing smoothly.

At the defense table, Eddie Baker plucked a three-ring binder from a brown leather satchel. To his right stood an imposing figure in an impeccably tailored gray pinstripe suit. He was tall and lean, with an angular jaw and short hair flecked with gray, and I knew instantly I was looking at Anchorage District Attorney Grant Fellows.

Fellows typically assigned cases to one of a dozen assistant D.A.'s, but these were not normal circumstances, for in deciding to try Rudy Skinner himself, Fellows was sending a clear message to the Native community: We're taking this case seriously. And if any credence could be given to news reports and coffeehouse chatter, he was sending another message as well: *Elect me as your next Governor.*

To his right and looking dapper in a beige suit sat Detective Mike Banner. As was the custom in criminal cases, the lead detective in the case, being most knowledgeable of the evidence, served as the prosecuting attorney's right-hand man during trial.

I walked forward through the swinging door to the defense table.

"Morning, Eddie," I said, adjusting my chair.

He glanced up, worry lines bisecting his forehead. "Hey, Sid."

I motioned toward Fellows. "I see they've brought in the big gun."

"More like the big ego," Eddie said.

A movement on my left caught my eye. Through a side door, a broad-shouldered Alaska State Trooper led Rudy Skinner to the defense table and unfastened his handcuffs and leg shackles. Rudy looked sullen as he settled into the chair between Eddie and me, wearing the clothes I had bought him at the thrift store. He offered me a nod and turned to Eddie, who was studying his notes.

"You don't return my calls," Rudy said loudly enough to turn heads in our direction.

"Keep your voice down, Rudy." Eddie leaned closer and whispered, "I explained to you that trial preparation takes time. I can't afford to talk to you every single day. If you have something important to convey to me, call Sidney."

By all means, call Sidney. Our operators are standing by.

Rudy swiveled his head in my direction. I nodded reassuringly. He pursed his lips as if to speak when the clerk's voice filled the room. "All rise!"

There was a low rumble as the courtroom's occupants rose to their feet. A wood-paneled door behind the bench swung inward, and through it a black-robed figure emerged. He was slightly stooped, with a broad rough-hewn face that was clean shaven and slightly tanned. The deep blue of his eyes was apparent even from where I sat, and above them a pair of heavy gray eyebrows perched like giant apostrophes. His splash of gray hair was slightly unkempt. Despite being, at age seventy-nine, Alaska's longest sitting judge, he retained a magisterial presence.

The judge eased his short, squat frame into his padded leather chair and surveyed the assembled masses.

"The Honorable Raymond Jeffries presiding," the clerk said. "Please be seated."

"The court will come to order," Jeffries said, pounding his gavel. He paused briefly as the room fell quiet. "We are here in the case of State of Alaska versus Rudy Skinner, case number 84127." He looked at the attorneys. "Gentlemen, do we have any issues to take up before I summon the jury?"

Eddie Baker and Grant Fellows stood in unison and said they did not.

"Are you prepared to deliver your opening statements today?" Both said they were.

"Very well." He turned to the clerk. "You may send in the jury."

The clerk picked up a telephone and spoke into it. Less than a minute later, a door on the right side of the room opened and, with every eye in the courtroom watching, eight men and seven women filed in and took theirs seats in the jury box.

The last three—two men and one woman—made their way to the back row, far right. These alternate jurors would sit through the trial and hear the evidence, but not take part in deliberations unless the judge dismissed one or more of the regular jurors. Once the clerk had sworn in the jurors, they sat back down, and a hush fell over the courtroom. The judge said, "Mr. Fellows, you may proceed."

The D.A. stood, buttoned his suit jacket, and strode to the lectern positioned between the two opposing counsel tables. "Ladies and gentlemen of the jury, I don't have a long and elaborate opening statement prepared for you. That's because the case before you is remarkably simple. As the evidence will clearly show, on the night of January fifteenth, the defendant Rudy Skinner, driving a pickup truck with a snowplow blade mounted on the front, struck and killed Willie Olson, the 23-year-old son of Native community leader Leonard Olson, in an act of willful murder."

Fellows paused for effect. The room was pin-drop quiet. "Contrary to what you may hear from opposing counsel, this was no accident. We know that because there is absolutely no evidence that brakes had been applied. No tire tracks to show the perpetrator had pulled over to check on Willie. None. What police did find when they arrived on scene was Mr. Olson's battered body . . ."

Fellows' oratory was interrupted by gentle sobbing somewhere behind me. I turned and found the source: a young Native woman sitting next to Leonard Olson in the front row. A sister of Willie's, perhaps. I was about to turn back around when I spotted Maria Maldonado at the far end of the front row. We locked eyes. I tried to read her but could not.

Fellows had paused, letting the girl's gentle sobs play like a movie soundtrack to the courtroom drama unfolding before us.

With pitch-perfect timing, he resumed. "Mr. Olson was not simply struck down by just any vehicle. Oh no. You see, the defendant, Mr. Skinner, operated a snowplow business, and his truck had one of those big steel blades mounted on the front. And when that blade struck Willie at fifty, perhaps sixty miles per hour, well . . . I don't have the words to describe what that blade did to Willie. When you view the police and autopsy photos, perhaps you can find the words. I cannot." He paused again.

"You may be asking yourselves, how do we know it was the defendant? Simple, ladies and gentlemen. The defendant, Mr. Skinner, told us he did it. You will hear the confession he gave to Officer Banner. You'll hear Rudy Skinner say, 'I killed him' in his own words."

"I want you to listen to the evidence very carefully. We're going to lay it all out for you in a very clear and concise manner. Now, Mr. Baker here is going to try to sell you on the idea that his client didn't really mean to confess. He'll even be calling an expert witness to say that Mr. Skinner gave Detective Banner a false confession."

The D.A. paused, letting his eyes bore into the jurors, each in turn. "Don't you believe it. The defendant confessed to this crime! Detective Banner, a highly experienced member of the police department, searched for the culprit like the dedicated officer he is and found only one suspect. That suspect confessed to this crime, and he's sitting right over there at the defense table."

Following the sweep of Fellows' arm, the eyes of the jurors panned over to our table. Rudy stiffened, and for a moment I thought he might leap over the table and tackle the D.A. in mid-sentence. I placed a hand on his left forearm and felt his twitching muscles relax. He eased back in his chair, and I uttered a sigh of relief.

"This case is a simple one," Fellows continued. "Listen carefully to the evidence and by the end of this trial you will conclude, as I did, that Rudy Skinner is guilty of murder in the second degree in the death of Willie Olson. And you will have no choice but to return a verdict of guilty."

As Fellows returned to his seat, I snuck a glance over my shoulder at Maria. She was bent forward, scribbling furiously in her notebook.

"Mr. Baker," the judge's voice boomed.

Eddie rose to the podium. "Good morning. Mr. Fellows told you this is a simple case and, on the surface, it might seem so. We've all heard the expression: the pure and simple truth. A compelling thought. We would all like the truth to be pure and simple, wouldn't we? And yet I am reminded of the words of the great playwright Oscar Wilde who said, 'The truth is rarely pure and never simple.'"

I turned and caught Fellows rolling his eyes.

What an ass.

I glanced at the jurors. *Their* eyes were glued to Eddie.

"We are, after all, here to seek the truth, are we not? And what is the truth? Are we—"

The shrill cry of a cell phone stopped Eddie in mid-sentence. All eyes in the room simultaneously embarked on a search-and-destroy mission to locate the offending sound, which seemed to emanate from somewhere directly behind me.

There's always one jerk in the crowd who didn't get the memo.

The phone rang a second time.

I swiveled around, determined to catch the miscreant red-handed, then realized with mounting dread that everyone in the gallery was staring straight at me—or rather, at the coat hanging off the back of my chair.

My coat.

Oh shit.

In one hurried yet smooth movement, I sprang to my feet, snatched up my coat, and made a b-line for the exit. A swift glance to my left revealed the ashen face of Eddie Baker. I believed, in that briefest of moments, that had Eddie been in possession of an ax, he would have gladly chopped me up into neat little pieces and stacked them like cordwood on my chair.

As I hit the swinging gate, the ringing of the phone rippled through the courtroom like the toll of angry church bells, followed by the judge's deep-chested voice. "I will not tolerate disruptions in my courtroom, Mr. Reed!"

Moving as fast as my legs and courtroom decorum allowed, I whizzed past visitor seating amid a chorus of chuckles and a sea of disdainful stares, past Maria, in whose face I saw a deep well of sympathy, and then through the double doors.

Eleven

The moment I passed through the second door, I fished my cell phone out of my coat and mashed the answer button in the middle of the fourth ring. Breathlessly I said, "Sidney Reed speaking."

There was no response at first, and I thought perhaps the caller had hung up, but then I heard the faint sound of breathing on the line—the fog of hesitation.

"I saw your notice in the newspaper," a woman's voice said, and my body stiffened. I'd almost forgotten placing the ad in the *Daily News*.

"You have information for me?"

She replied instantly. "I know who killed that boy." A kind of weariness ran through her voice—and something else. Was it fear?

As the import of her words took hold, adrenalin surged through my veins like warm honey. "I'm listening, Miss . . ."

"That's not how it's going to work. I'll tell you what I know, but on my terms. Is that understood?"

"Understood."

"Are you familiar with Happy Jack's?"

Dive bar downtown. I'd been inside a few times looking for witnesses.

"I know the place."

"Meet me there in half an hour."

"I'll be th—"

With a click she was gone. I checked my watch: 10:07. It was a fifteen-minute walk to Happy Jack's—ample time to get there and scope things out in advance.

I took the stairs to the lobby, donning my coat as I went. Outside the courthouse, the sun peeked shyly over the tops of the buildings, bringing with it ample illumination but precious little warmth, which would explain why the ranks of protestors had shrunk to half their former size. As I quick-stepped briskly down Third Avenue, though, my mind was not on the temperature but on the prospect of a break in the Rudy Skinner case. Rudy sure could use one of those. Life hadn't dealt him much of a hand so far.

Calling Happy Jack's a dive would have been a compliment. Dank and dingy, it was the kind of place you go if you're looking to score weed, or a hooker, or rendezvous with someone else's wife. I arrived fifteen minutes early, which gave me ample opportunity to get the lay of the land, to see if I was getting myself into something I didn't want to be in.

The place was dead, but then again, it was late morning. The drunks and dopers were still sleeping it off. I ordered an Amber at the bar from a grizzled old sourdough hunched over a small TV set watching a soap opera. I slid onto a stool and laid down a five. He brought the beer without comment. I sipped it and let my eyes roam over the dim interior.

Two men occupied stools at the far end of the bar, speaking in low tones. They ignored me, so I turned my gaze to the roughly dozen tables spread around the room. A middle-aged Native couple dressed in ragged coats, the kind you bought at the thrift store or fished out of a dumpster, occupied a two-seater. They chatted amicably, oblivious to my presence.

That left only a woman of about thirty with stringy bleach-blond hair that fell past her shoulders. A faux fur coat hung heavy on her too-thin body and was splayed open, revealing a low-cut red blouse and black leather miniskirt. The skirt made a half-hearted attempt to conceal a pair of exceedingly long legs shrink-wrapped in black mesh hose. She inhaled deliberately through a cigarette wedged between the index and middle fingers of her right hand. She exhaled even more deliberately, crossed her legs, and smiled. It didn't take much imagination on my part understand why.

Crap.

Hookers swarm Third Avenue like locusts. The cops and cold do a fair job of keeping them off the streets; inside is another matter. They can be good sources of information. This one, though, was going to be an annoyance.

Smiling back at her, I opened my wallet, fetched out a twenty and let it linger between my thumb and index finger. She stood and walked toward me, easing onto the stool next to me. Her teeth were stained and she reeked of cheap perfume.

She eyed the twenty like it was the Hope Diamond. "Buy me a drink?"

"I'll do you one better. The twenty is yours. All you have to do is leave."

She eyed the bill, then me, and frowned. "I don't get it. You want to pay me to go away? Why would you do that?"

"Why do you care?"

With only a moment's hesitation, she snatched the bill from my hand and stuffed it down her blouse. She made a show of buttoning up her coat, shot me a contemptuous look, muttered "You're weird," and stomped out the door.

I grinned and settled in for a wait. Thankfully, the Amber was cold. I finished it and ordered another. It was half gone when the entrance to the bar shot open, followed by a blast of cold air and the diminutive form of a woman wearing a beige parka. A matching hood concealed all but her eyes, cheeks, nose, and mouth. Just inside the door, she stopped and looked around. We locked eyes.

That's her.

I picked up my beer and followed her to a table in the far corner. She stood on the opposite side, staring at me with bright green eyes, her cheeks stung red from the cold.

"I'm Sidney Reed," I said. "You called about the ad."

She nodded.

I motioned toward the seat in front of her. "Please."

When she peeled off her coat, I saw that she was tiny and frail in faded blue jeans and a powder blue cashmere sweater. She had a roundish face and small nose, her jet-black hair swept back and held fast with a scrunchie. She was in her mid- to late twenties and attractive in a girl-next-door sort-of way. Worry lines carved grooves across her forehead. She fidgeted in her seat and wore an expression that said she'd rather be anywhere else than here talking to me. She looked even more frail nestled in her chair.

"You know who I am," I said. "May I ask who you are?"

Her eyes darted this way and that. Her face visibly tightened.

She's scared.

I glanced at my beer. "Where are my manners? Can I get you some—"

"Bloody Mary . . . please." Her voice was surprisingly deep for one so small in stature, and yet there was a softness to it that made me want to like her.

I caught the bartender's attention with a wave. "Can I get a Bloody Mary over here?"

"Sure, pal," he said.

I turned to the girl. "I appreciate you meeting me. It took guts."

"I haven't told you anything yet. I'm not even sure I will."

"I hope to convince you otherwise."

She didn't answer but fidgeted for the better part of a minute and seemed relieved when the bartender brought her drink. I asked for another Amber and he walked away. She brought the glass to her lips and drank with her eyes closed. She opened them and said, "My name is . . . Alice."

"Alice . . . ?"

"Just Alice."

"Pleased to meet you, Alice."

She lifted her glass and emptied it with a few swallows.

Just as the bartender walked up with my beer. I told him, "Another one for the lady, please."

"Sure thing, pal." He picked up my empty bottle and her now-empty glass and left.

I looked at her. "You said you know who killed that boy. Did you mean Willie Olson?"

She smiled faintly. "Can we dispense with being coy, Mr. Reed?"

I lifted the bottle to my lips and set it down again. "I would love it if we did."

"Good." The alcohol had already relaxed her considerably. "Yes, I mean Willie Olson. That boy your client is accused of killing."

She had my full attention now. Whatever this was, it wasn't a prank.

"I know who killed him and I'm willing to tell you all about it, but under no circumstances are you to bring me into it. Are we clear on that?"

"I don't have much choice, do I?"

"Not if you want to hear what I have to say."

At first glance she'd seemed frail as a robin's egg, but now I sensed an inner strength lurking behind those soft green eyes.

The bartender brought her drink and I handed him a twenty. He drifted away.

Alice gulped down half her glass like it was water and then leaned back and pinched her eyelids shut. "Does the name Travis Cooley mean anything to you?"

Travis didn't, but the name Cooley did. Anyone who worked around the Alaska legal system knew that name. "By any chance," I said, "is he related to Rance Cooley?"

She nodded. "He's the youngest of Rance's three sons." Her eyes darted around the room, as though he might be lurking nearby. "Travis and I dated for several years."

I browsed my mental filing cabinet. Rance Cooley owned and operated a junkyard and used auto parts business on the south side. It was rumored in law enforcement circles that he and his sons dealt in stolen parts and God knows what else, although the cops had never been able to pin anything on them. A few years ago, the state charged

Rance with threatening a man with a shotgun in a disagreement over the location of their respective property lines. I knew that because I'd been part of his defense team. His lawyer snared him a sweetheart plea deal with no time served.

Then I remembered something else. "Didn't Travis serve time a few years back for killing an airman from the base?"

"You have a good memory, Mr. Reed. Yes, he got drunk one night and lost control of his truck." Alice paused and wrapped her fingers around the cold glass. "The young man he hit had just gotten off his shift at Elmendorf. Going home to his wife and two-year-old son. Trav blew a point two-five on the Breathalyzer. The judge gave him five years. He served half that." She drank some more Bloody Mary. "I lost track of the number of trashy romance novels I read in the waiting room at Cook Inlet Pretrial." She paused and looked at me, doe-eyed. "He's a good boy, really. He just does stupid shit sometimes."

Don't we all.

I caught her gaze and held it. "Why are we here, Alice?"

She took a deep breath. "It was goddam cold that night, not fit to be out in. Snowing like crazy. An honest-to-gosh blizzard. Travis and I were at his dad's place on O'Malley. Maybe you know the place. They live in a big house back behind the auto parts store."

"I know where you mean."

"The old man was sitting in his big old recliner. He practically lives in that thing. Trav's brothers were in and out, doing this and that. We were watching one of those old-timey shows in black and white—*Beverly Hillbillies*, I think—when Trav's cell phone rang. When he hung up, he said he got called out on a job."

She saw my questioning look and said, "He had his truck tricked out for plowing driveways or whatever—new blade, lights, the whole shebang. There's good money in it during the winter months. Anyway, he headed for the door. I tried to stop him but—"

I interrupted her. "Why did you try to stop him?"

"The weather was flat out nasty, for one. I didn't want him going out in that. And, well, I just had a bad feeling about it, maybe because of what happened before, I don't know. He'd drunk quite a bit that night already and, well, he wasn't even supposed to be driving. His license was still suspended. We had words at the door. Finally, the old man tells me to shut up already and let him get on with it. When Rance Cooley talks, you listen. So . . . he went."

I understood what she meant. Rance was huge—six feet tall, broad of shoulder, with forearms like Popeye and a nasty temper. I remembered his lawyer explaining the terms of his plea deal to him. He'd sat eerily silent at first, cold, gray eyes fixed on a point I could not ascertain. Suddenly, his fury erupted at the mention of his victim's name as he unleashed, in a pronounced Oklahoma drawl, a rapid volley of obscenities, beginning with "That som' bitch!"

Rance Cooley was not someone you'd want to piss off.

Alice sipped, emptying her glass. "I figured he'd be gone a couple hours, but he was back in fifteen minutes, looking white as death. He just stood there staring at us until the old man said, 'Spit it out, boy!' Then Travis says he's driving down O'Malley in all that blowing snow, could barely see the road. He's almost to the Seward when he sees a guy standing in the road, looking at him, and he . . . Poor Travis, he . . . he hits him . . ."

Her voice, broken and trembling, trailed off into silence. Long delicate fingers picked nervously at the edge of the empty glass. "As long as I live, I'll never forget the look on his face. He just kept saying, 'I killed him. Oh my God, I killed him!'"

Alice took her napkin, wet from the perspiring glass, and dabbed her eyes. "Poor Travis. He looked like a lost little boy. He kept saying, 'What should I do? I killed him.'"

As she spoke I noticed her slim fingers caressing the tiny figure of a dolphin attached to a thin gold chain that dangled from her neck. A gift from Travis perhaps?

"Trav knew he should have stopped and helped that boy," she continued, "but a Cooley's first instinct when there's trouble is to run to family, and, well . . ." Alice hesitated, as though she had more to say but thought better of it. She slid a fingertip along the edge of her glass.

When she seemed to have run out of words, I said, "Why did you respond to my ad?"

She stared at her hands. "I'd managed to put that night out of my mind until they arrested your client. Then it got to nagging at me, especially when they said he confessed. It made no sense. I mean, why would he do that?" Her eyes danced in the dim light. "It got so I couldn't sleep, knowing that man was in jail for something he didn't do. Then I saw the ad and I . . . I had to call." She leaned back in her chair and sighed. Her small body seemed to lighten.

Goosebumps danced on my arm. Two days ago, Rudy Skinner's conviction for murder had seemed a foregone conclusion, but now fate had brought this slip of a woman to this seedy Anchorage bar and I very much wanted to believe she was going to save Rudy's neck.

"I'm awfully glad you did," I said. "It took courage."

"Please don't use that word. It's so patronizing. Anyone with a beating heart would do what I did. I just hope it will help your man."

Before I could reply, she scooted her chair back and reached for her parka.

"What are you doing?" I said as she got to her feet.

"I have to go." She said it in the most casual way.

"But we're just getting started. I don't even know your last name. You need to meet Rudy's attorney and—"

She froze, one arm in her sleeve. "No one can know I spoke to you. I thought I made that clear."

"I have to tell the attorney, otherwise there wouldn't be—"

"I said no one!"

You're losing her. Think of something.

I shot to my feet. "Alice, please. Give me two minutes?"

She paused, her eyes flittering wildly. The fear I'd seen earlier had returned with a vengeance. I held my breath.

She eased back into her seat. "All right, Mr. Reed. You have two minutes, but don't expect it to do any good."

How does one explain the criminal justice system in two minutes? It takes longer than that to grill a hamburger.

I took a deep breath. "I know you asked to be left out of it, but for your information to be of any value to my client, the jury has to hear it. And for that to happen, you have to testify."

"I don't understand. I've already told you everything I know."

"Telling *me* is not enough, at least from a legal standpoint. A jury has to hear it from you directly."

"But wouldn't that be hearsay? I didn't witness anything."

"Technically, yes. But there are exceptions to the hearsay rule."

She considered that for a moment. "What if Travis says it?"

"No good, Connie. Even if we brought him into court, he'd have a Fifth Amendment privilege. The judge would make him lawyer up."

She frowned. "This isn't what I was expecting. I thought if I told you, you could just, well, make things right for that man."

"I wish it were that simple."

She grew silent, lost in thought.

Don't screw this up. Get her name and address. Get her under subpoena.

"It really wouldn't be that bad, Alice," I said. "Just come in and tell the jury what you told me. Why don't you give me your address and phone number and we can—"

Her eyes flared. "No! He made me swear . . ."

"Who made you sw—"

Before I got all the words out, she was up and moving toward the door. By the time I was out of my seat, the door had swung shut behind her. I grabbed my coat and followed her into the biting cold.

I gazed about frantically. Fourth Avenue was thick with pedestrians.

Alice was nowhere in sight.

Panic gripped me. If I couldn't locate and identify her, Rudy Skinner was screwed and my name as good as mud. Goopy, slimy mud.

My eyes roamed anxiously over the sea of faces. I'd all but given up when I spotted her beige parka on the opposite side of the street, moving east through the crowd at a fast clip. I dashed into the street, darting between cars across three lanes of traffic and coming out on the opposite side at the spot I'd last seen her. Continuing up the street at a jog, I darted among the throng of pedestrians, an unforgiving wind stinging my face.

Huffing mightily, I pulled up short, wondering if she'd ducked into one of the storefronts. I was considering my next move when the roar of an engine drew my attention to an older model red Ford compact parked immediately to my left. A side look at the head of shiny black hair was all I needed.

It was Alice.

I straightened up and watched her ease into traffic, my eyes drifting downward to the blue-on-yellow Alaska license plate just above the rear bumper. I heaved out a plume of frosty air and reached for the pad and pen in my side coat pocket.

Twelve

I found Priscilla curled up on Molly's rocker when I came through the door. She glanced up, stretched, jumped to the floor, and walked toward me. She only made it halfway, plopping down on the rug.

"Guess what?" I said. "I know who killed Willie Olson."

She stared up at me and yawned.

"I know what you're thinking. Big fuckin' deal."

I hung up my coat, picked her up, and went over to Molly's photo sitting atop the thrift-shop bookcase, her freckled face frozen in time. "Wish you were here to see this."

The flashing light on the answering machine caught my eye, so I eased Priscilla to the floor and hit the playback button. A stilted, androgynously digital voice said, *You have one new message*, followed by a shrill beep. Eddie Baker's voice blared through the speaker: "Hey Sid, what happened to you this morning? You know better than to have your cell phone on in court. Jeffries was pissed. Anyway, I called to tell you I've got a ton of prep to do for tomorrow, so I won't be joining you at APD Impound. Briefing in my office at five. See you then. Oh, and don't forget to copy Rudy's business records." Another shrill beep and the digital voice concluded with, *Twelve thirty-seven p.m. End of new messages.*

I glanced at my watch. He'd called ten minutes ago. I went into the kitchen and opened the fridge, where I found a partially eaten package of bologna and a few slices of white bread. From these I constructed my version of a gourmet sandwich and, bottle of Amber in hand, plopped down on the sofa and mulled over my plans for the day.

It was almost one o'clock, which meant I had a little over two hours to kill before I had to be at the APD Impound to look at Rudy's truck. That might be just enough time to photocopy Rudy Skinner's business records. I mulled over the idea and promptly dismissed it, deciding it would be a better use of my time to search court records to learn all I could about Travis Cooley, Willie Olson's real killer—if Alice was telling the truth. The business records would have to wait.

As I wolfed down my sandwich, chasing it with gulps of cold beer, I pondered the morning's events. Placing that ad in the paper had been a spur-of-the-moment idea—a million-to-one shot. I shook my head and smiled. *Damn, I love P.I. work.*

I didn't quite know what to make of Alice. Her story had the ring of truth, but knowing that wouldn't do Rudy a bit of good if I couldn't get her under subpoena. Even then, Eddie would have to convince Judge Jeffries to allow her testimony. Alice was right about it being hearsay, but I was fairly certain it could come in as an exception to the hearsay rule. I was counting on Eddie to work his magic. All I had to do was find Alice and get her under subpoena.

I finished off the sandwich, took out my cell and punched in a number. On the second ring, the husky female voice of my old Army buddy, Lois Dozier, came on the line. These days she was an investigator for the state medical examiner's office.

"Hey, Sid. I was just thinking about you."

"Lucky me."

"Don't be a dickhead."

"Sorry. Why were you thinking about me?"

"A little bird told me you're working for the defense in the Willie Olson case. Am I right?"

"Guilty as charged."

"It's all everyone's talking about. Heck, it's the biggest trial we've seen up here in years."

"Actually, that's the reason I called." I paused a moment. "I need a favor."

"You have but to ask."

"I need you to run a plate for me."

"Shoot."

I read off the number.

After a pause, she said, "Care to talk about it?"

"Maybe. Buy you lunch tomorrow?"

"That's an offer I can't refuse. Mighty Moose at noon?"

"Make it one, will you? Eddie's going to want me in court."

"One it is. Assuming the plate number is legit, I'll have a name and address for you by then."

"Thanks, Lois."

I spent most of the next two hours at the courthouse sitting at a computer terminal and pouring over case files, learning everything I could about Travis Cooley.

The bulk of his troubles with the legal system centered around the consumption of alcohol. His first DUI, at the tender age of sixteen, had landed him in juvenile court. His second one, four years later, earned him thirty days in jail, a one-year suspension of his driver's license, and fifteen-hundred dollars in fines and court fees. His third DUI, coming only two years after the second, cost a young airman his life. Alice's description of the event had been accurate.

Travis was twenty-five years old when he walked out of prison. Lacking a valid driver's license, he was unemployable, so he went to work for his father. With three DUI's on his record, if he were to be implicated in Willie Olson's death, Travis would very likely spend the better part of his life behind bars. That was a powerful incentive to leave the scene of an accident, or not want to be found by a pain-in-the-ass detective.

The court files held no clues to the whereabouts of Travis or the identity of the mysterious Alice. If he had any brains at all, he'd be in the lower '48 somewhere, or maybe even Canada. I made a mental note to pay a visit to Rance Cooley's place, though I doubted I'd find Travis there.

As for locating Alice, I was counting on Lois Dozier.

* * *

The afternoon sun cast long shadows over the city as I exited the parking garage. Anchorage's efficient maintenance crews had done their work well, clearing the streets of snow and hauling it off in dump trucks to one of a dozen locations where it would sit—miniature mountains of dirty snow—until the warmer days of spring. In light traffic, I made it to APD Headquarters in fifteen minutes.

Looping through the parking lot out front, I spotted Detective Banner sitting behind the wheel of a dark blue Monte Carlo. I pulled into the space next to him and rolled down the window.

"Let's go," he muttered, sounding every bit as cold as he had the day before. I followed him down Elmore Road and past a series of non-descript municipal buildings and a vast yellow fleet of school busses. In a matter of minutes, he pulled alongside a huge slab-sided building the police department used to store and examine vehicles involved in criminal cases.

I stepped out of the Jeep and approached his car, motioning toward the building. "Skinner's truck in there?"

"Afraid not," he said, grinning a little too impishly. "It's in our outdoor lot." I swung around and saw what I can only describe as an ocean of automobiles, from sedans to pickups to panel trucks, all blanketed in snow and surrounded by a chain link fence. Quite a few were little more than twisted chunks of metal. I wondered if my Subaru was in there somewhere, wasting away.

Fucking moose.

"You got something to brush the snow off with?" Banner asked. I didn't and said so.

Banner exited the Monte Carlo, a bundle of keys in one hand, and reached in and got a snowbrush from behind the seat. "You're going to need this," he said, handing it to me.

He stomped off through the snow to the impound lot some ninety feet away. I grabbed my kit bag from the front seat and trailed after him to a pair of swinging gates ten feet wide and eight feet high. Each was held in place by a steel rod fitted into an opening in the ground and bound together with a heavy chain secured by a massive lock. I stood shivering as he fiddled with half a dozen keys until he found the right one, then jerked the rod loose from the gate on the left side and swung it outward in a half-circle, pushing a foot of loose snow along with it.

I followed him through the open gate and down a path two car-lengths wide that bisected the impound lot. As we trudged through the snow, it was apparent we were the first humans who had been here since the last snow—there wasn't a tire track or footprint in sight. I followed behind, letting him break trail.

Fifty yards in, Banner turned left past the skeletal remains of a VW Bug, its squat, rounded profile unmistakable under a foot of snow. A short way past it, he turned. "This is it."

Behind him stood a full-sized pickup truck with a snowplow blade attached to the front, the layers of white frosting giving it a ghostly appearance. I stared at it, then at Banner, and shivered.

God, I hate P.I. work.

I had to give Banner credit—he helped me brush off the snow. A lot of cops would have stood there, arms folded, and let me do all the work. I thought that was decent of him.

Underneath all that snow I found a faded red, older model Chevy pickup with a few bumps and scrapes but otherwise in good condition. Banner stood impassively off to the side as I photographed the truck from several different angles before moving in for close-ups of the blade attached to the front. Since the cops had already gone over it and come up empty, I was pretty sure I wouldn't find any incriminating blood or other organic matter. Still, you never know. It is the obvious things that are most often overlooked.

I knelt down beside the blade. Even with gloves on, numbness invaded my shaking hands, though Banner seemed unphased. I wondered absentmindedly if I'd developed an abnormal sensitivity to the cold.

With the afternoon light fading rapidly, I went over every inch of the blade. No blood. No nothing. I photographed it from multiple angles. Once I was satisfied, I then got out my tape measure and notebook and set to work measuring the distance from the ground to the bottom of the blade, on both ends and in the middle. I also measured the width and height of the blade itself, recording the numbers in my notebook.

As my last order of business, I opened the driver's door and poked my head inside. The bench seat and floor were clean. I got in, scooted over to the passenger side, and popped open the glove box. Inside I found a thin black folio. I examined the contents in the fading light.

There were two pieces of paper tucked neatly behind a clear plastic window. One was the vehicle registration and the other an insurance card that had expired six months earlier. Both bore the name Evelyn Waters and the address of Rudy's trailer in Muldoon.

I looked up and saw Banner stomping his feet, exhaling plumes of frosty air, and glancing at his watch. I took a last look around the truck's interior, checking underneath the visors and behind the seats. The vehicle was clean. Satisfied, I slid out the passenger door and approached Banner.

He asked, "All set?"

"Yep."

The homicide detective retraced his footsteps through the snow. He secured the gate and we trudged side-by-side back to our cars, snow crunching under foot. My encounter with Alice still very much on my mind. A thought occurred to me and I turned to Banner.

"What can you tell me about a guy named Rance Cooley?"

He jerked his head in my direction. "Why do you want to know?"

"I have to interview him on a case. I'd like to know what I'm getting myself into."

For the next few seconds, the only sound was that of boots crunching snow. At last he said, "Do you know Mel Denton in narcotics?"

I smiled to myself. Dent and I were hunting buddies. I'd gotten to know him several years before while working on a drug case. I said, "Yeah, I know him."

"Ask him about Cooley. Mention my name."

"Appreciate it."

We got back to the cars and I turned to him. "Thanks for letting me see the truck."

"The defense has a right to see the evidence. Just doing my job."

I swallowed hard. "I've been meaning to tell you, I'm sorry for the way I acted that night."

Darkness was closing in around us. We stood only a few feet apart and yet he seemed little more than a shadow. Plumes of frost billowed from his mouth. "I'm sorry about your wife, Reed, I really am, but the way you acted that night was bullshit. You not only impugned my integrity, you impugned the integrity of the entire department and the medical examiner's office. I wanted so badly to rearrange your jaw. I'd do it right now, except . . ." His words ended in a burst of frost.

"Except what?"

"Gail, my wife. I went home that night and told her about the call I'd been on. Described the scene and everything you'd said. I told her I felt like beating the shit out of you. She just listened patiently, let me vent. When I was finished, she said, 'How would you have acted if something like that had happened to me?' I thought about that for a long time. And you know what? I probably would have acted the same way you did." He paused, then added, "I'm still pissed at you, though."

"Your wife sounds like a good woman," I said through chattering teeth.

"She is."

We stared at each other through the gloom.

"So was mine," I said at last.

He gripped the door handle and paused, little more than a dark outline. "I hope you find what you're looking for, Reed."

Then he climbed in his car, slammed the door, and drove off.

Thirteen

I walked into Eddie Baker's office at 5 p.m. on the dot. He was leafing through a thick binder and munching maniacally on dry roasted peanuts he'd scooped out of a can sitting on his desk. Eddie never did anything halfway.

I ignored the straight-backed chairs in front of his desk and plopped down in an overstuffed couch off to Eddie's right. Without looking up he said, "Banner is a boy scout. He doesn't go to the john without checking the field manual. He's going to look good up there."

"He may be a boy scout," I said, "but he dicked up this case."

Eddie stopped chewing and looked up. "What are you talking about?"

I gave him the short version of my meeting with Alice. He listened, wide-eyed. When I'd finished, he said, "Jesus."

"My sentiments exactly."

He stood and turned to the huge window behind him. The sun had vanished, leaving a dense purple-blue sky with just a hint of orange as a reminder of daylight's passing. I felt pretty good about myself at that moment. I'd found Willie Olson's killer.

"Dammit, Sid," he said without turning around. "You always pull this shit on me in the middle of trial."

The thing about defense attorneys is, they spend a great deal of time and energy stitching together their case like an elaborate quilt. The last thing they need is the dog peeing on it, even if the end result is a more attractive quilt.

I summoned up my sarcastic detective persona and said, "Gee, Sid, you're the best. You solved the Willie Olson case. How can I ever thank you?"

He spun around. "All right, knock it off. What do you want, a medal? A woman calls you in the middle of trial, claims her boyfriend confessed to killing Olson, and you expect the state to give my client the keys to the city? Who is this woman, anyway?"

"I'm working on that. I don't have her last name yet, but—"

"You don't even know her name?"

"She's scared shitless, Eddie. Can you blame her?"

He shook his head. "She's worthless to me if I don't know who she is. I know you know that."

"Give me a little credit, Eddie." I stared at him hard, making no effort to conceal my annoyance. "I got her license plate number. I'll have her name and address by tomorrow."

He grunted and turned back toward window. After a long pause, he shot me a sideways glance. "I guess this trial has got me on edge. That was good detective work, Sid." He began to pace back and forth behind his desk, his thumb and forefinger on his chin like he was propping it up. "Okay. Once you've identified the girl, do a full workup on her and get her under subpoena. In the meantime, I'll figure out a way to get her testimony in."

"Sounds like a plan."

"And see if you can find Travis. If this Alice woman goes south on us, he'll be our backup witness. I'll have to find a way to use him regardless of the Fifth Amendment issues."

"What if I can get him on tape admitting to it? The D.A. would have to act on it, wouldn't he?"

"If the D.A. were anyone but Grant Fellows, I would say yes. He wants to be governor so bad he can taste it. He's staked his reputation on getting this conviction. Anything short of an airtight confession won't cut it." He stopped pacing and eyed me ruefully. "If you think you can get him to admit it then, by all means, have at it. All I'm saying is, don't pin your hopes on it."

"Okay. I'll see what I can do."

"Good." Eddie sank back in chair. "Anything else?"

"Yeah. I got a look at Rudy's truck this afternoon. I was—"

"Oh, I meant to thank you earlier for taking care of that. Find anything interesting?"

"Could be. I measured the blade. Let me see . . ." I took out my notebook and rattled off the measurements I'd taken at the impound. When I was done, I said, "We may be able to show these are inconsistent with Olson's wounds."

"What would you suggest?"

I raised an eyebrow. "Put me on the stand. I'll testify to the measurements, then you can argue the inconsistencies."

"You really think it will help?"

"What can it hurt?" His blasé attitude irritated me.

He idly flicked his fingers at the corner of his case file. "Grant will simply argue Rudy changed the blade, or drove a different truck."

"So what? Let the jury make up their minds."

"I'm just not sure about this."

He wasn't looking at me when he said it.

"What's not to be sure about? I'll get on the stand, talk about the truck and—"

"Sidney," he said quietly.

"What?" I sputtered in frustration.

"I'm not going to put you on the stand."

I stared at him. Saw the pity in his eyes. Like he'd just told a client he'd lost his appeal.

"But . . . why?"

Eddie cleared his throat. "Don't take this the wrong way. You're a great investigator, Sid. Hell, you identified Olson's killer and you've only been on the case for two days. I can think of a dozen cases I would have lost if it hadn't been for you. It's just that, well, you've been through a lot this past year—enough to throw anyone off their game. I'm worried you'll—"

"Fuck it up?"

He paused, choosing his words with lawyer-like precision. "If I know Grant Fellows, he'll do anything to win. I want this trial to be about Rudy Skinner's innocence, not about your . . . issues."

"What *issues*?"

"You know damn well what issues."

"Seriously, you don't think I can handle testifying about some measurements?"

"You're making this out to be more than it is."

I studied his eye movements. "What *aren't* you telling me?"

Eddie sighed. "I guess you have a right to know. Banner told Fellows about the brouhaha you two had after your wife died. Fellows warned me that if I put you on the stand, he'll argue that your testimony shouldn't be allowed because, well, you're unstable."

"It's absurd. Fellows is grasping at straws."

"I know that, Sid, but I can't afford to have him muddy the waters. And even if he doesn't succeed, once he puts it out there, well, you know. In any case, I can't afford to take the chance. It's nothing personal."

"My ass. This is my reputation we're taking about."

"My point exactly," Eddie said. "Like I said, Fellows wants to win so bad he can taste it. I see no point in helping him do it."

"Unstable," I mumbled, loud enough for Eddie to hear. I glanced up. "You don't think . . ."

"No, I don't. I wouldn't have asked you to work on a major murder case if I thought that."

"That's important evidence that needs to come in."

"Stop worrying. If I have to, I'll send my paralegal to the impound to get the measurements. Banner can freeze his ass one more time."

I nodded solemnly. I couldn't believe Banner had stabbed me in the back like that. After all that talk about how he would have acted the same way if that had happened to *his* wife. What a crock.

Eddie interrupted my thoughts. "You okay?"

"Sure, Eddie."

"Good. We have work to do." He tore off a sheet from a pad of yellow sticky notes and scribbled something. "Jim Hathaway, my expert on false confessions, is flying in on Sunday. Pick him up at the airport, will you? I booked a room at the Sourdough."

"Sure thing." I stuffed it in my shirt and headed for the door.

"By the way," he said. "Do you mind dropping by the jail? I happen to glance over at Rudy during openings and he looked like he was about to have an episode. He's not going to make any friends on the jury if he can't hold it together."

"Will do."

I was almost out the door when I heard: "And Sid?"

I swiveled my head around. "Yeah?"

"Good job finding that witness."

I nodded and walked out the door.

It was nearing 6 p.m. when I turned down my street, past the darkened interior of the Mighty Moose Café—Rachel closed up shop early on Tuesdays. I trudged up the stairs, the frigid wind burrowing inside my coat. I fumbled with the key long enough to feel the sting on my fingertips. Once inside I shucked off my coat and hung it by the door. Priscilla glanced up from Molly's rocker and just as quickly reassumed the position. I shagged a beer and anchored myself to the couch. My conversation with Eddie kept replaying in my head.

Fucking Banner.

I stared at the bottle but didn't open it. Instead, I picked up the phone and dialed the APD central number and asked for narcotics. There was a moment of silence, then a voice said, "Narcotics—Robinson."

"Mel Denton, please."

"I think he's around here somewhere. Lemme put you on hold."

Elevator music serenaded me until a gruff voice broke in. "Denton."

"Dent. It's Sid. Figured you'd be working late."

"Sid? Is it really you?"

"The one and only."

"I'd just about given up on you. How the hell are you?"

"Still stitching the pieces back together."

"And working again, from what I hear."

"That's the rumor."

"Glad you're back in the game, even if it is for the other team."

"Everyone's entitled to a rigorous defense."

"Good old Sid," he chuckled. "Still fighting for truth and justice."

"Hey, it's a dirty job—"

"—but someone's got to do it. Yeah, I've heard that one before. Now let's cut the chit-chat. You and I have a lot of catching up to do. Buy you a drink?"

"Hell yeah. How soon can you get away?"

"I was just about to walk out the door. Meet me at the bar in the Captain Cook in fifteen?"

"I'll be there."

Fourteen

I left my apartment and walked south to Fifth Avenue before turning west, into the mouth of a bone-chilling wind. Three blocks away, the Captain Cook Hotel's three towers, slabs of pale yellow trimmed in brown, dominated the downtown skyline. I held a gloved hand over my mouth to keep my lungs from freezing and made a mental note to pick up a scarf at the thrift store.

The Captain Cook is a treasured Anchorage landmark, the brainchild of an ambitious real estate developer named Walter "Wally" Hickel. When the 1964 earthquake leveled downtown Anchorage, Hickel built the opulent hotel upon its ruins. Later he served two terms as Alaska's governor.

At I Street, I slipped through the Cook's side entrance and started down a long corridor lined with paintings of Captain James Cook who, in the late eighteenth century, became the first person to map Cook Inlet. Even though it added several minutes to my walk, I enjoyed this route through the corridor connecting the hotel's three towers. It gave me a chance to warm up as I strolled past the various shops and restaurants.

At the hotel's sprawling main entrance, I paused to await my friend. A few minutes later, a massive pair of sliding glass doors swooshed open and a familiar figure strolled through.

The quintessential tough cop, Mel Denton was raw-boned and roughhewn, broad shouldered and fit, if you didn't count the paunch betraying his love of drink and prime rib dinners. His sports jacket and shirt always looked slept in and his tie dangled loosely around his neck like it didn't want to be there.

I approached him, right arm extended. "Good to see you, Dent."

"You too, Sid. You're looking well."

"Define well."

"Not dead."

"Works for me."

He motioned toward the bar. "I don't know about you, but I could use a stiff one."

I followed him into a large room—one of several restaurants at the Cook—dominated by a four-sided bar at its center. Booths lined one wall and there was a lounge area in the back. He made for the bar and we settled into a pair of stools away from prying ears.

A pretty girl in her mid-twenties, dressed neatly in a white blouse, black slacks and gray vest, made a beeline for us. She wore a name tag that said KATIE and flashed a friendly, white-toothed smile. "What can I get you gentlemen?"

Denton said, "Johnny Walker Black Rocks and whatever my friend wants." He saw me reaching for my wallet. "Put that away. I've got this."

She turned to me. "Sir?"

"I'll have the same, Katie."

"Can I get you guys anything to eat?"

"Yeah," Denton said. "Bring us two large orders of your famous buffalo wings, would you?"

Her smile widened. "My pleasure."

As she walked away, Denton turned to me. "It's really is good to see you. I thought I was going to have to find another hunting partner."

"I'm not sure I'm ready for that just yet."

His eyes narrowed. "You can't bring her back, Sid. At some point you have to let it go."

"I know that. It's just that I need to make sense of it."

"Don't even try," Denton said. "You'll drive yourself batshit crazy."

I could always count on Dent to cut through the bullshit.

"The thing is, I can't believe she'd take her own life."

"Can't believe it or refuse to believe it?"

"Is there a difference?"

He sighed. "I don't know."

At that moment Katie arrived with our drinks.

Denton placed two twenties on the bar. "Let me know when you need more, will you, Katie?"

"You got it," she said, adding, "Your wings will be up shortly."

As I watched her stroll away, my eyes were drawn to two lone figures sitting in the lounge area in a far corner of the room. One was District Attorney Grant Fellows, still in the suit he'd worn in court that morning. The other guy was unknown to me. His head was roundish and balding, his build pudgy in a rumpled tan suit. I turned back in time to see Dent sip his drink.

"Heard about your little dust-up with Banner." He smacked his lips.

I lifted my glass and held it. "What would you have done?"

"Probably the same thing. Anyway, Banner's a big boy. He can take it."

I sipped and mused, "I'll bet you guys were getting a padded room ready for me down at the station when word got out about what happened."

He eyed me sharply. "We all understood. Hell, it could have been any one of us." He paused long enough to take another drink. "Suicide is a strange thing. You can tell a mother her son was murdered and she'll accept it. Oh, it might take it a while, but she will eventually. But tell her that same son took his own life and she won't believe you—even when, deep down, she knew the signs were there. What they're thinking is, 'Billy would never do that.' And yet suicide is far more common than murder. Figure that one out."

Katie brought out a tray bearing two plates stacked high with chicken wings slathered in barbecue sauce, two sets of silverware, two small bowls filled with a white sauce, and a stack of napkins. "We make our ranch dressing in-house. Give a shout if you need anything else."

Denton rubbed his palms together in anticipation. "Dig in."

I watched, grinning, as he devoured one wing after another with cannibalistic fervor. In contrast, I nibbled. The wings were tasty and the home-made ranch a delight, but my thoughts were elsewhere. I waited until the culinary kamikaze sitting beside me stopped to wipe his fingers and slosh down a finger of Johnny Walker, then I cocked my head toward the back of the room where the D.A. was sitting. "What do you make of those two?"

Turning to look, he sniffed derisively. "Well, well. Grant Fellows and his trusty lap dog, Sergeant Fletcher. Fellows is a show-boater, a political hack. Word is, he's running for governor. I hope he wins, then we'll be rid of him."

"I take it you're not a fan."

"I'm not and I'll tell you why. A while back, one of my guys busted the son of certain state representative on a drug charge. Said rep complained to Fellows that it was a bad stop, which was bullshit. My guy did everything by the book, but that spineless motherfucker refused to back him up and the kid walked."

I sipped some Walker. "What about Fletcher?"

"Lou's a brown-nosing bastard. Bounced around the department, first burglary division, then narcotics, and finally robbery. Nobody wants to work with him. When the investigator job at the D.A.'s opened up, he jumped on it. Guys who were better qualified were passed over because Fletcher is such a kiss-ass." He snatched up a wing. "You know him?"

I shook my head. "Never seen him before."

"Fellows treats him like his little errand boy," Denton chuckled. "I think there's an umbilical cord connecting the two of them."

I polished off another wing, licked barbeque sauce off my fingers, and glanced at my friend. "I'm willing to accept that Molly killed herself. She had issues with depression. There was no evidence of foul play. It's just that . . ."

Dent leaned closer, eyes probing. "What?"

"Every time I try to let it go, my little voice starts talking to me. Like, what if somebody killed her to get back at me?"

"Get back at you for what? Trust me, Sid. That little voice doesn't know its ass from a hole in the ground. "

I managed a thin smile. "I'll bet you have that printed on a sign above your desk. Am I right?"

"I should. It's that good."

He hand-signaled Katie to bring two more drinks, then he said, "Look, Mike's a fine detective. Crosses all the t's, dots all the i's. He usually gets it right."

"Yeah, I know," I grumbled.

"You know what? I have a feeling it will never be over for you."

I didn't answer and we drank in silence. The whiskey slid down with increasing ease.

He glanced up from his plate. "How about we get to the real reason we're here?"

My lips curled in a grin. "I thought we were just two old friends having a drink?"

"We are. And you're too good a friend to shit a crusty old cop like me."

"Banner told you, didn't he?"

"Don't pretend you're surprised. You're not that far gone."

"No, I'm not—surprised or that far gone." I gulped down a mouthful of Johnny Walker, aware that he was staring at me, waiting. I said, "I heard a name . . . Rance Cooley."

"That's a name, all right." He stared forlornly at the remnants on his plate. "Sid, you're a good friend. I trust you more than I do some of the guys in my own department, but I need to tread carefully, seeing as how you're working defense these days. So, I have to ask—what's your interest in Cooley?"

"I'm not representing him, if that's what you mean."

"Well," Denton sighed. "Banner sent you to me. That says something." He lowered his voice. "What I'm about to tell you is close-hold shit, got it?"

I held up my index and middle fingers. "Scout's honor."

He frowned at the gesture. "I swear to God, if you fuck me on this . . ."

"I'm not going to fuck you, okay?"

He glanced around. "We've been getting good intel that Cooley's operating a meth lab, and I don't mean one of these kitchen sink type deals. I'm talking about a large-scale operation."

"At his place on O'Malley?"

He nodded. "We suspect it's in one of the out-buildings behind his house. We've tried getting a look-see, but the remoteness makes surveillance a nightmare."

"Informants?"

"He's way too crafty for that."

Dent stared at the empty glass, seeing something in it I couldn't fathom. He waved Katie over. "Another Johnnie for me and my friend."

When I raised an objection, he squelched it. "Man up and hang with me, okay?"

"Sure, Dent." I wasn't about to stop him now.

"Ever met him? Rance, I mean?"

"Once," I replied. "He pulled an assault charge a couple years back. I was part of his defense team."

"Property dispute with a neighbor. Old man named Boyd. Cooley came this close to sending Boyd to meet his maker."

"You know about that?"

"I know everything there is to know about that asshole."

When Katie brought our drinks, Denton laid another twenty on the bar. "Thanks for taking such good care of us, honey." She snatched up the note, smiled and walked away.

Denton watched her go, then said, "The oldest boy, Bo, runs the day-to-day operations. Ray, the middle son, handles deliveries, according to my sources." He paused to make sure he had my attention. "I don't know what your interest is, but let me tell you something. You don't want to fuck with these guys, Sid. Hear what I'm saying?"

"What about Travis?" I said, trying to sound casual.

Mel raised an eyebrow at the mention of the name. "He's something of an enigma these days. At one time we thought daddy was grooming him to take over the business. Then Travis killed that airman and disappeared." He launched into deboning the wing.

I took a drink, mulling over what he'd said. "Have you checked with probation?"

"Of course. He stopped reporting in eight months ago, so now he's got a warrant for a parole violation. He's officially gone underground."

"Strange, don't you think?"

"That whole family's strange. Came up here from Oklahoma when things got hot down there. Rance did a nickel for manslaughter. Taught the boys to cook meth when they were teens."

"Nice family."

"If your idea of a nuclear family is the Mansons."

I drank the last of my Johnny Walker and looked his way. "Maybe we can help each other."

Wiping his fingers with a napkin, he said, "I'm listening."

I collected my thoughts.

"I want to talk to Travis," I said finally. "Help me find him and maybe I can help you turn him."

"Turn him?" He seemed to mull that over. "Interesting idea. An old drug cop like you wouldn't throw that out there if you didn't have some basis for it."

"Just trying to be good citizen."

Dent gave me a sidelong glance. "I won't bother asking why you want him since you'll just hit me with the usual attorney-client bullshit." He emptied his glass. "Tell you what. I'll let you know if I hear anything, but don't get your hopes up. The man's a ghost."

He idly fingered the empty glass. "Just one thing, though. If you plan on going anywhere near the old man, I want a heads-up. We have an open case. And, if you happen to be on the premises and see anything that looks or even smells like a meth lab, call me and I'll have SWAT out there in thirty minutes."

"Will do." I slid off my seat and zipped up my jacket.

He gave me a sour look. "So soon? We're just getting started."

"Sorry to bug out on you, but I have to look in on my client. Thanks for the drinks, Dent."

"No problemo," he said with a wave of his arm. Almost as an

afterthought, he said, "Let's shoot us some ptarmigan this spring. What do you say?"

"We'll see," I said, smiling. I walked out through the hotel's giant double doors and into the unforgiving cold.

Fifteen

Twenty minutes later I was sitting in Visiting Room One at AJ, staring at the cold gray walls. I was tired, still buzzed from the scotch, and the guard was taking his sweet time rounding up Rudy. Eddie Baker's words still rang in my ears: *I'm not going to put you on the stand.* Where did he get off telling me that? How many times had I testified for him—twenty, maybe thirty?

The angry clank of steel interrupted my thoughts. Rudy Skinner came through the door wearing an orange jumpsuit, his arms and legs shackled. That could mean only one thing: Rudy had gotten in some kind of trouble, and was now in "Lockdown" status.

What has he done now?

Amid the squeal of metal on concrete, he dragged a chair up to the table and sat down. His face was drawn, his mouth curled in a scowl. "Bout time you showed."

"It's nice to see you too, Rudy."

He laughed, the sound amplified grotesquely in the claustrophobia-inducing cell. It was a nervous laugh, born of fear, or perhaps resignation. He tilted his head back, revealing a nasty purplish bruise on the side of his neck.

"Okay, what happened?" I said once the laughter had ceased.

He rubbed his hands nervously. "That fuckin' snitch Borman happened, that's what. Passed him in the hall after dinner and he had a shit-eating grin on his face, so I ask him if he wanted some. The motherfucker sucker-punched me! Can you believe it? Next thing I knew, we're both on the floor throwin' punches. Now, thanks to that rat, I'm on restriction." He jammed his elbows on the table and covered his face with his hands.

I felt for the guy. He shouldn't have let Borman push his buttons, but then again, he shouldn't have been in AJ in the first place.

I leaned forward. "Rudy, look at me."

He lowered his hands and gawked at me like I was his landlord there to collect back rent.

"I'm working on a lead."

He scrunched up one side of his face. "What kind of a lead?"

I hesitated telling him too much in case he decided to blab about it to his cellmate, nor did I want to get his hopes up unnecessarily in the event the whole Alice thing fizzled.

"A lead pointing me to Willie Olson's real killer."

A smile lit up his face. He seized my hand in a two-fisted handshake that shook my whole body. "Thank you, man!"

"You're welcome, I—"

"You did it. You saved my life!" His eyes moistened.

With effort, I reclaimed my hand. "Not so fast, Rudy. I haven't done anything yet."

His smile faded. "You're gonna get me out of here, right?"

"I'm doing my best."

He jumped to his feet, eyes twitching. "I'm going nuts in here."

"Sit down, Rudy," I ordered. He eased himself down. "Now take a deep breath and tell me about your snowplow business."

He set his jittery legs in motion. "What do you wanna know?"

"When Mr. Baker and I looked through your business records, we were surprised how organized they were. Each job documented with a call sheet. Neatly filed. Meticulous."

His eye movements stilled a bit. "That was Evelyn. She kept all the records." He looked away briefly and then back at me. "She took good care of me until the cops arrested me. Then the bitch left me. All those years together meant nothing, I guess."

"I noticed your truck is registered to her."

He shot me a hard look. "She never drove my truck. There's no way—"

"Relax, I'm not worried about that. I just want to know why."

"Insurance company won't cover me because of my record."

"And yet you drove."

"A man's gotta make a living, don't he?"

"I noticed you were constantly busy over the winter."

"Damn right I was. Every time it snowed, I was out there plowing."

"So it seems." I leafed through my notes until I found the entry for the previous day's evidence viewing at APD. "That's why I thought it was odd that there were no call sheets in the file for the night Willie Olson died. Any idea why that is?"

He scratched his head. "Um, no. Like I said, Evelyn kept the records."

"Any idea how I might find her?"

His faced contorted in a sneer. "How should I know? She moved out when they arrested me. I never wanna see that bitch again."

"She hasn't been to see you?"

"Fuck no. Not even a phone call."

"You have no idea where she might be? Think, Rudy. It's important."

His eyes roamed left to right and back again. "I think her sister Julie lives somewhere in town."

"What's Julie's last name?"

"I don't know," he said with a shrug.

"Where does she work?"

He shrugged again.

I expelled a sigh. "That's enough for now." I moved toward the call box, bolted to the wall behind him. "I need you to stay out of trouble. Can you do that for me?"

He stared at me, eyes watery. "Get me out of here, man, or I swear, I'm gonna kill somebody."

I placed a hand on his shoulder. "Listen to me. The state will finish its case on Friday, then it's our turn. See if you can keep it together until then, okay?"

"I'll try, Sidney."

It was the first time he'd called me Sidney.

I pushed the silver call button. The box squawked out, "Yes?"

"I'm done here."

"Okay," came the reply.

I turned to Rudy. "One more thing. Actually two. First, you really need to control yourself in court. Second, stay away from Borman. I mean it. If I hear you've been in so much as a pillow fight, I'll tell the officers to throw you in solitary."

He nodded sullenly. Hesitating, he said, "Mind doing me a favor?"

"What is it?"

"Can you check on my trailer for me? I know it's a piece of shit, but it's all I have. Will you do that? The key is under the mat by the door." He had the most forlorn look on his face.

"Sure, Rudy," I said. "I'll check on it."

The door clanged open obnoxiously and I stepped through it. "Hang in there, Rudy."

He didn't speak. He just stood there, looking lost as the door swung shut.

I pulled into my parking garage at 8:36 p.m. and stepped from the warmth of the Jeep Cherokee into the steely cold grip of an Alaskan night. Out in the sidewalk, each fall of boot on snow brought a corresponding squeak, a telltale sign that the temperature had fallen below zero. I crossed Third Avenue to G Street and climbed the rickety stairs. Once inside I made straight for the kitchen, along the way shooting a sidelong glance at Molly's rocker. Priscilla raised her head sleepily, yawned, and lowered it back down.

I fetched an Amber from the fridge, returned to the living room, propped my feet up on the coffee table, and kicked back. Thumbing the TV remote, I cruised the channels in search of something that would take my mind off the events of the day. I tried everything: fishing in Oklahoma, a woman selling real estate in L.A., *Hogan's Heroes* reruns, the Food Channel. I worked my way through a bottle of Amber and still nothing, so I switched it off.

I got another beer and returned to the couch. Between sips I kept thinking about my meeting with Alice. Lois had to come through with that name and address or Rudy was toast. I sank farther into the couch. It was threadbare, as befitted a thrift shop purchase, but it was comfortable. My eyelids drooped, then fluttered open.

I finished off the bottle, set it on the coffee table, and thought about giving Maria a call.

That ship has sailed, Sidney. Let it go.

I glanced at the bookcase that held Molly's framed photo. My eyes lingered there for a moment before dropping to the middle shelf, on which rested a compact disc player—another thrift store special—and a few dozen CD's. Some were Molly's that I couldn't bring myself to let go of. She had a thing for new age music. I didn't much care for it—I was more into John Lennon or a bit of jazz. I chose an album by a German guitarist and composer I liked a lot, started it up and sprawled out on the couch. I closed my eyes, letting the music take me . . .

The afternoon sun blazes over Flattop Mountain. Clouds dot the ocean blue sky like puffy white marshmallows. Two hundred miles to the north, a cluster of clouds mark but otherwise obscure the location where Denali—the Great One—rises twenty thousand feet above Alaska's interior. Hands tucked in my jacket pockets, I scan the horizon and then the sprawling city below it.

To my left, Molly sits on a large flat stone, feet drawn up against her body, her arms wrapped around them. She turns toward me, resting her head on her knees. The look on her face is utter bliss. Gradually, her eyes close. A warm wind blows her honey blond hair back in silken wisps.

"You know," she says after a while. "We don't do this enough."

"I know."

"You're always working."

The wind rumbles in my ear. I stare at her. "You want me to quit the business."

Her eyes flash open. She lifts her head. "That's not what I mean."

"What do you mean?"

"Just what I said. We don't do this enough."

"Oh."

Her smile fades. "What does that mean?"

"It means oh."

She blinks. "Oh."

She rests her head on her knees again and I look out over the city. I wish I could live in the moment the way Molly does. I'm forever looking either backward or forward. Assessing how I might have handled an interview better, or whether I should keep an eye on my client's husband on Saturday night, or wait . . .

"Sidney?"

"Yes?"

"Look at me."

I look. When she speaks, she keeps her head down though her eyes are focused intently on me. "If something ever happens to me, don't give up on life."

I think to myself, Why would she say that?

I say to her: "What makes you think I would, you know, give up on life?"

"I know you."

"Nothing's going to happen to you."

"How do you know?"

I lean close to her and whisper. "Because I won't let it."

She looks at me and smiles an angelic smile. Then the smile fades like the sunset. "There are some things you just . . . can't . . . stop."

Sixteen

That infernal invention, the alarm clock, rattled me awake at 7:30. My sleep had been fitful, interrupted by nightmares. Bleary-eyed, I rolled to my left, sending Priscilla cascading to the floor. She eyed me with justifiable indignance and slinked off to the rocker while I headed for the shower. Half an hour later I was downstairs in the coffee shop, standing in line behind a tall, skinny, twentysomething woman with autumn red hair. She placed her order and, glancing around, caught sight of me and smiled. "Do I know you?" Her cheeks were flush from the cold.

I made a pretense of pondering the question. "I give up. Do you?"

"That's funny." She held out her palm. "Sarah Wardlow, Alaska Public Defender Agency."

I shook her hand. "Sidney Reed, undertaker."

She eyed me quizzically. "I've never a met someone in your, um, line of work."

"Yes, well, we're a dying breed."

She hesitated, then burst into laughter. "You got me good."

Rachel Saint George's voice boomed from behind the counter. "All right, Sidney. Stop harassing my customers. Don't mind him, Sarah. He's been cooped up in a surveillance van too long." In reply to her questioning look, Rachel added, "Sidney is a private investigator."

Sarah's eyes brightened. "I've heard of you. You're working with Eddie Baker on the Rudy Skinner case."

"That's another one of my undertakings, yes."

She shook her head. "I can tell you're a handful."

She turned and collected a tall cup of whatever beverage she'd ordered and started toward the door. She paused to say, "We're keeping a close eye on the Skinner trial at the agency. Good luck, Sidney. It was nice meeting you."

"You too, Sarah."

As she glided out the door, I turned to face Rachel, who was watching Sarah's departure with interest. "She's cute, don't you think?"

Rachel frowned. "Leave it alone."

"Gorgeous red hair."

"You know I'm spoken for."

"What's the harm in looking?"

Her cheeks flushed. "Who said I was looking?"

"Rachel, your eyes were practically popping out of your head."

"I was doing no such thing. Your usual today?"

I grinned. "Sure." What little pleasure I extracted from life these days came from bantering with Rachel, who took it all good-naturedly and dished it out in equal measure.

I glanced at the counter. "No paper?"

"They're all gone," Rachel said. "With your salacious murder case hogging the headlines, the customers have been scooping them up like hotcakes."

"You don't say."

She nodded. "It made the front page again this morning." She looked at me and grinned playfully. "Saw your girlfriend's name on the byline."

"Maria?"

"Yep. Have you called her since the wreck?"

"I've been busy."

"Uh huh." She set a white mug on the counter. "Stop being a noodge and call her."

"It's a good thing you're getting paid for selling coffee and not advice." I reached for the cup. "You'd go broke in a week."

"Be glad it's free. And while we're on the subject of money, Monday is the first day of the month. You know what that means."

"Double punch day?"

"It means the rent is due, asshole."

"Don't worry, I'll have the money."

"Just thought I'd mention it."

Rachel turned to greet her next customer and I gravitated to my favorite table by the window. The table next to mine was occupied by an elderly man with a bulbous red nose and a wild slash of gray hair fastened in a ponytail. He wore a threadbare army field jacket and sat hunched over a mug of black coffee, lost in thought. A newspaper lay folded on the table.

I sipped from my mug and said, loud enough for him to hear, "Sure is cold out."

He glanced toward me. "Colder than a well-digger's ass." He paused. "It ain't politically correct to put it that way, but it paints a mighty accurate picture, don't it?"

"That it does." I leaned close to him. "Say, if you don't mind me asking, were you in Nam?"

His head jerked abruptly. "Yeah, I was in Nam. What's it to you?"

"Couldn't help notice the patch on your jacket. Artillery corps?"

"Why, yes." After a pause he said, "You, too?"

I shook my head. "Nam was a little before my time. Uncle Sam sent me to Germany."

"Doing what?"

"I was a cop."

"Military police or CID?"

"CID. I'm a private investigator these days."

He looked me over sharply, then stuck out his arm. "Jack Waits."

"Sidney Reed," I said, pumping his hand.

"Sorry for the reaction. I'm used to folks ignoring me, or worse." He grasped his cup with both hands and sipped coffee. "Working anything interesting?"

"I'm about to start a murder trial. My client's accused of hitting that Native kid."

He eyed the folded newspaper. "I was just reading about it. They say your boy confessed."

I sipped some mocha. "That's what they say."

He pondered that. "I gather there's more to it."

"There usually is."

He grinned for the first time. "Ain't it the truth?"

Calloused and weathered hands gripped the mug. The fingernails were broken in places and there was dirt wedged under them.

"Jack," I said. "You got a place to stay?"

He nodded slightly. "Got friends who put me up when I need a place. Nam vets, retired guys, and such. In a pinch there's Brother Francis."

I took out one of my cards and handed it to him. "Here's my number. I live upstairs here. If you ever need a place to crash, give me a call or come up and pound on my door." I gestured toward Rachel. "Just don't tell my landlady there. She doesn't like it when I bring home visitors."

His hands shook a bit as he stuck the card in his coat. "I'll remember that." He emptied the contents of his mug, rose from his chair, and sighed. "Onward and upward." He fetched a small khaki knapsack lying on the seat next to him and slung it over his shoulder. He began to walk away and then paused. "Pleasure meeting you, Sidney."

"The pleasure was mine, Jack."

I watched him move toward the door. Though he was hunched over, his gate was strong and deliberate. He went outside and I was about to turn away when I noticed a familiar figure coming in. Every part of her except for her face and hair were obscured by a huge coat that reminded me of a buffalo hide. But there was no mistaking the ocean of wavy auburn hair and the roundish face encircling two of the biggest brown eyes I'd ever seen.

She breezed in as if on a mission, scanned the sea of faces, and made a beeline for my table. She plopped down in the seat next to me, nearly out of breath. I tried unsuccessfully not to smile.

"Hi, Sidney. I'm so glad I caught you." Her voice held the warmth of a campfire.

"Hello, Maria." I made a herculean effort to sound casual. "Can I get you a cup of coffee?"

"Thank you, no." She paused, searching for the right words. "Look, I don't have much time. I just wanted to apologize for how I acted Saturday night. You were sweet . . . a real gentleman. And I was . . . well, I acted like a jerk."

"Yes, you did."

"I know. Those things I said, I . . . I didn't mean any of it. I was nervous about our date and stressed out about the accident and, well, I was mad at you. What I'm saying is, if you can find it in your heart to forgive me, I really would like to go out with you again. For the first time, I mean."

I'll be damned.

I pretended to mull over what she had said when in reality what I wanted to do was kiss her moist ruby lips. "You're in luck," I said at last. "I found another car. Hope you don't mind a rental."

She unleashed a smile that lit up the room. "Well then, it's settled. How about this Friday, say six o'clock? You know where I live."

"Sure, I—"

"And don't forget to make a reservation."

"Okay, I—"

"Do you have my cell number?"

"Hmm . . . I think so."

She frowned and whipped out a business card. "I know you have it, smarty pants, but just in case you lost it, my cell number is on the back."

I stuffed her card in my jacket as she rose from her seat.

"Sidney?"

I looked up into those fathomless brown eyes. "Yes?"

"Will I see you in court this morning?"

"Unless I see you first."

"Good." A broad grin puffed out her cheeks. "Gotta run!" With that, she practically flew out the door, leaving a wisp of perfume behind. I leaned back and sipped mocha, letting the scent of her caress my nostrils and thinking that maybe the day wouldn't be so bad after all.

Seventeen

An air of anticipation hung in the courtroom like a fine mist. From my seat at the defense table, I scanned the sea of faces assembled in the packed room: there were television and newspaper reporters, relatives of Willie Olson and his supporters in the native community, and members of the general public, all waiting for the show to begin.

Maria Maldonado, chestnut hair flowing down her back in silky waves, was writing in her notebook. Her head popped up and our eyes met. A smile flashed beneath chocolate brown eyes.

I smiled back.

To my right, Rudy Skinner, wearing the thrift shop jacket I bought him, shuffled his feet nervously. To his right, Eddie Baker browsed through a thick black binder. At the prosecution table, District Attorney Grant Fellows chatted jovially with Detective Banner, whose grin in response to the D.A.'s banter struck me as forced.

Once the jury was seated, the clerk picked up the phone and Judge Jeffries soon appeared.

"All rise!" the clerk ordered, followed by, "The Honorable Raymond Jeffries presiding."

Jeffries coughed and said, "Please be seated." As the room quieted, his probing blue eyes swept the room like a hawk scanning a corn field. I held my breath as his gaze fell briefly on me before moving on.

Satisfied that all was well in his domain, he rapped his gavel and in a voice that managed to sound equally authoritative and reassuring, said, "The court will come to order." He recited the case name and number for the record and glanced up. "Gentlemen, do we have any issues to take up?"

Both attorneys said they did not.

"Very well," Jeffries said. "Mr. Fellows, call your first witness."

"Judge, the state calls Sarah Adams."

A slight woman in her thirties emerged from the back of the room and strolled through the swinging door toward the witness box. With her shoulder-length black hair, she looked prim and petite in a red sweater and gray knee-length skirt. There was a small lapel mic lying on a stand in the box. The clerk instructed her to clip it to her blouse and then led her through the oath. At its conclusion, Adams said "I do."

The clerk instructed, "State your full name for the record, spelling your last name."

"Sarah Ann Adams, A – D – A – M – S."

"Please be seated."

Adams lowered herself and cast her eyes about nervously. She'd probably never testified in court before. I knew from experience how intimidating it could be.

Fellows stepped up to the lectern. "Good morning, Mrs. Adams. What is your occupation?"

"I teach first grade at Taku Elementary School."

"I admire that. Teachers are undervalued in our society."

The small talk was Fellows' way of putting his witness at ease, but he was also playing to the jury, making himself appear likeable. One of *them*.

"Now, Mrs. Adams, I want you to think back to the night of January fifteenth. Please tell the jury what you remember about that night."

Hands planted firmly on her lap, Adams narrowed her eyes and took a deep breath. "I had taken my son—he's a senior in high school—to his basketball game. They were playing Dimond that night. It was snowing pretty heavily after the game, so I cleared off the windshield and we started for home. When we got to the O'Malley Road exit, I could barely see the road. I'd gone maybe a quarter mile up O'Malley when I saw a dark shape lying in the road."

She paused, her voice cracking.

"Take your time, Mrs. Adams," Fellows said softly.

I glanced at the jury. All fifteen sets of eyes were fixed on the witness, a portrait of collective empathy at the drama playing out before them. I swiveled toward the rear of the courtroom. In the far corner, the television camera with its zoom lens recorded every murmur and inflection. In the gallery, all eyes remained laser-focused on Adams.

"I pulled to the side of the road as best I could—there wasn't much of a berm. I told Daniel to stay in the car. The wind was blowing so hard, I had difficulty opening the door. The shape was half buried in snow but when I got to within a few feet, I knew . . ."

"Knew what, Mrs. Adams?"

"I knew it was . . . a body."

She'd been looking down at her hands, avoiding eye contact, but then she looked up at Fellows. "It was a man . . . He wasn't moving. And there was blood . . . I just knew he was dead." She shook her head slowly, her voice barely a whisper. "There was nothing I could do for him, poor man." She stared dreamily toward the rear of the courtroom. Then she straightened her back. "I got back in the car, called 9-1-1, and waited for the police."

Dramatic as it was, in the scheme of things her testimony didn't contribute in any significant way to the case against Rudy Skinner beyond establishing how the victim was discovered. What it *did* do was help tell a story for the jury. And that, the D.A. knew, he had to do in order to secure a conviction.

Fellows asked a few follow-up questions and sat back down.

Judge Jeffries lifted his chin. "Mr. Baker, you may inquire."

Eddie moved quickly to the podium. "Good morning, Mrs. Adams. I'm sorry you have to appear here under these circumstances. I have just a few questions. Did you touch or physically examine the body in any way?"

"No, sir."

"Did you see anyone else around there?"

"No."

"See any footprints or tire marks?"

"No, but there was drifting snow everywhere, and it was quite dark. My attention was focused on that poor man."

"Thank you. I have no further questions."

Jeffries said, "Mr. Fellows, any redirect?"

Fellows stood up. "No judge. The state now calls Bill Stansfield."

Sarah Adams walked off and the tall, lanky college kid I'd interviewed on Monday strolled to the stand. Willie Olson had made the mistake of crashing the arrogant jock's frat party, an action that not only earned him an ass-kicking but led to his death on that lonely snow-swept road. Like Adams, his testimony served little purpose other than to help weave a story line about the night Olson died.

Fellows' direct examination lasted barely ten minutes. He avoided confronting Stansfield about the beating he and his buddies had given Olson. So did Eddie Baker, who, when offered the podium, simply said, "I have nothing for this witness."

"Very well," the judge said. "Mr. Fellows?"

The prosecutor rose from his seat. "Your honor, the state calls Dr. Thomas McGrady."

I turned to the back of the room in time to see the double doors splay inward and a stooped and frail-looking man shuffle through. He was heavy-jowled and saggy-cheeked and his head was topped with a wisp of kinky white hair. Pushing eighty, McGrady had served as the state medical examiner for over twenty years. He was competent enough, although he tended to err on the side of helping the prosecution when afforded the opportunity. My friend, Lois Dozier, was one of McGrady's investigators and, as Grant Fellows slow-walked McGrady through a recitation of his credentials, I found myself growing impatient to meet her for lunch and hopefully learn the identity of the mysterious Alice. I glanced at my watch: 11:47 a.m.

The M.E. droned on about Willie Olson's injuries in gruesome detail. With sloth-like speed, autopsy photographs were identified, marked, and introduced into evidence. I checked my watch every ten minutes.

As the doctor's testimony labored on, I began to notice a dull whapping sound. On about the fifth slap I glanced under the table and saw Rudy's foot see-sawing back and forth. The sound I'd been hearing was his dangling foot banging against the table leg. It was just loud enough to be worrisome. I leaned over and whispered. "Watch the foot, Rudy."

His body stiffened. The offending sound faded and died.

Eddie's cross-examination was fortuitously brief—we weren't contesting the fact that a snowplow killed Willie, only the assertion that Rudy had been driving the truck that killed him.

Fellows finished with McGrady at 12:37 p.m. and, as the D.A. had no redirect, that was it for the day. The crack of the judge's gavel set the room in motion, unleashing a rumble of voices. As soon as the court deputy led Rudy back to his cell, I sidled up to Eddie. "I'm glad we stopped when we did. Rudy was getting edgy."

He nodded. "Where are we at on identifying this source of yours? The one who claims she can identify Olson's killer?"

"Working on it. I'll brief you at our five o'clock."

"Oh, I almost forgot. I've got a conference call at five. Let's make it four-thirty."

I had noticed a weariness in his voice earlier, and now I could see that his eyes were bloodshot, as if someone had dribbled beat juice in them. I told him, "You look tired, Eddie."

"I tend to look that way when I don't sleep."

"That's all right," I said, trying to sound reassuring. "I tend to look that way when I do."

Eighteen

Inside the Mighty Moose Café, the aroma of fresh brewed coffee was a welcome respite from the stuffiness of Judge Jeffries' courtroom. At the counter, Rachel was speaking with a squat woman with sandy blond hair that reached the middle of her back. I smiled knowing it was Lois Dozier.

Fifteen years ago, I was an Army CID agent stationed in Germany, working major drug cases. I was looking to recruit someone for my team who was experienced, savvy, and familiar with the area—someone I could trust. I went to the local provost marshal, explained what I needed, and he gave me Sergeant Lois Louise Dozier, a military police investigator with a good rep. We became fast friends and made some major cases together. Eventually, at my urging, she applied for the Criminal Investigation Division and was accepted into the program.

Lois and I ordered lunch and made small talk until our sandwiches appeared on the counter under the ORDER PICKUP sign, then plopped down at my favorite table by the window.

I rubbed my palms together in anticipation. "So, what did you find out?"

Lois put down her sandwich. "What is it with you?"

I stared at her. "What do you mean?"

"I mean, you only call me when you need something, that's what."

I leaned back in my chair.

Do I really do that?

I dipped a spoon into my potato soup and set it back down. "Lois, I'm a schmuck. These last few days have been—"

She held up her hand. "Okay, stop." She softened her voice. "You're not a schmuck. Hell, I don't even know what that means."

She bit into her tuna salad sandwich while I gulped spoonfuls of soup and glanced her way every few seconds, feeling like I'd kicked the cat. At length, she set her sandwich aside and reached for her purse. She took out a torn scrap of paper and laid it on the table in front of me. It read: *Alice Elizabeth Crawford, 5008 Taku Street, Apt #8.*

I stuffed it in my shirt pocket, sipped some more soup, and glanced up at her. "Lois, I—"

"Will you just shut the fuck up? Running the plate was easy. That's not the point. I'm not looking for a thank you, like I just sold you some Tupperware." She glanced out the window, lost in thought. I felt like crawling under the table.

She shifted her gaze back to me. "We go way back, you and me. Remember the good times we had in Germany? The drug busts we made? The parties we got drunk at?"

"How could I forget?" My mind sailed back to a happier time. I loved Germany and its people. I'd often told Molly I would take her there someday. It never happened.

Lois chuckled. "Remember that time we all went on that Rhein cruise and you were so drunk you almost fell off the dock?"

"You never stop reminding me," I said with a grin.

She sipped her iced tea. "I guess what I'm saying is, I miss the old Sidney."

I shifted my gaze to the saltshaker on the table. It was the cheap kind, clear glass with a silver lid. "I miss him, too."

"And I miss seeing you at the ADA meetings."

She was referring to the Alaska Detectives Association, which I'd been actively involved with prior to Molly's death. I smiled at the memory of countless luncheons, bad jokes, and hangovers.

I managed to say, "We had some great times, didn't we?"

She wiped her mouth with a paper napkin. "Then we're in agreement. You're going to end this perpetual pity party and get your shit together. Are we clear?"

"You don't think I want to? You think I like living like this, in a crummy apartment—"

"You know I can hear you, right?" Rachel's voice boomed from behind the counter, accompanied by a stern look.

I shot her a glance and lowered my voice. "I *am* back in the game. I've had two cases now. I feel like things are returning to normal."

"Normal? You're seeing a shrink."

I felt a tightness in my temples. "Lots of people see a psychiatrist."

"Bullshit."

"I'm pulling myself together."

"Bullshit. Have you looked in the mirror lately?"

"What are you talking about?"

"When's the last time you shaved?"

I scraped my fingers across my stubbled chin. "I'm going for a more rugged look."

"Your eyes are bloodshot. When's the last time you had a good night's sleep?"

"You're acting like my mother."

"You're right." She sighed and lifted her glass. "I don't mean to do that."

We sat and nibbled at the food on our plates for a good five minutes without saying a word. Near the end of my egg salad, I pushed my plate aside. Something was gnawing at me from the inside, something I had no control over.

In between bites she caught me staring at her and stopped in mid-chew, waiting for me to say something.

"The thing is," I said, "What if everyone got it wrong? The cops, the M.E. It's been known to happen."

She stared at me hard. "Don't do this."

I turned toward the window, stared at the spider-web pattern of frost at its edges. "I'll never rest until I know."

"Sid, I'm begging you. Let it go."

An inner voice implored me to *Shut the fuck up*. I ignored it and said, "You really want me to let it go? Let me see Molly's autopsy report. With my own eyes."

In some part of my brain, I thought it was a fair question. If I could resolve the doubts I had about Molly's death, maybe then I could put my mind to rest once and for all.

Lois's eyes drifted slowly to her plate and in a voice that rose only slightly above a whisper said, "Molly committed suicide, Sidney. She killed herself and there's nothing you or I or anyone else can do to change that." She got up, pulled on her coat, and looked down at me with sad eyes. "When you're ready to grow up, give me a call."

And then she was gone.

I trudged to the parking garage and sat shivering behind the wheel until the Jeep sputtered out its first breath of warmth. I pulled out of the garage onto Third, took a right on E Street and hung a left on Sixth. The downtown lunch crowd was out in force, bundled up in their wool and Gortex and bobbing in and out of restaurants and stores, oblivious to the cold. I whizzed past them, leaving the downtown behind. Sixth Avenue soon morphed into the Glenn Highway, one of two thoroughfares feeding into the city of Anchorage—the Glenn from the north, the Seward from the south.

If you never leave the city of Anchorage, it's easy to forget you're in Alaska, but then you see the snow-capped Chugach Mountains and you remember. They popped into view as soon as I hit the Glenn Highway and my spirits lifted.

There had been a time when they'd lifted Molly's too. I know for a fact they did. We'd gone skiing at Alyeska Resort and she'd been so happy. We were making a life up here. But something had happened to change all that and I couldn't figure out what it was. I didn't know how to make Lois understand that.

Out over the sprawling city, plumes of smoke and steam rose into the sky like miniature streamers. I didn't need to have the window rolled down to know it was cold outside. It *looked* cold.

I exited the highway at Boniface Parkway, took the first right, then looped back around to where Taku Drive paralleled the Glenn. On its south side—the side facing away from the Glenn—Taku was lined with drab, nondescript two- and three-story apartment buildings, one after the other. I slowed down, watching for house numbers. Halfway up the street I spotted a wooden sign emblazoned with the words SOURDOUGH APARTMENTS.

The apartment complex consisted of two identical two-story buildings facing each other and painted a washed-out teal blue. The one on the right was number 5008. There were half a dozen vehicles parked in numbered spaces along the front. I nosed the Jeep forward until I came to an older model red Ford Fiesta parked in space number 8.

Alice's car.

I glanced around for a place to park and saw some vehicles butted up against a grove of trees to the rear of the property. There was a rusted-out Chevy van that had seen better days, a Jetstream motorhome sitting up on blocks, and a black Ford pickup, confederate flag sticker affixed haphazardly to the front bumper, backed into the space between them.

I pulled in next to the Jetstream and killed the engine. The time was 1:37 p.m. After patting my inside coat pocket for the subpoena I'd filled out for Alice, I got out and went up to the middle door and pushed it open.

I found myself in a darkened hallway that smelled of mildew and cigarettes, apartments 3 and 4 flanking me. By my calculation, that would put Apartment 8 on the third floor. I followed the hallway to a darkened stairwell and climbed to the top, where I saw a wooden door with a metal "8" nailed to the middle of it. Just below that was a peephole.

A push of the small white button to the left of the door elicited a muffled buzz. I squinted through the peephole and saw a vague shadow emerge from the depths. I stepped back and heard the slap of the deadbolt. The door creaked opened the width of an open hand and a woman's face peeked around it, eyeing me curiously.

Her lips were slightly parted, her eyes wide and blue, and her hair was blond as a Palomino's. Whoever she was, she wasn't the same woman I'd met at Happy Jack's.

In a soft, earthy voice, she said, "May I help you?"

"I'm here to see Alice Crawford."

"And who are you?"

"I'm Sidney Reed."

"Are you sure you're in the right place?"

"I'm always in the right place, even when I'm not supposed to be."

She flashed a mischievous smile. "Hold on, then." The door closed, the security chain rattled, and the door opened again, this time to its full width.

So did my mouth.

The woman standing before me might have pranced straight out of a men's magazine, and I don't mean *Popular Mechanics*. She wore designer low-rise blue jeans, and I do mean low—the waist band leveled out several inches below the curve of her bare hips. Above the waist band, her tan stomach was flat as a ping-pong table, and in the unlikely event someone failed to notice, a tiny blue stone glinted from the delicate recess of her navel and, from it, a silver chain dangled like a fishing lure. Higher up, rising above the slope of her rib cage, a gauzy white tube top struggled to contain a most impressive pair of breasts.

When my lizard brain allowed my eyes to roam higher, I saw an attractive woman with classic high cheekbones and silky-smooth skin. She stood with her right hand on her right hip, which was cocked jauntily to one side.

"Hi there," she said. "I'm Alice Crawford. Won't you come in?"

Nineteen

My mouth was still open when "Alice" turned and headed down a long hall with enough hip action to power a modern kitchen appliance. I followed her like a heat-seeking missile, remembering somehow to close the door behind me.

This should be interesting.

The hallway was dimly lit, its walls covered in posters of Marilyn Monroe, Jayne Mansfield, and other Hollywood sex symbols from days gone by. We passed three closed doors and emerged, as if from a tunnel, into a brightly lit and spacious living area. To my left, behind a long breakfast bar, there was a full kitchen which led to a small art deco dining table and chairs, and to my right, a sparsely though elegantly furnished living room. Two windows offered a view of the sister apartment building across the way, and beyond, the Chugach Mountains thrown in as a bonus.

Her voice emerged from behind the breakfast bar. "Would you like coffee?"

Okay, I'll play along.

"I'd love some."

While Alice busied herself making coffee, I wandered over to a glass-covered coffee table, where I found issues of *Cosmopolitan*, *The Hollywood Reporter*, and a Caribbean cruise brochure. I picked up the *Cosmo*, noting a label on the front cover bearing Alice Crawford's name and address. I roamed over to a shelf with a framed photo of a smiling couple in a lush mountain setting. The woman in the photo was Alice—blond Alice. The man was a head taller, ruggedly handsome, and sported a full black beard.

"That's my boyfriend, Bo," she said from across the room.

The name set off alarm bells in my head. *Bo Cooley, perhaps?*

I turned to find her setting two steaming cups on the table.

"I hope you like yours black," she said. "I don't keep cream or sugar in the house. They go right to my hips."

I don't know about the cream and sugar, but my eyes definitely went there.

"Black is fine," I replied, and went to the table and sat down. I glanced around. "You have a nice place."

"It'll do for now. If things go as planned, I'll be in Hollywood come spring."

"You're a model?"

"Exotic dancer," she corrected. "But my agent is working on getting me some lucrative modeling gigs. I'm going to be an actress." Her eyes brightened. "Hey, would you like to see my portfolio?"

Before I had a chance to answer, Alice bounded into the living room. A moment later she placed a black binder in front of me. "Have a look," she said with unabashed pride.

The cover was of leather and on it was printed, in silver letters, PORTFOLIO OF ALICE CRAWFORD. I peeled back the cover to find several dozen plastic sleeves with glossy photos sandwiched in between. Some were color, some black and white, and all were of Alice posing in a variety of settings and states of dress—and undress—ranging from standard portraits and outdoor scenes to "boudoir" shots in bikinis or lingerie. In a few of them she wore nothing at all. To my untrained eye, at least, they appeared to be professionally done, capturing her natural beauty, not to mention every square inch of her impressive anatomy.

I closed the binder and looked up to find Alice eyeing me like an expectant schoolgirl. "Well?"

"What can I say? These are stunning, Alice. They're really beautiful."

"Thank you, Sidney! I thought they came out quite well. This," she pressed the portfolio to her ample chest, "is my ticket out of this godforsaken wasteland."

"I wish you luck." I couldn't help but be taken with her enthusiasm—and naivete. She acted like we were old friends when, for all she knew, I could be Ted Bundy. I smiled inwardly at the strangeness of it. I'd been there for all of ten minutes, had seen photographs of her naked as the day she was born, and she had yet to ask me what I was doing there.

Alice reached for her coffee cup and held it in suspension, gazing dreamily out the window.

I cleared my throat. "Alice, the reason I'm here . . ."

"Yes?" She jerked her head around, seeming to pop out of a trance. "I'm sorry, how silly of me to ramble on like some star-struck ditz. Please, I'm all ears."

I'd been mulling over possible cover stories from the moment I'd stepped through the door. I tried one on for size. "I was downtown yesterday running errands and as I was getting ready to pull out into traffic—I was parked on Sixth—the car in front of me backed up and clipped my bumper, then sped off without stopping. Luckily, I managed to write down the license number. I asked a police friend who owed me a favor to run the plate. Your name and address came up and so . . . well, here I am."

I sipped some more coffee and smiled. "Don't worry, though. The woman who was driving had straight black hair so it couldn't have been you."

Her expression changed abruptly from cautious curiosity to one of recognition. She mumbled to herself, "Connie."

"Connie?"

"My roommate, Connie Zwick. Against my better judgment, I lent her my car yesterday."

"Anchorage is not a good place to be without a car," I observed.

"Yes, well, she *had* her own car but sold it to pay bills, including her share of the rent."

"I take it she's not working now?"

"Not for several months."

"Hmm. That doesn't bode well for getting my bumper fixed."

"No, it doesn't." She glanced up, eyes wide. "I hope you're not expecting *me* to cover it."

I flashed an appropriately shocked look. "Certainly not." After a pause I said, "What if *I* spoke with her? Perhaps she and I could work something out."

"Be my guest." She frowned. "She's not here at the moment."

"Maybe later, then." We sipped coffee in silence and then I said, "If you don't mind my asking, how did you two meet?"

Her hand dove inside a bejeweled gray handbag looped over the back of her chair and pulled out a pack of cigarettes. "Mind if I smoke?"

Before meeting Molly I'd been a three-pack-a-day smoker. She made it her mission in life to get me to quit—and succeeded. Now I hated the smell. I waved a hand. "Help yourself."

She lit up, inhaling and exhaling with half-closed eyes. "A mutual friend approached me earlier this year and told me Connie had been in some kind of trouble. They wanted to know if I would take her in. I said I would, on the condition she help me with the rent."

"What kind of trouble?"

"They didn't say."

"When was that?"

Her baby blues darted up and to the right. "Mid to late January or thereabouts."

I felt my skin tingle—that was right about the time Olson was killed.

"Who was the friend?"

She squinted through the smoke. "You ask a lot of questions."

"I find it's the best way to get answers."

She studied me with a lopsided grin that was incredibly sexy and took a long drag on her cigarette. I sensed I'd reached the point beyond which she wouldn't go.

"I've bothered you enough, Alice." I pushed my chair back and stood up. "I should be going."

"Nonsense," she said. "You've hardly bothered me at all."

"I must not be trying hard enough."

She unleashed a disarming smile. "You know, you're pretty cute."

"Yeah, I know. It's a curse."

"That depends on how you look at it." She plopped her still-smoldering cigarette into her coffee cup and rose from her chair in slow motion, her tanned, toned body uncoiling like a serpent's. "Thanks for putting up with my chatter. Come and see me sometime at the Wild Stallion. I dance there Thursday through Saturday night under the name Stormy."

"Bo won't mind?"

She grimaced. "On any given night a hundred guys watch me dance naked. I doubt he'd notice one more. Besides," a tinge of regret crept into her voice, "he's too busy to come and watch *me*."

I was tempted to ask what Bo was too busy doing, but thought better of it. Instead, I said, "If you were my girlfriend, I'd be in the front row every night."

She hit me with those penetrating blue spotlights and was about to reply when the melodic notes of a cell phone's ringtone sent her reaching for her handbag. She fished out her phone and tapped the answer button. "Hello? Oh, hi. Yes of course . . . No, I haven't seen her since . . . Now look, I agreed to . . . That's not fair! . . . Oh really?"

I couldn't make out the caller's words but his anger seeped through the wires loud and clear. Alice bit her nails furiously, tapping a bare foot against the floor as she struggled get a word in edgewise. At one point she glanced at me in alarm and then back at the phone. "Why, that's ridiculous, I . . . No, I haven't . . ."

Phone in hand, she pushed past me and peered out the window toward the spot where I'd parked my car. Her eyes grew wide. "You fucking SOB. You have that low-life brother of yours watching me. Why am I not surprised? . . . Oh no? His ratty-ass Ford is parked outside right . . . He's not watching me? Alice shot me a sidelong glance. "There's a man here, yes, but . . . No, he's got nothing . . . that's just . . . Bo, you're being . . . Connie bumped his car and . . . Hello? Bo?"

Alice glared at the phone. "Fucking bastard." She cast her gaze full on me, her face fraught with anguish. "Okay, who the fuck *are* you?"

"Like I said, I happened to be downtown and . . ."

"Stop, okay?" Her eyes locked on mine. "Bo knows you met with Connie. Now tell me what the hell is going on."

Someone followed Connie to Happy Jack's. Now they know I'm here.

I sighed. "I think you'd better have a seat, Alice."

"Sure, fellah, I'll have a seat." She pivoted toward the kitchen. "But first I'm going to need something stronger than coffee."

Five minutes later we were sitting at the table again. Alice poured chardonnay from a mostly-full bottle into a pair of rather nice wine glasses and studied me between sips, her pouty lips growing poutier the more she drank. She crossed her legs and waited.

I took a drink of wine and said, "I'm not at liberty to tell you the whole story, except to say I'm a private investigator trying to help a guy who's on trial for murder."

"Help who?"

"His name is Rudy Skinner."

"Don't know him."

"It doesn't matter. What matters is, I need some answers."

"You lied to me."

"Couldn't be helped. I had to know what I was dealing with."

"Okay," she sighed. "What do you want to know?"

"Who told you to keep an eye on Connie?"

Her eyes lowered. "My boyfriend, Bo."

"Bo Cooley?"

She nodded.

"What for?"

"I'd like to know that myself." She emptied the contents of her glass and refilled it. "Bo came to me and said his brother Travis had a friend who was in some kind of trouble and needed to lie low for a while. The deal was, Connie would come live with me and I was supposed to keep an eye on her. He didn't say why, but the implication was, she might hurt herself."

"Did you believe that?"

"Not really."

"And still you let her move in?"

"Well, yeah, sure. Bo wanted me to. But I insisted she pay half the rent. That was *my* deal."

I sipped some wine. "Okay. How has it been working out?"

Alice shrugged. "All right, I guess. She's quiet. Keeps to herself. At first Travis came by to check on her—really check on her, if you know what I mean. But then he stopped coming around and she got all weepy on me. She really missed him."

"How well do you know Travis?"

Alice shrugged. "He's Bo's little brother. I see him around, that's about it. Can't say that I know him, really."

"What's Connie like?"

"Quiet." She hesitated. "Come to think of it, though, she started acting weird a few days ago."

Must have been when she saw my ad in the paper.

"Weird how?" I asked.

"Pacing around like a nervous Nellie, always looking out the window. She drove me nuts."

"Did you ask her what the problem was?"

"I did. She told me to mind my own business. Pissed me off."

Alice leaned back in her chair and sipped wine. "All I know is, I better get some rent money soon or I'm going to kick her out." The alcohol's effects were beginning to show as a faint blush on her cheeks.

I caught her eye. "Who's watching your apartment, Alice?"

Her face clouded over. "That would be Bo's brother Ray, the family errand boy."

"You don't like him?"

Her eyes turned cold. "I hate him. He's mean." She gestured toward the window. "He's out there right now. Fucking asshole."

"Why would he want to watch *your* place?"

"He wouldn't unless someone told him to. Ray doesn't tie his own shoes without permission. It had to be Bo, or his old man."

"You mean Rance."

Her eyes probed mine. "Yeah, that's right."

"Okay. Why would *they* want to watch your place?"

"Beats me. Must have something to do with Connie." She paused. The wine glass wobbled in her fingers. "They think I don't know what they're up to, like I'm just some dumb blonde."

I perked up at that. "What do you mean?"

She cast a knowing look. "I mean, I hear things."

"What things?"

Her eyes danced from left to right, then she blushed. "Sometimes I talk too much." She set her glass on the table and lit up a fresh cigarette. Fingers shaking, she said. "Is Ray still out there?"

I glanced out the window. A thin gray plume spewed from the Ford's tailpipe. I turned and nodded. She puffed in silence.

"Any idea where Connie is now?" I asked.

"I haven't a clue. She was gone when I woke up this morning."

"Is that normal for her?"

"No, not really. When I get up she's usually sitting at this table drinking coffee, but not this morning. Figured she was out looking for a job." She stared at the glass, tapping the side with her painted fingernails and sending ripples through the clear fluid.

"Mind if I have a look at her room?"

"Be my guest." She got up from her chair and headed shakily down the hall, hips pumping. As we walked she said, "What does your guy have to do with the Cooleys anyway?"

"I wish I could tell you, but I can't."

She paused at the first door on the right. "Yeah, well, I'm getting tired of being jerked around by these Okies."

"Why don't you leave?"

"Leave Bo or leave Alaska?"

"Both. Get a fresh start somewhere else."

Her mouth formed a pencil-thin line. "I wish I could."

I thought her comment odd, given her earlier one about expecting to be in Hollywood in the spring, but I brushed it off.

Alice opened the door and went inside. I followed her into a small bedroom with canary yellow walls, a twin bed that was unmade, and a dresser and chair. There was a closet with its door standing open and a single window facing north toward Taku and the Glenn Highway beyond.

Alice made a B-line for the closet. "That bitch!"

I followed her and saw empty hangers dangling from a long wooden rod. A flash of white drew my gaze to the dresser, its top bare except for a single sheet of paper, which I picked up. On it was written a few hastily penned lines:

Alice—

I have to leave. I'm sorry there's no time to say goodbye.

Connie

Alice plucked it out of my hand and read it. "That little bitch!"

I bent down and pulled the drawers out one by one. They were all empty. I straightened back up and my eyes fell on a small metal waste basket beside the desk. It was empty save for a crumpled piece of paper at the bottom. With my back to Alice, I snatched it out of the basket and stuffed it in my coat.

When I turned around, Alice was clutching Connie's note tightly in one hand, distress etched on her pretty face.

"Looks like she left in a hurry," I said.

Alice didn't answer. I don't think she heard me.

Twenty

I shuffled out to my car, keeping one eye on the black Ford and the dark, bearded figure of Ray Cooley hunkered down behind the wheel. My first instinct was to get in his face, but I decided instead to play it cool and see what happened.

I got behind the wheel and fired up the engine. It was a little past 2:30 p.m.—enough time to hit the courthouse before meeting with Eddie. I reached into my coat for the scrap of paper I'd pulled out of the trash. Scrawled on it was the word "Mona's" and a telephone number. My mouth curled in a smile. Perhaps I'd caught a break. I stuffed it back in my pocket.

I pulled out of the complex and hung a left on Taku, intent on taking a series of side streets south to Debarr Road and then east on Fifteenth Avenue, a route that would take me to the *Daily News* building. I wanted to drop in on Maria and tell her how glad I was to see her that morning.

The route I chose zig-zagged through a residential neighborhood. Not only was it the quickest route to the newspaper office, it would also make it easier to spot a tail. Sure enough, after the first couple of turns, I noticed the black pickup tagging along. Whenever I made a left or right, he mimicked my move. When I sped up, he kept pace. I lost sight of him when I made a right on Debarr, a busy four-lane.

I arrived at the *Daily News* building, went inside, and headed straight for the phone on the wall. When I punched 3-5-7 into the black handset, the call went straight to voicemail, but I let it play through so I could listen to Maria's melodic voice.

I left there and drove to my parking garage, alert for a tail. I didn't detect one. I parked the Jeep and walked briskly down Third Avenue, the afternoon sun stinging my eyes until I stepped into the welcome shadow of the Nesbett Courthouse. Named for Buell Nesbett, the first Chief Justice of the Alaska Supreme Court, the five-story slab of nondescript, rectangular granite occupied a city block cattycorner from the Captain Cook Hotel.

Frost puffing out of my mouth, I rounded the north side of the building to the main entrance on the southwest. I glanced around for any sign of protestors. Seeing none, I went inside, through security, and crossed the lobby toward the records section. A series of windows lined one wall. Behind it, records clerks answered questions, date-stamped and processed filings, handed out legal forms, and pulled court records.

I ignored them and sat down behind a computer terminal, one of several lining the opposite wall and made available to members of the public to look up cases. I typed Rance Cooley's name and punched the return key. The computer spewed out a laundry list of hits, the majority of them traffic violations. Skipping over those, I came across the assault case arising from the property dispute I had worked on. No need to dwell on that one. That left an old DUI—driving under the influence. That didn't interest me either.

I typed in another name: COOLEY, BO. Rance's eldest son had three traffic violations and a misdemeanor assault. I ripped a blank "Record Request Form" from a pad next to the terminal and filled it out for the assault case. Repeating the process for Ray Cooley, I found two assaults cases and filled out request forms for those as well.

Next, I entered Connie Zwick's name and hit "Return." The screen responded with: NO RECORD FOUND. That was fine by me, since no record meant there was nothing for the D.A. to attack if she were to testify in court—unless, of course, she had a record in another jurisdiction. Grant Fellows, I knew, would run her name through NCIC, the FBI's National Crime Information Center database. If she had priors anywhere else, he would find them and, under the rules of discovery, would be obliged to share the results with Eddie Baker.

Evelyn Waters was next on my list. Her search produced five

hits—three traffic offenses and two drug cases. I filled out request forms for the drug cases and was about to take them to the window when another thought occurred to me.

I placed my fingers on the keyboard and typed: MALDONADO, MARIA. My index finger hovered over the return key. I held it there, my mind drifting back . . . remembering.

Molly and I were having dinner at a Tucson restaurant. We'd been dating for several weeks and our relationship had gotten pretty serious. Something had been eating at me all day and I couldn't hold it in any longer.

"I have a confession to make," I said, fidgeting with my wine glass. "I had you checked out."

She stared, wide-eyed. "Oh you did, did you?"

I nodded, feeling a bit foolish.

"You know, relationships are built on trust," she said.

"If it makes you feel any better," I replied, "I didn't find anything." She grinned mischievously. "Neither did I."

I smiled at the memory, then stabbed the return key. Two cases populated the screen. The first was a ticket for speeding. I smiled again and shook my head.

I'll tease her about it when the time is right.

I stared at the second entry and my smile faded.

It read: NAME CHANGE. I tapped the return key with some slight apprehension and the detail screen appeared. It said simply: FILE SEALED. I leaned back in the seat and stared at the screen. I wasn't surprised that the file was sealed—that was typical in name change cases. What *did* surprise me was the fact that it existed at all. She'd shared a bit about her past, but I had the feeling there were things she didn't want me to know. Now this.

With that new nugget of information to occupy my thoughts, I got in line to wait for a records clerk. A bookish, bespectacled young man motioned for me to step forward.

A few minutes later, five blue file folders bunched under my arm, I made my way to the reading room next door and sat down at one of two large tables in the middle of the room. The time was 3:48 p.m. I'd have to hustle if I was going to make my meeting with Eddie.

Eddie's head was buried in a thick trial binder when I walked through the door.

"You're late," he said without looking up.

"I thought trial went well this morning."

"Don't change the subject. I expect you to be on time."

It was a funny comment coming from him, but I didn't laugh. "I was doing research at the courthouse. It took longer than expected."

"That's not my problem."

"You're still mad about the other day."

"Yeah, I'm still mad."

"You'll get over it."

"I might, if you tell me you have Alice Crawford under subpoena."

"I do not."

At last he looked up. "Dare I ask why?"

"Because Alice Crawford is not who we're after." He listened stone-faced as I explained that it was actually Connie Zwick and not Alice who heard Travis confess to killing Willie Olson. I left out certain superfluous details, such as my examination of Alice's portfolio.

When I was done, he leaned back in his chair. "I don't give a flying fuck if her name is Marie Antoinette. Just tell me you can get her under subpoena."

"I'm damn sure going to try," I assured him. "The question is, can you wave your magic attorney's wand and get her testimony admitted if she does appear?"

"I think so. I reviewed the Alaska Rules of Criminal Procedure and for good measure called the state bar. They concur with my assessment that her testimony comes in as a statement against interest, so Jeffries will probably let her testify. And to demonstrate my confidence in *your* abilities, I plan to put her on the stand on Monday, right after I'm done with Dr. Harper."

I wished I shared his confidence. I let him finish scratching some notes on a legal pad and then I said, "There's one more thing."

"What is it?"

"We need to track down Evelyn Waters."

He eyed me curiously. "Why?"

"To ask her about Rudy's business records."

"I don't see the point. The records we examined suggest he didn't work that night, or if he did, he destroyed the record to make it look he didn't. Either way, my sense is we need to leave it alone."

"But what if he *was* working that night?"

"That's exactly what I'm afraid of. If he was working anywhere near where Olson was killed, then Rudy's fucked." He suddenly glanced up. "You're not suggesting what I think you're suggesting?"

"You have to admit, it's possible."

"Yes, and it's possible I'll win draw the Lucky Lotto number, but not likely. Banner is a Boy Scout, you said so yourself. I'm not going to argue to the jury that he hid exculpatory records, so you can forget it."

Hesitating, I said, "I found something interesting at the courthouse."

He glanced up, his impatience showing. "And what's that?"

"Evelyn was busted on a felony drug charge last spring. The case worked its way through the system. You'd expected to see a plea deal, right?"

"Probably."

"Well, guess what happened?"

"Just tell me, okay?"

"The A.D.A. filed a deferred prosecution. No reason given."

"So? It's done all the time."

"He filed this one two days after Rudy was arrested."

Eddie rubbed his chin. "You're right, that *is* interesting. What do you think it means?"

"I'm not sure, but it bears checking out."

He leaned back and sighed. "Okay, fine. Find Evelyn and interview her, but I don't want you wasting too much time on it. I'd rather you focus your efforts on finding Connie Zwack, or Zink, or whatever her name is. Do you have any leads?"

"One. I think she called a cab from Alice's apartment this morning. All I have to do is find out where she was dropped off."

"That doesn't sound very promising."

"Trust me, Eddie."

Bundled up against the cold, I strode briskly to the parking garage and fired up my gas-powered Grizzly. It was time to pay a visit to my old friend, Mona Charles.

The moment I learned Connie disappeared from Alice's crib without being seen, I realized she must have been desperate to get out of there. She must have known she was being watched. What to do?

The answer to that question was on the scrap of paper I fished out of her wastebasket. Sometime during the night she'd packed her bags, then called for a cab—not for out in front of the building, but on Taku Street, away from prying eyes. Discarding the note the way she did had been careless, but Connie must have figured Alice was too ditzy to realize its significance even if she saw it.

My admiration for Connie Zwick, aka Alice, was growing by the hour.

Mona's Midnight Cab Company occupied a dilapidated single-story building on a side street in Spenard—an older and somewhat seedy section of Anchorage, known for its raucous nightlife. There was no sign or phonebook listing telling me where to find Mona's, but I didn't need one. I knew the place well.

Mona Charles was a legend in Anchorage taxicab circles. Barely five feet tall, of uncertain age and lineage, irascible, a chain-smoker, and possessing an encyclopedic knowledge of the city's streets, alleys and buildings, Mona had come to Alaska a quarter century ago from God knows where. I came to know her the same way every other private eye and police detective did—by seeking her out for information.

Lots of people take cabs. Knowing where they take the cabs *to* can be very valuable information. Mona was willing to share that information with the right person.

When I got there at 5:25 p.m., Mona was leaning over a small wooden table with an older-style telephone, a yellow pad, a bouquet of pencils in a clear plastic cup, and an ashtray overflowing with cigarette butts sitting on top. A tattered city map hung precariously from a cork board above the desk. A few feet away, an ancient space heater rattled and whined—I suspected its warranty had expired sometime during the Carter Administration.

Mona sat in an old wooden swivel chair, one hand hovering over the desk mic, the other holding a smoldering cigarette. She keyed the mic and issued a crisp command, dispatching one of her drivers to the southside. I waited until she finished the call and said, "I see you're still doing it the old-fashioned way."

She replied in a gravelly voice, "At my age, I'm happy I can do it at all."

My mouth broadened into a grin. "It's good to see you, Mona."

"And you as well, Sidney Reed." She studied me through a gauzy curtain of cigarette smoke. "I was sorry to hear about your wife."

"Thank you," I managed.

"Of all the cops, private eyes, and bounty hunters that traipse through my door, wanting this or that, you're about the only one who bothers to show their appreciation. Last Christmas it was this ashtray, the year before, a calendar. I think there was a bottle of wine in there somewhere. The calendar and wine are long gone, but as you can see, I still have the ashtray."

"No big deal."

She drew a leathery hand to her mouth and coughed. "It is to me."

The phone shrieked. Her husky voice answered, "Mona's Cab." She scribbled on the pad. "I'll have someone there in ten minutes." She hung up as I strolled over to the table.

She keyed the mic. "Stan, you copy?"

"I'm all ears, Mona."

"Couple arriving on Alaska Air. Can you take 'em to the Cook?"

"Sure thing, gorgeous."

Mona lifted her finger off the mic. "Now then, what can I do for you, dear boy?"

"You picked up a fare early this morning on Taku."

She exhaled a mighty cloud of smoke and stabbed her cigarette into the ashtray where it joined the other dearly departed butts. "I didn't take the call and I've been here since seven. Must have been on Ziggy's watch. Let me see . . ." She flipped back through the tablet on her desk. "Here it is. Call came in a little after 2 a.m. Ziggy dispatched Ted Collins. He's one of my new guys. Can't seem to keep drivers. You wanna drive for me, Sidney? Course not. The fare requested pickup at the Sourdough Apartments, with a drop-off in Mountain View." She scribbled the address on a sticky note and ripped it off the pad and handed it to me. It read: 781 Parsons Ave.

"I owe you one, Mona," I said, stuffing the note in my coat pocket.

"When you win the lottery, buy me a nice place on the Hillside."

"You'd hate it there."

"The hell I would." She peered over her glasses, then scrawled out another note. "In case you need to talk to Ted." As I reached for it, she admonished, "Don't call him before six—he'll bite your head off and I wouldn't blame him. Tell him I said it was all right." Then she gave it to me.

"Thanks, Mona."

"Don't mention it, Sidney Reed."

As I opened the door to leave, she was answering another call.

Twenty-one

The house at 781 Parsons Avenue was a pale-yellow one-story with a fenced-in front yard. Street lighting offered just enough illumination so that I was able to unlatch the gate without sustaining bodily injury. I walked briskly up to the front door, knocked, and waited. Scuffling noises drifted from inside and then the door was opened by a woman who was somewhere north of sixty, with a nest of silver-gray hair and a gaunt face. I sensed she was younger than she looked, aged prematurely by a lifetime of hard living.

The woman eyed me warily. "What do you want?"

"My name is Sidney Reed. I'm here to see Connie."

"What do you want with her?"

"She's not in any trouble, ma'am, but I do need to speak with her."

"Well, she's not here."

"I'm pretty sure she is."

"And I said she's not here. Now, if you don't leave, I'm going to—"

"It's all right, Mama." Connie emerged from the shadows.

"Hi, Connie," I said as we locked eyes. "Or is it Alice?"

The woman glanced questioningly at her daughter.

Connie said, "Come in, Mr. Reed." When her mother didn't move she said, "Christ, let the man in, Mama." Begrudgingly, the woman stepped aside and braced me with a cold stare.

I followed Connie into a small, drab living room that reeked of cigarette smoke and wet dog, although if a dog lived there, I saw no immediate evidence of it.

"You promised me you wouldn't bring your friends here," the older woman chided.

Connie rolled her eyes. "He's not a friend, Mama." She turned to me. "This is my mother, Beatrice Phillips. She's pleased to meet you, I'm sure."

I nodded. "Nice to meet you, ma'am."

The older woman scowled.

"We can talk in my room." Connie led me down a dark hallway and through a door and into a small bedroom with walls painted robin's-egg blue. She walked over to a twin bed by a small window and sat down. I settled into a rickety wooden chair and stared at Connie Zwick. She seemed more fragile than when I'd first laid eyes on her. Her eyes were puffy, her complexion pallid.

"You have to excuse my mother. She's not well."

I spoke curtly. "It would have saved us both a great deal of trouble if you'd told me your real name when we met. I might have been more inclined to believe your story."

In truth, I *did* believe her story. I just hated being lied to.

She stared at her hands. "I told you the truth, Mr. Reed. What you do with the information is up to you. I can't involve myself any more than I have already."

"I really wish you'd call me Sidney."

"I doubt you'll be here long enough."

I ignored that. "Do you know Ray's watching Alice's place?"

She shuffled her feet and nodded.

"Is that why you left in such a hurry?"

She nodded again, then stood and paced the room.

"I'm pretty sure Ray followed you to the bar."

"Shit." She said it to herself more than to me.

"He knows you met with me."

Her eyes darted skittishly. "Shit shit shit."

"This isn't just about Travis hitting that kid, is it?"

Her feet stopped moving. She stared down at me. "They're afraid."

"Who are *they*?"

She sat down and rested her palms on the bed. "Rance and his sons are afraid of what I know."

"And what's that?"

"They cook methamphetamine. They're drug dealers."

Well, this is just turning into a damn mess.

I asked her how she knew. Her green eyes didn't waiver one bit. "I've seen their lab, okay? Big concrete building out behind the house. Travis showed it to me. Heard them talking too, about buyers, deliveries . . . things like that."

It was my turn to pace the room. All I had to do was give her the subpoena to appear in court on Monday and get out of there. That's what Eddie would want me to do. He'd tell me my only duty was to my client, and that meant getting my witness in front of Rudy's jury. I had no "official" obligation to do anything else.

Except it wasn't that simple. Not for me.

I stopped pacing and looked at her. "What can you tell me about the Cooley family?"

She considered the question. "Well . . . Mr. Cooley—that's what I always called him—pretty much runs things. He's a big man, very intimidating. When I first met him I thought, Shit, this man hates me, but Trav must have convinced him I was all right because after a while he let me stay at the house. Eventually he warmed up to me. One day, out of the blue, he said I could call him Rance if I wanted to. Huge milestone, right?"

I nodded. Knowing Rance the way I did, I had to agree with her.

"Then a weird thing happened. One day I was alone with him in the house. He'd been drinking quite a lot that day—he likes to sit in that big ol' recliner and drink beer—and out of the blue he told me I reminded him of Kate, his dead wife. It was sweet in a way, but it also kind of creeped me out. That was right about the time I was allowed to move into the house and live there with Trav."

"What did Bo and Ray think of you being there?"

"Bo never liked having me around. I think I make him nervous. He sees himself as the ramrod of the place and me as someone he can't order around. There might also be some jealousy there, too, because his dad liked me."

"And Ray?"

Her face clouded. "Him I try to stay away from."

"Alice told me he's mean."

"He's mean, all right." She gave a slight shudder. "I've heard him threaten people and I see the way he looks at me. I know that look well. I make it a point to never turn my back on him."

I stopped moving and looked at her. "Tell me about the drugs, Connie."

She gripped the bed a little tighter. "They were pretty careful around me, but every once in a while, I'd hear things. Enough to know they were up to something. I didn't care, really, as long as they didn't involve me in it." She paused a moment. "Trav's room, where I stayed, faces the back of the property. Sometimes at night I'd hear things and get out of bed, or I'd be up walking around because I couldn't sleep, and I'd look out the window. And I could see a big concrete building through the trees with a red light over the door. Quite often I'd see trucks pulling up to it, people coming and going and the like. So I asked Travis what was in there and he told me."

"That it was a meth lab."

"Yeah. He said it like it was no big deal. Later, though, he warned me not to tell anyone. He said bad things would happen if I did." She sighed deeply. "It was Bo's idea to have me stay with Alice after Travis hit that boy. I think he'd realized by then that I wasn't just some airhead like his bimbo girlfriend. I think I made him nervous, like maybe he saw me as a threat."

I nodded. "Makes sense. They needed someone to keep an eye on you. They see you as something of a loose cannon."

I sat down and scooted my chair close to her.

Here goes nothing.

I took out the subpoena and gave it to her. Her eyes ping-ponged between me and the yellow piece of paper until she finally unfolded it. Then they widened in alarm as she read the words.

"Are you out of your fucking mind?" Her voice rose and carried through the thin walls.

"You all right in there, Connie?"

"Yes, Mama," Connie called back shakily. "Everything's fine."

But she wasn't fine. I saw it in her eyes when she turned slightly, the dim light from an overhead bulb revealing a tear perched high on her cheekbone. She clutched the yellow paper in a death grip. "Sidney, you can't ask me to testify."

Handing out subpoenas had become so routine for me over the years, I never considered what it felt like on the receiving end. Now, though, there was no mistaking the terror in her eyes.

"I'm not asking, Connie." I pointed to the paper in her hands. "That's a court order." As soon as I said the words, I wished I could take them back. I wished I could take that subpoena and march over to Eddie's office and tell him to stick it where the sun don't shine. But I couldn't, and for one simple reason: Rudy Skinner's life was hanging in the balance.

She looked right at me, eyes moist and pleading. "You really don't get it, do you? If they knew I was talking to you now, they'd kill me."

I caught sight of a slight movement—her hands were trembling. I waited until her eyes darted in my direction.

"What aren't you telling me, Connie?"

Her eyes flared wide, filled with some unseen terror. She hesitated, looked away, and spoke. "That night . . . after Travis came back to the house . . . after he hit that boy . . ."

"Yes?" I prodded.

"Rance and the boys, they . . . they made it go away."

I leaned forward. "What do you mean?"

"I mean they hauled Travis's truck into the yard and cut it up."

"How? How did they do that, exactly?"

"With torches, hammers, whatever they had. Took them most of the night. When they were done, there wasn't a piece of metal left bigger than a washtub. Rance dug a great big hole with a backhoe and they buried what was left."

I conjured up a mental image of the four men cutting up an entire pickup truck and burying the pieces as a blizzard raged all around them. The implications hit me like a runaway train: Father and sons not only knew what Travis had done, they were accessories after the fact in the murder of Willie Olson. And I'd just ordered Connie to testify against them in open court. No wonder she was so damn scared.

Connie had her head bowed and was staring at the floor.

"You saw them do all that?"

"I didn't have to. I know they did."

"How do you know?"

"Travis told me the whole story later, okay?"

I leaned back in my chair and exhaled audibly. "But you didn't actually see it."

"No, I didn't see it, but I know he was telling the truth. I could see it in his eyes."

She saw it in his eyes. Terrific.

"Is that when Rance threatened you?"

She shook her head. "No, that was earlier. When he heard what Travis had done, he called his sons into the kitchen and they talked amongst themselves for maybe ten minutes. Then the boys left and the old man came over to where I was sitting. I'll never forget what he said—'You listen to me now, Connie. You don't know a goddam thing, understand? Not a goddam thing.' His words chilled me to the bone. Then he made me swear not to tell a soul."

Her lower lip quivered. "After making me swear, he got all fatherly on me. Patted me on the shoulder and said Travis was going away, but not to worry, he'd find a new place for me to live." Her eyes flashed fire. "They think I'm someone they can order around."

She paused to wipe the remnant of a tear from her eye. Once again, I couldn't help but admire the gutsy little woman sitting before me.

"When I saw Travis two days later, he was a mess. Smelled like a brewery. That's when he told me what they'd done to his truck. He told me to pack up my shit and get out. Just like that. Mind you, I'd been living there with him for more than a year. That really hurt."

She folded her arms tightly to her chest. "I asked him where I was supposed to go and he told me I was to move in with Alice. The way he said it, I didn't have much choice in the matter. It's what had been decided. So that's what I did." She turned her gaze on me. "Please don't make me go to court, Sidney. Make Travis talk."

I thought for a moment. "Assuming I can find him, what makes you think he'd talk to me?"

"Because he's not like them," she shot back. "He hates himself for what he did. He wants to make it right, I know he does. He just needs help doing it, that's all."

I didn't find her words very reassuring. I didn't know Travis, but I knew enough about human nature to know he probably wasn't going to risk going back to prison to help some guy he didn't know.

The voice inside my head screamed at me to just leave the subpoena and get the hell out of there. But another voice said it wouldn't hurt to find the guy. I didn't think he would turn himself in, but maybe I could get him on tape admitting to what he'd done. An admission like that might convince the D.A. to drop the charges.

There you go again, trying to be the knight in shining armor.

"Okay," I sighed. "How do I find him?"

Her eyes panned back and forth like searchlights. "Last I heard, he was staying with a friend in a cabin somewhere in Knik."

Knik, so-named because of its proximity to the Knik River, is an hour's drive north of Anchorage. Lots of folks were living off the grid out there, I knew.

I reached in my coat for my notebook. "Who's the friend?"

"They call him Big Tooth. Don't know his real name."

"Ever met him?"

"Just once." A trace of a smile dusted her lips. "At the Lazy Dog Saloon in Palmer—Trav's favorite place. God, the two of them were shit-faced that night, and rowdy like—"

"I get the picture. What does he look like? Big Tooth, I mean."

"Tall and skinny. Long, straggly dark hair—I doubt it's ever touched a comb. Full beard and moustache."

"A hundred guys out ther look like that," I lamented.

She grinned. "Not like this guy. You see, there's a reason they call him Big Tooth." She pinched her front tooth with her fingers.

"He's got this big gold tooth in front. When he opens his mouth, you can't miss it."

"Okay, so what does he do?"

"He runs a body shop on the Old Glenn, and . . ."

"What?" I said.

"I think he runs meth for the Cooleys."

I jotted it all down. "Do you have a photo of Travis?"

"Got one in my purse." She reached for the tan bag on the desk beside me and withdrew a small, wrinkly snapshot. It showed a tall, lanky, clean-shaven kid wearing a baseball cap and standing next to a pickup. He had a long thin face and pointy chin. I was pretty sure I'd recognize him if I saw him.

"Mind if I keep this?"

"Help yourself. I'd like it back, though."

I stood up. "I have to get going. Will you need a ride to the courthouse?"

"You're really going to make me testify?"

"Monday morning at ten." I saw the panic in her eyes and added, "It really won't be that bad. We'll put you on the stand and—"

"You really don't get it, do you? This—" she waved the subpoena in the air "—is my death warrant."

"You don't know that."

"I know Rance Cooley. He may like me, but he'll do anything to protect his family and that business."

"Well, let's hope you won't need to testify."

"Can you promise me that?"

"Of course not. Look, I'll let the attorney know of your concerns. If I can find Travis and convince him to cooperate, it's possible we won't need your testimony, but I don't think I need to tell you that's a longshot." I watched the worry lines spread across her forehead. The truth was, I'd grown fond of Connie. She reminded me of Molly.

"I'll find Travis," I said in the most reassuring voice I could muster. "In the meantime, give me your phone number so we can keep in touch."

"I'll have to give you my mom's number. I don't have a cell phone."

I wrote the number on my copy of the subpoena, then I handed her one of my old business cards with my cell number on it.

"Call me anytime, day or night, okay? I mean it, Connie. If anyone gives you any trouble, if you see anything suspicious, call me."

She stuffed my card in the rear pocket of her jeans. "I'll show you out."

At the front door I said, "This is a good thing you're doing, Connie."

"Tell me something, Sidney." She stared up at me, sadness etched in every line on her face. "Who's going to protect me when Rance and his boys find out what I've done?"

She closed the door without waiting for a reply.

Twenty-two

When I left Connie's place, I was tired and hungry. I wanted very much to go home and crash, but I'd made a promise to Rudy Skinner that I'd check on his trailer, and so I left Mountain View and headed east.

The east end of Anchorage is known euphemistically as Muldoon, after the bullet-straight four-lane highway that cuts through the middle of it. While Muldoon's reputation was less unsavory than some other parts of the city, its collection of half-empty strip malls, strip clubs, bars, fast food restaurants, dilapidated apartment buildings, and even more dilapidated trailer parks seemed unlikely to increase the city's chances of making it onto a list of best places to retire.

I followed the busy thoroughfare south for roughly two miles until I caught sight of my destination on the left—the trailer park where Rudy Skinner had lived prior to his arrest. I knew it well, having gone there chasing down witnesses more times than I cared to remember.

The moment I pulled into the complex, the Jeep's tires slipped into a pair of deep, uneven ruts in the dirty snow, like grooves in a scratchy vinyl record. The management hadn't seen fit to plow the road, which left individual trailer owners no choice but to take matters into their own hands and push the snow toward the nearest available space. I threaded my way through the rows as best I could in the evening darkness, deftly dodging the many parked cars.

I located Rudy's trailer, parked astride a huge mound of snow, and killed the engine. Number 324 was an older model single-wide with tiny windows and a single door in the middle. The only trace of illumination spilled from a half moon overhead, its eerie indigo light reflecting dimly off the surrounding snow.

I grabbed a flashlight, then felt for the Ruger under my seat and stuffed it in my coat. No use taking chances in this neighborhood. I got out and slogged up to the trailer through two feet of undisturbed snow. With just enough light to make out the outline of the door, I scraped off the step with my boot, exposing a heavy rubber mat. I lifted it up and found the key underneath, just where Rudy said it would be. I slipped inside, thumbed on the flashlight, and found the light switch.

I stood in a sparsely furnished living room with a royal-blue loveseat and two matching chairs, small coffee table, and a flat panel T.V. perched on a small wooden stand. The acrid smell of cigarettes assaulted my nostrils. The place was desperately in need of a good airing out. It was just warm enough to prevent the pipes from freezing.

To my right, the kitchen was separated from the living area by a narrow partition. Some cabinets had been pulled open but otherwise it was neat and clean. A folding card table and matching chairs had provided a utilitarian dining experience. The table was bare except for a single sheet of yellow paper, which I realized, on closer examination, was a copy of the search warrant left behind by APD officers.

I drifted back through the living room to the opposite end of the trailer, where I found a bathroom and two bedrooms, one of which had obviously been used as an office. Starting there, I found a small desk, a printer stand, a straight-backed chair, and a filing cabinet. The desk and filing cabinet drawers were pulled out. I found pencils, pens, a stapler, tape dispenser, envelopes, bond paper, and some bottles of whiteout in the desk. One drawer of the filing cabinet held various forms, all blank. The other drawers were empty. There was an ill-defined dust outline on the printer stand. I guessed there had once been a computer and printer here but someone else had them now. The APD had Rudy's business records, I knew. The closet was empty.

I drifted into the bedroom and switched on the light. A queen-size bed dominated the small room; a large chest of drawers had all of its drawers pulled out. The top two drawers were empty; the bottom two held socks, briefs, t-shirts—men's clothing. Against one wall there was a vanity, painted light blue, with a large mirror mounted on top. I sat down in the chair adjoining it and stared into the mirror.

You're looking old, Sidney. Old and tired. Lois was right.

A glint of light drew my gaze to the surface of the vanity. It was a long blond hair. All of the drawers were open and empty. I left the room and stuck my head in the bathroom. The drawers under the sink were empty. There was a crusty bar of soap on a ledge in the shower, but no feminine products in sight.

"Who's in there!" a husky voice demanded.

I tensed, stuck my hand in my coat, and felt for the Ruger. Slowly, I peeked my head out the bathroom door. Whoever it was, he was standing just outside the trailer door, beyond my vision.

"Don't make me say it again! I've got a twelve-gauge cocked and ready. Now come out nice and slow or I'm calling the cops."

There was just enough nervousness in his voice to make *me* nervous. *This is all I need. Some trigger-happy asshole with a shotgun.*

I started across the living room, keeping low, my hand glued to the Ruger. I stopped halfway to the door. "You there," I said. "My name is Sidney Reed. I'm a private investigator. This trailer belongs to my client, Rudy Skinner. I'm checking on the place for him. That's what I'm doing."

"You got some I.D.?"

"Yeah, I got I.D. Hold on."

I fished out my P.I. credentials that I'd bought online expressly for situations like this. It was strictly for show—the state of Alaska licenses hairdressers but not private eyes.

I took aim and sent the case skidding across the floor like a foosball puck. It came to stop at the open door and a hand snatched it away. I sat down in one of the navy-blue chairs and waited.

Moments later, the self-appointed neighborhood watch commander said, "Good enough, Mr. Reed. I'm sorry if I put a scare into you. It's just that we've had a number of—"

"Forget it," I interrupted. "Come inside where it's warm."

"Don't mind if I do," he replied with evident relief.

He was of medium height and thin, with a thick mat of dark hair, streaked with gray and combed straight back. Probably in his late fifties or early sixties. He looked me over, nodded, and leaned his shotgun against the wall near the door. It was a Mossberg pump-action 12-gauge. He stomped across the room, his boots dropping chunks of snow, and handed my credentials back. The trailer's floor shook under him.

"Name's Frank Leslie," he said.

I stood and we shook hands. "Sidney Reed."

"Don't usually come on like gangbusters, but I like to keep an eye on things. When I saw somebody in Rudy's trailer, I had to check it out."

"Don't worry about it, Frank. Come on in and take a load off."

I sat back down as Frank eased into the blue chair opposite. "This about the death of that Native kid?"

"It is." I stretched out my tired legs. "You live next door?"

"Going on twelve years now. Moved in right after my discharge."

I grinned faintly. "I had a feeling you were ex-military."

"Didn't know it showed," he chuckled. "Sergeant first class, retired. Should have made master sergeant but I got busted from staff down to buck sergeant after I punched a guy. That kind of set me back career-wise."

"Tough break."

He shrugged. "The L.T. had it coming."

"They usually do."

He arched an eyebrow. "You served?"

"Retired warrant officer, CID."

His face lit up like a Christmas tree. "Military cop. Why didn't you say so, chief?"

"No need to call me chief. Sidney's fine."

"Whatever you say, chief," he said, laughing.

I laughed too and found myself liking Frank Leslie immediately. I said, "Do you miss it?"

"Hell, yes. I loved keeping those Hummers and deuce and a half's running at forty below. My motor pool was the best on Fort Rich while I was there. We had a great group of guys." He stared longingly at the room, as if his old crew might suddenly materialize. "Sure miss 'em."

I'd known lots of guys like Frank. After twenty or thirty years living with their military "family" and having every need provided for—food, shelter, medical services—they become, in effect, institutionalized, in much the same way prison inmates do. When it comes time to retire, many have trouble coping on the outside. Some never do.

"You married, Frank?"

Pain crinkled his face. "Was. I lost Edith almost three years ago."

I kicked myself for bringing it up and sputtered out, "Sorry to hear it."

"How about you, Sidney?"

A knot formed in my gut—I *really* wished I hadn't brought it up. "Molly's been gone almost a year now. They say it was suicide."

Frank cocked his head. "You sound like you don't believe it."

I stared at my snow-clogged boots. "I suppose I don't want to."

"I hear you."

Neither of us spoke for a minute. I was suddenly in a foul mood. Dark images from last December tried to push their way to the surface and I forced them back under.

Frank suddenly grinned and reached into his coat and pulled out a silver flask wrapped in a faded leather pouch with a faded U.S. ARMY logo on its side. He twisted off the cap and handed it to me. "I keep this handy for cold nights."

"Good idea," I said, and tilted the bottle up to my waiting mouth. It was scotch whiskey. Good scotch whiskey. I handed it back and said, "Tell me about Rudy."

He paused to take a drink and stared past me. "I liked him, at least at first. He and Evelyn—that was his woman—were decent neighbors, though I can't say I approved of their lifestyle."

"Lifestyle?"

"Rudy had a nasty drug habit, come to find out. Oh, he was nice enough most days, but when he was tweaking—I think that's what they call it—he got pretty crazy. That wouldn't have been so bad, except for the way he treated Evelyn."

"Like how?"

"He was mean to her. Never saw him hit her, but I had my suspicions. But even if it was just verbal abuse, she didn't deserve that."

"Tell me about Evelyn."

He lifted the flask and drank some before handing it to me. "Nice lady. Too good for Rudy, in my opinion. Mind you, she had her problems, too. She was busted for possession, oh, maybe a year ago. I think she got probation for it."

"When did they move in?"

"Five years ago maybe, but don't quote me on that." I passed him the flask and he paused to drink from it. "Don't get me wrong. When he's sober, Rudy's a decent enough guy, and a hard worker when he wants to be. Did pretty well for himself with his snow plowin'. Not that he could have managed it without Evelyn keeping him straight. I believe she had an accounting degree or certificate. Something like that."

"What does she look like? In case I need to find her."

He gazed at the ceiling. "Blond, about my height, early forties. Nice figure. Wears her hair long and straight."

"Was she around when the cops searched the place?"

He scrunched up his face. "No, that was the odd thing about it. I'd just come back from Roy's—I like to tip back a few now and again—and noticed a dark sedan parked behind Evelyn's Honda. That made me curious cause she don't get many visitors. I walked up there and heard a man's voice. He was loud and mean, ordering her around. She wasn't happy about it, neither. I'm thinking, this guy's trying to force himself on her or whatever, so I pound on the door. And this guy opens it and tells me to fuck off."

"Can you describe him, Frank?"

He looked thoughtful. "No, not really. I just saw his silhouette."

"And then?"

"I told him to have Evelyn come out where I can see her or I'm gonna call the cops. He laughed and said he *was* the cops. I called bullshit on that. That set him off. He came out of the trailer and shoved a badge in my face. Said if I didn't leave he was going to arrest me. I told him I'm not going anywhere until I know Evelyn's all right."

Frank paused and took a pull on the flask. "That's when he said something that raised the hair on the back of my neck. He said, 'Mess with me and I'll be your worst nightmare.'"

"Did you get a better look at him when he came outside?"

He shook his head. "No. It was just too damn dark. And he was wearing a hat, so his face was kind of hidden. Definitely a white guy. About your size, maybe a little bigger. Sorry I can't remember more."

"You're doing fine, Frank."

"What bothered me was his manner. The guy was creepy."

"What do you remember about the car?"

"There I can help you. I *know* cars. It was a late model Chevy Malibu, dark blue or black."

"Was he alone?"

"Far as I could tell."

"What happened then?"

"He just stood there staring at me until I went inside my trailer." He passed me the flask.

I drank and said, "You peeked out your window, didn't you?"

He smiled. "Bet your ass I did. He went back inside. Came out ten minutes later and drove off. Evelyn packed up and left right after that."

I passed the flask back. "Did you talk to her before she left?"

"Better believe it. She told me to mind my own business."

He leaned back and emptied the container. "Whatever that cop said to her, it scared the bejesus out of her. Early next morning, a couple of APD units pull up and searched the place."

"Did they take anything?"

"Far as I could tell, just a couple of cardboard boxes."

"What about the cop who came the night before? He take anything?"

He thought for a moment. "I don't think so."

"Any idea where she might have gone?"

He shook his head. "All I can tell you is, she left in one hell of a big hurry."

I sat there in silence, lost in my own thoughts. I felt warm inside from the alcohol.

Frank broke the silence. "You know, Sidney, I don't get a lot of visitors anymore." He held up the empty flask and smiled. "What would you say to a refill?"

I replied with a smile of my own.

Twenty-three

pg 169 - half way through book

Rachel Saint George studied me with a frown. "Bad night?"

It was 8:30 a.m. Thursday morning and we were sitting by the window of the Mighty Moose Café, mugs of steaming black coffee in front of us. A freight train chugged back and forth between my ear drums. I looked at Rachel, bleary-eyed. "What gave you that idea?"

"You're drinking black coffee instead of mocha, which you only do when you're nursing a hangover. Also, you look like you just clawed your way out of a cement mixer. Seemed like a reasonable deduction."

"Keep it up and the city will give you an honorary detective badge."

"Don't be an ass. What's bugging you?"

I shifted uneasily. "Had a little too much to drink last night, that's all."

She cocked her head. "I don't think so. What are you trying so hard *not* to tell me?"

I demurred.

She pressed.

I drummed my fingernails on the mug. "You're a woman."

"Thanks for noticing."

"What makes a woman change her name?"

"Well . . ." She paused to gulp coffee. "Either she's hiding from someone, or . . ."

"Or what?"

"Or she's running away from someone or something."

I mulled that over.

Rachel stared thoughtfully. "Are we talking about Maria?"

I hesitated before saying, "We are."

"Oh." She drank more coffee. "You two still going out tomorrow?"

"We are." I glanced at my watch. "I have to get to court." I stood up and turned to go, then stopped and looked at her. "Thanks, Rach."

"Mind if I offer a bit of advice? Speaking as a woman who likes women, of course."

"By all means, offer away."

"Don't bring it up. Let her tell you when she's ready."

I twirled that thought around in my head. My roving eyes landed on my mug, untouched and steaming on the table. "By the way, thanks for the coffee. Save it for me?"

Rachel smiled impishly. "Fuck you."

A bone-chilling wind stung my face as I trudged along Fourth Avenue in the predawn dark. I was more than a block away from the courthouse when the drone of chanting voices filled the air. I crossed H Street and a dark mass of humanity materialized beneath the cold white streetlights. Shouts of "Justice for Willie!" soared above the traffic noise like a flock of squawking birds.

Approaching the fringe of the protesters, I surveyed the scene. The crowd had doubled both in size and intensity since yesterday, and there was a change in tone that I found unsettling. It was etched on the faces of the protesters and in their voices, and as I stood among them, their frantic shouts piercing the frigid air, an unease gripped me.

These guys are really worked up.

The bulk of the crowd was gathered around a young, charismatic Native man, his head shaved nearly bald, yelling into the crowd. He looked familiar but I couldn't place him. I eased closer in an effort to hear what he was saying.

". . . sick and tired of white men fishing our rivers, hunting our caribou, raping the ground we walk on, the ground Mother Earth entrusted us with, to extract gold and oil!"

He paused for effect and, as if on cue, the chanting subsided and a hush fell over the assembled throng. "Most of all, I'm sick and tired of them killing our Alaska Native brothers! It's time we demand justice. Justice for Willie!" Dozens of JUSTICE FOR WILLIE! signs pumped up and down, echoing the shouts of the participants.

Soon enough, the crowd quieted and the young Native man continued. "My brother lost his life because he believed we are *all* brothers. He went to a party looking for friendship but instead found ridicule and hate. They turned him away, left him to wander alone on a busy highway in a blizzard. Had the people at that party welcomed Willie as a brother instead of treating him as an object of ridicule, he would still be alive. I stand here seeking justice for my brother, Willie Olson. Justice for Willie!"

The crowd echoed his refrain: "Justice for Willie! Justice for Willie! Justice for Willie!"

I didn't linger. The day's trial session was scheduled to begin in less than ten minutes. I turned in the direction of the courthouse entrance and had taken only a few short steps when a raspy voice behind me shouted, "Hey you!"

I swiveled around. Barely five feet away stood a Native man in his twenties. His straight black hair and long narrow face were partially hidden under a pullover cap. His dark, depthless eyes bore into me.

"Yeah, you."

I was pretty sure the curl on his lips was not a smile.

He said, "I saw you sitting next to Willie's killer in court yesterday."

I didn't need this. My head throbbed like a drumbeat and I had to get to court. I had started to turn when the man next to him spun around. It was the guy stirring up the crowd. Mr. Charisma.

"What is it, Tommy?" he said.

Tommy poked a finger in my direction. "That's one of the guys helping Skinner, Woody."

It dawned on me at that moment that Woody and Tommy were Willie Olson's brothers—the *Daily News*, in its coverage of the demonstrations, had quoted both men extensively. The way they were glaring at me, you'd have thought *I* murdered Willie—with my bare hands.

"Who are you?" Woody demanded.

I didn't answer.

He half-grinned. "You have a name?"

"Yeah. My parents gave it to me."

Woody Olson's smile faded. "So, you're a funny man."

I shrugged. "What can I say? It's a curse. Now, if you'll excuse me, I'm due in court right about now."

I turned to my right and hadn't taken two steps when a powerful hand grabbed my left shoulder and spun me around. I used the spiraling force generated by the pulling motion to dodge the blow I knew was coming. Tommy Olson's right fist missed the side of my head by an inch. With my flattened palms, I marshaled all the power in my 45-year-old body and shoved him between the shoulder blades. He shot forward and hit the pavement with an audible *oomph*!

The shouting and drumming came to an abrupt halt. The throng of protesters gathered around us in a semicircle, their expressions ranging from curiosity to acrimony. Woody Olson stared slack-jawed at his brother, then at me.

"I get why he's pissed," I said to him, "so I'm willing to let this go. But you'd better keep him the fuck away from me. I've got a bitch of a headache."

Tommy sprang to his feet and maneuvered into a fighting stance. His brother rushed forward and body-blocked him. "Let him be, Tommy. He's not looking for trouble."

"He's defending that killer!" Tommy growled, trying to muscle his way through. "I say we kick his ass." He turned to face the crowd. "Who's with me?"

No one seemed inclined to join the fray, with one exception: Another young Native man, this one short, squat, powerfully built, a stringy goatee sprouting from a weak chin, stepped forward. "I say we teach his white ass a lesson." His jaw flexed in anticipation.

Just then a familiar woman's voice bellowed from the fringe of the crowd. "Stop! Leave him alone!"

Here we go.

I half turned to see Maria Maldonado elbowing her way through the throng of protestors. The cold had painted her cheeks red and her lips purple. I had an overwhelming urge to kiss both.

She reached my side, worry etched on her face. "Sidney, what's this about?"

"I was just conveying my condolences to the Olsons on the loss of their brother. Isn't that right, fellas?"

"That's right," replied a stone-faced Woody Olson.

Tommy, effectively restrained by his brother, glared at me, his face contorted in anger.

Woody addressed the group: "All right, everyone, show's over. Let's get back to it." He herded his brother away and the chanting resumed as though nothing had happened.

I looked at my watch: 8:56 a.m. "Let's go," I said, urging Maria toward the courthouse entrance. "The show's about to start. The one *inside*, that is."

"What happened back there, anyway? I thought they were going to hurt you."

"I had it all under control."

"It didn't look that way to me."

"Keep talking, will you? I just love the sound of your voice."

When I walked into the courtroom at two minutes past nine, the judge hadn't yet entered, so in a hushed voice I exchanged greetings with Eddie Baker and whispered the news that Connie Zwick was under subpoena. When I said hello to Rudy, he launched into a rant about jail cuisine and informed me he was no longer under lockdown status.

Judge Jeffries made his entrance a few minutes later. After dispensing with the preliminaries, he said, "Mr. Fellows, you may proceed."

The District Attorney straightened his tie and stepped up to the podium. "Your honor, the state calls Michael Banner."

The clean-cut APD detective strode smartly to the witness chair, the clerk swore him in, and for the next hour Fellows led him deftly through a chronology of the APD's investigation of Olson's death.

To avoid the expense and tedium of calling every officer who worked the case, Alaska's court rules allowed the lead detective to testify to the investigative efforts of the officers in his charge. Banner was impressive, having testified in numerous cases during his career, and any first-year A.D.A. could have sleepwalked through direct examination. On many occasions I'd seen Banner deflect some pretty nasty cross with ease. The man was unflappable.

When it was Eddie's turn at the podium, he went after Banner on three facets of his investigation: his efforts to track down the truck that had struck Olson, his handling of the snitch, and his interview of Rudy and the elicitation of his supposed confession. Eddie sought to sow doubt in the minds of the jurors about the thoroughness of Banner's investigation, while setting the stage for his expert witness to testify.

At one point during Fellows' direct he had tried to get Banner to say that marks on Olson's clothing were a match for the snowplow blade on Rudy's truck. Eddie put the matter to rest when it was his turn at the podium. "Detective, you're not suggesting to this jury that the impact pattern left on Mr. Olson's body is in any way a match to the defendant's vehicle, are you?"

"No, I am merely suggesting that his vehicle cannot be excluded."

"Thank you, detective. No further questions."

The exchange reminded me of Eddie's refusal to put me on the stand, which I thought was a mistake. I felt I could handle whatever Fellows threw at me, and besides, arguing reasonable doubt in closing remarks was not the same thing as presenting hard physical evidence refuting the state's theory. I was still stewing about it when the judge dismissed Banner.

Fellows returned to the podium. "At this time, the state calls David Borman."

A trooper led the state's star witness through a side door and over to the witness box. Clad in blue prison garb, his ankle and wrist chains clanked noisily in the otherwise still courtroom. The reactions of the jurors ranged from mild interest to outright contempt. I saw a female juror scrunch up her nose at the sight of him. It was why I went to the trouble of buying jackets and ties for my clients.

The moment the jailhouse snitch made his entrance, Rudy's left hand gripped his thigh, as if holding his leg in place. He mumbled something under his breath. I scooted my chair closer until I was mere inches away and whispered, "Take it easy, Rudy."

He turned slightly but kept silent.

Once Borman had settled into the witness box, the trooper said something to him before fading into a corner of the room. The clerk said, "Mr. Borman, clip the mike to your shirt and remain standing, please." After leading him through the oath, she said, "Please state your full name, spelling your last name."

"David Borman. B – O – R – M – A – N."

"You may be seated."

"Mr. Borman," Fellows began, "where do you currently reside?"

"At the, uh, Anchorage Jail." A smile arced across his florid face. "Temporarily, that is."

Chuckles were quickly silenced with a whack of Jeffries' gavel.

"And where were you prior to that?"

"Hiland Mountain."

"You're referring to Hiland Mountain Correctional Facility in Eagle River, isn't that right?"

"Yeah, that's the place."

"Did you have a cellmate during your stay at Hiland Mountain?"

Borman pointed a beefy finger at our table. "Yeah, that guy sitting right there. Rudy Skinner."

Rudy stiffened. I touched his left arm and whispered, "Easy."

"I see," Fellows said. "And during the time Mr. Skinner was your cellmate, did you two have occasion to engage in conversation?"

"Yeah, we talked all the time."

"What about?"

"Pretty much everything. Women. Booze. You name it."

"Did he tell you what he did for a living?"

"He said he drove snowplow. During the winter, of course."

"Did Mr. Skinner ever mention hitting someone while driving his snowplow?"

Eddie Baker shot out of his seat. "Objection . . . leading."

"Sustained." Jeffries cast a distasteful glance at Fellows.

Fellows said, "Mr. Borman, do you recall seeing a story in the newspaper about a young Native man who had been struck and killed while out walking?"

Eddie stood. "Again, judge . . . leading."

"I'll allow it."

"Well, Mr. Borman?"

"Yeah, sure, I remember that. It was a big story."

"And did you mention it to Mr. Skinner?"

"Yeah. When he said he plowed snow for a living, I got to thinking about that kid that was killed. I asked Rudy about it."

"And what did he say?"

"Nothing really. The way he was acting, you know, all quiet. I thought it was suspicious."

Eddie stood up. "Judge, if the witness is going to entertain us with his suspicions, perhaps Mr. Fellows would prefer to schedule a séance instead of actual testimony."

Fellows shouted "Objection!" with dramatic fervor.

The judge spoke in his commanding baritone. "I once heard a man say, 'Can't we all just get along?'" Tilting his chin toward Eddie, he said, "Mr. Baker, I see you're trying to match Mr. Fellows in the theatrics department. It may be acceptable in drama class, but not in my courtroom." He turned to the witness. "Mr. Borman, please confine your remarks to things you either heard or witnessed. Now, let's try this once more, shall we?"

The exchange was a portend of things to come. As the D.A. led Borman through his testimony, it was clear that his star witness delighted not only in being the center of attention, but aggravating Rudy in the process, which he accomplished using subtle facial gestures directed toward the defense table.

Nor did Borman let up during Eddie's cross-examination. He

was so effective, in fact, that by the time Eddie was wrapping up, Rudy could no longer contain himself. When Borman mentioned something that he claimed Rudy had said, Rudy shouted, "You're a fucking liar!" Heads snapped in our direction.

Jeffries glared. "Mr. Baker, control your client!"

Eddie's head swiveled toward Rudy, then me, and finally back at the judge. "My apologies, your honor. It won't happen again."

"I'm holding you to that, Mr. Baker. Please proceed."

As Eddie continued with cross, I squeezed Rudy's arm and whispered, "Look at me, Rudy. If you can't control yourself, the judge will tell that trooper over there to shackle your wrists and gag you. Is that what you want? Now, this jury is just itching to lock your ass up for the rest of your life. Don't give them an excuse to do it."

Rudy stared, wide-eyed, cheek muscles twitching. I hoped like hell he still had enough functioning brain cells to process what I had said. He reached across with his right hand and placed it on mine. He nodded his head shakily. "It's all good, Sidney. I'm fine . . . really, I am."

By the time Eddie was done with David Borman, the smugness that had permeated the convicted felon had all but disappeared. He'd painted Borman as a conniving opportunist who manipulated Rudy in order to broker a deal for himself. I could see it on the faces of the jurors. Despite Rudy's brief disruption, I thought the day had gone well.

As Eddie stepped away from the lectern, Judge Jeffries turned to the D.A. "Mr. Fellows?"

"Judge, I'd like to reserve my redirect for a later time."

"Very well." Jeffries pounded the gavel. "Court is adjourned until 9 a.m. tomorrow."

As the courtroom emptied, I checked my watch: 12:30 p.m. That gave me half an hour to get to my shrink appointment. Eddie took his time filling his satchel, seemingly lost in thought.

I wanted until he and I were the only two left in the room, then I said to him, "I won't be able to make our briefing today. I have an appointment. Then I'm headed out to the Valley to look for Travis."

He nodded, a dejected look on his face.

"Cheer up, Eddie," I said. "Your cross of Borman was brilliant."

"Give me a break. Any first-year law student could smoke Borman like a cheap cigar." He looked at me. "The thing you've got to get through your head, my intrepid investigator, is that this jury wants to punish someone for what happened to Olson, and today Rudy made it a whole lot easier for them."

"Oh yeah? They're not the only ones who want a piece of Rudy." I filled him in on my encounter outside the courthouse that morning. "Some folks in this town would hang him from a lamppost if given half a chance."

"It doesn't help that he's a pain in the ass," he said with a snicker.

"You have to play the cards you're dealt, Eddie. It is what it is."

"You're a philosopher now?"

"Well, I did study Kierkegaard in college."

"Wow, I'm impressed."

"That I studied Kierkegaard?"

"That you went to college."

"Fuck you, Eddie."

Twenty-four

Twenty minutes later, I was on the eleventh floor of a Midtown high-rise, approaching a door containing two lines of precise gold and black lettering which read:

ELLIOT P. RUNDLE, MD

PROFESSIONAL PSYCHIATRIC SERVICES

I went inside and approached a reception desk, behind which sat a woman of about sixty, looking prim and proper and stern, a hive of raven-black hair streaked with gray cemented in place. She wore spectacles set so near the edge of her nose, they seemed in danger of falling off if she so much as sniffed. An expensive-looking wooden placard bore the name MS. TALMADGE. She glanced up as I approached.

"Sidney Reed?"

I nodded.

"You're seven minutes late, Mr. Reed. Let me remind you of our policy." A bony index finger, tipped with a perfectly manicured fingernail, pointed at a sheet of paper taped to the front of her desk. It read:

PATIENTS ARRIVING MORE THAN FIFTEEN MINUTES LATE MAY,

AT OUR DISCRETION, BE BILLED AND THEIR APPOINTMENT

RESCHEDULED!

I recalled reading somewhere that you can't bill someone for a service not performed, and was tempted to tell her so. Instead, I smiled inanely and said, "Oh, good, I'm eight minutes early."

Her mouth tightened. "Your reputation precedes you, Mr. Reed, and not in a good way. Unlike my predecessor, I will not tolerate any shenanigans, such as using subterfuge to gain access to the doctor."

This was a not-so-subtle reference to my first appointment with Rundle. In an effort to get in to see him, I'd finessed my way past

Ms. Talmadge's younger and decidedly more gullible predecessor. Rundle had not been amused.

"By the way, whatever happened to Melanie?" I asked casually.

She sniffed. Her glasses remained in place. "Dr. Rundle felt a change was in order. That's all I'm at liberty to say. Now please have a seat. He will be with you shortly."

I strolled over to the waiting area, where half dozen chairs were set around a glass-topped table that held an assortment of magazines arranged in neat little stacks. I picked up a copy of *Guns & Ammo*, wondering idly if a firearms magazine was appropriate reading material for mental patients. Not that I thought *I* was a mental patient—just those other people.

I didn't have long to ponder the question because just then Rundle's door burst open and the doctor walked through it, followed by a chubby, balding man hunched over so far, he was looking almost straight down.

"... worry about a thing, Carl," Rundle was saying. "I'll see you in two weeks."

Carl shuffled toward the elevator. Rundle turned in my direction. "Sidney, please come in."

I caught Ms. Talmadge's eye, made a show of fingering my watch, then tilted my head toward the departing figure of Carl. She sniffed and turned away.

I stepped inside Rundle's now-familiar office. It was spacious and infused with light from a window that took up one entire wall. Rundle retreated behind an enormous cherry desk and reached for a green file folder. "Have a seat," he said, his manner pleasant yet brisk.

I ignored the offer and walked over to the window, which featured a panoramic view of the Alaska landscape. I needed to gather my thoughts. After two sessions, I couldn't say we'd made any progress to speak of, but these sessions gave Rundle a chance to work off a debt he owned me for a surveillance job. Despite the lack of progress, I still held out hope he might be able to help me.

"How have you been?" I heard him say.

"Busy," I replied off-handedly. "I'm in the middle of a trial."

"Then you're working again. How do you feel about that?"

"I'm working again. Anyway, what you're really asking me is whether work takes my mind off the death of my wife."

"Well . . . does it?"

I turned and began pacing back and forth. "I suppose, a little . . ."

"You seem to have something on your mind, Sidney. Why don't you have a seat and tell me about it?"

I sat down and stared at him across his desk, which was big enough to double as a ping-pong table. "I have a client charged with the hit-and-run killing of a Native man."

He raised an eyebrow. "Oh yes. I've been following that case in the paper. Go on."

"I'm providing trial support. It's an easy gig, really, except . . ." I hesitated. "I've learned that my client is innocent."

"You don't think he killed the boy?"

"I know he didn't."

"You think the state got it wrong."

"I do."

"And you want to make it right."

I leaned forward in my seat. "It's not a question of wanting to. I have to."

"I see." He scrawled something in the file, then leaned back and scratched his chin. Flicked his fancy Mont Blanc pen, trying to keep me off balance. That's what these guys do.

Impatiently, I scanned the bookcases behind him.

Shouldn't we be talking about Molly?

At last he spoke. "Why do you have to make it right?"

I felt my lips part involuntarily. "What do you mean?"

Another sharp click of his pen. "My question is a simple one. You said you have to make it right. Why is that so important to you?"

"Isn't it obvious?" I said it a little too loudly. "He's innocent. I can't let the state convict him. It wouldn't be right. You can understand that, can't you, Doc?"

Of course he can, I thought to myself. *He's humoring me. That's what these guys do.*

Rundle stared, waiting for me to speak. I smiled. It was slight, but Rundle caught the look. "Why did you smile just then?"

"I was thinking about something Dad used to say."

Rundle seemed amused. "What did he say?"

"He said, if you wrong someone in some way, make it right, because you may not have a chance to later."

"He died when you were just a boy, as I recall."

"Massive heart attack." My mouth felt like sandpaper. "I was ten."

"I'd say he taught you well." He paused, chin resting on splayed fingers, eyes fixed, thinking. "In our last session, you mentioned reading Molly's diary. Tell me more about that."

I was wondering when he'd get around to asking about my dead wife. "I was going through some papers and came across it. I've been reading the various entries, trying to . . . well, figure things out."

"What things?" He sat in rapt attention, his pen now silent.

I gave him a brief summary of some of the diary entries: her struggle with the long Alaskan winters, musings about my work as a private investigator and the long absences the work too often required, her sometimes cryptic notations about her volunteer environmental work and the people she worked with. I concluded by explaining that she'd been taking medication to treat depression, after being diagnosed with Seasonal Affective Disorder.

"If I understand you correctly—please pardon my directness— you're trying to figure out why your wife killed herself?"

I nodded and lowered my gaze to the carpet. It had a colorful paisley pattern to it. When I raised my head again, Rundle had leaned back in his chair with his hands clasped behind his head, looking up at the ceiling.

"You sound as if Molly's death is a puzzle you have to figure out."

"That's exactly what it is," I replied.

"You really think so?"

"Don't you?"

"I think you're avoiding the real issue."

"You don't think I should read her diary?"

He tapped his pen on the desk. "I didn't say that. By all means, read it. Just don't expect that anything you find in it is going to help you regain your former life. The answers you seek are inside of you; not your wife's diary."

The answers you seek are inside of you? Rundle was sounding more like a Shaolin monk than a psychologist. I got up and returned to the coolness of the window, my gaze directed at the distant landscape, the true wildness that lay beyond the limits of the gray, bland city. As the old-timers—in Alaska we call them "sourdoughs"—are fond of saying, *Anchorage is only one hour from Alaska.* It was Alaska's wildness that Molly loved so much. Savage yet simple, like a snowplow blade on a cold winter's night.

"Sidney, are you listening to me?"

No, I'm not, you dime store shrink.

I turned from the window. "I'm listening."

He held my gaze. "You'll tie yourself up in knots trying to figure out why she committed suicide. Death is final. She's not coming back, regardless of anything you or I might do. The sooner you come to grips with that, the sooner you can get on with your life."

What Rundle was saying sounded an awful lot like what Lois Dozier had said, and *her* advice had been free.

I strong-armed my thoughts away from the sight of my wife's limp and bloodied body. Lois and Rundle were both right, of course. Molly wasn't coming back. But that didn't mean there couldn't be justice.

Or retribution.

Throughout our previous sessions, I'd never told Rundle about the feeling that had found a happy home deep in my gut, like a sleeping monster. I'd hardly acknowledged it myself, and yet it festered there all the same. The feeling that someone had done this to her and *that* someone needed to pay for it.

But what if this feeling was merely an excuse I had created to hold on to her? What if my monster was a creature of my own making?

I looked up at Rundle. "I know she's not coming back. I'm not that delusional." I paused, collecting my thoughts. "It's true, I blamed myself for her death, but the more I read through her diary, the more I realize I have no business putting all that on my shoulders."

"Good! That's an important realization."

"Still, I can't bring myself to let it go." I tried to finish the thought, then realized I had a mass of phlegm lodged in my throat. I swallowed it. "Honestly though, Doc, I don't think I'm making any progress."

"You're not giving yourself enough credit, Sidney."

"If you say so."

"You're working now and *that's* progress." He folded his hands atop the open file folder. "Why don't you try making new friends, perhaps go out on a date?" He peered over his gold frames. "Allow yourself to have fun."

"Actually, I'm seeing someone now." I said it almost too quickly, like a student desperate to please his teacher.

"Yes." He glanced through his notes. "I recall you saying something about a love interest. How is that progressing?"

I decided to spare him the gory details of my attempts to have dinner with Maria. Instead I said, "We have a date for tomorrow night."

"Excellent." He penned something in my file.

Suddenly I remembered. I said, "There's something else, Doc."

"Yes, Sidney?" He didn't look up.

"I've been having these nightmares."

He set his pen aside. "Tell me about them."

Rundle listened intently as I described in detail my recurring dream in which Molly ends her life with a pistol shot. I concluded by saying, "They never go away, these . . . visions."

He leaned his elbows on the desk and pressed his fingers together. "You know, these nightmares you've been having, coupled with other things I've observed with you, may be symptoms of Acute Stress Disorder or Posttraumatic Stress Disorder."

I came alert. "You think I have PTSD?"

"It's not out of the question. Think about it, Sidney. You arrive home after a long night on the job, no doubt tired and stressed out, and—please excuse my frankness here—you discover your wife has been shot in the head. Witnessing such an event would no doubt traumatize anyone."

A lump formed in my throat like a millstone.

"You display other symptoms as well. Avoidance of work, feelings of detachment, and, by your own admission, you blame yourself for what happened to her."

My eyes were drawn to the floor under his desk. There was Molly's lifeless, bleeding body, lying at my feet on Rundle's paisley carpet.

It's not real ... not real.

My hands trembled. Sweat pooled in my palms.

Don't ... look ... down.

I heard the sound of Rundle's voice far off in the distance. "You do, don't you, Sidney?"

I swallowed great gulps of air, tried to slow my breathing.

"Sidney? Are you all right?"

"Sure, Doc. What did you say?"

"I was saying, you blame yourself for what happened to her. That might also suggest a diagnosis of PTSD."

I glanced at the carpet. Molly's body was gone. I nodded.

He leafed through the file. "Now, I don't recall asking this in our prior sessions, but ... are you drinking?"

He's reading me like a cheap novel.

"I drink quite a bit of beer. Harder stuff on occasion."

"During the day?"

"I guess I'm pretty fucked up, aren't I, Doc."

"Not at all. You're having a surprisingly common reaction to a highly traumatic event. All too often, PTSD is viewed as a character weakness rather than an illness." Rundle sighed and glanced at his watch. "Well, I think this is a good place to stop. We've made real progress today, Sidney. In fact, we may have reached a turning point."

He scribbled a few hurried lines in his file, put aside his pen, and stood up. Seeing as how we'd only been in session for thirty minutes,

I thought perhaps it was his subtle way of telling me I'd exhausted my line of credit. By my calculation, he still owed me an hour and I told him so, adding, "I hope you haven't forgotten our arrangement."

"I haven't forgotten, Sidney. It's just that I'm running behind today. I'll make it up to you."

We moved into the lobby, where Rundle said to Ms. Talmadge, "I want to see Sidney again in a month." To me he said, "Good luck tomorrow night," and winked for good measure. We shook hands and he retreated to his office. Watching him go, I thought to myself that Rundle wasn't such a bad guy, just a little full of himself.

Hearing Ms. Talmadge clear her throat, I turned around.

"The earliest I can get you in," she said, "is the second week of January. Will that do?"

I felt a flexing in my gut and replied, "That's more than six weeks away. I have to see him before Christmas."

Her questioning eyes searched mine, but I think my reaction surprised me more than it did her. I didn't tell her Christmas Eve was the anniversary of Molly's death, even though I felt the weight of it pressing down on me like a big slimy rock.

"Please try," I said. "It's important."

Ms. Talmadge regarded me without speaking, lowered her gaze to the appointment book on her desk, and then looked up. "Well . . ." she said at last, "I suppose I could see if someone is willing to switch with you. Give me a couple of days to work on it. I'll call you."

I thanked her and turned toward the door. Her strident voice stopped me in my tracks.

"In the future, Mr. Reed . . ." She paused.

"Yes?"

"Please be on time."

Twenty-five

I left Midtown behind and followed the Glenn Highway north toward the Matanuska Valley, in search of Travis Cooley. If Connie Zwick was to be believed, it was he and not Rudy Skinner who struck and killed Willie Olson on a wind-blown evening last January. To free Rudy Skinner, I had to find Travis.

The Glenn Highway is the primary artery north out of Anchorage, a human pipeline for the many thousands of commuters residing in bedroom communities from Eagle River to Willow. The drive is pleasantly scenic, although not quite so pleasant during rush hour, when thousands bail out of the city en masse. The drive can be downright ulcer-inducing when blowing snow and icy roads create a demented version of bumper cars.

Thankfully, it was too early for rush hour and the sky was clear and sharp. With conditions like these, you can often catch glimpses of Denali, the mountain formerly known as McKinley, in all its glory. To my dismay, chunks of blue-gray clouds were gathered along the northern horizon like huddled sheep, obscuring North America's highest peak.

Once I had passed Birchwood, clusters of houses and apartment buildings gave way to undulating forest to my left and the Chugach Mountains to my right. Farther north the majestic and vaguely foreboding Alaska Range loomed. I crested a rise and sprawled out before me was the Matanuska-Susitna Valley.

To Alaskans, it is Mat-Su, or simply The Valley. Here, the mighty Matanuska and Knik Rivers converge and spill into Cook Inlet, the surrounding area forming a vast area of wetlands, mudflats, grasslands, and upland birch forest. The fertile soil and mild, sunlit summers inspired the government to transplant a few hundred farmers from the Upper Midwest in the 1930s. Their descendants still reside there.

The Glenn descended out of the mountains onto the valley floor, where it swung to the east and narrowed to two lanes. On my left lay the vast expanse of the Palmer Hay Flats, where each winter herds of moose gather, taking advantage of the ready food supply. To my right, the imposing edifice of Pioneer Peak rose more than a mile from the valley floor to its snow-covered crest.

A few miles on I exited the Glenn Highway in favor of the Old Glenn. Unlike its newer namesake, which swings north across the hay flats and crosses both the Knik and Matanuska Rivers, this narrow two-lane continues east for several miles, straddling the south side of the Knik River. Now, for the first time since leaving Anchorage, I felt I was in the midst of wilderness. Ignoring the single-digit temperatures, I lowered the window to hear the sweet music of the river.

The Old Glenn Highway swept abruptly north across the roiling Knik and continued in a ramrod-straight line through dense forest. A wall of trees gradually gave way to homes and side roads and the trappings of civilization. I was approaching The Butte, an unincorporated community named for a 900-foot-high geological formation that bore the name Bodenburg Butte.

A single-pump filling station and store no bigger than a single-car garage emerged from the trees to my left. The place was devoid of a name or other visible markings, except for a small handmade sign that read CASH ONLY. I pulled alongside the pump and went inside, an anemic-sounding bell announcing my presence.

An elderly woman, sixtyish, with straggly gray hair appeared from the back. She was stooped and wore a green plaid shirt with the sleeves rolled up. I could see she had been attractive once, with an angular face and high cheekbones, but the years had not been kind to her.

She looked me over, starting at my boots and working her way up, then out the window at my car. She stepped behind a small counter. "I s'pose you need gas."

I nodded. There was something in her manner that I liked.

"It's cash only," she said.

I pulled out a ten and handed it to her. "Let it ride."

She shot me a glance that held a trace of mischief. "I don't see too many folks from the city with a sense of humor."

"I was raised on a farm. Comes with the territory, I guess."

"I s'pose it does."

"I'm Sidney Reed."

"Clara Ann Lamott." Her mouth curled in a grin. "*My* folks had a sense of humor."

"They must have been farmers."

"Through and through. Came here in thirty-five. Dad blew his brains out in forty-nine, two years after he had me. Can't say as I blame him."

Her words sent a chill through me as I thought about Molly. I shook it off and said, "I'm sorry."

"Don't be. He was a no-good drunk. Mom found herself a nice man who was good to us."

I was beginning to like Clara Ann. "Maybe you can help me," I said. "I'm looking for a man named Travis Cooley."

"Don't know him," she replied without hesitation. "And I know most everyone in the Butte."

I showed her the photo Connie gave me. "Does this help?"

She glanced at it. "Not in the least."

"How about a guy they call Big Tooth?"

Her eyes narrowed into slits. "Him I know. Real name's Robert Murphy. Knew him when he was just your average juvenile delinquent. These days he runs an auto body shop two miles up the road here called B.T. Auto. B.T. stands for Big Tooth, you see. Clever, don't you think? Why do you suppose they call him Big Tooth?"

Before I could answer she pointed a finger at her open mouth. "Because he's got a big gold tooth that sticks out in front. That's what we out here in the Butte call irony."

I couldn't resist grinning at that.

She studied me closely. "What do you want with him?"

"I'm a defense investigator working on a murder case. I need to find Travis Cooley. I was told Big Tooth could lead me to him."

She stared out the window and sighed. "Like I said, I don't know Travis, but I can tell you you're not going to get anything out of Big Tooth unless there's something in it for him."

"Tell me about his shop, Clara Ann."

"Not much to tell. He fixes cars and sells meth. They say he's the biggest dealer in the Valley. I don't know about that. I never touch the stuff. Lots of folks do, though. Just not me."

"He must be clever to get away with it."

"He's clever enough. Anyway, who's gonna tell?"

"You seem to know a lot about it."

"I see his wrecker driving up and down this road half dozen times a day." She paused. "Let me ask you something, Sidney. If you ran an auto body shop out here in the Valley, why would you tow a junk car all the way out here from Anchorage and then all the way back again the next day? Does that strike you as cost effective?"

"Not really."

"You're damn right it's not."

"Why are you telling me all this?"

"Because you asked and because I don't like him." Her lower lip shook. I glanced down at her hands. They were shaking, too.

I looked at her steadily. "What happened, Clara Ann?"

Once more her gaze took her out the window, where the low November sun threw flaming red light against the trees on the far side of the road.

Without turning she said, "He raped a girl and never answered for it, that's what happened."

Silence filled the room.

I swallowed hard. "Did she report it?"

Her head snapped in my direction. "She wanted to, but he threatened her if she said anything. She told me. That's as far as it went. I begged her to let me drive her to the troopers or the doctor, but she wouldn't have it. But he'll answer for it one day. He'll damn sure answer." She wiped away a tear with the back of her hand and threw me a sharp glance. "Now why in hell did I just tell you that?"

"People tell me things. I guess it's why I'm good at what I do."

Dead silence followed. She stared through the glass for so long, I began to wonder if she knew I was still there. I shifted my weight and said, "I'm sure the girl appreciates that you tried to help her."

She blinked and looked at me intently. "You'd think she would, seeing as she's my daughter. But she don't."

Way to go, Sid.

I cleared my throat. "Well, uh, I think I'd better hit the road."

She came alert, smiling sadly. "I'm sorry to vent on you like that, Sidney. I don't get many customers, and the few I do get ain't paying to listen to me."

"Well, it was a pleasure all the same."

"Come by any time, Sidney."

"Thanks, Clara Ann."

I left a ten on the counter and walked out to the Jeep. Her sad face looked out at me through the window as I drove north.

Twenty-six

B.T. Auto was a flat-roofed concrete slab of a building, with two narrow bays and a single door in front. The initials B.T.A. were hand-painted crudely in black on a four-by-eight sheet of plywood hung slightly off kilter above the door. I admired the subtlety.

I cruised slowly past, turned around in someone's driveway, and returned for a second look. A red Ford pickup, a black Chevy with a snowplow attached, and an older model Buick sedan were parked in front. In the rear, a tow truck stood idle. Across the street, dense woods and shrubs lined the road. No side roads or driveways—no place to set up a stakeout. So much for surveillance.

I decided to make one more pass and looked for someplace to turn around. A hundred yards or so down the road there was a boarded-up building. I did a one-eighty in the gravel driveway and doubled back north on the Old Glenn. As I was approaching B.T.A. again, I saw a man exit the building and walk over to the black pickup, his right hand clutching a package. He matched Connie's description of Big Tooth perfectly. My pulse quickened.

I cruised past, maintaining a lazy pace and eyeing the rearview mirror. A moment later the pickup popped into view and turned in my direction. I sped up to forty-five and held it there. In a matter of seconds, the truck was hugging my bumper, its plow blade looming in the rearview mirror like a great wall of steel. He laid on the horn and sped past me like his ass was on fire.

Andrea said this thing runs like a pissed-off grizzly. Let's find out.

I punched the pedal to the floor and the engine roared, shoving my body deep into the seat. Squeezing the wheel, I drew a bead on the pickup, now little more than a black dot on the road ahead. I leaned on the pedal and the speedometer climbed . . . sixty . . . seventy . . . I wondered how long I could keep this up.

At eighty the black dot began to grow larger. When I had pulled to within seventy-five yards behind him, I eased off the pedal until I was keeping pace.

Big Tooth held speed as we whizzed through the Butte, slowing only for turning vehicles or slower drivers. In due course the trees on my left fell away, exposing the wide, chalky white bed of the Matanuska River, its primary stream cutting down the middle and breaking off into spidery rivulets along the edges. Gradually we left the Butte behind as we followed the Old Glenn toward the pioneer town of Palmer, home of the Alaska State Fair. I knew it well. Molly's sister, Barbara, was a resident.

The black pickup sped across the Matanuska River Bridge and then slowed as we approached the Palmer city limits. I inched closer so as not to lose him in city traffic, realizing the move was a double-edged sword—closer proximity increased my chances of getting burned. Luckily, this guy showed no interest in what was behind him. He seemed to be on a mission.

He hooked a left at Alaska Street—Palmer's main drag. I followed suit.

What are you up to, Mr. Murphy?

I didn't have to wonder long. The pickup slid alongside the curb in front of the Blue Light Bar. I did likewise, leaving three car-lengths between us, and killed the engine. Reaching into my kit bag, I took out my digital camera and aimed it at the pickup. The driver hopped out, package in hand, and I clicked the shutter as fast as my discount-store point-and-shoot would allow. Seconds later, he rounded the front of the truck and dashed inside the bar.

It was almost 4 p.m. I noted the time and the pickup's license plate number in my notebook, settled back in my seat, and waited for Big Tooth to come out. Less than five minutes later, Murphy exited the bar. He glanced around furtively, climbed into the truck's cab, hooked a U-turn, and headed back in the direction from which he'd come. I made an identical maneuver, following at a discreet distance. At the Old Glenn he signaled a right turn, toward the Butte.

I debated whether I should follow him and quickly decided I should. If Connie was correct that Travis lived in a cabin with Big Tooth, this was a golden opportunity to find Mr. Cooley.

By the time I made my own right turn, Murphy was already a quarter mile up the road. I leaned on the gas pedal and caught up to him just past the bridge. To my right, the river reflected the golden glow of the setting Alaska sun.

I wish you were here to see this, Molly.

I seriously doubted Murphy was admiring the view. The man was moving like he had a mama grizzly nipping at his heels. I leaned on the gas pedal, struggling to keep up.

Soon the truck's brake lights flared bright red and swung sharply left onto Clark-Wolverine Road, coursing up a steep hill. The road, I knew, stretched for miles into the backcountry, with many side roads and tight spots. I kept as far back as I could without losing him.

Two miles in, the Chevy pivoted right onto a narrow road, unnamed and unpaved. I suddenly felt very exposed but I had no choice but to follow dutifully behind. As the Cherokee bounced along on the snow-covered surface, I gripped the wheel with growing unease. If Murphy hadn't noticed my headlights by now, he wasn't the drug dealer I suspected him to be. For all I knew, this was a dead-end road and I was headed into a trap. I reached under the seat for the Ruger and set it on the passenger seat next to me.

We'd gone three quarters of a mile when he pumped the brakes and jerked the wheel to the left, leaving the narrow road. I felt like I was in a tunnel—there were no driveways or other places to turn around or pull off. Snow-filled ditches lined the roadway. If the Jeep got in there, it wasn't coming back out. I had no choice but to keep driving nonchalantly past, trying not to look like I was strolling down Fourth Avenue with my pants down around my ankles.

As I neared the spot where he'd disappeared, a wall of trees gave way to a clearing with a log cabin set in the middle of it. The black

Chevy was parked directly in front of the cabin and Robert Murphy was standing on the front stoop—staring directly at me.

We locked eyes.

Busted.

Or maybe not. There is a paranoia-inducing aspect to surveillance—a tendency to assume that if your subject so much as glances at you, you must be burned, even if you haven't been. Then again, most of my subjects are cheating spouses, not drug dealers, and most live in suburbia, not in cabins in the middle of nowhere. And his was more than just a casual glance. So, yeah, I was busted.

I continued for another mile with no sign that the road was going to circle back around to the Old Glenn anytime soon, or at all. I cursed myself for not having a topo map of the Valley. I decided to reverse course and head back in the direction from which I'd come.

Darkness folded in around me, my rental car's halogen beams stabbing the inky blackness. As Murphy's cabin neared, I eased off the accelerator, debating whether I should stop and see if Travis was there. Arriving at the clearing, I saw a thin rectangle of light streaming from a window, but what got my blood pumping was what I didn't see.

Big Tooth's Chevy was gone.

I drove on, sweaty hands clutching the wheel. I told myself, without much conviction, that Murphy had probably gone for pizza, or drinks, or to his girlfriend's house.

More likely, to find me and kick my ass.

I dismissed these thoughts as P.I. paranoia. There were dozens of places he might have gone. I decided to look at my situation philosophically. I now had a good lead on where Travis was holed up. Better I should come back during the day, while Murphy was at work. In the meantime, it was still early in the evening, plenty of time to head back to Palmer, say hello to Barbara and make nice. Tell her I—

Wham!

With a sickening crunch of metal, something immense and muscular slammed into the Jeep's passenger side with the force of a berserk wrecking ball. Instantly the passenger-side airbag exploded like a rifle shot, then just as quickly deflated, a ghostly apparition in the dark interior. The Jeep stopped cold. A deathly quiet followed.

I felt a slight vibration and realized the car was still running. Breathing a sigh of relief, I peered through the passenger side window. No sign of my attacker.

Murphy's there, waiting in the dark.

He'd known I'd have to return the same way, so he had decided to send me a message. He'd driven up the road, backed into a neighbor's driveway, killed the lights, and waited.

And now *I* waited, listening to the sound of my own breathing, my heart pounding in my chest. Then I heard it—the mad roar of an engine, the frantic spinning of tires on ice—high-pitched, like a demonic scream . . .

Wham!

The Cherokee lurched under a second impact amid the sound of buckling steel and slid sideways, as if pushed by a giant hand, slowly yet inexorably toward the maw of the ditch waiting in the darkness.

Think, damn it, think!

I was on a collision course with the ditch, but I knew from the tortured scream of the tires that Murphy was having trouble getting traction on the ice-covered road. I saw a chance, if only a slim one. If he let up on the gas pedal, even for a second, the Chevy's death grip on the Jeep would be lost, giving me just enough time to accelerate out of there. It was a question of luck and timing.

My headlights exposed the black gash of the ditch as it loomed closer and closer, and I was helpless to do anything except wait for the Jeep to tumble on its side like an upended coffee mug.

Without warning, the Chevy's tires stopped screaming. Its engine faded into an idle.

It's now or never.

I punched the accelerator, and it was the Jeep's turn to scream, its tires spinning like banshees, fighting to gain traction.

Move, you sonofabitch, move!

But it didn't move; it just sat there, tires whirling frantically.

I gripped the wheel and braced myself for the impact I knew was coming.

It never came. Instead, the Jeep leapt forward so fast, the front wheels seemed to lift off the road. The car fishtailed briefly before gripping the road and racing forward as if shot from a cannon. I glanced in the rearview mirror and saw the Chevy's headlights blink, but they didn't move.

From then on, I never looked back. At Clark Wolverine Road I hooked a left, ignoring the stop sign, and pegged the speedometer until I hit the Old Glenn. Only then did I ease up on the pedal and cast a sharp eye on the rearview mirror. I was alone.

There was a good-sized pull-off just past the bridge. Molly and I used to park there and hike down to the riverbank to fish. I pulled to a stop and got out and looked back across the bridge. Seeing no one, I got back in the car and sat for a minute, listening to the sound of my own labored breathing. I turned on the cabin light and surveyed the damage. The side airbag lay sprawled across the passenger seat like a dead animal. Both the front and rear doors were pushed inward noticeably, though not as bad as I might have thought. Both windows were spider-webbed but remained intact. I lifted my hand up to chest level. It quivered slightly.

I dug into the kit bag for my flashlight, got out, and went around to the passenger side. Sweeping the flashlight's beam along the crumpled passenger side, my attention was drawn to a pair of vertical indentations bracketing the damage area. One cut a vertical line through the rear side panel; the other made a similar pattern behind the headlamp assembly—the tell-tale fingerprint of a snowplow blade.

A blade just like the one mounted on Robert Murphy's black Chevy.

Surveying the bent and twisted metal, I shook my head slowly. Two cars totaled and three airbags deployed in one week. I was compiling quite an impressive driving record. I wondered idly what Andrea would say when I returned the car and asked for another.

I got back in and drove to the Alaska State Troopers' Palmer

Station to report the accident. Through a round metal speaking port, I told the dispatcher behind the glass, a pretty gal with short, bobbed hair and a pleasant smile, that I wanted to report an accident.

"When and where did the accident take place, sir?"

"Twenty minutes ago, on some no-name back road off of Clark-Wolverine."

"Why did you leave the scene, sir?"

"Didn't have much choice," I said. "Somebody tried to run me off the road. I didn't think it would be wise to stick around."

Her face registered alarm. "All right. I'll need your driver's license and registration. Let me get an investigator up here. One moment, please."

I slipped the requested documents under the glass. She took them and walked through a door in the back. Less than a minute later, she emerged from the back with a tall, clean-cut trooper in tow. He was a head taller than me and a much younger man, probably not that long out of the academy.

"I'm Investigator Hartman," he said, and we pumped hands.

"Sidney Reed."

"Jim," the dispatcher said, looking up at Hartman, "this gentleman says someone tried to run him off the road somewhere off Clark-Wolverine."

Hartman's face clouded. "That so?"

I nodded.

"Okay, let's have a look at your car."

After he photographed and diagrammed the damage to the Jeep, I dutifully went through the routine of answering questions and being helpful while he took my statement. My being helpful did not include telling Hartman my suspicions about Murphy or that I'd been tailing him. Instead, I informed him that I'd been scouting out real estate. I saw no point in muddying the water.

I didn't get out of there until almost 7 p.m. I feared Hartman was not going to let me drive away, given the amount of damage, but I managed to convince him it was safe to operate and, besides, I planned to return it to Last Frontier Car Rental the next morning. The dispatcher handed me a copy of the accident report and wished me luck.

It went without saying I was going to need it.

Twenty-seven

Barbara Harper lived in a quaint little two-story just off Palmer's main drag, not far from the old Mat-Maid Dairy. I parked out front and killed the engine. The last time I'd seen her was Thanksgiving Day, almost a year ago. When we'd last spoken, some six weeks before, she'd hung up on me. I wasn't expecting a warm reception now.

I knocked, waited, and knocked again. The door swung open.

Barbara squinted into the cold night. "Sidney! What a pleasant surprise."

"Hi, Barb. It's good to see you."

"You too." She raised a hand in welcome. "Please, come in."

I followed her inside. Like all self-respecting Alaskan homes, hers had an arctic entryway. It was small—just big enough for boots and coats—but it served its purpose. I shucked mine and joined her in the living room. It was small yet cozy, with a couch and matching chairs, coffee and end tables, and a brick fireplace. Throw in a Faulkner novel and a mug of hot chocolate and you had my idea of nirvana.

She stood by the sofa. "What can I get you? I'm a tea drinker myself but I have some instant coffee hiding in the cupboard somewhere, and there's hot chocolate as well. I know that's a favorite of yours."

It used to be, when Molly was alive.

She and Bob were teetotalers, which explains why she didn't offer beer. Or maybe it was because she didn't want me drinking. I decided not to ask.

"Hot chocolate will be fine."

She smiled. "Make yourself comfortable."

I sank into the couch and glanced around the room, feeling oddly out of sorts. I hadn't expected her to be so nice, given the level of acrimony that had infused our previous phone call. Barb had taken her sister's death hard, and I believed—for no good reason other than my own post-traumatic paranoia—that she blamed me for Molly's suicide. I expected her to be mad at me. Perhaps, on a subconscious level, I *wanted* her to be mad at me.

What would Doc Rundle say about that?

An assortment of noises drifted in from the kitchen, so I crossed the room and peeked my head in. Barbara was pouring boiling water from a copper-bottomed kettle into two large white mugs. She wore jeans and a sleeveless beige blouse. Her bare arms were lean and her skin silky smooth, just like Molly's. Unlike Molly, her hair was straight, long, and dark brown, almost black, and a red scrunchie held it together in a ponytail. She was somewhere near forty, but you wouldn't know it to look at her slim figure and light, springy step. She was an attractive woman.

I said, "You look good, Barb."

She turned her head slightly and blushed like a teenager. "Thank you. Bob spent a ton of money on a weight room in the basement but I'm the only one who uses it."

"I take it he's on the slope?"

She sighed. "He has one more week up there."

I knew her story by heart. She was barely out of high school when she married Bob Harper, a bright college boy with an engineering degree. A headhunter recruited him to work on the 800-mile-long Trans-Alaska Pipeline project. That led to a permanent position on the north slope of the Brooks Range, euphemistically called "The Slope." The pay is *very* good, but comes at a price: Three weeks on, one-week off. Many marriages don't survive it. Apparently theirs did. With what Bob made, they could easily afford a fancy home on the Anchorage Hillside, but chose instead to live in sleepy little Palmer. I admired them for that.

She crossed the room and handed me a mug. I took it and we locked eyes. Hers were a lustrous blue-gray and rimmed with tiny crow's feet and almost imperceptible sadness. She'd learned to hide it well. I thought I saw something else in them, but wasn't sure.

"Why don't we talk in here?" she said.

We sat down across from each other at a narrow breakfast island. I silently wished I'd gotten there when the low winter sun was still streaming through the row of south-facing windows and six-thousand-foot Pioneer Peak was visible, rising like a stalwart sentry above the valley floor, powdered with glistening snow. The sight of it could take a dead man's breath away. A photograph of the iconic mountain—complete with red barn in the foreground—graces just about every Alaska calendar that's ever seen print.

"I see you're still a daydreamer."

I turned at the sound of her voice. "I was remembering the view out those windows."

Her eyes brightened. "When I first saw the mountain, I knew this was where I wanted to be."

I nodded and lifted the mug for my first sip.

She cradled her mug in her fingers. "You're looking good yourself, Sidney."

"I'm wearing a hangover and a day's worth of stubble. If you like, I can recommend a good eye doctor."

She chuckled. "You always did make me laugh."

I shot her a look. "Not always."

The smile faded. "About that phone call . . . I didn't mean to—"

"Yes, you did." I paused to clear the lump in my throat. "What you said was true. Every word of it. I was distant. Never there when she needed me."

"Sidney, don't do this."

"Let me finish." I scooted off my stool and began to pace the floor, Barb tracking my every move with sad eyes. "A while back, I found Molly's diary in my closet. I couldn't bring myself to read much of it at first, just bits and pieces. Recently, though, I've been reading more of it and I realize how selfish I've been. I wasn't there when she needed me. She might be alive right now if—"

Barbara came off her seat, eyes afire. "Stop blaming yourself, for crissake! Damn it, I hate when men do that!"

Her reaction pushed me back a step. She was just getting started.

"When is it going to penetrate that thick skull of yours that the earth does not revolve around Sidney Reed?" She paused at the window. "Master private eye! Reader of men! You think you know people, do you? Allow me to give you a little lesson."

I should have gone straight back to Anchorage.

She opened the fridge, took out a bottle of cabernet and set it on the counter, then opened a cabinet and reached for two wine goblets. She returned with the bottle and glasses and sat back down. So did I.

She filled the glasses, studying me for a reaction. "Surprised?"

"I thought you and Bob—"

"Didn't drink? I venture to say there are a great many things you don't know about me."

"I won't argue with you there."

She lifted her glass in a toast. "To Molly."

I raised my glass. "To Molly."

She inhaled deeply. "Bob and I have been distant for years. Did you know that? No, you didn't. I didn't mind his work schedule at first. I fell into a routine, kept myself occupied. But in time it wears on you. Those long dark winter months get longer and darker with each passing year." She paused. "Then the loneliness sets in."

I cringed, imagining how Molly must have felt when I was gone so much of the time.

"I did my best to deal with it, I really did. But then . . ." A tear meandered down her left cheek. I lost sight of it when she raised her glass and sipped some more wine. Quite a bit more. "He wasn't as good at deleting his voice mails as he thought he was."

I stared at her. Her eyes were red and listless.

"I found out the day I called you. She's the administrative assistant to the operations manager. I gather she's had affairs with a number of the men." She paused, her voice cracking. "Do you have any idea what the ratio of men to women is on the slope?"

I didn't have those statistics handy. Anyway, I was pretty sure it was a rhetorical question. "Why didn't you tell me? I would have—"

"Would have what? Driven up here and comforted me?"

An awkward silence choked the air. We sipped from our respective glasses, exchanged uncomfortable glances, like we were on an awkward prom date.

I broke the silence. "So, why don't you leave him?"

"And give up what I have? Not on your life! I love this place and I'm damn sure not going to let *that* bitch have it." She paused to sip wine. "No, I'm not going to leave him. What I am going to do is keep this little nugget of information to myself for the time being." She shot me a look. "I don't have to tell you—"

I held up a palm. "Your secret is safe with me, Barb."

"I know." She smiled faintly. "You've always been discreet." She lifted her glass and drank, dropping her gaze to the white casual shoe dangling loosely from her toes. "We never really know someone as well as we think we do. Not really." Her eyes shot up and pierced mine. "That goes for you, too. You didn't know Molly as well as you think you did."

I bristled at that. Molly and I were best friends, lovers, companions—the whole shebang. I knew her, all right. "I know what she wrote in her diary," I countered.

In a very casual way, she tilted her head back, emptied her glass, and poured another. "Tell me, does her diary say anything about wanting to kill herself?"

I thought back to the many sleepless nights I'd spent reading it. "No, not directly."

With one long gulp she emptied the contents of her second glass of wine and looked at me, eyes glazed over. Gone was the good housewife, Molly's prim and bossy older sister. Her face flushed, and with eyes that seemed to glow now she said, "I never believed the official bullshit about her committing suicide. Why do you?"

I stared at her in disbelief. "I thought you *had* accepted it?"

"Not hardly." Her mouth curved into a sad smile. "Just ask Bob.

I rampaged through the house like a moose with an attitude. Threw dishes. I even yelled at the dog."

"If you felt that way, why didn't you speak out? Say anything?"

"Are you kidding? I let loose on everyone but the mailman. I'll bet the medical examiner's ears are still ringing."

I remembered my own rampage, not realizing I hadn't been alone. "And what did he say?"

She laughed disdainfully. "He said the evidence pointed to suicide and asked if I had anything to refute that. I said I know my sister. He gave me the speech about how no one believes their loved one would ever do such a thing, blah blah blah. That ended the conversation."

I stared at her, not knowing what to say.

"I would have kept on until hell froze over if it hadn't been for Bob. He told me to let it go before it devoured me, like it has you. He was right, it would have."

I stared dumbly at my glass. "I didn't realize how you felt."

She snickered. "Of course not. You were in your own little world." She lifted the bottle. "Here, have another. Let's get shit-faced, shall we?"

"Better not," I said, waving her off. "I have to drive to Anchorage."

Her eyes flashed. "You could . . ." She looked away with a snap of her head. She set the bottle aside and regarded me. "You never let it go, did you? Molly, I mean."

"I did for a while."

"I don't think you can. Something inside you won't let you, and that's what worries me."

I downed the last sip. "You shouldn't worry."

"But I do." She paused, then gave me a sidelong glance. "Are you still seeing Rundle?"

"Yep."

"Is it helping?"

"I don't know. Probably not."

"Know what I think?"

"I know you're going to tell me."

"I think your problem is, you never let yourself mourn her. Have a good old, open-the-floodgates-here-it-comes cry. You haven't done that, have you? Of course not. Men don't cry."

"Sometimes they do."

She filled both our glasses. "Bullshit."

I'd never heard her swear before. I found it vaguely amusing, even refreshing.

"It's hard for men. Bob's that way, too."

"I suppose." I hesitated, then sipped from my glass, thinking what a blur the past year had been.

"Have you been to see her yet?"

I cringed slightly. I wasn't sure why, but I didn't want to tell her I wasn't ready to visit Molly's grave. At least, not yet.

"I've thought about it."

"You really should go. It would do you a world of good."

"I'll think about it."

I glanced at my watch and began a slow slide off my stool. "Barb, I really have to—"

"Are you . . . seeing anyone?"

Well, this has just been one surprise after another.

I slid back into place.

"Sort of. We're going on our first date tomorrow night, in fact."

"That's good, Sidney . . . really good." She drank some wine. "How did you two meet?"

"She interviewed me for a story."

Her eyebrows arched. "She's a reporter . . . how nice."

In her inebriated state, I don't think she realized how sarcastic she sounded. I had a feeling she was about to hold a pity party and I was the guest of honor. I made a show of looking at my watch, slid off my stool, and told her I had to go. She put down her glass and led me to the front door where, without warning, she flung her arms around me and gently sobbed. I patted the small of her back, feeling awkward. After she'd had a good cry, she broke off the embrace and kissed me on the cheek.

"Goodbye, Sidney." She wiped a tear from her eye. "Don't be a stranger, okay?"

I nodded. She opened the door and I walked to the Jeep. She was still standing at the door when I drove away.

I was on autopilot most of the way home. The evening was clear, southbound traffic light, though even now, at 8 p.m., the headlights of northbound commuters formed what appeared to be one continuous string of glowing white bulbs stretching for miles and miles.

I enjoyed driving at night. The darkness has a way of stripping away the bullshit and revealing the stark reality of things: light and dark, right and wrong, life and death; peeling back the extraneous and allowing one to focus on what matters. By the time I'd reached the Palmer Hay Flats, my head had cleared enough to realize the afternoon hadn't been a complete waste of time.

I fetched my cell phone out of my coat and punched a number I had on speed dial. The chief of APD Narcotics answered on the first ring.

"Dent, it's Sid. Got a minute?"

"Sure. What's up?"

"I've got a name to run by you. Robert Murphy, alias Big Tooth."

"You better believe I know that guy. We think he's Cooley's primary distributor in the Valley. Works out of an auto shop in the Butte. How does he tie in with your case?"

"Remember me telling you I'm searching for Travis Cooley? I heard he and Murphy are close."

"Murphy and the Cooleys are tight, for sure."

"That's what I figured. Thought you might like to know, I saw Murphy drop off a package at the Blue Light Bar in Palmer this afternoon."

"The Blue Light, you say? I'll write up a sheet on it."

"Can you keep my name out of it, though?"

"No problemo. I'll say it came from a confidential informant."

"One more thing. I spoke with someone who says the Cooleys are shipping product from Anchorage to the Valley in junk cars. Pretty clever when you think about it."

"Not that clever. We got a tip on that a few months back."

"You don't say."

"We're working it."

"I'm sure you are."

"It takes time to put together a big drug case."

"I know that."

"I know you know. And Sid?"

"Yeah?"

"Be careful. These guys aren't fooling around." Then he broke the connection.

I said to no one, "I'm not either."

Twenty-eight

I woke Friday morning to the hammering beat of Buddy Rich banging out a drum solo inside my auditory canal. I decided not to wait for the encore performance, but when I tried to lift my legs to get out of bed, I felt a weight pressed against my ankles.

It was Priscilla, and she was even less inclined to seize the day than I was. I regretted stopping by Annie's for a twelve-pack, but it was a long drive from the Valley, and I couldn't stop thinking about Barbara's revelation that she didn't believe her sister had committed suicide. It kept playing over and over in my head like the Zapruder film. Next thing I knew, I had a flotilla of empty Corona bottles lined up on my coffee table.

Carpe fucking diem.

I cajoled Priscilla into exiting the bed, got up and did a hard-target search for the aspirin, swallowed four of the little white tablets, chased them with cold water, and stumbled into the shower. It was 8:13 a.m.

Rachel Saint George set aside the morning paper. "It's not looking very good for your client." We sat at my favorite table by the window.

I sipped black coffee from a hand-fired ceramic mug, savoring the taste. The aspirin and cold shower had done their work well.

"I almost feel sorry for the poor schmuck," she continued. "But, come on! Blabbing to a cellmate that you did it?" She paused to sip from a mug emblazoned with the words RACHEL ROCKS.

I set my mug on a coaster. "Things aren't always what they seem."

"Tell me about it. I thought hell would freeze before I'd see you in here before 9 a.m."

"I'm seizing the day."

"You'd better try seizing it a little harder. You may not have noticed, but your client's going down in flames." She jabbed the paper with her index finger. "Your girlfriend's been giving me all the lurid details."

"I wish you'd stop calling her my girlfriend. We haven't even been on a date."

"You haven't been on a date *yet*." Her eyes lit up in amusement. "I have a feeling tonight's your lucky night."

"Have your fun."

"Seriously," she said, "this has gone on long enough."

"I was thinking the same think about this conversation."

"Somebody has to worry about you." She drank from her mug, smacking her lips appreciatively. "Where are you taking her, anyway?"

"Giorgio's."

She rolled her eyes. "That's twice now you've tried to take her there. Give it up."

"What are you, superstitious?"

"As a matter of fact, I am."

"Well, I'm not. I like it there."

"I seem to recall it was Molly's favorite restaurant."

I gave her the slant eye. "You know it was."

"Mind if I make a suggestion?"

"Is there any way to stop you?"

"Take her someplace new and make it *your* place."

"That's a really fine suggestion."

Her lip curled. "But you're not going to."

"No, but it's a really fine suggestion."

"Ass."

I sipped coffee and looked at her. "Now can *I* say something?"

"If you must."

"Leave the psychoanalysis to my shrink. It's what I pay him for."

"I surrender." She sighed. "What's on your agenda for today? Other than your big date, I mean."

"Picking up a new car, then I'm off to court. After that, I thought I might, um, visit Molly."

Her eyes widened. "After all this time?"

"After all this time."

She thought for a moment. "I think it's a good thing."

"You really think so?"

"Uh-huh, I do. Maybe now you can put her death behind you and move on with your life."

"We'll see," I said, though I doubted one visit to the cemetery would accomplish that feat.

She raised an eyebrow. "Why do you need another car?"

"I got t-boned out in the Valley yesterday."

"The hell you say! Are you all right?"

"I'm fine, although now I'll be late for court."

"Need a lift?"

I shook my head. "Believe it or not, the Jeep is still drivable—barely."

I downed the last of my coffee and stood.

"By the way," she said as I turned to go. "Storm coming. Be careful out there. Oh, and Sid?"

"Yeah?"

Her lips curled up in a crooked smile. "Go get 'em, tiger."

Andrea was flipping around an OPEN sign on the front door of Last Frontier Car Rental when I walked up. Seeing me, she grinned and held the door open, and I slipped inside. "Good morning, Sidney! I wasn't expecting you back quite so soon. Come in out of the cold."

I slipped through the door and watched with heartfelt male admiration as she made her way behind the counter, clad as before in black skin-tight yoga pants, evidently her work attire of choice. A red V-neck sweater displayed more than a hint of cleavage. Bright hazel eyes studied me as I approached. "What do you think of the Jeep?"

"Great car," I began, taking a deep breath. "Unfortunately, I'm going to need another one."

Her face contorted in a frown. "Something wrong with it?"

"It's fine vehicle. It's just that, well, I wrecked it."

Her pouty lips parted. "You wrecked my new Jeep?"

"Yeah. But the good news is, the side airbag works great."

"That's not funny, Sidney. What happened?"

I sighed. "I was in an accident. Actually, it wasn't an accident at all. Someone ran into me quite deliberately." I handed her the police report. "Here, have a look."

She read it and looked at me, her eyes wide. "You poor man." She came around the counter and hugged me, strands of hair tickling my nostrils. Her soft breasts brushed against my chest. "You might have been killed. Driving one of *my* cars!"

"Really, I'm fine." I patted her back reassuringly.

"All right, let's have a look." She grabbed a clipboard and stepped outside. I followed close behind. Although Anchorage was still bathed in darkness, outdoor lighting exposed the Jeep's disfigured right side. She surveyed the damage, scrawling notations on a form. When we came back inside, she scribbled furiously at her desk before strolling to the counter. She released a long sigh.

"As a matter of policy, we don't typically rent another car to a customer after they've wrecked the first one. However . . ." She leaned forward, drawing my gaze to the gentle slope of her breasts peeking out playfully above the V-neck. ". . . it just so happens, I like detectives."

"In that case, I wish I'd wrecked the car sooner."

She chuckled and pulled out a form from under the counter. "Let's get you another car."

"Thank you." I smiled and picked up a pen off the counter. I paused and said, "You wouldn't by chance have a Subaru, would you?"

"Don't push it," she replied. "You're lucky to be getting a car at all. However, since I happen to like you, I'm giving you a brand-new Toyota Camry. It's the newest addition to our fleet. *Please* bring this one back in one piece."

"Yes, ma'am."

Twenty-nine

The now-familiar chants of protesters filled the cold morning air as I rounded the courthouse's western façade a few minutes before ten. The dozen or so men and women lining Fourth Avenue were, compared to yesterday's crowd, a picture of serenity. I hurried past them, breezed through security, and took the curved metal staircase to the second floor. There I was greeted by the sight of several dozen people chatting in the hall.

Wading in among them, I spotted a thick mane of wavy auburn hair. The woman wearing it was facing away from me and chatting with Tommy and Woody Olson. I was about to tap her on the shoulder when Tommy Olson began eyeing me like a hawk sizing up a tasty rabbit.

The woman turned and her mouth widened into a broad smile. "Sidney! How are you?"

"I'm good, Maria. Listen, you're busy, so I'll just—"

"Don't leave. I was just discussing—"

Without warning, Tommy Olson lunged toward me. I braced myself for the assault, but Woody grabbed him by the arm before he'd gone half a step and said, "Little brother, why don't you pick us up a couple of soft drinks from the snack bar?"

Tommy yanked his arm free. "Anything you say, *big* brother."

As the younger man stalked off, Woody turned to Maria. "Please excuse my brother, ma'am. He's a bit of a hothead. His behavior yesterday was inexcusable, but perhaps you can appreciate his frustration. It's been a difficult time for all of us." He glanced at me. "My apologies to you as well, Mr. Reed. I know you have a job to do. Now, if you'll excuse me, I must speak with my brother."

As Maria watched him retreat down the hall, I moved closer and caught the scent of her. When she turned around, we were practically nose to nose. Her eyes were brown like coffee beans.

"You're staring at me," she said quietly.

"You'd better get used to it, Ms. Maldonado."

"I prefer Maria."

"So do I."

"You're pretty sure of yourself, aren't you?"

"I am when I know what I want."

"And what's that?"

Just then the courtroom door swished open behind her and a somewhat agitated Eddie Baker cast his gaze up and down the hall before settling on me. "There you are," he said. "We need to talk." He stalked off down the hall.

I turned to Maria. "I'm being summoned. See you tonight?"

Her face lit up. "You bet. But, uh . . ."

"What?"

"You should arrange for a police escort—just in case."

"Very funny. Moose are everywhere, you know. And we were in a snowstorm."

"You were going too fast."

"Was not."

"Sidney!" Eddie's voice boomed down the hall.

I said goodbye and hurried to a small interview room at the end of the hall. I followed Eddie inside and closed the door. He shuffled his feet nervously and then looked at me.

"Fellows completed his direct of Borman this morning. Everything was going fine until Rudy decided to have one of his outbursts. It was all I could do to keep Jeffries from locking him up. We won't be so lucky next time. When we go back in there, you need to keep him under control."

"I'll try."

He uttered an audible sigh of relief. "Okay." He started to leave, but then paused. "Were you able to get another car?"

"Yep, the rental company's been very good to me."

"Good. Oh, and one more thing. I was thinking about this witness of yours. Connie, is it? I want to meet her before I put her on the stand. Can you bring her by my office tomorrow at ten?"

"I'll see to it."

"She may be Rudy's only hope."

We left the room and walked toward the courtroom. I was about to go inside when I noticed Leonard Olson's lanky form approaching me. *Oh shit, now what?*

"Mr. Reed?" the older man said. "May I have a word with you?"

I glanced toward the door. "I'm expected in court."

"Please. This will only take a minute." Without waiting for an answer, he shuffled over to a bench a short distance away and sat down on the shiny wood surface. I followed and sat down beside him.

"May I call you Sidney?"

I told him that would be all right.

"My name is Leonard Olson."

"I know who you are, sir. I saw you speaking with a TV reporter the other day."

"Yes. I seem to be a celebrity." His head drooped slightly. He appeared to be lost in thought. "Sidney, I want to apologize for the way my son Tommy behaved outside the courthouse the other day. That is not the way I raised my sons. He's always been hot-blooded, but he's taken the death of his younger brother especially hard. I certainly do not condone his behavior, I only ask that you consider what he's been through when judging it."

The elder Olson sat ramrod straight, looking dapper in tan slacks, white shirt, and navy sports jacket. His face was weathered, his hair thin and graying. I couldn't help but admire his quiet eloquence.

"I appreciate it, Mr. Olson, but no apology is necessary."

When I started to get up, he touched my arm. "If you will indulge me a moment longer."

I eased myself down.

"You might be curious as to how I know your name." He paused, perhaps anticipating a reaction. Seeing none, he continued. "I doubt you recall, as it was some years ago, but you helped defend my nephew Sam Williams against a charge of sexual assault."

I remembered Sam. He lived in one of the villages—I couldn't recall which one. He and some of his friends had spent the day drinking when, according to the state, they decided to have sex with Sam's 16-year-old cousin without bothering to ask if that was what she wanted. Sam's defense was that it was consensual. The jury didn't buy it and Sam was convicted and received a twenty-year sentence. I remembered thinking at the time that Molly, had she known about it, would have been dismayed at the part I'd played in defending Sam Williams.

Olson said, "I appreciated the care you took investigating Sam's case. I guess what I'm trying to say is, I hold no animosity toward you. I know you're just doing your job." He rose to leave.

"Mr. Olson, wait."

He turned, eyebrows arching as he did. "Yes?"

"It's probably unethical for me to tell you this, but I'm going to anyway."

Olson eased his thin body onto the stiff wooden seat. "Tell me what?"

I gestured toward the courtroom door. "Despite what you've heard or may hear in that room, Rudy Skinner did not kill your son."

Olson's eyes never left mine. "Then . . . who did?"

As I looked into the eyes of this distinguished gentleman, I had an overpowering urge to tell him everything. God knows he deserved the truth. I wanted to tell him Travis Cooley killed his son, and that he was going to pay for what he'd done. But I couldn't. The fact of the matter was, I shouldn't have been talking to him at all.

At last I said, "I can't tell you who killed your son. Nor can I offer any assurance that the person who did will be held accountable for his crime. At least, not legally. All I *can* tell you is, Rudy didn't do it."

He stared down at his feet, then at me. "I appreciate your candor, Sidney. If you don't mind me asking, why are you telling me this?"

"I don't know. I guess I just thought I should."

He looked away, his thoughts inaccessible to me. At last he said, "This man, whoever he is, may have ended my son's life, but hate and prejudice and indifference killed him."

I nodded slowly. "In a way, maybe we're all responsible for what happened to Willie."

Olson lifted his chin, rose from his seat, and began to walk away. He paused and glanced back at me. "Something you said struck me. You said you couldn't assure me my son's killer would be held *legally* accountable for his crime. Interesting distinction, I thought."

He smiled faintly and retreated down the hall, his heels tapping out a lonely rhythm.

Inside the courtroom the rows of seats were stuffed like sausage casings. More spectators leaned against the wall in back, while others lined the wall to my right and filled the spaces in between. I craned my neck for a glimpse of Maria, but she was lost somewhere behind a sea of bobbing heads. All eyes were riveted to Eddie Baker, who stood at the podium cross-examining David Borman. I pushed my way through the swinging gate and hurried to the defense table. Rudy was focused on Eddie's cross, his nervous left leg temporarily immobile.

Across the aisle, Detective Banner was whispering something in District Attorney Fellows' ear, while a portly Lou Fletcher looked on from his chair next to Banner, wearing the same rumpled tan suit I'd seen him in at the Captain Cook Hotel.

Judge Jeffries, his eyeglasses perched near the end of his nose, cast his regal gaze from the bench as Eddie led the witness line by line through his statements to the police, shining a spotlight on the slightest inconsistency.

"... and so Rudy was trying to tell you he hit a dog, isn't that right?"

"No ... well, yes ... I'm not—"

"Come on, Mr. Borman, which is it?"

Fellows leapt to his feet. "Objection! Your honor, please instruct counsel to allow Mr. Borman to complete his thought for the jury to hear."

Eddie Baker's face was deadpan. "Was that a thought? I'm sorry, judge. I couldn't tell."

Fellows' face reddened. "Your honor!"

Jeffries sighed gravely. "Lighten up on the theatrics, Mr. Fellows. The objection is sustained. Mr. Baker, save the sarcasm for closing arguments, if you don't mind."

And so it went. I glanced at Maria hunched over her notebook in the first row. She saw me and smiled.

Maybe there's a chance for us after all.

Swiveling back around, I glanced at Rudy and shuddered. His eyes were bloodshot, the left one twitching uncontrollably. In a voice that was whiny and strained he said, "Borman's telling lies about me."

I lightly touched his arm. "Don't let him get to you, Rudy."

"He's lying!"

"Lower your voice and listen. You have to promise me you'll keep it together. Let Eddie do his thing. Can you do that?"

His eyeballs seemed to float upward. "Sure, Sidney. Don't worry, I'm fine . . . really."

I didn't find his words terribly reassuring but, to my great and pleasant surprise, he kept it together through two hours of cross, redirect, and recross, although at one point the sound of his nervous leg banging against the table drew warning stares from Eddie. When Borman left the stand, Rudy glared at him so fiercely, I thought he might leap across the table and tackle him.

As a trooper took Borman away, Fellows rose to his feet. "Your honor, the state rests."

"Very well." Jeffries turned to the jury. "I'll see you folks back here Monday morning. Please refrain from discussing the case. By the way, the weatherman is predicting yet another snowstorm, so be careful out there." He pounded his gavel and the courtroom rumbled with a sound like distant thunder.

I turned to Rudy. "I checked on your trailer like you asked.

Everything looked good to me. Your neighbor has been keeping an eye on the place."

"Who, Frank? I saw him hitting on Evelyn." After a pause he said, "Did you see her?"

"No, Rudy. Evelyn moved out, remember?"

"That bitch," he said with a grunt.

"Hang in there a little while longer. This will all be over soon."

Rudy seized my arm. "You gotta get me out of here, Sidney. I can't take it anymore!" His eyes were wild and pleading.

A state trooper rushed forward. "Get your hands off him, Skinner!"

I glanced up with an icy stare. "It's all right, officer. We're just having a discussion here."

"Yeah, well, I need to get him down to holding," he said with a look of indignance.

I turned to Rudy. "Relax. I'll see you on Monday."

Once he'd been led away, I turned to Eddie. "I'm worried about Rudy. He's hanging by a thread."

Eddie stuffed a binder into his valise and sighed. "I know. You just worry about getting Connie here on Monday."

At that moment Lou Fletcher got up from the prosecution table and stepped into the aisle. We locked eyes and he bared a crooked smile. "Don't look so glum, Reed," he said. "You can't win 'em all."

That was weird. He doesn't even know me.

As I stared at Fletcher's retreating figure, I said to Eddie, "Don't you think that was weird? What's his deal, anyway?"

Eddie looked up, following my gaze. "Who, Fletcher? Ex-cop, now Grant's attack dog. Ignore him—he's an asshole."

Out in the hall, I spotted Maria standing off to one side, recorder in one hand, interviewing Grant Fellows. Fletcher stood off to one side. I sidled up to the group.

"Thank you for your time, Mr. Fellows," Maria said, the interview apparently over.

"I'm always happy to accommodate the press." Fellows smiled. "Now if you'll excuse me."

What a phony, I thought as the D.A. trounced away.

Maria saw me and brightened. "Sidney! I'd love to chat, but I've got to get back to the paper and file my story. I'm so looking forward to tonight." She seemed to glide down the hall.

A voice behind me said, "You've got yourself a real hottie there, Reed."

I whirled around to find the D.A.'s pudgy assistant leering at Maria's retreating figure. My body stiffened. "Fuck you, Fletcher."

The detective balled his fists. Was Fletcher seriously wanting to duke it out with me in the courthouse? Granted, the man had a good twenty or thirty pounds on me and, although a good portion of it was attached to his midsection, I suspected he could hold his own in a fight. Still, I was confident I could take him. Either way, it was a dumb idea. If I were to hit a badge in the courthouse, whether I had started it or not, I'd end up keeping Rudy company in AJ for the weekend. And that would mean strike three as far as any relationship with Maria was concerned.

"You say something, Reed?"

I stared hard at him. "You should show a little more respect for women, Fletcher. You really should."

His eyes roamed over me, sizing me up. Then, ever so slowly, he relaxed, it having dawned on him, I suppose, that the outcome of such a contest was, at best, doubtful.

"Be careful, Reed." He took a step forward. "Mess with me and I'll be your worst nightmare." He trudged off at a stiff, lumbering gate and disappeared down the stairs.

I slowly descended to the first floor and stepped out into the late November cold. I stopped and looked around. A dozen protestors waved signs along the street. I thought about my scuffle with Tommy Olson the day before and his lunge at me earlier that morning. Now I'd almost traded blows with a municipal police officer. Had I always been so combative?

I struck off east down Fourth Avenue, stopped, and glanced up at the sky. Slate gray storm clouds billowed ominously, as if spoiling for a fight. I frowned, wanting so badly for my date with Maria to go well. The last thing I needed was the weather to screw it up. I resumed walking, lost in thought.

Fucking Fletcher.

His comment about Maria had really pissed me off. Not only that, something else he said had stuck in my head like a broken record and was bothering the hell out of me: *Mess with me and I'll be your worst nightmare.* It was a threat anyway you slice it, and it had come from a police officer. The way Fletcher said it was . . . well, creepy. But there was something else, too.

The words sounded eerily familiar. I was sure I'd heard them before, but where?

I shuffled east toward my apartment. I'd gone maybe a dozen yards when it hit me. Clear as day, I saw the weathered face of Army veteran Frank Leslie as he wiped a dribble of whiskey from his chapped lips, eyes alive with the memory of his encounter with a nameless cop outside Evelyn Waters' trailer. The officer's dire warning had chilled Frank Leslie to the bone: *Mess with me and I'll be your worst nightmare.*

That nameless cop now had a name.

Thirty

There's no deep, dark secret to finding people—what we in the P.I. business call skip tracing. Most of us leave a trail of breadcrumbs wherever we go, and it's easy to follow them if you know where to look. The skip tracer's bag of tricks includes things like motor vehicle and Alaska Permanent Fund Dividend records, credit header information (the top portion of a credit report, containing a subject's current and prior addresses), and voter registration records. But database searches cost money, and money was in short supply since I'd stopped accepting clients. I could pay another P.I. to run her name but that would take time, and time was something I didn't have a lot of, either.

If I really wanted to find Evelyn Waters before Rudy Skinner's trial was over, I needed another way.

The answer came to me as I hooked a left on G Street: Evelyn must have filled out a forwarding address form when she moved out of her and Rudy's trailer. Forgetting about home, I made a beeline for the parking garage and drove across town to the Muldoon Post Office.

The U.S. Postal Service guards forwarding address records like the IRS guards tax returns. You need a criminal subpoena or court order to access them, so I filled out a subpoena form for Evelyn Waters and handed it to the clerk behind the counter. He studied it with a puzzled expression.

"Wait here," he said, and disappeared through a door. A short time later, a tall man with a thin body and thinning hair appeared. "I'm Postmaster Phillips," he said. "How may I help you?"

"I'm Sidney Reed, an investigator working a case currently in trial. I attempted to serve this witness, but she seems to have moved."

I pointed to the name on the subpoena. "I'm going to need her forwarding address so I can serve this."

He peered at the form. "Hmm . . . appears to be legitimate. You understand, we only forward mail for up to a year after an address change."

"It hasn't been that long," I countered. "You should have it."

"Very well," he said with audible sigh, as if I were asking for the Magna Carta. "Let me check." He returned in less than five minutes, sticky note in hand. "Here you go."

The address Evelyn filed with the postal service was in an upscale neighborhood on the west side, less than a mile from where Molly and I had lived. I took Northern Lights Boulevard across town to the Turnagain Heights subdivision and a sprawling brick ranch with a spacious front yard, now covered in snow. I parked in the driveway and walked up to a heavy wood door with a big brass knocker in the middle of it. I opted instead for the plain white buzzer to the right. An attractive woman in her mid to late forties with rust-colored hair and expressive gray eyes opened the door.

"Yes?" she said.

"Evelyn Waters?"

Her eyes narrowed slightly. "Who wants to know?"

In my line of work, you size people up quickly. Sometimes you're wrong, but that's the chance you take. I went for the straightforward approach. "My name is Sidney Reed. I'm an investigator representing Rudy Skinner in a murder case."

She glanced uncertainly over her shoulder and then at me. Sizing me up. Perhaps thinking: How much should I tell this guy?

"I'm Julie, Evelyn's sister," she said at last. "I'll get her."

She left the door slightly ajar and retreated into the house. From where I stood, I could see a bleached white interior with polished wood furnishings, suggesting a level of affluence Julie possessed and her sister did not. Voices drifted from somewhere inside, rising and falling in waves. I used my hand to widen the gap in the door and leaned my head in.

"No . . . Julie, no . . . I won't!"

"Evelyn, please . . . at least hear what he . . ."

"No, Julie. Rudy . . ."

The muffled exchange continued for a short while and then Julie came back, her gray eyes apologetic. "I'm sorry, Mr. Reed. This has been a difficult time for my sister, as you can imagine. The strain has been, well, almost unbearable."

"Julie, for God's sake!" came a shrill cry from somewhere just beyond my vision, followed by the woman hurling it.

Evelyn Waters was an older version of her sister, with the same reddish hair, build, and bone structure, but, unlike Julie, her beauty had faded with time, drugs and alcohol having taken their toll. I saw it in her pale complexion and the dark lines etched around her eyes, which darted nervously from me to her sister. "I told you to send him away."

Julie locked eyes with her sister. "Don't forget yourself, Evie. This is my house."

"Ms. Waters," I said, "I was hoping to talk to you about the night Willie Olson died. I think you might be able to—"

"Mr. Reed, is it? As my well-meaning younger sister should have told you, I am not able to assist you. I'm sorry about Rudy's current situation, but it is of no concern to me. We were already in the process of breaking up prior to his arrest."

"Well, you kept his business records."

"Which the police now have."

"I know, I saw them. I was wondering why there was no call sheet for the night Olson died."

She stared at me. Something unmistakable pooled in her eyes for the briefest of moments. That something was fear.

"I don't know anything about that. Now, I insist that you—"

"Why did Detective Fletcher come to see you?"

Her face turned ashen. "I'm sorry, I don't . . ."

"Oh, I think you do."

Evelyn Waters looked everywhere—at her feet, her sister, the ceiling, everywhere but at me. Frustrated, she said, "I'm not at liberty to talk to you. You must go now." She hurried from the room, her feet clattering down the hall.

Julie eyed me sadly. "I'm sorry, Mr. Reed. My sister has been under so much stress . . ."

I handed her my business card. "If she should change her mind, please have her call me."

On any given Friday afternoon in Anchorage, commuters are on a single-minded mission to exit the city as quickly as possible. On this day they were no doubt additionally motivated by the canopy of ominous-looking clouds hunched over the city, engorged with snow and poised to dump it on top of them.

The weather was the last thing on my mind as I followed the Seward Highway south through the city. I was after Travis Cooley. True, we had Connie Zwick ready to testify, but Eddie wanted Travis as a backup, and what Eddie wants, Eddie usually gets.

I had what I thought was a good lead—namely, the cabin where I'd followed Big Tooth the day before—but when I was driving back from the Valley, another thought had occurred to me: Why not ask Rance Cooley? After all, I'd helped Travis' dad with his own criminal case a few years back. Who knows? He just might give me a lead to the whereabouts of his son, provided I limit my inquiry to Travis' whereabouts and assiduously avoid any mention of drugs. I thought it was worth a try, anyway.

I took the O'Malley exit and soon passed the spot where Travis struck and killed Willie Olson. A mile or so further on, I came to a battered metal sign that read NORTHERN LIGHTS AUTO PARTS and a long and winding drive that dipped in the middle and ended in a series of buildings at the top of a small rise.

I passed slowly up the drive, flanked by a veritable sea of junk cars, and parked in front of a gray steel-sided building, the name of the business painted above the door in fading black letters. I got out and looked around. A six-foot-high chain-link fence surrounded the entire property, while a separate section of fencing divided the parking lot from a larger area behind it. Surveillance cameras stared down from atop it at twenty-foot intervals. These were state of the art.

Northern Lights Auto Parts, I knew, was one of the more prominent suppliers of used parts in the state, so it didn't surprise me that Rance had installed a high-tech security system. What *did* surprise me was that his fancy security system did not appear to be protecting his huge inventory, but rather the buildings in the back of the property, behind that big fence.

I strolled over to the fence and noticed there was both a pedestrian gate and an adjoining vehicle gate that could be activated by a keypad from either side. Pretty fancy for a used auto parts business, I thought. Beyond the fence stood a two-story home and, beyond that, more buildings.

One in particular, several hundred feet away, caught my eye. It had what appeared to be a fairly elaborate venting system, judging by the ductwork attached to the roof and sides. Recalling what Connie had said about her observations when she'd lived with the Cooleys, I turned my gaze to the house, then back again. I edged toward the small gate.

"Sidney Reed!" Rance Cooley's unforgettably throaty baritone boomed behind me and I turned.

He was just as I remembered him. Broad of shoulder, with a roundish frame. Sheathed in tan Carhart coveralls, he reminded me of a whiskey barrel. His ears and nose were red from the cold, his unkempt hair and beard as white as the snow at his feet. But I noted a weariness in his eyes and a stiltedness in his gate that hadn't been there the last time I saw him.

"Rance Cooley." I glanced around. "Quite a place you have here."

"It suits me." His stare was both unwavering and unreadable. "What brings you to my neck of the woods?"

"I was hoping you could help me. Can we talk?"

He stood there, unmoving. I thought maybe he hadn't heard me. Then he waved his hand. "Come on."

With surprising speed for a man of his circumference, he led me through the gate and into the house through a side door. The obligatory arctic entryway smelled of mud and sweat and motor oil. I followed him through another door and into a spacious but over-crowded kitchen, with outdated cabinetry and shelves that sagged and a large sink with old school fixtures. I noticed an open doorway off to the side with stairs that led down—into a basement, perhaps?

Rance paused in front of a fridge befitting someone his size and yanked open the door.

"You a beer drinker, Sidney?"

"On occasion."

Grunting in reply, his beefy hand snared two bottles of Pabst Blue Ribbon from the cavernous interior. He handed me one and continued through an open doorway into a dimly lit room that I judged, based on its size and furnishings, to be the living room. The walls were swathed in blue and brown paisley wallpaper that had no doubt been attractive in a prior era but was now faded and peeling. An oversized beige couch and matching chairs had likewise seen better days. They were worn and faded, and the corners showed signs of having been chewed by a large animal.

"Have a seat," Rance said, though he didn't say where. He gravitated to an outsized leather recliner with built-in cup holders, one of which held a remote-control unit with an attached cord than ran underneath his chair.

The big man eased into the recliner with an audible sigh, plucked the remote out of the cup holder, and thumbed one of the buttons. With a whir, the chair tilted backwards and stopped. He issued a satisfied grunt, and I thought I discerned a wince of pain.

"I have it set so it stops at the same spot every time," he said with a satisfied grunt. He wheezed audibly, each exhalation painful to the ear.

I eased myself into the couch adjacent to an end table, where I set my beer. On the wall opposite, an episode of *The Andy Griffith Show* played on a flat screen T.V., the sound muted.

I glanced at Rance, his ponderous body filling every square centimeter of the recliner, and suddenly remembered Connie's description of the night Willie Olson died. I pictured, in my mind's eye, her pleading with Travis not to go out in the storm raging outside, and Rance, impatient with the rancor interrupting his enjoyment of *The Beverly Hillbillies*, ordering her to let Travis "get on with it." I looked past Rance to the kitchen beyond, where father and sons had huddled to discuss how to clean up the mess Travis had made.

I let those images go and said, "How are you getting along with your neighbor these days?"

"Boyd? I haven't killed him yet, if that's what you're asking." He lifted the bottle to his lips and drank, then set it back down. His hawk-like eyes studied me. "I appreciate you helpin' me with that legal matter, but somehow I don't think you came all the way out here to talk about old times."

"No, I didn't. Actually, I was hoping you might help me get in touch with Travis."

He swigged some more beer and looked at me hard. "Now what would you be wantin' Travis for?"

"I'd like to ask him a few questions . . . for a case I'm working on." I lifted the bottle to my lips, trying to appear unconcerned. "It'll only take a couple of minutes."

"A case you're working on," he repeated.

His fist tightened around the stem of the bottle and he coughed with a rumble that came from deep down in his lungs. It suddenly occurred to me that maybe this wasn't such a good idea.

"You must think we're all a bunch of fuckin' hicks here." His voice had turned guttural, his face reddening. "I saw you lookin' around, checkin' the place out. Tell me, Sidney, what do you think we do here?"

I missed Molly so much. She had a way of keeping my worst instincts in check, softening my tendency toward confrontation. When she left, so had much of my self-restraint.

"I don't know," I said with a shrug. "Sell used auto parts. Cook meth."

I half expected him to sick a Doberman on me or kick me down the stairs. Instead, he burst into laughter. Unadulterated, side-splitting laughter. I drank more beer and waited for it to stop. When it did he cleared his throat. "Almost forgot what a funny guy you are."

"You should catch my act at the Sullivan."

He coughed again, this time for the better part of a minute. When the coughing fit ended, he said, "I took Travis off his leash a long time ago. He's no longer my responsibility."

At that moment a lanky young man with shaggy black hair and a shaggier beard poked his head through the kitchen door. He was clad in grimy coveralls and I recognized him immediately as the guy in the black pickup watching Alice Crawford's place. His round dark eyes bore into me with what I can only describe as consummate hatred.

"Pa," he said, "Bo and I need help with that tranny. Could you—"

"Mind your manners, boy. We have company." Rance turned to me. "This is my son, Ray."

I displayed a purposeful smile. "We've already met, sort of. Ray seems to have an peculiar interest in my comings and goings."

Ray balled his fists but remained silent.

Rance got up out of the recliner with painful slowness and addressed Ray in a voice that could peel the paint off a barn door. "Wait for me outside." Ray left the room and Rance turned to me. "Travis no longer lives under my roof. I'm not inclined to tell you any more than that. Now, you did me a good turn once, but I think maybe you ought to leave while the atmosphere is friendly. Goodbye, Sidney Reed."

I rose from the couch. "Thanks for the beer. I'll let myself out."

"No, sir." His voice grated like a chunk of rusty iron. "I'll be letting *you* out."

Thirty-one

The moment he saw me, the starched-looking private first class standing post at the main of Fort Richardson strode stiffly out of the guard shack. He was somewhere around the same age I was when I enlisted in the Army so many years ago. I handed him my retired military I.D. card. He studied it.

"Good morning, sir. Where are you headed this morning?"

"The national cemetery."

"Sir, I notice your vehicle does not have a post registration sticker. Is there a reason?"

"There is. I was in an accident a few days ago. This is a rental. Tell me, private, have you ever lost a car that meant the world to you?"

He grinned sheepishly. "Why . . . yes, sir. I loaned my MG to a friend so he could go on a date. He called later that night to say he'd totaled my car. To make matters worse, it was the other guy's fault and he wasn't insured. My insurance company canceled me."

"Sucks, doesn't it."

"Roger that, sir." He handed back my I.D. "Have a pleasant day and be careful, sir. The roads are slick in spots. Black ice."

I returned his salute and drove a mile and a half before turning right on Sixth Street, then right again on Davis Highway. A mile down Davis I saw a large wooden sign on the left and I felt an involuntary tingling in my skin.

I made the left onto East Valor Drive, following as it bent through the trees. Dense woods gave way to a huge expanse of open field. I pulled to the side of the road, shoved the Camry into park, and stared.

Fort Richardson National Cemetery is an uncommonly beautiful place. I'd first laid eyes on it the summer we arrived in Alaska. The image of its vast fields of green, the snow-capped Chugach Mountains in the background, had burned itself into my memory. I could see now that it was no less beautiful in winter, the endless rows of perfectly-aligned grave markers jutting above a wide powdery carpet like silent sentries, each stone topped with a wedge of snow.

The day I brought Molly here, we'd spent a resplendent Sunday afternoon exploring Fort Richardson. We spotted the sign for the national cemetery and decided to check it out. During our slow drive-through, she was unusually quiet. I had begun to pull away when she said, "Let's not go just yet. I want to look around."

I'd never been any good at telling her no, and being curious about her interest in the place, I nodded, parked the car, and for the next hour or so we wandered among the rows. When we met back up I found her gazing longingly at the mountains.

"It's so beautiful here," she said.

"Yes, it is."

"I was just thinking . . . why don't we come here?"

"What do you mean, *come* here? Like for a picnic?"

"No. I mean, when it's our time."

I frowned. "You shouldn't be thinking about that. You have your whole life ahead of you."

"My dad used to say, always plan ahead."

"Colonel Harper was a good man. But why here?"

"I don't know," she said, shrugging. "It just feels right to me."

That was Molly, through and through. Knowing further argument was futile, I reserved a plot for the two of us, never imagining she would occupy it before me.

I set the car in motion and drove until I came to Freedom Road. There I hooked a left and rolled slowly past row after row of identical round-topped stones before pulling to a stop adjacent to Section FF. I killed the engine and sat for a moment, listening to the sound of my breathing in the crowded confines of the Camry's interior.

She'd been buried on a day much like this one, with storm clouds threatening to release another layer of white. A priest from the post chapel had said words over her grave, but I didn't hear them. My mind had been somewhere else.

I got out and tromped off through the snow to Molly's grave. Crouched down on one knee, I swept away the snow with my gloved hands. Like the hundreds of other gravestones, hers was a plain slab of white marble three and a half feet high. Upon it, beneath a simple engraved cross, was written the words:

MOLLY CATHERINE REED

DEVOTED WIFE

DAUGHTER & SISTER

LOVED BY ALL

I stood looking down at the stone, my shuffling feet tamping out a flat spot in the snow, and cleared my throat with a nervous cough. "Hi, Molly. I'm sorry it took me so long to visit you. The thing is, I went to see Barb last night. She convinced me it was time to . . . you know."

I rubbed my gloved hands together and shuffled my feet some more, until pretty soon I had carved out a near-perfect semi-circle in front of the marble. "Priscilla's fine. She spends most of the day racked out on your rocking chair. By the way, some asshole broke your rocker, but I had it fixed. It's good as new. Well, almost."

A gust of wind slapped my face and I looked toward the southeast. Above the snow-laced trees, the Chugach Mountains were partially obscured by clumps of sinister-looking clouds that seemed to thicken even as I watched.

"Rachel says there's a storm coming." I half-grinned at what I'd just said. "Um, that's right, you don't know who that is. She's my landlady, Moll. Yeah, after what happened, I sold the house and moved into an apartment downtown. I had a rough time there for a while, but I'm better now. I guess you could say Rachel takes care of me. Not that way. She plays for the other team, if you know what I mean. She's just a good friend."

I swallowed hard. "Speaking of friends, I . . . have a date tonight. Her name is Maria. She's nice, Moll. You'd like her. If you were here, you'd be telling me to move on already, so here I am, moving on."

Moving on? Who am I kidding?

"Well, uh, I should be going. I've got a case I'm working on. There's this guy on trial for murder, but he's innocent, Molly. He didn't . . ." It suddenly dawned on me that I was starting to get worked up, the way I sometimes did when she asked me about my work. I smiled at the thought. "Anyway, I gotta go, but I'll be back. I promise."

I was about to turn away when I caught sight of something dark peeking through the snow. I grabbed for it with my gloved hand.

It was a single red rose, its barbed stem about ten inches in length. It looked fresh, as though it had only recently been placed here, but by whom? Barbara, her only living blood relative, hadn't said anything about a recent visit. It must have been a friend.

I placed it gingerly on the ground and returned to my car. As I was pulling away from the cemetery entrance, my cell phone jingled. It was Connie Zwick. I pulled to the side of the road and stabbed the answer button. "Connie, what's up?"

"Sidney?" Stress rippled through her voice.

Shit, now what?

"What's wrong, Connie?"

There was a pause, her labored breathing filling the empty space. "Someone's watching me."

"Slow down, Connie. Start from the beginning."

I was sitting in Connie Zwick's bedroom at her mother's home in Mountain View. She sat on the edge of her bed, just as she had when we last spoke two days before. Her hand, smoldering cigarette notched between two fingers, trembled noticeably. She brought the cigarette to her lips and drew smoke into her lungs, held it there, and exhaled a billowy cloud of gray fumes.

"Mom and I were eating breakfast in the kitchen when I looked out the window and saw Ray's truck parked across the street." Stress-induced furrows zigzagged her forehead.

"Are you sure? There are lots of black pickups in this town."

Who was I kidding? *Of course* it was Ray. We both knew it.

She shook her head furiously. "The same truck was parked outside Alice's place. It was Ray, all right. He found me, Sidney."

A shrill voice seeped through the door. "Are you smoking in there, Connie? I won't have smoking in this house!"

"I'm talking to someone, Mom!" Connie rolled her eyes. "She can't stand the smell. I opened the window, but that woman could smell a mouse pass gas." She took another drag, using her cupped hand as an ashtray, then shook her head slowly. "I knew them Cooley boys were trouble. Travis is the only one worth a damn."

"You've got them on edge, Connie. That's all."

Her jaw visibly tightened. "If they fuck with me, I'll fuck with them. I know enough to put the whole bunch of them away."

An idea occurred to me. "You really want to get back at them?"

"Damn right I do."

"You think you could you draw a sketch of the place? Where the buildings are, what's in them, that sort of thing?"

She nodded. "Switch places with me." I moved to the bed and she took the chair. Pulling open the desk drawer, she took out a small notepad and pencil and began to scribble. Two minutes later, she surveyed her handiwork. Satisfied, she tore the sheet off the pad, swiveled around, and handed it to me. "That's pretty much all I remember."

I looked at the sheet of white paper and its series of lines, squares, and circles, some with writing next to them. With the memory of my earlier visit as a reference, I was able to pick out the drive leading up to the property, the auto parts store, and the home. I pointed to a square, larger than the others, in roughly the spot where I'd seen the building with the air vents on the outside. Connie had written the letter L next to it. "Is that the lab?"

She nodded forcefully. "That's it."

I pointed to a smaller square near the lab. "What this?"

"A shed of some kind. I think they store fuel in there."

"And these?" I indicated several smaller, unmarked structures.

She squinted at the drawing. "The circle near the lab is a big propane tank. These two smaller squares behind the lab are buildings of some kind. Sheds, maybe." She dragged her finger along a line that meandered past the buildings and over to the edge of the paper. "This drive leads out the back of the property. Trav call it their escape route."

Connie handed me the map and I stuffed it in my coat pocket. The plan I'd conjured up in my head was to introduce her to Mel Denton and let him deal with the Cooley's meth operation.

"Travis never wanted to be a part of their dirty business, Mr. Reed. But he was Rance's son. Rance always said, 'blood is blood.'"

She got up and paced around the room. "I think that's why Trav drank so much. He hated who he was. I remember him telling me he saw his dad kill somebody in Oklahoma. Can you imagine a young boy seeing something like that? Never talked much about it, but I know it weighed on him. A lot of what happened down there did. That's why he wanted no part of it. He wanted to go his own way, but he was terribly conflicted. He wanted to please his dad. And, well . . ."

"What?"

"He missed his mom. No one said much, but I could tell she was a big part of that family. Trav told me his dad was never the same after she died."

"What happened to her, Connie?"

"Cancer, I think. Like I said, he didn't like to talk about it."

I checked my watch and was shocked to learn it was twenty past four. There was no way I could drive out to Big Tooth's cabin to look for Travis and get back time for my date with Maria. It would have to wait until tomorrow.

Connie sat back down on the bed. Seeing the worry in her eyes, I put my hand on hers. "Okay, here's the plan. I'll pick you up at quarter to ten tomorrow morning and take you to meet Rudy's attorney. Then I'm putting you up in a hotel until Monday. You'll be safe there. Pack a suitcase for a couple of nights away. How does that sound?"

Her eyes lit up. "You'd do that for me?"

"Are you kidding? You're my star witness."

"What are you gonna do, Sidney?"

"Find Travis. See if I can get him to come forward."

Connie absentmindedly fingered the gold chain encircling her slim neck. "When you do, tell him I miss him, will you?"

"I will."

She suddenly realized her hand was still nestled in mine and gently pulled away. She reached for the necklace encircling her slender neck. A slender digit slid along the length of the chain until it reached the dolphin figure dangling at the end. Her green eyes locked pleadingly on mine. "Promise me you won't hurt him, Sidney."

She really loved the guy. I felt a sharp stab of remembrance as an image of Molly lying on the floor pushed its way into my thoughts. I forced it back out. "I promise."

I glanced at my watch again. I had barely an hour and a half to get home, shower and change, and pick up Maria.

"Connie, I've gotta run," I said as I got up from my chair. "Just stay put here tonight. Don't go anywhere. You're safe here for now. If you see Ray again, or anything suspicious, call me."

"What if he follows us to the hotel tomorrow?"

"That's not going to happen. Trust me."

By the time I got back to my apartment it had begun to snow. My roommate Priscilla greeted me with an affectionate leg rub. I topped off her water and took a quick shower. Staring at my image in the mirror after I'd shaved, combed my hair, and spritzed cologne on my neck, I decided I passed muster.

Back in the living room, I collected my coat and went to the rocker and scratched Priscilla behind her ear. "Wish me luck," I said, glancing at Molly's photograph on the way out the door.

Outside it was full dark, and the thick snowflakes seemed even thicker under the cold white vapor lamps. I reached the bottom of the stairs as Rachel was exiting the Mighty Moose. She walked up and looked me over. "Not bad. If I were into men, I might be interested."

"That's just about the nicest thing anybody's ever said to me."

"Don't get used to it." She offered a crooked smile. "By the way, where are the flowers?"

"Flowers?"

"Sid, for fuck sake, I know you've been out of the dating scene for, like, decades, but you can't not take her flowers. It's Dating 101, dude."

"I knew that."

"Loretta's is just around the corner on Fifth. If you hurry, she might still be open. Buy the woman a dozen red roses."

"Thanks, Rach. What would I do without you?"

"Become a recluse. Now go get yourself laid." With that she took off in a hurry down G Street. I followed her at a slightly slower pace, rounded the corner, and entered Loretta's Bloomery. Ten minutes later I came out with what Loretta assured me was an arrangement dazzling enough to impress any woman.

Threading my way through heavy Friday afternoon traffic, I switched on the Camry's radio and surfed the dial for a weather report. I wished I hadn't. A foot or more of snow was expected in the Anchorage area. A travel advisory was in effect.

The Skinner case invaded my thoughts. Eddie was presenting his defense on Monday. We had a magic bullet in Connie Zwick, but would she hold up in court? In the short period of time we'd spent together, I'd grown fond of her. Truth be told, she reminded me of Molly. Perhaps it was her vulnerability, perhaps her spunk. She'd shown a lot of brass coming forward, but she was afraid. I began to wonder if I should have checked her into a hotel that night. I decided to drive by her mom's house after my date with Maria and check on her.

Then there was the matter of Evelyn Waters. I was convinced she had information important to the case, but she was scared. Had Lou Fletcher threatened and, if so, why?

I grinned. I was looking for reasons to take my mind off my date with Maria. I didn't want to admit I was nervous. Forty-five-year-old men aren't supposed to get nervous before about a date.

I was pretty sure it was a rule.

Thirty-two

Maria lived in an older but well-maintained condominium complex in Midtown called Mountain Terrace, its quaint, wood-shingled units freshly painted bluish-gray and separated for privacy. I'd visited the complex several times before interviewing witnesses and liked how the units were laid out.

By the time I arrived it was snowing quite heavily, clumps of thick powder roosting on the Camry's windshield as fast as the wiper blades swept them away. I located Unit 27 without difficulty, slipped into visitor parking, and strolled up to the first-floor apartment, flowers at the ready.

I pressed the buzzer, the door opened, and I stared.

"Hi, Sidney," Maria said, her eyes dark and animated. She was ready to go: A black wool coat covered all but her slender neck. Wavy russet hair spilled like a waterfall across her shoulders and down her back. The sweet smell of jasmine swirled around her.

Now that's a beautiful woman, I thought to myself.

I said, "Taking my breath away is becoming a habit with you."

She smiled coyly. "I certainly hope so."

I held out the flowers. "I brought you these."

"They're lovely, thank you! Hold on, let me find a vase." She disappeared but soon returned and looped an arm through mine and we strolled to the Camry.

"Where to?" she said once we were on the road.

"Giorgio's on the south side."

"Ooh, I've heard good things about that place."

"You like Italian?"

"I *love* Italian."

Mindful of what had happened the last time she'd been in my car, I adhered assiduously to the speed limit while still managing to steal glances at her nylon-wrapped legs, on display up to mid-thigh.

"You look stunning, Maria," I said. "If you don't mind me asking, why do you hide it?"

"I'm not hiding it now," she said with a sidelong glance.

"Definitely not, no. What I mean is, um, when you're on the job you dress . . ."

"Like a Hobbit?"

I smiled at her reference to Tolkien's iconic characters. "Why do you say that? You're a beautiful woman."

"My neck is too thin. It looks like a pencil."

"I love your neck. Just admit it, you're a babe."

She gushed at that, but then her face darkened. "It's important to me to be taken seriously as a reporter. The newspaper business is a man's world."

"I don't know much about that world," I admitted.

"It's not just the newspaper business. It is a man's world, period."

I switched subjects to the weather and before long we arrived at Ristorante Giorgio. Molly and I had dined here often, and despite Rachel's admonition, I wanted to share it with Maria.

It was a light crowd for a Friday night, a happenstance I attributed to the looming snowstorm. That was fine by me. Soon we were seated at a candle-lit table for two in front of an elegant stone fireplace, traditional Italian music wafting through the air.

Playing the role of knight in shining armor to the hilt, I pulled her chair away from the table. She winked playfully and nudged her coat off her shoulders, revealing a sleeveless black cocktail dress that caressed her delicate curves. I thought to myself: *Damn.*

I sat down in the chair opposite and stared at her, feeling for the first time in a very long while that something was finally right with the world. A server delivered menus and glasses of ice water. Moments later, a tall, thin fortysomething woman with a pleasant face, dressed in black slacks and a white frilly blouse, approached our table. "Good evening. My name is Francesca. I'll be your waitress for the evening." After exchanging pleasantries, Francesca handed us each a wine list. Maria deferred to me and I ordered a bottle of Cavaliere d'Oro Chianti.

Maria glanced around the dim, cozy interior. "Mmm . . . I love the atmosphere in here. Did, uh, you and Molly come here often?"

"It was our favorite place."

She sat in silence, biting her lower lip.

"What's wrong?" I said.

"I need to ask you something. Are you . . . over her?"

Feeling my chest tighten, I lowered my gaze. "I don't think I'll ever be over her."

Her lips tightened. "I'm sorry, that must have sounded cruel. I didn't mean it come out that way. I'm—"

"I know what you meant, and it's a fair question. To tell you the truth, I don't know."

She hesitated. "So, why did you ask me out?"

"Actually, you asked me out."

"You're right, I did. Well, then, why did you accept?"

"Because I'm attracted to you."

"That's your only reason?"

"Do I need more than one?"

She giggled. "No. I suppose not."

Francesca returned with the Chianti and filled our glasses. "I'll be right back with some bread," she said and drifted toward the back.

We toasted "To us" and sipped wine. It tasted so damn good, I wondered why I wasted my money on Corona, or, for that matter, why I drank beer at all.

Maria peeked over the top of her menu. "You're really attracted to me?"

"Since the moment we first met."

She smiled bashfully, her eyes dancing in the candlelight.

Francesca appeared with a basket of warm bread and took our orders. Maria asked for vegetable lasagna and I opted for the veal parmigiana. Soon we were chatting easily and laughing and drinking like old friends. She was intelligent and down to earth and made me feel at ease.

When our salads arrived we attacked them hungrily, and for a while the only sounds were the murmur of other voices and the deep baritone of some nameless Italian crooner.

I refilled her wine glass. "What led you into journalism?"

She considered the question. "When I was still in high school, I read a story in the newspaper about the Mexican drug gangs and all the violence associated with them. It made such a huge impression on me, I decided then and there I wanted to be a journalist. My school counselor helped me apply for a scholarship to the Walter Cronkite School of Journalism and I was selected."

"You certainly seem well suited to it. What brought you to Alaska?"

Her eyes shot up and to the left. "I saw a *Daily News* job posting online," she replied quickly. "Um, you have a pretty cool job. Private investigation, I mean. How did that come about?"

I shrugged. "After twenty years as an Army cop, it seemed like a natural transition."

"Well, I think it's sexy. I liked being on surveillance with you that time."

A few months back I was staking out a guy's house. Maria was there for the same reason. She saw me and jumped in my car.

"It wasn't a surveillance, it was a stakeout. A surveillance is when you follow people around. A stakeout is—"

"All right, smarty pants, I get it. My point is, I had fun doing it with you. Let me help you with the Rudy Skinner case."

"I can't do that, Maria. We shouldn't even talk about it."

She reached for her wine glass. "Why not?"

"Well, for one thing, it would be a conflict of interest. We're both working on the same case, each with a different agenda and for different employers. Then there's the matter of attorney-client privilege, although that's my problem, not yours. And then—"

"There's more?" she said, frowning.

"The most important reason of all. I work ALONE."

She was about to respond when Francesca arrived with our food. "Bon appétit," I said.

Maria picked up her fork, and attacked her entrée. She had deftly evaded my question about why she came to Alaska, then changed the subject. Could her obfuscation have something to do with her changing her name? I was dying to ask her, but resolved instead to take Rachel's advice and wait for Maria to bring it up when she was ready.

She must have gotten over my earlier comments, because soon she was smiling at me in between morsels of pasta. For my part, I enjoyed her company. I found myself wanting to trust her, something that did not come easy for me. And as I nibbled away at my meal, I found myself thinking about Evelyn Waters.

I set my fork aside. "There is one thing you could do for me."

Her eyes shot up from her plate. "Yes?"

"I probably shouldn't ask you . . ."

"Come on, Sidney. What is it?"

"Well, okay. I want you to interview someone for me."

Her eyes widened. "Who would that be?"

"Rudy Skinner's girlfriend, Evelyn Waters. Well, ex-girlfriend. I have a hunch she might be able to provide my client with an alibi for the night Willie Olson was killed. She wouldn't talk to me, but I have a feeling she wants to talk to *someone*."

Maria speared a piece of asparagus with her fork. "You'd think she'd want to help him."

"I was thinking exactly the same thing."

"So why would she talk to me and not you?"

"Because you're irresistible."

She shot me a withering look. "Be serious."

"I *am* serious. I don't think she trusts men. You, on the other hand, are a woman."

"Thanks for noticing."

"What I mean is, she might find a woman less threatening."

"I have found that to be true." She paused to drink wine. When she was done, she curled her mouth. "There's more, isn't there? I mean, for you to want little ol' *me* to help *you*, well . . ."

I smiled—at her spot-on imitation of a sexy southern belle, *and* because he'd seen right through my poker face. "I think I know why she's afraid."

"I'm all ears."

"And they're adorable ears, but I can't tell you. Not until I know for sure what's going on. Anyway, that shouldn't concern you. Your job is to get her to talk. Find out what she knows."

"All right," she said after another sip of wine. "I'll do it."

"Good." I pushed my peas around the plate with my fork. "There's just one thing."

"What's that?"

"If what she says ties my client to Olson's death, you can't print it."

She wrinkled her nose. "You're asking me to sit on a story. I can't—"

"No, Maria. I'm asking you for a favor, not as a reporter but as a friend. Look, if you can't do it, just say so. I'll understand."

She thought for a moment. "Say no more," she said at last with a forceful nod of her head, "I've got this." She raised her glass in a mock toast. "This makes us partners, right?"

As I started to object, Francesca came and took our plates. We waved off dessert menus.

Maria had taken to lazily twirling her glass, grinning as if in response to a private joke. Her eyes suddenly flittered upward. "Perhaps I can help you with other things, too." Her voice rose almost imperceptibly.

"What things?"

"I don't know . . . private eye stuff?"

"Maria, we talked about this. I don't think it's a good idea."

She slid her index finger along the rim of her glass. Her eyes shifted from the glass to me and then back again. "So . . . what if it's not?"

Just then, something soft and yielding touched the side of my ankle and I flinched. That something meandered past the upper reaches of my sock to bare leg, removing all doubt that the something was

Maria's nylon-covered toes. She proceeded to rub her foot up and down the side of my leg, in the process pushing my sock down lower on my ankle. My heart thumped.

Be cool, Sidney.

"Maria, I would love to work with you, but . . . well . . . I'm just not sure—"

"I can help you?" she finished. "Sidney, I spend four hours in court every day watching a boring trial and then go to the office and spend hours sitting at my computer. That's my life. Does that sound exciting to you? I need adventure." Her foot shinnied up my leg like a cat fleeing a Doberman. "I need it *bad.*"

My leg jerked reflexively upward and struck the underside of the table.

Maria smiled, cat-like.

"You're enjoying this, aren't you?"

"The question is, are *you* enjoying it?" She gazed at me dreamily. The candle flame flickered like a Tiki Torch in her bottomless eyes. Her foot meandered back up my leg.

"Tell me, Sidney . . ." Maria's hands came across the table and rested on mine. "When was the last time you had . . . fun?"

At the word "fun," the cleft of her foot came to rest on my crotch and I blurted out "Whoa!" several decibels louder than intended. Heads swiveled in our direction. My face reddened.

Like a guardian angel, Francesca approached our table. I waved my arm like a distress signal and she came and smiled down at us. "My, don't you two make a lovely couple!"

I grinned sheepishly. "Check please."

Thirty-three

I woke expecting to feel her against me. Instead, I was alone. I yawned and stretched myself awake. A faint pre-dawn light seeped in through Maria's east-facing bedroom window. Her smell lingered in the sheets, much as our night together lingered in my memory.

For all my earlier trepidation, it had been all right. Well, better than all right. Driving her home after dinner, my little voice had said, *Don't press your luck. Kiss her and call it a night.* But she'd met my sputtering attempts at gallantry with, *It's too dangerous to drive home in this weather.* My little voice said I would be a fool to disagree.

Once in a great while, my little voice gets it right.

So, we spent the night together and it was good. Afterwards came the realization that I had been with a woman who was not Molly and the world had not ended. Far from it. Still, I felt a twinge of guilt that I couldn't quite shake no matter how hard I tried: I'd been unfaithful to Molly.

That thought was soon swept away by the sight of Maria in a robin's-egg blue bathrobe waving a spatula. "Good morning, lover," she said in that marvelously soothing voice of hers. She made a beeline for the bed, bent down, kissed me, and whispered, "You talk in your sleep." Then she did a one-eighty and left the room.

Talk about what?

I eased my middle-aged body out of bed, gravitated naked to the bathroom, and stepped into the shower. Under the hot jets of water I tried in vain to recall what I might have said in my sleep, as if my brain were a broken-down juke box I was trying to kick back to life. I gave it up as a lost cause, shut off the water and toweled off, returning my thoughts to Maria. Our lovemaking had been spirited and passionate. How long had it been since Molly and I . . .

Don't go there.

I checked the time on my phone and noted with relief that I had over an hour before I had to pick up Connie and take her to meet Eddie Baker. I dressed hurriedly and headed for the kitchen, lured there by the aroma of sizzling potatoes.

Maria's kitchen was small and sparse, yet charming in its own way. There was a small window, with a hint of cold blue morning light, and a small white table and, resting upon it, a glass of orange juice and a plate piled high with scrambled eggs, home fries, and slices of toast. I smiled. My idea of a gourmet breakfast was a peanut butter sandwich.

I could get used to this.

Next to a small white fridge was a stainless-steel sink. Maria stood leaning over it, the blue bathrobe snug around her waist. I approached silently and put my hands on her hips and leaned close to her ear. "Thank you for breakfast."

She trembled slightly and turned to face me. "You're, um, welcome."

I untied her robe and slipped my hands around her bare waist. Her skin was silky smooth. I pulled her to me and our lips touched.

And then my cell phone rang.

Shit.

She sighed in frustration. I released her and fished the phone out of my pocket. Lois Dozier's name appeared on the display. We hadn't spoken since our Wednesday luncheon—the one she'd walked out on.

I looked at Maria. "I have to take this."

She frowned.

I pushed ANSWER and heard, "Sid, Lois." The tension in her voice leapt out of the phone.

"Lois, about the other day—"

"Save it," she said tersely. "I need you here on Lake Otis Parkway, a mile south of Tudor Road. ASAP."

"I'm fifteen minutes away. I'll—"

Click.

This can't be good, I thought.

I turned to Maria. The look in her eyes told me she already knew, but I said, "I have to . . ."

"I know." She displayed an understanding smile, but the sadness in her voice reached into my chest.

"This shouldn't take long. How about we take in a show later? Maybe dinner."

"I'd like that." Her robe still hung open, revealing a long, narrow strip of olive skin and faint, indistinct shadows. My hands found her waist and I kissed her long and hard. I eased away from her and she cinched up her robe.

"Don't worry," she said. "I'll talk to Evelyn this morning."

I nodded and glanced at the table. "Sorry about breakfast. It looks awesome."

She grinned. "I put Martha Stewart to shame."

"Martha Stewart's got nothing on you, babe."

We walked hand in hand to the door and kissed again.

"I had a nice time," I said.

"Me, too." Her big browns studied me. "Be careful, will you? The roads will be a mess."

"I'll be all right."

I opened the door to the sting of frigid air. An ocean of white shrouded everything. I zipped up my coat and set off down the walkway, my boots shoveling two feet of powdery snow.

"Sidney?" Maria's voice seemed to snap in the crisp morning air.

I turned to see her standing in the doorway, looking very serious. "Yes?" I said.

"Watch out for moose."

The Camry more closely resembled a snow sculpture than a car. I dug through a layer of snow, found the door handle, and fired up the engine. It took some rooting around under the seats and in the trunk, but I finally located a long-handled brush. It took a good five minutes of vigorous brushing and scraping before I'd shed the car of snow and ice and was able to pull out into the street.

It took considerably longer than fifteen minutes to reach Lake Otis Parkway. The side roads were all but impassable, but I made it to Northern Lights Boulevard. Road crews were out in force, plowing and loading snow onto dump trucks, two lanes of traffic reduced to one narrow swath. I chafed at the slow procession of cars in front of me, thoughts of Lois's ominous phone call filling my head. I feared the worst.

When I finally made the turn onto Lake Otis, the sun was cresting in a blaze of glory over the Chugach Mountains to the southeast. A mile or so past Tudor, the road swept into a gradual curve to the left, and when it straightened out, a half dozen flashing red lights came into view. I felt a twinge in my gut as I drew closer.

I counted two APD squad cars, an ambulance, and a government sedan. Lois Dozier was leaning against the door of the sedan. To her left, a group of officers stomped their feet near a huge snow berm that had been pushed there by city maintenance crews during a frantic night of road clearing. A uniformed officer directed traffic, shooing along rubberneckers. When I came to a stop, he approached the Camry and eyed me with a bored look. "Keep it moving, sir."

"Sidney Reed. Investigator Dosier called me."

He glanced her way. She waved me over.

"Go ahead," he said.

I pulled up next to her car and got out. "What's this about?"

Lois wore a thick gray parka, the furry ruff of the hood framing her red-cheeked face. She stepped away from her car. "Walk with me."

We shuffled toward the officers huddled some twenty yards away. Lois spoke in a measured tone, the chill in her voice matching the chill in the air. "A little over an hour ago, a northbound driver saw something sticking out of that snowbank over there. He pulled over to check it out and saw a leg with a boot attached to it. He called 9-1-1 and they called the M.E.'s office. They were digging her out of the snowbank when I arrived on scene."

The huddled officers parted like a curtain to reveal, some ten feet beyond, a body laid out on a tarp. During my drive there, I kept telling myself it wasn't so. Someone had got their wires crossed. But now, as I approached the prone figure, saw the long wave of jet-black hair, flecked with snow and ice, and the beige parka, its matching hood askew beneath her, I knew what I had known all along.

Connie Zwick's slight frame appeared even slighter than I remembered, as if shrunk by the cold. Her face, once vibrant and warm, was now alabaster white and surreal, the eyelashes festooned with ice crystals. Open, bulging eyes seemed locked in eternal disbelief.

Blood rushed to my temples and bunched there like fists. I stifled an overwhelming urge to scream.

Lois spoke in that calm and clinical way of hers. "This is preliminary, of course, but given the nature of the injuries and position of the body, it would appear she was struck by a municipal snow removal truck as she walked along the road sometime last night." She turned, her dark eyes nearly lost under her parka's hood. "There's just one problem."

"What's that?" I replied, only half listening.

"We don't know who she is. There was no identification on the body. We only have this. I found it in her coat pocket."

She handed me a small white card. I stared at it.

It was my business card.

When I looked up Lois was staring at me. "Who is she, Sid?"

Her voice trilled hollow, like a distant echo. The words I'd spoken to Connie only hours before came flying back at me like bullets.

You'll be safe here? Who was I kidding?

"Sidney . . . talk to me."

A sharp pain stung my left forearm. Lois's hands were squeezing it. "Dammit, Sidney. Who is she? Who *is* she?"

The coffee maker gurgled crankily next to the copy machine in Lois Dozier's second-story office. I watched numbly as she opened an overhead cabinet, took out a pair of mugs imprinted with the official logo of the Medical Examiner's Office, blew the dust out of them, then peered inside each to make sure it was clean. When the gurgling stopped, she filled the mugs to the brim.

I sat in a plain straight-back chair opposite her desk—a good investigator never lets a witness get too comfortable—and glanced around the room. Her office wasn't exactly spartan, but it wasn't opulent either: desk, filing cabinets, printer, coffee maker, and a panoramic view of the Chugach Mountains as a reminder—as if one needed reminding—that this was The Last Frontier. It suddenly occurred to me that, although I'd known Lois for years and considered her a good friend, this was the first time I'd been in her office.

Lois handed me a mug. "Sorry. All I have are these things. If you need a fill-up, help yourself."

I nodded but didn't smile.

Lois settled in behind her desk and sipped coffee. "Well, old friend. I'm all ears."

"What do you want to know?"

"Some facts would be nice. All you've given me so far is the name Connie Zwick. Tell me the rest of it, starting with how she came to have your business card in her pocket."

On the drive from Lake Otis, I hadn't given much thought to what I was going to say, or not say. All I could think about was Connie's broken body lying on the frozen ground. How she'd put her trust in me and I'd failed her. Now I had a few questions of my own, but I'd have to wait until I found the people who could answer them.

"She was someone I interviewed for a case I'm working on. I gave her my card. It was a routine thing."

"For the Willie Olson case?"

"That's right."

"How does Alice Crawford figure into it?"

I spoke in a slow, measured tone. "When I first met Connie Zwick, she told me her name was Alice. She wouldn't give me a last name, so I followed her to her car and snagged her license plate number.

When it came back registered to Alice Crawford—thanks to you—I assumed that's who she was."

"Assumed? You remember what they told us in the Army?"

"Yeah, I remember. It makes an ass out of you and me. Now, do you want to gloat some more or can I keep going?"

She waved her hand. "Be my guest."

"I went to the address you gave me, only to discover the *real* Alice Crawford. Turns out Connie Zwick was Alice's roommate. She had borrowed Alice's car for her interview with me. You getting this?"

Lois looked at me. "I'm normally pretty slow after spending all morning investigating a dead body, but I think I've got it."

I sipped coffee and set the mug on her desk. "That about covers it."

"Not hardly, my friend. What was Connie a witness to, exactly?"

"You know I can't tell you that."

Her face creased in anger. "I've got a dead girl and you're giving me some attorney-client privilege bullshit?"

She was referring to the legal principle, deeply engrained in American jurisprudence, protecting communication between attorneys and their clients. It applies to anyone working with the attorney, such as their investigator. It pissed off Lois that I was invoking it now.

As she stared at her notepad, I braced myself for a lecture. She stiffened herself with gulps of coffee. "Why do you suppose she wanted to conceal her identity from you?"

"I'm not sure. I think maybe she had a lot of unpaid parking tickets. Can I go now?"

Lois's eyes burned with thinly concealed rage. "We go back a long way, you and me. Hell, I wouldn't have this position if it weren't for you. But now I've got a job to do. There's a dead girl lying in a refrigerator downstairs. On Monday the M.E. is going to perform an autopsy." She leaned back and clasped her hands behind her neck. "All I ask is that you be fucking straight with me."

Lois was a good friend and a professional colleague. She deserved the truth. But I was too angry, both at myself and at whomever had done this to Connie, to worry about helping Lois complete her report.

The only thing on my mind was getting out of that office and going after Connie's killers.

I said, "Sorry, Lois, but I can't."

"So that's it, then? Fine. You just better hope the autopsy reveals no evidence of foul play or you'll be talking to a homicide detective." She leaned forward, her dark eyes boring into me. "Now get the fuck out of my office."

I set the mug down with a thud on the edge of her desk and made for the door. When I reached it, I turned and looked at her, searching for something clever and witty to throw back at her. I came up short on both counts.

"Your coffee sucks," I said, and walked out.

Thirty-four

Eddie Baker was writing something in a file when I walked into his office. He glanced up, saw that it was me, and returned to what he was doing. "Where have you been?"

The dead can be so thoughtless when it comes to the living, I thought to myself. I moved to the edge of his desk. "I just left the M.E.'s office. Connie Zwick is dead."

"Connie Zwick?" He stopped scribbling, eyes probing mine. "What happened?"

"They pulled her body out of a snowbank on Lake Otis Parkway early this morning, that's what happened." My temples were still throbbing.

"Yeah, that was one hell of a snowstorm last ni—"

He never finished the sentence. A vicious swipe of my left hand sent a stack of case files crashing to the floor. He came out of his chair like a rocket. "What in hell is wrong with you?"

"I see I have your attention now. I wasn't sure you heard me say the cops found your star witness frozen like a popsicle by the side of the road."

He stared at me. "Sidney, I'm sorry. I'm on my last nerve with this damned trial. I've been struggling with my closing remarks. You've obviously been through a lot this morning. Sit down and tell me about it . . . please."

He relocated the stack of file folders from the chair next to his desk and I slumped into it.

"How about some coffee?"

"I don't want any fuckin' coffee."

"Suit yourself. I'm getting some." I watched him as he gravitated to the coffee maker, filled a plain white mug, and returned to his desk, not bothering to clean up the mess I'd made. "Okay, tell me what happened."

I heard myself tell him how I'd arranged for Connie to meet him in advance of her planned testimony on Monday, about the early morning call from Lois, and my identification of Connie's body. I concluded with the heated meeting in Lois's office. All the while, the image of Connie lying dead in that snowbank pervaded my thoughts like a demented daydream that refused to go away.

"Sid, I am truly sorry. You worked your ass off to get her to come forward. To come this far, only to lose her in a tragic accident—"

"It was no accident."

"I thought you said—"

"I said the M.E. thinks it *looks* like an accident. It wasn't. Connie was murdered."

Eddie straightened his spine. "What makes you say that?"

"For starters, she had no reason to be where they found her. She was staying at her mom's, lying low. Didn't have a car. I . . . told her to stay put. I think someone lured her out of the house, killed her, and left her on the side of road for the city plow to do the rest. Whoever did this probably figured the cops would conclude she froze to death and that would be the end of it."

"You may be right, but the why doesn't really matter at this point, does it? She's dead and we have no witness."

"It matters to me! She came forward at great personal risk to herself, to help someone she didn't even know. That took guts."

Eddie stared at me as if I were his crazy uncle, the one who sits down at the dinner table in his skivvies, convinced the government is poisoning his toothpaste.

Sucking air deep into my lungs, I stared past Eddie toward Sleeping Lady Mountain, awash in a palette of pinks and blues, as if the morning sun had set it ablaze. I still vividly remembered Molly staring dreamily at that mountain and saying, *She looks so peaceful lying there.* But all that beauty was lost on me now. The only thing I felt was rage. My body reeked of it. Rage at Connie killers, but even more than that, rage at myself for letting it happen.

Eddie said, "I've seen that look before. You get it when you're about to set out on one of your crusades. That's not going to help Rudy, so forget it."

His words bounced off me like rain off a tin roof.

"Sid, are you listening to me? I know you're upset, but we need to get past this and move on. Now pull yourself together and focus on picking up Dr. Hathaway at the airport tomorrow and getting him to court Monday morning. Rudy Skinner's counting on us. Say you're with me."

I didn't reply.

"Dammit . . . say *something*."

I got up out of the chair and stood over him. "Fuck you, Eddie."

The pale yellow house on Parsons Avenue looked no less pale in the light of day, though now a miniature mountain of new snow stood between the street and the front gate. I wasn't the first visitor that morning—at least two others had gone before me, breaking trail to the front door. I suspected the trail breakers were members of the Anchorage Police Department, there to deliver the bad news to Connie's mother. I rang the bell and soon enough the door opened.

One look at Beatrice Phillips' tear-stained face told me I was right. Stooped and frail in a faded blue robe, she glared at me. "You! Haven't you done enough already? Go away!"

"Mrs. Phillips, please. May I come in?"

She answered by retreating into the house, leaving the door open. I followed her inside.

"I'm kind of busy right now, Mr. Reed. I have to make arrangements to bury my daughter."

"Please, Mrs. Phillips. Tell me what happened."

"What happened? My daughter's dead, that's what happened!"

"Why did she leave the house?"

Her eyes narrowed into dark slits. "You ought to know. You're the one who called her."

My dry lips parted. "What are you talking about?"

She flittered about the room, sputtering out words in between gentle sobs. "You called her . . . Said it was urgent . . . Said you had to see her right away."

"Mrs. Phillips, please. Slow down and start from the beginning. Tell me about the call."

She slowed, but never stop moving. "The damn phone woke me just after five—I know, I looked at the clock. I don't answer no damn phone at five in the morning. I heard Connie pick it up and talk to somebody. I wanna know who's calling so damn early, so I get out of bed and she's standing in the living room with her coat on, fixin' to fly out the door. I said, Whoa, girl, where you off to? Don't you know we just had a big snow storm? And she said the detective called her and she had to go meet him. She said it was urgent."

"The detective?"

"She was talking about you. I heard her say the name Sidney."

"How was she supposed to meet me? Did she call a cab?"

"She said you were picking her up. Said you told her to walk down to Bragaw Street. That you'd meet her there 'cause they hadn't plowed the roads—" She froze. "You didn't call?"

"No, ma'am."

She sank into a faded old Salvation-Army-looking couch, mumbled something, and buried her head in her hands.

I stared down at her. "Where's your phone, Mrs. Phillips?"

"God help me! I shouldn't have let her go nowhere!"

"Mrs. Phillips, I need to see your phone."

She pointed feebly toward the dim hallway. "On that little stand."

It was an old Sears touch-tone phone with a small digital display. I scrolled through the incoming numbers until I came to one time-stamped 5:07 that morning. There was a pencil and scratch pad next to the phone. I wrote down the number, tore the sheet off the pad, and stuffed it in my coat. When I returned to the living room she was sitting on the couch, her face buried in her hands, rocking back and forth. She kept saying, "My baby! My poor baby!"

I cleared my throat. "Mrs. Phillips, don't erase any numbers on your phone until the police have a chance to examine it, okay?" I hesitated. "Ma'am, I'm terribly sorry. You daughter was a fine woman. You should be very proud of her." But the words sounded hollow to me. I could only imagine how they sounded to her.

Suddenly she turned her shell-shocked gaze on me. "You brought this on! You killed her! Get out! Get out of my house!"

She was still screaming when I got to my car.

It was almost noon when I swung by my apartment for a change of clothes and to brush my teeth. Priscilla came off her rocker to greet me but my idea of reciprocity was a scratch on the head and a quick hello. I was in and out in ten minutes. I resisted the urge to pop into the Mighty Moose, for as much as I would have liked to chat with Rachel and pick up a mocha, I knew she'd want to grill me about my date with Maria. I wasn't in the mood.

As I descended the stairs and crossed the street to the parking garage, a stiff north wind assaulted me, the opening volley of a cold front—the kind that so often follows a late fall snowstorm. If experience was any kind of guide, the next few days were going to be god-awful cold.

The Alaska Range was uncommonly beautiful, and under other circumstances I might have enjoyed the scenery. But now as I fired up the Camry and zipped north on the Glenn Highway, I was oblivious to it, just as I was to the road crews laboring to clear the previous night's snow dump, and to the dozen or so ditch divers littering the median strip separating the north and south lanes. Nor was I thinking about Molly, or Maria, or Rudy Skinner. The only person on my mind was Connie Zwick. I wanted answers and I knew someone who might be able to provide some: Travis Cooley.

With one eye on the wind-swept highway, I plucked my cell phone out of my coat and scrolled through "Favorites" until I found what I wanted. Lois Dozier answered on the first ring.

I said, "You still love me?"

"Jury's still out. You aggravate the shit out of me sometimes."

"I know, but I need you to run a reverse phone for me."

"You've got a lot of fucking nerve."

"Connie Zwick was murdered. Someone lured her away from her mom's house, claiming to be me. *That's* who killed her."

There was an audible gasp on her end. "Jesus, why?"

"She was going to testify Monday in the Skinner case. Somebody didn't want her talking."

"Testify to what?"

"Sorry, Lois. I wish I could, I really do."

There was a long pause. Then, "What's the number?"

I told her.

"Call you back in five," she said before the phone went dead.

It rang four minutes later. Lois said, "Call came from a burner phone. Untraceable." When I didn't reply she said, "I assume you'll be contacting Homicide?"

"Sure thing."

"Sid, I'm warning you. Don't pursue this on your own. It's a murder case now."

"I'll be in touch."

Thirty-five

Robert Murphy's cabin was all but buried in snow when I got there at quarter past one. Atop this ocean of white, ice crystals sparked in the midday sun and wood smoke belched from the cabin's chimney. His black Chevy was nowhere in sight. Nor had I seen it when I drove past B.T. Auto ten minutes earlier.

Where are you, Big Tooth?

Someone had cleared a wide swath of driveway in the front of the cabin, so I backed the Camry up against the front porch in case I needed to beat a hasty retreat. I reached under the front seat for the Ruger, stuffed it in my parka, stepped out of the car, and trudged to the front door, dry frigid wind stinging my face. I raised a fist and banged on the door.

No answer.

I pounded the heavy wooden slab a few more times. When no response came, I turned the knob and pushed. The door squeaked open. I called out, "Travis! You in there?"

No answer.

While I was weighing the pros and cons of going inside and having a look around, I heard the sound of wheels on snow behind me. My muscles stiffened. I turned just as a now-familiar black Chevy pickup rigged with a snowplow blade pulled to a stop in front of the Toyota. A gangly figure in dirty coveralls sprang out of the cab and strode toward me. I easily recognized Robert Murphy from his full beard, his slow, loping gate, and his pissed-off expression.

Murphy came and stood so close to me, I could smell his rancid breath. His stringy black hair flapped in the icy wind. His mouth opened in a sneer, revealing a row of rotting teeth—suggestive of a meth addition—and the single gold tooth I'd heard so much about. It disappeared behind a purplish upper lip.

"What the fuck are you doing here?" he demanded.

What I wanted was Travis Cooley, but I found myself thinking about Clara Ann Lamott in her little one-pump gas station and what Murphy had done to her daughter. I reached deep into my soul and put on the best imitation of a concerned look I could muster and said, "Robert Murphy? I'm here to tell you you're in grave danger. The Methodists are looking for you. I'm afraid we don't have much time. I need to get you into the Jehovah's Witness Protection Program ASAP. I'll be escorting you to one of our safe houses. Let's go."

First, Murphy looked at me like I was nuts, an assessment I would have had a hard time disputing. Then he smiled. Finally, his neck muscles twitched, his jaw tightened, and his left arm uncoiled like a spring and flew at my jaw.

I don't know if it was his drug habit or the extreme cold, but he was way too slow. I dodged his fist handily and launched a kick to the side of his knee. He dropped like a bag of wet sand. Before he fully understood what had just happened, I had a knee on his chest, a hand against his throat, and the Ruger pointed at his head.

"Travis Cooley. Where is he?"

Plumes of water vapor shot from his nostrils. His pain and fear-stricken eyes darted left to right. "I don't know anyone by that name."

I sighed. "Let's try again." I pressed the barrel hard against his cheek. "Where . . . is . . . Travis?"

"Fuck you!" Murphy sneered, his famous tooth jutting out of his mouth like a golden chisel. I saw it as a golden opportunity and dashed the butt end of the Ruger against the twinkling tooth. The lanky drug dealer cursed and spat a mouthful of ruby red blood into the snow, along with his tooth. "Goddam motherfucker!"

I stood up, keeping the Ruger leveled. "Put snow in your mouth. It'll stop the bleeding."

He glared at me.

"Do it, Robert. Would I lie to you?"

Hesitating, he scooped up a handful of snow and shoved it in his mouth. He held it there briefly, then spit it out. "Fuck, that's cold."

"No doubt. Now, unless you want to lose another tooth, tell me where to find Travis."

Venom seemed to ooze from every pore in his body. "He's at the Lazy Dog Saloon, okay?"

"Where was he last night?"

His face took on a puzzled expression. "Last night?"

"Yeah, where was he?"

"He was here."

"All night?"

"Yeah, all night."

I slipped the Ruger into my pocket. "Know a good dentist?"

"Fuck you." He eyed me like a wounded animal. "You're gonna pay for this." He made a credible effort to get up, then stopped with a grunt and clutched his knee. "Fuck, that hurts!"

"You're going to need medical attention for that knee. I trust you've been saving wisely. That tooth ought to be worth a couple hundred bucks."

He glared up at me. "Who the fuck *are* you, anyway?"

"I'm the guy you tried to run off the road."

"That was *you*? You were following me, motherfucker!"

"You know something, Robert?" I smiled down at him. "You're going to need a new nickname. What do you think about Toothless?"

The Lazy Dog Saloon was a wood-framed building with one of those squared-off false fronts, painted midnight blue and located midway along Palmer's main drag.

I stepped inside and paused, letting my eyes adjust to the dim interior. The voice of Clint Black belting out "Killing Time" mingled with the bitter smell of cigarette smoke. A bar ran the length of one wall and, behind it, rows and rows of liquor bottles. As for the rest of the place, there were a dozen round wooden tables, each with a complement of four wooden chairs. None of those were occupied, but it was only 4 p.m. I figured the place would be packed by ten o'clock.

Three men sat at the bar, each by himself. I fished in my pocket for the photo of Travis that Connie had given me and studied it, then studied the three men. The one sitting at far end of the bar could be a match, I thought. I walked up to the bar, near where the bartender was wiping a glass over the sink. He saw me in the mirror and turned. He was a pudgy, thick-haired man with muttonchops, thick moustache, and a beard he could have used to mop the floor.

"Nice place," I said. "You the owner?"

"Owner, manager, you name it. The name's Matt Simmons."

"Sidney Reed." I held out my hand and he shook it.

I laid a five on the table. "You got Corona . . ." I hesitated. "No, wait. To hell with Corona. You got Amber on tap?"

His mouth arched in a grin. "Does a grizzly shit in the woods?"

I grinned. "Fill a mug for me, will you, Matt?"

"You got it."

Matt went to work and I turned toward the end of the bar. The age seemed right. He was thinner than his picture and had a few days' worth of stubble, but otherwise it was him. Long bony fingers were wrapped around a half-empty glass. He was staring straight ahead.

Matt returned with a frosted mug topped off with a lofty head of foam. He seemed eager to stay and talk, so I said, "Seems kind of dead in here."

"Not for long. By eight o'clock, you won't be able to have a conversation without yelling."

I lifted the mug and nodded to my left. "The guy at the end of the bar looks like he doesn't have a friend in the world. What's his story?"

He leaned across the bar. "Name's Travis. Used to be a regular. Haven't seen him much lately, though. Came in around lunchtime, sat down in that spot right there, and ordered a bottle of Jack. Hasn't moved since."

"You say he used to be a regular?"

"He and his girlfriend, Connie. Cute little thing. They never missed karaoke night. She was a good singer. Him, not so much. Haven't seen her in a good long while."

"Maybe I'll go over and say hello."

He grimaced. "I'm not so sure that's a good idea."

"I'll be all right." I picked up my beer and went over and sat on the stool next to Travis.

Without looking at him I said, "Hello, Travis."

He turned his head slowly. "Mister, there's nothing you can possibly say to me that would encourage me to interact with you in any way, so fuck off." His speech was slurred yet surprisingly coherent, the way inebriates sometimes are.

"My name is Sidney Reed. I'm a private inves—"

"I told you to fuck off."

I decided to skip the formality of establishing rapport and said, "I thought you might like to know Connie's dead."

With a quickness I would not have expected for someone as soused as he was, Travis lunged from his stool, his long bony fingers encircling my neck. In an instant we were on the floor, his adrenalin-fueled hands squeezing the life out of me. I grabbed his wrists and yanked with all my strength, but he had the advantage. I dared not let go, for fear he'd crush my windpipe. His face held a crazed look. His open mouth revealed a grillwork of yellowed teeth and his breath a sickening mixture of stale food and whiskey.

I rolled left and then right, to no effect. A shout rang in the distance. A much closer voice bellowed, "Get off him!" Travis's face blurred and seemed to drift away.

In an instant the pressure on my throat eased, the weight on my body lifted, and I lay gasping for air. I heard Matt say, "All right, Travis, knock it off." I propped myself up on one arm and looked around. The bar owner had Travis's arms pinned behind his back. He jerked his body in protest but the fight had gone out of him.

Someone helped me to my feet. When I tried to thank him, a croaking sound sputtered out. Travis and I stood a few feet apart, exchanging glares. Matt turned to me. "I don't know what you said to him and I don't care. I don't allow this crap in my place. If you want to file an assault charge, I'll be glad to back you up."

I stood there, chest heaving. My throat felt like Mohammed Ali had been using it for a punching bag. "It's okay," I said at last. "Let him go."

Matt released his hold on Travis and said, "Don't ever pull this shit in my place again, understand?"

Travis nodded, dropping his gaze to the wood floor.

"I've a mind to kick you out of here just the same," Matt said.

"I've got a better idea," I said through a sore windpipe. "How about fixing us both a cup of coffee?"

Thirty-six

Travis and I sat at a table near the window. He sipped coffee with his elbow pressed against the table, his head resting on an open palm. His free hand wobbled slightly as he raised his cup to his lips. I thought I heard him groan.

"You're gonna feel like shit in the morning," I said.

He regarded me with bloodshot eyes. "Why didn't you turn me in?"

"You're no good to me in jail."

He groaned something inaudible. "Who the hell are you anyway?"

"I told you, I'm Sidney Reed."

"What do you want from me?"

"I need your help. More to the point, Rudy Skinner needs your help. And I need some answers."

"You're not making any sense, pal." He drank some coffee.

"My client Rudy Skinner is on trial for the murder of Willie Olson. Ring a bell?"

His eyes shot back and forth. "That's got nothing to do with me."

I made a show of rubbing my neck. "You know, I think I might have permanent muscle damage. Maybe I should have Matt call the cops after all . . ."

"All right, all right. I'm listening."

"Good." I sipped coffee. It was better than Eddie's, although that wasn't saying much. "Rudy's attorney hired me. When I dug into the case, I realized Rudy might be innocent, so I asked myself, if Rudy didn't kill Willie Olson, who did? Follow me so far?"

He flashed a wary but curious look. I took the lack of a no as a yes.

"I ran an ad in the paper asking for information about what happened that night. I wasn't really expecting a response, so you

can imagine my surprise when I got a call. Care to take a guess who
it was from?"

Travis didn't answer, but I could tell I had his undivided attention.

"If you guessed Connie Zwick, you win the prize."

"You're a liar!" Travis slammed his fist on the table, sending jets
of coffee sloshing out of our cups.

"Just shut up and listen, will you? Connie told me everything.
How you got called out on a job during that big January storm and
hit a man walking on the road. That man was Willie Olson. Your
old man told you boys to cut up the truck and bury it. Any of *that*
ring a bell?"

Travis stared out the window into the fading light, his bloodshot
eyes providing a hint of the agony roiling behind them. His jaw
tightened, though he didn't speak.

"I doubt you meant to kill him. There was a blizzard raging, you
could barely see the road. Suddenly there's something there, right in
the middle. It's too late to stop—"

"What the fuck do you want from me—a confession? No thanks,
pal, I've been to prison. I'm not going back. No fuckin' way."

I took another sip and watched Travis sulk for a long minute. A
part of me felt sympathy for him. I had no doubt he was sorry for
what he'd done. Nor did I doubt he loved Connie. I asked him how
he'd learned of her death.

His head sagged. "A friend heard it on the radio. They said it was
an accident."

"Her death was no accident."

He came out of the slouch quickly. "What are you talking about?"

"Connie was murdered."

"Murdered?" His face twisted oddly. "I don't believe it."

"I don't care if you believe it or not, it's true. To be honest, I
thought *you* killed her."

"Me? Are you nuts?" He pounded his fist on the table. "Why
would I kill her? I loved her!" His voice boomed across the room,
turning more than a few heads.

"Obviously to stop her from testifying against you."

His face reddened. "I could never hurt Connie . . . never!" He buried his face into the table.

"Relax, Travis. You didn't kill her." I massaged my neck. "I deduced it the moment you tried to choke me to death."

He lifted his head. "Sorry about that. Ever since I heard about her death I've been—"

"Acting crazy?"

"You gotta believe me, mister. I didn't kill her!"

"The name's Sidney Reed. And I know you didn't kill her, Travis. You have an alibi. You weren't in Anchorage last night."

He appeared to perk up suddenly. "Then who did?"

"You tell me. You knew her a lot better than I did."

I let him mull that over while I went to the bar to ask for refills. I came back and sat down. "Let me see if I can help. Who wouldn't want Connie talking to the police?"

He stared straight ahead for a long while before speaking. "You think my brothers did this?"

"Or your dad."

He shook his head vigorously. "No fucking way. He wouldn't—"

Matt brought our coffees and I handed him a five. He shifted his gaze between the two of us and left. As soon as he was out of earshot, Travis spoke. "My Pa and my brothers would never hurt Connie. They know what she meant to me."

I sipped tentatively on the hot liquid. "If you say so."

He displayed a look of defiance. "We had plans, Connie and me."
Molly and I had plans, too. That's life.

"Let me ask you something, Travis. If you loved her so much, why did you send her to live with Alice Crawford?"

"That wasn't my doing. I wanted to take her with me and start fresh somewhere, but Pa wouldn't have it. He said I had to lay low somewhere. He told Bo to take Connie someplace and keep an eye on her, so he had her stay with Alice."

I sipped coffee and waited.

"I never wanted us to be apart. She stuck with me through all the dumb shit I did." He paused to sip coffee. "The thing is, Pa liked Connie, but he was afraid she might, I don't know, get me to go straight or something."

The afternoon light exposed a spider web of dark red lines intersecting the white parts of his eyes. I could almost feel his coming hangover. He shifted his gaze toward me. "Are you going to turn me in?"

"How would that work, exactly? I can't prove you did anything. No, Travis, the only person who can turn me in is you."

"I'm sorry about your client, Mr. Reed. I wish I could help him, I really do, but I'm not going back to prison again. I can't."

"Maybe there's a way to help him without doing jail time."

"I don't follow."

"Come to Anchorage with me and meet Rudy's attorney."

His eyes narrowed. "What for?"

"Eddie Baker's a smart guy. He might be able to figure out a way to get Rudy out of this mess without you becoming directly involved."

He shook his head. "No way. I'll get there and you guys will turn me in to the cops."

"That's not going to happen. Like I said, there's no basis to arrest you. Once we're done, I'll drive you back here, or anywhere you say."

He stared hard. "Give me one good reason why I should."

"Because Rudy didn't do what they said he did, that's why."

"You want me to help some gacked-out loser? Fuck him. He doesn't deserve my help."

Anger bubbled to the surface. "Like you didn't deserve Connie?"

He jumped to his feet, knocking over his chair in the process. "Hey, fuck you, buddy! You don't know anything about me. I loved Connie. She—"

I let my voice fill the room. "Spare me the self-pity. Connie risked her life to help a guy she didn't even know. What have you done with your life except sell drugs?"

The low rumble of barroom voices had faded into silence as all eyes swiveled toward our table. Behind the bar, Matt ceased wiping a glass with a towel and stared. Travis realized he'd become the center of attention and with the slow, jerky movements of an inebriate, righted his upended chair and sat down. "You know about that?"

"Yeah," I said. "I know all about it."

Travis shook his head slowly. "What can I say? Some kids' dads sell life insurance, some work in a bakery. My dad cooks meth." He chuckled bitterly. "It's what I was taught to do. Pa expected his sons to be a part of it."

I understood all too well about fatherly expectations. My dad wanted me to be a farmer. Had he not died when I was still a boy, I might still have been back in Ohio milking cows. But then I wouldn't have joined the army or met Molly or been sitting at that table with Travis.

"We always have a choice, even if it's not a very appealing one."

"Easy for you to say," Travis replied. "You don't know my old man."

Seeing no point in a response, I quietly sipped coffee. Then a thought occurred to me and I said, "I saw Connie just yesterday."

Travis came full alert, as though my words had sobered him up more than the coffee. "You . . . saw her? What did she say?"

"She told me to tell you she misses you."

Travis pressed his head into the table and wept, his gentle sobbing strangely at odds with the rattle and laughter of the bar patrons. As I watched him, I thought to myself, *He and I aren't all that different. He lost someone he loved dearly and now he feels detached and alone.* I could definitely relate.

I waited until his whimpering had faded away. "I don't care what you've done, but I do care about Rudy Skinner, and so did Connie. What do you say, Travis? Will you help me?"

He didn't move for a long time. Then, slowly, he lifted his head and stared out the window, his thoughts somewhere I couldn't fathom. At length he lifted his cup, then set it back down on the table. Steam from it drifted up into the smoke-filled room.

"Okay," he said. "Let's go."

Thirty-seven

On the way out of Palmer I pulled into the McDonalds drive-thru and ordered Travis a couple of hamburgers and a large coffee. I wanted him to be as sober as possible when he met Eddie. Soon we were heading out of town, past farmers' fields and the state fairgrounds. The sun dipped low, the evening sky lush with reds and yellows. We were on the great expanse of the Palmer Hay Flats when he crumpled up a sandwich wrapper and spoke. "You really think Connie was murdered?"

"I know she was."

He sat in silence for several more minutes. Then, out of the blue, he said, "I never wanted any part of Pa's drug business."

"Connie told me the same thing."

He twisted his head at the mention of her name. "His plan was for me to take over when he retired. He thought Bo was too undisciplined and Ray too stupid to do it. But Ma was dead set against it. With Bo and Ray, she relented, but not me. She made him promise."

"Why was that?"

"I suppose because I was her favorite. I dunno."

"But you're back in it now."

I heard him sigh. "After Ma died, Pa tried to keep me out of it. Once we got up here, though, my brothers pushed him to have me help out. By then he'd changed. It was like he didn't care anymore."

"Blood is blood," I said. "Isn't that what your dad used to say?"

"Connie told you that? That's what he said, all right. It was the family motto, sort of."

"So, you drank to make the pain go away."

"What are you, my shrink now?"

"You were drunk when you hit the airman from the base. The one with kids."

"Yeah, I hit him." His voice steadily rose. "Paid for it, too."

"Then you killed Willie Olson."

"The dumbass was in the—hey, what are you trying to do, entrap me or something?"

"Relax, Travis. I'm just trying to understand you, that's all."

We drove on in silence. The Camry climbed out of the flats as darkness descended upon us. I used the quiet time to think about what I was going to do with Travis. I still had the reservation I'd made for Connie at the Hotel Captain Cook, but wasn't sure I could get him to use it, or stay put if he did.

I glanced to my right. My passenger's rhythmic breathing told me he was asleep. I took out my cell phone and punched in Eddie Baker's number. When the call went to voicemail, I said in hushed tones that I'd located Travis, was putting him up in a hotel overnight, and would bring him to the office in the morning. As I ended the call I wondered whether I could deliver on what I'd just said.

We passed the Birchwood exit some minutes later and I heard a moan. Travis yawned and stretched. "My head's fucking killing me. Got any aspirin?"

I said I didn't. It was several more minutes before he spoke again.

"You probably think Pa's just another drug dealer. Can't say I'm proud of what he does, exactly, but strange as it sounds, I think he found something he's good at and was proud of doin'. Kate—my Ma—hated what he did, but loved him all the same. She softened him, I think."

"What was she like, your mother?"

"Kind and generous. A good cook, too. Always baking something. When us boys asked her to bake us an apple pie, she didn't make just one. No, sir, she'd bake four of 'em, one for all of us, and the rest she'd give away to folks. That's the kind of woman she was."

"If you don't mind my asking, what happened to her?"

"It was one of those things." His voice betrayed a profound sadness.

"One day she started coughing. Didn't think anything of it at first, but then it got worse. Before long, she couldn't get out of bed. By the time Pa took her to the doctor, it was too late. The cancer had spread everywhere."

I thought about my own mother, who'd died of kidney failure in an assisted living facility. When dad passed away shortly after my tenth birthday, mom was already showing signs of dementia. She was unable to take care of me, so I was sent to live with relatives. She was placed in a home soon thereafter.

"Had to be rough on you boys, losing your mom."

"It was, but I think it hit Pa the hardest. He didn't seem to give a shit about anything after that." He glanced my way. "I guess you know he served time down there for killing somebody."

"Yeah, I knew about that." I briefly described working for Rance following his arrest for assaulting his neighbor. "The D.A. knew all about it, so I figured we'd better know, too." I glanced his way. "Is it true you witnessed it?"

"Yeah, I seen it." A shaking in his voice hinted at the trauma. "I was pretty young when it happened. When they let him out, he went back to cookin' meth. By that time the state drug cops were watching him pretty close, so he decided it was time for us to clear out and come north."

I heard Travis chuckle to himself. I asked him what the joke was.

"When we left Oklahoma, Pa wanted to have the last laugh on the cops, so he wired the whole place with explosives. He learned all about that shit in the Army. Once we were all packed up, he drove the motorhome to the end of the drive, stopped, and blew the whole fucking place to smithereens."

Talk about a dramatic exit, I thought. I said to Travis, "Think he'll ever quit the business?"

"I don't know. Pa always said he wanted to buy a couple acres on the Platt River, build himself a cabin, and spend his last days fishing. I don't know, though. I'm worried about him."

"Why worried?"

His voice deepened slightly. "First off, his health was never that good to begin with. He's overweight, drinks, smokes, and spends all day in a room breathing those nasty chemicals. Lately, though, he's been coughing a lot. Something's not right."

"What do you think it is?"

"Couldn't say, but I'm worried."

We climbed the hill at Eagle River, a silent reminder that Anchorage was close at hand. I said, "I took the liberty of setting up a meeting with Rudy's attorney for tomorrow morning. In the meantime, I have a room for you at the Captain Cook."

"I don't know, Mr. Reed." The tension in his voice was palpable. "I need time to think this over."

"Look, why don't you take the room? If nothing else, you'll get a good night's sleep in a nice hotel, free of charge. See how you feel in the morning. And if you decide to help yourself to one of their monogrammed bathrobes, I promise I won't tell."

"I suppose that would be okay," he said with a sigh.

We flew down the wide expanse of the Glenn Highway. An eight-foot-tall chain-link fence appeared on the right, separating Fort Richardson from the highway, erected decades before to help cut down on the sort of car-moose dust-ups that had destroyed my beloved Subaru.

Another idea began to twirl around in my head. I glanced at Travis. "There is one more thing you can do for me."

"What's that?"

"Help me get inside the compound. Take a look at the lab."

His head snapped in my direction. "Why? So, you can have the cops go in and bust up the place?"

"Something like that."

"That's a really fucked-up idea."

"I thought you wanted to get away from that life? Make amends?"

"Yeah, but I'm not about to betray my family and ruin their livelihood."

"Even if they murdered Connie?"

"There you go again with that murder shit. It's ridiculous!"

"You really believe that? Tell me, then, who else had the motive?"

He shook his head vigorously. "I don't buy it."

He fell silent, so I decided to leave it alone. In the quiet that followed, I began to wonder if I'd made a mistake broaching the idea. A few minutes later, as we approached the Muldoon exit, he said, "Pull off here and find a gas station, will you? I have to piss like a racehorse."

Without comment, I signaled a right turn and looped around until I was heading south on Muldoon Road. I pulled into the first station I came to and parked next to the building. As soon as Travis had gone inside, I punched in Mel Denton's cell number. He answered on the first ring. "Hey, Sid. What are you up to on a Saturday night?"

"I could ask you the same thing, pal."

"I'd like to say I'm sitting in front of the tube—or whatever they call televisions these days—drinking a cool one, but instead I'm stuck in a surveillance van watching scumbags."

"Tough break. Speaking of scumbags, remember our conversation about the Cooleys?"

"You bet I do. Biggest ice dealers in South Central Alaska. You got something for me?"

"Yeah. Confirmation Rance Cooley's cooking meth in a building behind the main house. My source has seen the lab. Appears to be a pretty sophisticated operation. I did some recon the other day and they've got surveillance cameras all over the place."

"Man, I'd love to get a warrant and shut that operation down."

"What would it take?"

"For a warrant? Eyeballs on the inside. Something I can take to a judge."

"Would *I* do for confirmation?"

"Sure, but how the hell you gonna get inside?"

"I'm working on that."

"That's a pretty ballsy move. Hope you know what you're doing."

"So do I." I peeked out the window, but saw no sign of Travis. "Can you have a team on standby in case I can make it happen tonight?"

"Tonight? Well, yeah, if it means taking down Rance Cooley, you bet I can."

"Good. Tell your guys to watch for my signal."

There was a pause, then: "Hey, Sid. You sure about this?"

"Not really."

"Good old Sid. What's the signal?"

I mulled that over. "Just tell them they'll know it when they see it."

Denton ended the call. A few minutes later Travis walked out the door carrying a small plastic bag. He looked pale when he got in the car.

I stared at him. "You buy out the store?"

"Picked up a few snacks, is all. And a bottle of aspirin." As if to prove his point, he took an aspirin bottle out of the bag, opened it, tapped some pills into his palm, and put them in his mouth. As he stuffed the bag in a pocket of his floppy coat, I noticed his hand shake and asked if he was all right.

He shot me a sharp glance. "You never had a hangover?"

"More times than I care to admit."

He fidgeted. "Can't help thinkin' about Connie and how horrible it must've been, you know?"

"Yeah." I didn't pursue the matter, but something in his demeanor seemed off, although I wasn't sure what it was.

I got back on the Glenn Highway and continued west toward downtown, all the while trying to think of a way to get into Rance's lab. If Dent's boys raided the place, I was sure they'd find enough evidence to put the Cooley boys away for a good long while.

Travis was quiet as I neared downtown. I caught the light at Bragaw Street and turned to look at him. He had his arms folded across his stomach. I hoped, with all the whiskey he'd drunk, his McDonalds meal didn't end up on the floor of my rental. For my part, I was tired and hungry and missing Maria. I had a great and sudden urge to hear her voice.

While I pondered those things, Travis began to moan.

I glanced his way. Shadows clouded his face. "You all right?"

"I don't feel so good, Mr. Reed."

"We're almost there."

He moaned again, louder this time. The light changed and the Camry surged forward.

"Man, I'm gonna be sick. Pull over, will you?"

"Yeah, okay." Along that stretch of highway there were two lanes in each direction and the speed limit was forty-five. I check my mirrors and switched to the right lane.

"I need you to pull over RIGHT NOW."

We were adjacent to a fleabag hotel across from Merrill Field. It was a favorite of hookers and drug dealers. I pulled in and pointed the car to a space along the east side of the building. "Go around back," Travis ordered. "I'm not gonna puke where everyone can see me."

I steered around behind the building where there was a good-sized parking lot that was half empty and poorly lit. I pulled into a space and he bent over and groaned like he was at death's door.

"Help me out, will you?"

I got out and went around to the passenger side and opened the door. All I could think of was, *Please don't puke in the car.* He had a queer look on his face as he rose up out of his seat.

That's when I heard footsteps behind me.

I heard them too late.

As I turned to my left, a crashing blow to the back of my head turned my whole world pitch black.

Thirty-eight

My first sensation upon waking was not of cold—although it was bitter cold—but of burning; the burning one feels when skin is pressed against cold steel. Burning one side of my face and the fingers of one hand. My second sensation was of bouncing, as if I were lying on one end of a trampoline and children were jumping up and down on the other, my body jerking with each jump.

Darkness and motion.

The bed of a pickup.

Flashes of white flew past—street lights.

The memories came back in spurts: The drive from Palmer . . . the stop for aspirin . . . the fleabag hotel . . . footsteps . . . darkness.

My head throbbed from the inside out. Someone had clobbered me good.

Travis was the only earthly human who knew where I was and where I was going. There was only one possible explanation. He'd called his brothers from the gas station. They'd been waiting for me at the hotel. The Cooley boys had blindsided me.

Sidney, you dumbass.

Pain morphed into anger.

I took stock of my situation and didn't much like it: I lay on my side in a fetal position, arms bound behind me, feet tied at the ankles. I strained at the ropes, but it was no use. They were fastened nice and tight.

I pried my cheek off the frigid metal and felt the sting of sub-zero air pouring into the truck's bed, as if on a mission to find every square centimeter of exposed skin. I couldn't rise to my knees or turn or do much of anything, so I gave it up and lay still.

Conserve your energy. Wait for an opportunity.

A streetlight zipped past, then another. I listened to the throb of the truck's engine, inhaled the stink of the exhaust, felt each seam in the pavement vibrate through my bones.

To take my mind off the cold, I tried to discern where I was, as Sherlock Holmes might: the telltale sound of construction work, the thump of railroad tracks, seams in the pavement. Except I had no idea how long we'd been driving, no points of reference. And this was twenty-first century Anchorage, not nineteenth-century London.

Still, I listened. After a period of driving in a straight line, we arrived at what felt like an off-ramp, followed by another straightaway, and then a gradual uphill incline.

East toward the Hillside maybe?

I decided it was a pointless exercise. I'd learn our destination soon enough.

After about fifteen minutes, according to my brain clock, the truck screeched to a stop. Muffled voices merged with the crunch of boots on snow. The tailgate dropped and the beam from a powerful flashlight blinded me. Then I heard the now familiar voice of Ray Cooley.

"Home sweet home, Mr. Reed," he said.

Rough hands seized my legs and yanked me from the truck. My fingers, numb with cold and wedged beneath my buttocks, skidded painfully across the truck's bed. The pain was excruciating.

As my digits scraped the icy metal, they encountered what felt like a thin piece of wire or chain. I trapped it between two pinched fingers and worked it into the nest of my palm. A moment later I dropped off the end of the bed, landing hard onto the snow-packed ground, as if my old schoolmaster had taken a fifty-pound paddle to my rear end. I grunted in pain.

Bo Cooley spoke. "Take him to the shed and don't untie him until you get there."

"Why not just leave him tied up?" Ray cut in.

"If he freezes like that, there'll be rope marks on him. The cops'll know he didn't die natural. Take his coat off, too."

Did he just say the word DIE?

It was all lights and shadows and stomping feet. Then I heard a car drive up. Two pairs of flashlights swiveled toward the sound. It was my rented Camry pulling alongside the pickup. Its twin halogen beams revealed the grimy facade of Last Frontier Auto Parts, settling the question of where we were.

Travis stepped out of the Camry and joined our group.

"Thanks a lot, Travis," I said snidely.

"Nothing personal, Mr. Reed. I couldn't let you hurt my brothers."

"It doesn't get any more personal than murder. Keep your—"

"I hate to interrupt your little reunion," Bo snapped, "but we have work to do. Ray, unhook his feet, unless you want to carry him to the shed."

Ray stooped down and took a folding knife out of his coat and cut the rope binding my ankles. He got back up and held his light on me.

"You mind getting that light out of my face?" I snapped.

Ray smirked in response.

I heard movement behind me. A moment later, powerful hands grabbed me by the armpits and yanked me to my feet. I pulled at my wrist restraints, to no effect.

"Save your strength, Mr. Reed."

"Shut up, Ray." The voice behind me was Bo Cooley's.

"Yeah, shut up, Ray," I said.

Ray's smile faded. He shoved me hard and I fell backward. I braced myself for a rough landing that never came. Bo caught me and began pulling me backwards. I tried using my feet, but couldn't keep up. Bo just dragged me like a rag doll, my heels scraping the frozen ground.

We came to a gate I recognized as the one I'd passed through on the way to the Cooley house the day before. Ray followed behind, keeping the light on me the whole time.

Bo, now huffing from the exertion, told Travis to park my car by the shed. Travis walked off without comment as Bo dragged me through the gate. Although I couldn't see him, the eldest Cooley sibling's frozen breath spewed out above me like a fog machine. Ray closed the gate and followed behind us, his boots squeaking with each footfall. Whatever these guys had in store for me, I knew it couldn't be good.

Watch and listen. Wait for an opportunity.

"You guys know this is kidnapping, right?" I said.

"Feel free to file a complaint," Ray said with a chuckle.

We came to a stop and I twisted my head around to see where we were. It was a small shed of some kind, fashioned from sheets of corrugated metal. Bo let go and I fell on my ass. The tromping of boots. A door squeaked open. Bo lifted me up by the collar, which had the effect of pulling the front of my shirt tight against my windpipe. I gasped for air as he dragged me through the doorway. My left foot caught on the door frame, sending ribbons of pain shooting through my Achilles tendon. I belched out an *Oomph*.

"Watch yourself, Mister Reed," Bo said. "Lots of hazards hereabouts."

These Cooley boys are nothing if not polite.

Bo dragged me to the middle of the room, let go, and my rear hit the concrete floor. Ray followed us in, his flashlight casting eerie shadows everywhere. I sucked in air and felt it sting my lungs. I heard a sharp click as Ray reached for a light switch next to the door. Nothing happened.

"I took out the fuse," Bo said flatly. "Don't want him pulling some MacGyver shit." He withdrew a large hunting knife from a sheath on his belt and knelt down next to me. The glare from Ray's light glinted off the blade. Bo sneered. "It's been nice knowing you, Mr. Reed."

I closed my eyes, bracing myself for what I knew was coming—the steel blade drawn across the jugular, the spurt of warm blood, the rapid loss of consciousness . . .

I'm coming, Molly.

Two seconds . . . three . . .

Powerful hands yanked my arms viciously upward behind me and held them there. I felt the cold steel of the blade scrape the sides of my wrist, then a quick jerk upward. My arms dropped to the floor as the rope fell away. I rubbed my now-freed hands together in an effort to get the blood flowing again. It didn't seem to help—they were quite numb. My heart pounded in my chest.

I'm in some deep doodoo here.

I heard the sound of automobile tires on snow. A moment later Travis came into the shed and surveyed the scene. Ray told me to take off my coat, waving his Glock to emphasize the point.

"Shouldn't we leave his coat on?" Travis said.

"He won't be needing it," Ray sneered. "Take it off, Mr. Reed."

I stared up into the glare of his light. "Fuck you, Ray."

Before I could react, his boot slammed against my left shoulder. Though my parka softened the blow, I cried out.

I heard Bo say, "Jesus, Ray," and his powerful hands pulled off my coat. He walked over to where Ray was standing, still holding my coat, and looked down at me. "Might as well make yourself at home, Mr. Reed. You're not going anywhere. Not for a while, anyway."

"Yeah," Ray chuckled. "Chill out."

"You have him well trained, Bo," I said. "A few more years and he'll be housebroken."

Ray's face curled into a sneer and he launched a kick at my head. I was ready this time, and twisted my neck to the right. His boot clipped the left side of my face. I felt teeth rip the meaty flesh inside my mouth and I spat blood.

Bo seized his arm. "Knock it off! If the cops find marks on his face, they'll get suspicious."

"Who cares?" Ray jerked his arm free. "After the city plow hits him, he won't have a face."

Bo ignored that. "We're wasting time."

The two of them started for the door. The moment they turned away, I looked down at the piece of metal still clasped in my palm, realized what it was, and my eyes grew wide.

Travis, who'd been standing silently off to one side, started after them. "Psst . . . Travis," I whispered. "Take a look at this."

Hesitating, he stepped forward, his light full on my face. I extended my open palm and the tiny piece of metal glinted in the harsh light. He peered at my palm, unsure at first of what he was seeing. Moving in for a closer look, his eyes bulged in recognition. "Toss it on the floor."

I did and he snatched it up. "Where'd you get this?" he demanded.

"In the bed of Ray's truck. Must have fallen off when they forced her to get in and . . ." I let the words trail off, but he got my meaning.

He stared at the small chain, his face a muddle of rage and betrayal.

Ray, who was waiting at the open door, said "Hurry up, Travis. Let's go." He then noticed his brother was clutching something and shuffled forward. "What have you got there, little brother?"

Travis glared at him. "Connie's necklace, *big* brother. The one I gave her the night of that big storm in January. You remember that night, don't you, Ray? You had a delivery to make, but then you saw how nasty the roads were, so you asked me to go in your place."

Ray's air of defiance faded like confetti in the wind. "Um . . ."

Travis moved unsteadily toward Ray, his nostrils snorting out plumes of frost. "What was it doing in the bed of your fucking truck?"

The color drained from Ray's face. "Trav, I can explain."

"So can I. You killed her and dumped her on the side of the road like a piece of trash."

"That's not the way it—"

"Like a fucking piece of trash!"

Travis thrust his arms out at Ray's chest, pushing him back.

Ray's face turned livid. "All right . . . yeah, I killed her. You're goddam right I did! The bitch would've talked!"

Travis launched himself like a missile, plowing into Ray's midsection and propelling the two of them against the side of the tin shed. Ray's flashlight spun away in one direction and died. His gun rattled across the floor in another.

The sole remaining source of light in the room now directed its eerie beam away from me and toward the door, leaving the two combatants little more than dueling shadows. Their grunts and labored breathing filled the interior of the shed.

I'd heard Ray's Glock skid across the floor, so I crawled in the direction of the sound, careful to avoid the two men flailing and kicking nearby.

The moment I began moving I knew something was terribly wrong. My fingers and toes were now throbbing unbearably, and the shaking in my body had progressed to a near-constant shudder. The stark realization hit me that I was becoming hypothermic. I had to get someplace warm—and fast.

I crawled with abandon, hands flailing about, in search of the Glock. I rubbed my fingers raw sliding them across the rough, frigid concrete. I'd almost given up when I was hit with a blinding light and a voice as cold as death.

"Going somewhere, Mr. Reed?"

Bo Cooley stood in the doorway, gun and flashlight trained on me. "Stand up," he ordered.

I rose to my feet on wobbly legs.

"Show's over, assholes," he said, eyeing the two men sprawled at his feet. "Time to kiss and make up." Sweeping his flashlight back and forth, Bo watched with amusement as his brothers rose to their collective feet amid grunts and moans.

As his roving light traversed the room, a glint of something reflective drew my attention to the floor near my feet. I saw nothing at first, but then, as the beam of Bo's flashlight swept past, I realized what it was: Ray's Glock lay on the floor near my left foot.

"All right," Bo said, addressing his brothers. "What's this about?"

Travis, sporting a nasty-looking cut on his right cheek, glared at Ray, who dabbed at a bloody lip with the backside of his glove.

"He knows about Connie," Ray said.

Bo stared icily at Ray before turning to Travis. "I know you cared about her, little brother, but we didn't have much choice. She was a threat to us. To the family."

Travis dabbed at the cut on his cheek, huffing loudly. "Blood is blood, right, big brother?"

"That's right," Bo shot back.

I inched closer to the gun, my body shaking uncontrollably.

Bo rested a gloved hand on Travis's shoulder and in a placating voice said, "Why don't you come on in the house? Pa's cooked up a pot roast."

The youngest Cooley pulled away, hesitated, then gave a terse nod. Bo turned toward the door and the others followed close behind.

The moment their flashlights turned away, I stooped down to collect the Glock, steadying myself on the hard cement floor. I wrapped my fingers around the gun's pistol grip, but something wasn't quite right. I couldn't seem to coax my index finger through the trigger guard. Frustration morphed into panic. I glanced up and saw Bo leading the others through the doorway.

Ray, following close on Bo's heels, suddenly froze.

"What is it now?" Travis snapped.

"I don't have my gun. Must have lost it when you—"

At once, two powerful shafts of light hit me like searchlights from a prison tower. I must have been a sight: on my knees, shaking like a leaf, the Glock held limply in my right hand.

"Shoot the motherfucker, Travis!" Ray hollered.

"No!" Bo snapped. The Marlboro-man-like figure stepped through the door, surveying me with an amused expression. "Look at him. He's not a threat to anyone." He crossed the room and took the gun from my wobbly hand, then handed it to Ray. "Try not to lose it this time."

Ray sneered and tucked the Glock in his pants. He glanced sideways at Travis. "Why didn't you shoot?"

Travis just stared at me with an expression I couldn't read.

Bo looked askance at Ray, then turned to me. "I give him an hour—two at most. Come on, let's go."

The three men filed out. Ray was the last one through the door. He stood there for a moment, grinning. "Goodbye, asshole."

When he slammed the door, the walls trembled with a sound like distant thunder.

Thirty-nine

I listened as their footfalls scuffled away, until the only sound was the rhythmic huff of my own labored breathing. The taste of blood lingered in my mouth. I probed the fleshy inside of my cheek with my tongue and found the narrow slash left by Ray's kick.

That guy has issues.

Then again, so did I: Locked in a room with no heat or light, the thermometer hovering well below zero. Prognosis: grim.

I thought back to my first few days in Alaska. I was a tenderfoot—a *cheechako*, as Alaskans like to say—assigned to the CID office at Fort Rich. Like all new arrivals, I was required to undergo cold weather and winter driving indoctrination. They'd herded a group of us into a room and in came a tall, lean soldier with a Mississippi drawl.

Ladies and gentlemen, welcome to Alaska. My name is Sergeant First Class Rafferty. I'm here to teach you how to survive in an arctic environment, so listen up.

Sergeant Rafferty offered some introductory remarks and then treated us to a graphic slideshow depicting the myriad possible fates awaiting anyone failing to heed his instruction—hypothermia, frostbite, trench foot—to the accompaniment of a somber narrative, complete with dramatic pauses.

The minute you fail to respect the harsh arctic environment, mark my words, it WILL bite you in the ass.

Pause.

Can someone tell me the number one killer in Alaska? Anyone? Who thinks it's freezing to death?

Six hands shot skyward. Hands on hips, Rafferty shook his head sadly, as if he were about to reprimand a roomful of recalcitrant first graders on their unacceptable playground behavior.

Ladies and gentlemen, I assure you, if you are in the field without proper clothing or shelter at forty below zero for any length of time, you will not have to worry about freezing to death. Why? Because hypothermia will kill you first.

I stood on quivering legs and shuffled through the inky blackness to where I knew the door to be and twisted the knob. Locked.

I felt my way along the corrugated metal wall until my aching fingers brushed some sort of wooden handle. It was a tool of some kind, perhaps a shovel or pick. Surely something I could use to force open the door—a heartening prospect. I gripped the handle and ripples of pain snaked through my fingers. I slid my hand along the handle and felt the end. It was a garden rake.

Oh well, better than nothing.

I hobbled with it toward the door, the shaking in my body now spasmodic and unceasing. My worst fear had been hypothermia but now it dawned on me that, while hypothermia might be my worst fear, it's not the only one.

As your core body temperature drops, ladies and gentlemen, your motor skills become increasingly impaired.

Quickening my pace in the all-consuming darkness, I misjudged the distance and slammed into the corrugated metal wall. Momentarily dazed, I let loose a sigh and, tightening my grip on the rake, jabbed blindly at the door—how many times, I don't know—until some logic center in my brain told me to wedge it between the door and frame.

You may find yourself behaving irrationally.

I reached for the door and realized with mounting dread that the door was there, I just couldn't feel it. In fact there was no feeling left in my fingers at all, only the peculiar soft scraping sound they made as they brushed the surface of the metal.

I swept my hand in an ever-widening arc, searching for the door-frame, but it wasn't there. It wasn't anywhere. I wasn't anywhere near the door—I'd missed it entirely. Now, for the first time, raw panic seized hold of me.

Christ, what's happening to me?

I inhaled deeply, sucking in air in an effort to calm myself. Instantly I felt a burning sensation deep down in my lungs.

Listen up, because this is important: When exposed to subzero temperatures, always cover your mouth and nose with a balaclava or scarf. If you don't, your lungs could freeze.

I reached for the bottom hem of my flannel shirt, a move that sent ripples of pain through my fingers. I tried again and managed to lift the shirt to my mouth. With the flannel covering my mouth, I inhaled slowly but deeply, counting breaths until I reached ten.

The feeling of panic slowly subsided, as did the shaking of my body. These were now replaced by a great tiredness. I leaned against the side of the shed, gripped by an overwhelming urge to rest from my exertions.

That's what I need . . . rest.

I slid down the side of the shed to the floor and the shaking eased up even more. Sergeant Rafferty's chiseled face appeared, his eyes now red and saucer-like.

The one thing you must never do is fall asleep. Fall asleep and you die.

I chuckled at the thought. Who could sleep in this place? The memory of my dead Subaru filled my head, reminding me that Rafferty's slideshow had included photographs of automobiles horribly crushed after colliding with moose. A person would have to be pretty stupid to do something like that. I laughed at that, the sound falling flat in the tin shed. Rafferty's face reappeared, ever stern.

What are you laughing at, soldier? You think this is funny?

No, Sergeant. Nothing funny about it.

I relaxed even more, an odd feeling of contentment enveloping me. Feeling suddenly quite warm, I reached for the zipper of my coat.

I'm not wearing a coat.

I chuckled giddily, the way a pot smoker might, and the warmth embraced me like a blanket. Thoughts of Molly appeared. Her face, with its smile and sea of freckles. I wished for her to be with me now. Knowing her, she'd want to sing me a song. She had a beautiful singing voice, like a songbird. I imagined her offering something by Simon and Garfunkel, her favorite.

A winter's day-ay-ay, in a deep and dark December, I am alone . . .
I heard a sound, so faint I thought I might have imagined it.
I have no need of friendship, friendship causes pain . . .
I heard it again, only louder. A light padding sound, growing louder still. Memories of Ray's kick came rushing back. Fear gripped me.
They're coming back. Where's the damn rake?

The now-distinct crunch of boots on snow drew steadily nearer, then the jangle of keys and the scream of metal reverberating along the shed walls as the door was thrust open.

A beam of light stabbed the darkness. I shifted awkwardly to my right, my gaze falling on a shadowy figure, its face bathed in pale gray moonlight.

"Mr. Reed?" A pause. "Thank God you're alive."

I tried and failed to raise my hand to shield my eyes from the flashlight's glare. I mouthed the word "Travis?" but nothing came out.

"It's me," he replied.

The beam shifted and he came full into view. One arm held a bundle, which he laid on the floor. Then he shined the light on my hands. "You're in a bad way, Mr. Reed. We need to warm you up."

He picked up the bundle that was my parka and, with what seemed like great effort, fed my arms through the sleeves and zipped it shut. "Come on, let's get you out of here before they come back. Can you walk?"

I didn't answer because in truth I didn't know. He gripped my arm and pulled me to my feet.

"Your car's outside. Key's in the ignition. I'll need to open the gate."

"I don't think . . . I can drive."

"I'll drive you."

"I'm not leaving."

"Oh yes you are. My brothers want you dead."

"I'm not leaving."

"You're not making any sense. You need medical attention."

"Just get me someplace warm . . . will you?"

He stared at me uncertainly, clouds of water vapor spewing forth with each breath he took. "You're not in any shape to travel. I'll take you to the basement, but we'd better hurry."

He started for the door and I took a step after. My legs gave way beneath me. Reacting quickly, he caught me before I hit the ground. I gripped his shoulder and he led me outside, pausing to lock the door behind us.

We stumbled through the snow, the Cooley home a vague eerie shadow in the distance. My fingers and toes ached. I steered my thoughts to Maria and our time together the night before. I imagined the warmth of her body, the softness of her lips . . .

Travis's words invaded my thoughts. "I'm sorry about that business at the hotel. Pa raised us to believe you always back up your kinfolk. I guess I felt I had to warn them." We clomped along in relative silence until he spoke again. "I was confused and pissed off. I didn't want to believe my brothers would hurt Connie. I still can't believe it."

After what seemed like an eternity, we arrived at the rear door of the house. "Better keep quiet from here on in," Travis said. "I'm not sure where Pa is, but Bo and Ray are inside watching TV."

He latched onto my arm and we ascended the steps. I gritted my teeth as my weight fell on my left foot. Tears stung my eyes. We made it up the steps, through both doors, and into the mud room.

There we paused. The chatter of voices drifted in from the living room. He guided me through the mudroom door and to the left, pausing at the top of the stairs I'd noticed earlier. I heard the door leading from the kitchen into the living room open, accompanied by the mocking refrain of the soundtrack from *The Good, The Bad, and The Ugly*.

Ray's unmistakable nasal voice said, "You want another beer, bro?" followed by a barely audible "You bet" in reply.

I waited in the shadows, heart pounding, as the fridge door opened, then closed. A moment later, the music receded into the background, signaling Ray's departure from the kitchen.

Travis whispered, "You should be safe in the basement for the time being. Get yourself warm." He added pointedly, "Once they realize you're not in the shed, you'd better be somewhere else."

We descended the narrow staircase into the darkness below, our boots clomping heavily on the wood steps. The slightest amount of pressure on my left foot brought tendrils of pain shooting up my leg. At the bottom of the stairs, Travis yanked a string dangling from the ceiling and the space filled with light.

It was a typical basement: dusty, smelling of mildew, and packed with stuff. He led me behind the stairs where some crates were stacked. I eased myself down onto one of them, relieved to be off my feet.

"I'll try to keep them inside as long as I can. When it's safe, I'll be back for you."

Travis turned and snapped off the light and tromped up the stairs. He pulled the door shut, leaving me in darkness once again.

"Mr. Reed?"

My eyes fluttered open. "What? Where . . . am I?"

Travis Cooley's face came into focus. "You're in the basement. Don't you remember?"

I didn't answer. Light from the lone bare bulb shone through the narrow slats of the basement steps, casting eerie shadows about. My mouth was dry, my fingers and toes throbbed, and my body shook uncontrollably. "How . . . long was I . . . asleep?"

"About an hour. You've got some color back in your face, at least. Here, drink this."

He unscrewed the cap on a bottle of water he was holding and handed it to me. When I reached for it, my hand curled into a grotesque-looking claw and I winced. I peered at my hands in the light and blanched. My fingertips were all, to varying degrees, swollen and reddish-purple in color.

"Shit," I muttered to myself.

Travis stared at the misshapen, discolored digits and frowned. "I'm afraid it's frostbite, Mr. Reed." He held the water bottle to my lips and I drank with abandon. "We need to get you to a hospital as quickly as possible."

That hour of sleep had revived a few brain cells. Sergeant Rafferty was gone, and some of the old Sidney was back. Travis was right. The frostbite on my fingers required immediate medical attention. No doubt my toes were just as bad as my fingers, maybe worse. But I had no intention of leaving. Not yet.

"Ray and Bo are pretty settled in right now," Travis said. "I told them to wait another hour, you'll be pretty far gone by then. That *should* buy us enough time to get you to your car and out of here. I'll drive you to a hospital and—"

"I told you, I'm not leaving, so get that idea out of your head."

"You're not hearing me. We need to leave *now*."

"Not until I finish . . . what I came to do."

"And what's that?"

"I need to get inside your dad's lab."

He stared at me like I was crazy. "What the hell for?"

"So I can . . . shut it down." My teeth wouldn't stop chattering.

His face drooped. "That's Pa's livelihood you're talking about."

My anger flared. "What the hell is . . . wrong with you? Those guys killed Connie, damn near killed me, and you're . . . worried about their livelihood?"

"Pa's lab means everything to him. I'm not prepared to take that away. Besides, you're in no condition to do much about it anyway."

"I'm not asking for permission, Travis. I'm telling you what I'm going to do." I muscled myself into a standing position. "You can either help me or get out of my way."

Those were pretty bold words, considering that a stiff wind could have knocked me over at that moment. If Travis wanted to stop me, he wouldn't have much trouble doing it.

Travis pushed his palms against his forehead and combed them through his thick mop of hair. "Bo and Ray will shoot your ass on sight—you know that, right?"

"They can try."

"You're one stubborn SOB, Mr. Reed." He reached in his coat and fished out the Glock. He stood motionless, his face unreadable.

I stared at the business end of the barrel and stiffened.

Oh shit.

"All right, Mr. Reed," he said at last, "what's the plan?"

I felt the tension drain out of me. "First off, give me the damn gun."

"Right. I'll bet you can't even fire the thing."

"I'll manage."

He sighed and handed it over. "What am *I* supposed to do?"

"Keep your brothers busy upstairs." I stuffed the Glock in my parka. "Can you do that?"

"For a while, sure."

"A while is all I'll need."

We came out from my hiding place. At the foot of the stairs, Travis grabbed me by the sleeve and we locked eyes. "Pa's probably in the lab. Don't hurt him, okay?"

"I'll do my best."

I followed him up the stairs. It was like climbing the Empire State Building—ten steps felt like ten thousand. The stinging in my fingers and toes was intense, and my hands were all but useless, but at least I was able to walk unaided, provided I kept my weight off my toes.

At the top of the stairs, Travis stopped and listened. Satisfied, he gave a nod and watched with sad eyes as I limped through the mud room and out the back door.

I stood on the top step to give my eyes a chance to adjust to the darkness around me. A stiff, unforgiving wind sent shivers up my spine. Glancing upward, millions of stars flickered in the night sky.

My body trembled—I was obviously still hypothermic—and yet I found the cold strangely invigorating. If I had any sense at all I would have gotten the hell out of there right then. The Camry was parked in front of the shed with the keys still in it. All I'd have to do was crash through the gate or drive out through the escape route Connie had talked about.

Connie. I couldn't get the image of her out of my head. That slip of a girl, her soft green eyes so full of fear, telling me what happened to Willie Olson. She was the reason I couldn't leave. I'd dragged her into this with the ad I put in the paper and now she was dead.

Yeah, Doc. I have to make it right.

I scanned the terrain. There was just enough ambient light to make out the outline of the shed where, were it not for Travis, I'd have ended up a popsicle. Farther back and to the right there was the larger building that housed Rance's meth lab, a single red light glowing above the door.

I flipped up the hood on my parka and limped off in that direction, thankful the wind was at my back. Each step brought a fresh blast of pain. I tried to trick my mind away from the physical discomfort by thinking of Maria, replaying the previous night over and over in my head.

And then I was there. The building was roughly the size of a two-car garage and windowless, its walls fashioned from concrete blocks and painted a dull gray, sheet-metal vents spaced at intervals around it. As I approached, my nostrils were assaulted by an odor resembling ammonia mixed with cat piss. There was a steady hum I guessed came from an exhaust fan.

My plan was simple: Get inside, confirm that methamphetamine was actively being manufactured there, and somehow get a signal to Mel Denton's drug squad. I had an idea about that.

I groped in my pocket for the Glock. I hefted it and frowned. I was able to hold it by the grip, though just barely. I tried looping my finger through the trigger guard and failed. My finger was just too swollen. The only thing I *could* do was hold the gun in my hand. I might as well throw it at Rance, for all the good it would do.

Fuck it, I thought. *I'm going in.*

I stepped up to the dark gray slab and reached for the door handle.

Forty

I inched open the ponderous steel door. Through the widening gap, a bright shaft of light stabbed the darkness. I slipped silently through the opening and got my first look at Rance Cooley's meth lab.

The same pungent odor that had assaulted my nostrils outside permeated the place. The interior was lit up like a department store, with multiple rows of florescent lights crisscrossing the ceiling. A workbench traversed one wall, and upon it stood a dizzying array of bottles, jars, containers, and vials, some filled with chemicals, others empty. All were neatly arranged. Lengths of rubber tubing protruded from some of the bottles. A stainless-steel sink stood against the far wall, and there were three small video monitors perched above the workbench at its far end. I was too far away to make out the images being displayed.

To my right, a separate room protruded out from the wall some five feet and ran the entire length of the building. A door, midway along its length, stood slightly ajar.

I remained motionless for two full minutes, alert for the slightest sound. In sharp contrast to the oppressive cold outside, the building's interior was uncomfortably warm, and I felt the first beads of sweat erupt on my forehead. I resisted the urge to remove my parka.

Hearing nothing but the incessant thrum of the exhaust fan, I shuffled forward, keeping a wary eye on the door to my right. Each step was pure agony, and I was constantly shifting my weight to relieve the pain. Perspiration puddled in my armpits.

As I approached the middle of the room, my eyes were drawn to a number of cellophane bags containing a white powder, laid out in three neat rows on the bench at the far end. I counted eighteen bags. Despite my discomfort, I smiled as I remembered fondly my days working drug cases in Germany as a CID agent.

I moved in for a closer look. A faint scuffling sound stopped me in my tracks. I froze.

"Sidney Reed!" An all-too-familiar voice boomed like thunder. "Turn around nice and slow."

I turned around nice and slow. Rance Cooley's corpulent body filled the doorway of the side room, a double-barrel sawed-off shotgun clutched in his beefy hands, its shiny blue barrel pointed at my chest. The khaki trousers he wore were deeply stained, his sleeveless undershirt discolored and ringed with sweat.

"Now give me the belly gun. You won't be needing it."

I tossed him the Glock, wincing as I did. He caught it one-handed and stuffed it in his belt. "Kind of surprised to see you here, Sidney, but I suppose I shouldn't be after yesterday's visit." He looked me over with the thoroughness of a meat inspector after a national recall. "I must say, you don't look well."

"Your sons gave me the no-frills tour."

"We're not used to visitors round here."

"I wouldn't think so." I surveyed the room. "I must say. This is the cleanest drug lab I've ever seen. I'm impressed."

His thick, silvery eyebrows arched. "I take pride in my work. Not many cookers have a degree in chemistry. Hell, most of 'em don't know a glass pipette from a beer stein. They're cooking their shit in soda bottles off the backs of Harleys. I make a quality product."

He let out a low, guttural cough. He looked spent. I decided to keep the conversation going, under the wafer-thin logic that, if he was talking, he'd be less likely to shoot me. I asked him how he ended up in the business.

His head tilted and I thought I saw a twinkle in his eye. "I always figured I'd end up working for one of the big pharmaceuticals. Uncle Sam had other plans, though. They trained me as a combat engineer and I loved it. Let's face it, how many jobs are there where you get to blow shit up?" His face darkened. "Then they sent me to Vietnam. Ever been to Nam, Sidney?"

I shook my head. "That was a bit before my time."

"Of course. Well, Sam sent me there in seventy-two. Met a fellow Oklahoma Sooner named Jack Wakefield. A real character, Jack. Once he got to trusting me, he told me how a man could make good money cookin' meth. The two of us made it out alive somehow and we set up shop outside Oklahoma City. Did quite well for a while. Unfortunately, Jack got to likin' his own product a little too much. Started seein' snakes in his bed 'n shit. One day he put a gun in his mouth, and that was that. By that time, though, Bo and Ray were helping me run things. Didn't need Jack no more."

Another round of coughing ensued. He took out a handkerchief while still holding the shotgun. I noticed flecks of red against white when he put it back in his pocket.

"What made you leave Oklahoma?"

"It was different things. Course you know, I killed a man and did time in the state pen. Had drug agents crawlin' up my ass after that. Then the Mexican gangs came and ran out all but the small operators and . . ." He paused to stare absently at his thick, sausage-like fingers. ". . . when my Kate passed, there was nothin' left for me down there anyway." He glanced up. "I know you know what it's like, losing the thing that's most precious to you." He studied the look on my face. "Yeah, I read about your wife's death in the paper. We both know that pain, don't we, Sidney?"

Even as he said the words, Rance's chin drooped. "Kate wasn't afraid of dying. She was afraid of leavin' me alone on this earth. She was a pious woman, but some days she cursed the cancer, the doctors, and the lord, all for taking her away from me. Cursed 'em for cowards. That's what kind of woman she was."

His fingers gripped the shotgun so tight, his knuckles shone white as the hair on his head. Seeing this huge man crumble at the loss of his wife triggered my own frightful memories. In my mind's eye I saw Molly lying dead in our bedroom like it was yesterday. I saw police detectives taking measurements and dusting for fingerprints as uniformed officers led me forcibly from the room. I saw those things with such intensity that, for a just few moments, my physical pain evaporated.

I vowed then and there that, if I came out of this alive, I'd find out what happened to Molly, or die trying.

Rance broke in. "When a man loses someone like her, it's like the pin's been pulled on a grenade. When that happens you've only got two choices. You can put the pin back in or let the damn thing explode." His eyes seemed to glaze over, his thoughts somewhere I couldn't fathom. I had no clue what he'd been through in Nam, but it was obvious the death of his wife had affected him deeply, and in ways I couldn't begin to comprehend.

As he spoke, I noticed his grip on the scattergun loosen ever so slightly. I calculated the distance and the odds and decided it would be foolish to try to overpower him. The throbbing in my hands and feet had worsened, as had the nausea. There had to be another way.

"Tell me about the night Travis killed Willie Olson."

Rance came alert. "That was some shit-ass bad luck. What kind of a dang fool walks down the middle of a highway in a snowstorm? Travis for sure ain't no angel, but he ain't no killer neither. My Kate loved him dearly. Trav was her favorite. On her death bed she made me promise I'd take care of him, so when he walked in the house that night lookin' like a lost puppy, all I could think was, she'd never forgive me if I let her boy go back to prison. So we got rid of the truck—buried the evidence, so to speak. And that was that."

"Except for Connie."

He bit his lip at the mention of her name. "Always knew deep down Connie was a do-gooder, but figured all I had to do was remind her to keep quiet. I misjudged the woman." He said it with a hint of pride.

"That wasn't all you did, was it, Rance? You told Bo to give her a place to stay."

He smiled weakly and coughed. "I always knew you were a good detective. Yeah, it seemed like the prudent thing to do for the time being. As much as I liked Connie, I couldn't let her stay here after I sent Travis away. Bo thought she was getting a little too curious."

"Travis and Connie loved each other. Why didn't you let him take her with him?" I was tempted to add, *If you had, she might still be alive*, but decided against it.

Rance's face darkened. "I was of a mind to let him, but Bo argued against it. He felt like she would get Travis to turn himself in, or worse. So I convinced the boy it would be better for everyone if they split up until this business with the Native kid blew over." He shook his head sadly. "I almost thought it had when the cops charged your boy with Olson's murder. Figured Travis was home free . . ."

He paused, bushy eyebrows drooping. ". . . until I noticed a certain item in the newspaper a few days ago."

I managed a weak smile. "You must've shit a brick when you saw my ad in the newspaper."

"Yeah, I spent a few sleepless nights wondering if Connie would call the number." He shot me a look. "Didn't know that was your idea 'til you showed up at Alice's place." His eyes dropped to his hands again. "A real do-gooder, Connie. It's why Kate loved her. Prob'ly why Travis loved her. She was the best thing that ever happened to that boy."

He fell silent, a kind of melancholy settling over him. Then, just as quickly, it passed. "When the ad appeared, I had Bo tell that stripper girlfriend of his to watch her extra close, and I had Ray follow her to see who she met up with."

"I must say, his surveillance skills leave a lot to be desired."

Rance nodded solemnly. "That boy'd fuck up a soup sandwich if he ever got near a kitchen."

Images of Connie lying in the snow invaded my thoughts. I gritted my teeth in anger. "Why did you have to kill her, Rance? She wasn't a threat to—"

Rance lunged forward, swinging the shotgun menacingly. "You think I killed Connie? You fucking think that? She was the only good and decent thing in this house!"

I recoiled at the suddenness of his outburst. Even Rance seemed surprised by his own passion, if not embarrassed by it. He took a moment to catch his breath. "She reminded me a lot of Kate, she did. That woman—" The sentence ended in another agonizing coughing fit.

"Sounds pretty bad," I remarked.

"Lung cancer," he wheezed. "Stage four. The folks at the VA give me four months. If I'm lucky."

I stared slack-jawed at Rance Cooley as this latest news sank in. I felt exhausted and weary. I glanced glumly at my swollen, purplish fingers. The room began to move under me, and for a moment I thought yet another earthquake was hitting the state. My legs wobbled.

"You all right there, Sidney?" Devoid of its usual hardness, Rance's voice sounded strange.

I fought to steady myself. Gradually, the dizziness passed, though my legs continued to wobble.

"Grab that stool behind you," he said.

I limped the few steps to it and sat down.

"Stay with me Sidney. This will all be over soon."

What the hell does that mean?

Rance issued a stuttering cough. "Will you excuse me?" He took his right hand off the shotgun and reached for something just inside the door of the anteroom. Holding his hand there, he said, "Bo, you there?"

A moment later a speaker cackled. "Yes, sir."

"I need you and Ray in the lab ASAP. Is Travis with you?"

"Yes, sir, he's here."

"Bring him along."

"Can't it wait, Pa?" Ray's voice broke through the static. "The movie's almost—"

"Turn off the fuckin' TV and get in here—now."

"Yes, s—"

Rance pulled his hand away. "You have kids, Sidney?"

"No, I'm sorry to say."

"Don't be sorry. Nothing but pains in the ass."

My brain was trying to sort out what Rance was up to when the room began to sway again.

Keep it together, damn it.

We waited in silence. I found it a struggle staying upright on my seat. All thought of escape had drifted away, replaced by lethargy. All I wanted now was for the pain to go away.

I wanted it all to just . . . go . . . away.

Forty-one

The door to the laboratory flew open and banged against the wall. Bo and Ray stepped through, Travis and a blast of frigid air at their heels. One look at me, then at their dad holding the shotgun, and their eyes grew wide.

"What's this about, Pa?" Bo's gaze shifted nervously. "What's *he* doing here?"

Rance stood a few steps away with the shotgun now angled toward the floor. His voice boomed with new authority. "Sidney and I were just having a discussion. He'd like to know why you two killed Connie." He glanced knowingly at me, then back at his sons. "So would I."

I almost fell off my stool.

Bo and Ray exchanged wide-eyed glances.

"He's lying, Pa," Bo blurted out. "Ray and I—"

Rance held up a beefy palm. "Hold it right there, son. What have I told you about lying?" He leveled the shotgun. "Now tell him the truth or, so help me God, I'll give you both barrels."

"He's telling the truth, Pa," Ray chimed in. "We don't know anything about that."

Rance's neck muscles visibly tightened. "Boy, you must think I'm dumber than a dog turd. Inside this room here . . ." He gestured toward the door behind him. ". . . there's a box on the wall. Think of it as a fancy intercom. Amazing, the things you can find on Ebay. With this gadget I can hear everything you say in that house. For instance, I heard you knuckleheads discussing how you lured Connie out of her ma's house and put her in the shed, then you stuck her in a snowbank on Lake Otis and waited for the municipal snow crew to finish the job. You planned to do the same with Mr. Reed here."

Fear swept over the faces of his sons like a dark cloud. Travis balled his fists, his face reddening with rage.

Rance said to him, "Sorry, boy. Always figured you for the weak one, but I had it wrong. You were the only one worth a damn. Your ma knew it, bless her soul. Finest woman who ever walked God's earth and that's a fact."

Ray spoke up. "What are you gonna do, Pa?"

Rance lifted his head and blinked rapidly, as if awakened from a trance. "What I shoulda done a long time ago." His eyes shifted from Ray to Bo. "I'm shutting her down, boys."

Bo stared blankly. "You mean . . ."

"The whole damn thing. I'm done. It's gettin' too hot for us here."

"Bullshit!" Ray practically screamed the words.

Rance coughed hard. "Mind your tongue, boy."

"Now hold on, Pa," Bo said. "Don't Ray and me have a say in this?"

"No. This ain't a democracy, son. We clear out of here and start someplace else. We've done it before."

"You're just gonna leave all this here?" Ray said.

"Remember Oklahoma, boy?" Rance's weathered mouth curled in a grin. "My escape plan?"

I recalled what Travis had said on the drive from the Valley. About how his dad had blown up his lab down there. I had wondered idly if it were true. I wondered now where he'd hidden the explosives.

Bo smiled. "Yeah, that's what we'll do."

Ray cocked his head at me. "What about *him*? You can't just let him walk out of here."

"Who, Sidney? Hell, he ain't gonna tell nobody."

"He knows too much," Ray sputtered. "He'll—"

"You don't wanna test me today, boy!" Rance fumed. He turned his gaze on Travis. "Come here, son."

The youngest Cooley went and stood next to his dad.

"See to it Mr. Reed gets safely to his car. You got that, boy?"

"Yes, sir," Travis said.

The youngest Cooley came and stood next to me.

Rance looked at me. "You'll wanna have those hands and feet looked after. I know frostbite when I see it."

Even as he spoke, I felt myself slipping into unconsciousness.

Hold on, Sidney. You can do this.

Rance said, "Travis, there's about seventy-five thousand dollars in an ammo can on the shelf in the basement behind some camping gear. Got a big red X painted on it, like on a first-aid kit. After you get Mr. Reed to his car, take the money and get out of here."

"What?" Bo and Ray shouted in unison.

Bo leveled his gaze at his dad. "With all due respect, Pa, that money's ours too."

Rance didn't flinch. "And there's plenty more of it. No need to get greedy. You both know Travis ain't cut out for this life. That money'll give him a stake. Now get goin', Travis, or you'll be carrying Mr. Reed on your back."

"Go where, Pa?"

"Far away as you can. Start a new life somewhere. Clean yourself up. Find a good woman and take care of her."

"What about you, Pa? What are you gonna do?"

"Don't worry about me, I'll be fine. Now you better hurry."

I slid off the stool and my legs buckled, the room spinning like a carnival ride. Travis swung an arm around my rib cage, steadied me, and led me awkwardly to the door.

Bo and Ray, jaws set, barred the way.

Rance motioned with the shotgun. "Step aside, boys."

"We're not letting him go," Ray growled. "He knows too much."

"I mean it, son," Rance said, his voice strained yet ominous.

For a long moment, no one spoke. I was drenched in sweat, drifting in and out of consciousness. Ray kept looking at Bo, who finally said, "Let 'em go," and pulled Ray roughly aside.

Travis twisted the knob on the door, paused, and glanced back at his dad, who simply nodded. Travis, in turn, offered an awkward nod to his brothers and pulled open the door. The last image I had as we left the building was of their angry, bewildered faces.

Outside, a blast of sub-zero air slapped my face. I doubled over and vomited a quantity of pasty yellow slime into the snow.

"That's some nasty looking shit, Mr. Reed," Travis said, his face contorted.

I stood in silence, chest heaving, waiting for the next volley. It never came. Once my eyes had adjusted to the darkness, I let him know I was ready and we followed the beaten path through the snow, Travis half pulling, half dragging me along. He grunted from the exertion.

Eventually—I don't know when, for I had lost all sense of time—we paused to rest, the two of us exhaling great clouds of condensation into the night air.

"You're . . . a heavy man . . . Mr. Reed."

"I've . . . been meaning to—"

A deafening explosion shattered the stillness, knocking me to the ground like a giant hand. Almost immediately, a blast of warm air passed over me and was gone. Raising myself up on my elbows, I jerked my head around and saw a pit of roiling fire and steel gray smoke in the place where the Rance's laboratory had stood moments before. A mushroom cloud billowed up from the ground and into the trees, the burning limbs crackling in the frigid air. I stared numbly at the smoldering ruins.

Rance had executed his escape plan.

The sound of moaning turned my head. Travis was hunched over on his knees, his gloved hands covering the back of his head. I crawled to him and asked feebly if he was all right. In response, he began pounding his fist into the snow.

"Pa!" he bellowed. "Why?" He hammered his fist again and again. Eventually, he stopped pounding and just sobbed.

"Travis?" I grabbed his arm and shook it. He looked at me dumbly. I suddenly had an image of Mel Denton's drug squad spotting the fireball and charging up the road, guns drawn.

"We need to go," I said. "Cops will be . . . swarming all over this place in a few minutes."

He pulled me to my feet, and we slogged on through the snow.

We arrived at the shed and Travis muscled me into the passenger seat of the Camry. He went around and slid behind the wheel and fired up the engine.

I glanced his way. "Aren't you going back for the money?"

His jaw tightened. "Fuck the money."

Travis didn't stop to open the gate, he just plowed right through it. I winced as the front bumper crumpled. Even in my delirium I wondered what I would say to Andrea about the damage to the Camry's front end.

Soon enough, I put those thoughts behind me. I remember pulling onto O'Malley Road, but I drifted in and out after that. I vaguely recall streetlights drifting past, and sirens, and the soft rumble of the engine. I remember the car jerking to a stop, and Travis saying "This man needs help," and people I didn't know lifting me out of the car and placing me on a gurney. I remember passing down a long hallway, as if through a tunnel.

Everything was so very white.

Forty-two

I woke to the pallid whiteness of a hospital room and the pungent odor of disinfectant. A woman's face peered down at me. She was attractive, with a roundish face and sympathetic smile, her dark hair pinned back.

"Good morning, Mr. Reed," she said in a bright, cheery voice. She wore hospital whites and a nametag that said HOLLY. Rhymes with Molly, I thought absentmindedly.

I felt relaxed and surprisingly well, though slightly woozy and a little nauseous. Covered to my armpits in a sheet, the one part of my body I could actually see—my hands—were bandaged.

"Where am I?" My voice made a strange sound, my throat like sandpaper.

"Alaska Regional Hospital. You were brought in last night."

Brought in?

I remembered a very cold dark room and an explosion. The dots connecting the two were missing.

"What day is it?" I asked.

"Sunday."

"Morning or afternoon?"

Her eyebrows tilted. "Why, morning. A little past seven."

Something squeezed my left arm—a blood pressure cuff, set to trigger at intervals. A catheter protruded from the other arm. I traced it to a bag hanging from a stainless-steel rod.

"Morphine," Holly said, as if reading my mind.

"Makes me nauseous."

"It's a common side-effect. Believe me, you want the morphine." She set a bedpan atop the portable table beside the bed. "Just in case."

I asked for water. She filled a glass from a pitcher and brought it to my mouth. Instinctively, I raised my bandaged arm. There was no discernable feeling in my fingers. I sipped the water.

"Why am I here, Holly?"

She gave me a strange look. "Why, you're being treated for frostbite. Beyond that, I'll let Dr. Canalis explain your condition and treatment. Rest easy. The doctor will be in soon."

Holly left, and shortly thereafter a stoutly built woman with frizzy hair and thick black glasses lumbered in with a clipboard under one arm and a small paper bag under the other. She pulled up a chair and sat down.

"Good morning, Mr. Reed. I'm Ms. Danby, Hospital Administration." She studied me over the top of her spectacles. "It seems you are a bit of an enigma. Dropped off at the emergency entrance in the middle of the night in a rather distressed condition. I don't suppose you remember who did that?"

Yeah . . . Travis Cooley.

I shook my head.

"It was all quite mysterious, although the man who dropped you off—we're all calling him the mystery man—did give us your name. He was—"

"What can I do for you, Ms. Danby?"

She cleared her throat. "I see you've been a patient of ours in the past, Mr. Reed. However, I still need to see some documentation: driver's license, insurance card, that sort of thing."

"You'll find my ID in my wallet, but I don't know—"

"I'll check with the nurse. For now, what is your date of birth?"

I told her, adding, "You should have a copy of my retired Army ID card on file."

"We do." She jotted something and stood up. "I wish you a speedy recovery, Mr. Reed." She started out the door, then paused. "Oh, I almost forgot. The gentleman who brought you in asked us to give you this." She set the bag gingerly on the small, moveable table next to the bed and walked out.

I pulled on the table until it hovered over my lap and reached for the bag. It was small and brown, with grease stains near the bottom and the yellow McDonalds logo on each side. A light came on.

I bought Travis a sandwich in Palmer.

I flipped the bag upside down and the keys to the Camry and a folded-up piece of paper tumbled out. I picked up the note and spread it open in front of me. It read:

I left your car in the big lot behind the hospital. Sorry I couldn't stick around. Thanks for everything. Travis

I read it twice more before drifting off to sleep.

"Good morning, Mr. Reed. I'm Dr. Canalis. May I call you Sidney?"

The doctor was young, trim, and athletic and reminded me of Dr. Kildare from reruns I'd seen on cable T.V.

I lifted my bandaged left hand. "How many did you lop off, doc?"

He grinned. "Thankfully, none."

"Good. I hope one day to learn to crochet."

That produced a chuckle. "You're a lucky man, Sidney. You were admitted with a body temperature of ninety-five degrees Fahrenheit. In other words, you were hypothermic."

"Ninety-five doesn't seem all that bad."

"No, it doesn't. We tend to think, only three and a half degrees below normal, how bad can it be? But it is. Had you been exposed to those temperatures much longer, it could have proven fatal. We put you in a warm-water bath, administered a tissue plasminogen activator to restore blood flow, and gave you an antibiotic to ward off infection. Once we got your temp back to normal, we could deal with the rest of it."

"The rest of it?"

"Your fingers and toes suffered first- and second-degree frostbite. First degree is mostly redness and swelling and should heal with proper treatment. But some of your digits also have blistering, which moves you up to second-degree. We will need to watch those a little more closely, but if you do the follow-up I prescribe, you should fully recover. "

"That's it?"

"That's the worst it. Your ears, nose and cheeks have some blanching—what we call frost nip. I expect those areas to heal fine on their own. I'll give you some salve for those; send you home with a fact sheet and instructions on following up."

"So when *can* I go home?"

"Well, you had a nasty crack on the head. I need to rule out a concussion."

"I'm fine, doc. Really."

He touched my arm. "Hang around another day for me. If everything looks copasetic, I can probably let you go in the morning."

I nodded. "How about taking me off the morphine?"

"No problem. I'll have the nurse switch you to Motrin."

As he was getting up to leave, I said, "Doc, I wonder if you could do something for me."

Half an hour later, Rachel Saint George walked in. "Came as soon as I heard." She took one look at me and her face went pale. "What have you gone and done to yourself now?"

"A little frost nip," I said. "Nothing serious."

"Uh huh. Well, I have to call bullshit on that one, my friend. They've got you wrapped up like a steaming pile of fish guts."

"There's a nice image."

"Spill it, Sid. What happened?"

She shook her head slowly as I recited the short version. "Trouble follows you everywhere."

"What can I say? I'm an enigma."

"Wrapped in a bologna sandwich."

"Did you call Eddie Baker for me?"

She squinted at me. "What happened to *your* phone?"

"Well, did you?"

"Yeah, I called him."

She inquired again about my phone, but before I could answer, the tall gangly figure of Eddie Baker loomed behind her, looking like he was ready to burst.

I said, "Rach, this is—"

"You must have been bonked in the head but good," Rachel said. "Eddie's been coming to my shop for years."

"Right, I knew that."

Eddie acknowledged Rachel with a nod and gawked at me. "Jesus, Sid. What happened? I've been trying to call you all night. And what's up with your phone?"

"Repossessed," I said.

Eddie said, "Are you kidding me?"

Rachel grinned. "Yes, Eddie, he's kidding." She slung her handbag over her shoulder. "I'll leave you two to talk legalese. I've got a coffee shop to run."

"Thanks, Rach," I said weakly.

It was then I noticed Rachel had a rolled-up newspaper under one arm. She laid it on the table. "Check out the story on page one. It may help speed your recovery. And get well soon, will you? You make up one quarter of my customer base."

I managed a grin as she left the room.

Eddie's eyes widened. "You haven't seen the paper yet?"

"No, Eddie, I tend not to be in a reading mood when I'm pumped full of morphine."

"I owe you an apology. This damn trial had me pulling my—"

"Jesus, Eddie. Will you just spit it out?"

"I'm trying to tell you, the state is dropping the charges. The AG's office called a short while ago to tell me officially. Rudy's going to be a free man."

I stared at him, dumbstruck. "How . . ."

Eddie looked at me like I'd missed the invention of the automobile, the Apollo moon landing, and the demise of bell bottom jeans and the Hoola Hoop. "Just read the damn story, will you?"

He tossed the paper on my lap. The lead headline hit me right between the eyes:

Anchorage District Attorney implicated in scheme to hide evidence in murder trial

I looked up at Eddie, but he just smiled. My eyes returned to the page.

By Maria Maldonado

Anchorage District Attorney Grant Fellows conspired with an investigator in his office to hide evidence in the Rudy Skinner murder trial, a *Daily News* investigation has revealed.

Fellows is prosecuting Skinner for the January 15 hit-and-run killing of Willie Olson.

The allegation came to light when a source close to the defendant told the *News* of offering the D.A. documentary evidence proving Skinner could not have killed Olson.

According to the source, Sergeant Lou Fletcher, an APD officer assigned to the D.A.'s office, confiscated the evidence from the source and threatened retaliation if the evidence were disclosed to anyone.

Unbeknownst to Fletcher, though, the source kept a duplicate copy of the documents which, upon review by the *News'* investigative team, appeared to show Mr. Skinner was nowhere near the scene of Olson's death at the time it allegedly took place.

Alaska law requires prosecutors disclose any information favorable to the defendant, and judicial ethics rules forbid the prosecution of a defendant if the state lacks a good-faith belief in the defendant's guilt.

The documents allegedly offered to Fletcher were never revealed to Skinner's defense team, the *News* has learned. The state rested its case on Friday without mentioning the exculpatory records. Fletcher was seen sitting next to Fellows throughout the trial.

The state alleges Skinner struck and killed Olson shortly after the Native man left a private party on O'Malley Road. David Borman, a former cellmate of Skinner's and the state's key witness, testified Skinner admitted to killing Olson. The state promised Borman a reduced sentence on an unrelated charge in exchange for his cooperation.

A spokesperson for Office of the State Attorney General called the *Daily News* allegations "disturbing" and promised to issue a response "once we've had a chance to thoroughly review them." The AG's office has not responded as of press time today.

The Anchorage D.A.'s office declined to comment. Calls to D.A.

Fellows were routed to his voicemail. Eddie Baker, Mr. Skinner's defense attorney, could not be reached for comment.

Fellows, who has been exploring a run for governor next year, took the unusual step of prosecuting the Skinner case himself. Fellows recently told a local television news reporter he "felt compelled to act as an advocate for all Native Alaskans."

Fellows' recent appearance at the Alaska Federation of Natives Convention has been widely viewed in political circles as a testing of the waters among Alaska's indigenous population, who make up seventeen percent of Alaska's voters.

An eighteen-year veteran of the Anchorage Police Department, Fletcher has had six ethics complaints lodged against him in his career, a source in the department told the *News*.

Both Olson's death and Skinner's trial have focused renewed public attention on Alaska Native issues such as homelessness, discrimination, and joblessness. Willie Olson's father, Leonard Olson, is president of the Oomingmak Native Corporation and an outspoken advocate for Alaska Native rights.

The trial of Skinner is scheduled to resume Monday with the defense presenting its case. If convicted of second-degree murder, Rudy Skinner could face up to ninety-nine years in prison.

What effect, if any, the allegations against Fellows and Fletcher will have on the trial is as yet unknown.

I sank back into the pillows, a contented smile on my face.

I'll be damned—she did it.

Memories of our night together came rushing back, only to be interrupted by the sound of a throat clearing. I'd forgotten Eddie was still in the room. I looked up to see him grinning like a Cheshire Cat.

"It was craziest thing, Sid. Edith and I had gone out for a late dinner. When we got home after midnight there were half a dozen messages from Maria what's-her-name, but it was too late to call her back. Then I saw the paper this morning and I felt like I'd been hit in the head with a crowbar. Tried calling you, but kept getting your voicemail. You need to check your phone once in a while, pal."

"I'll keep it in mind," I said.

"Your landlady called me like half an hour ago and told me where you were. I was on the way here when the attorney general called me."

"Get to the point, will you, Eddie?" I hit the morphine trigger.

"I'm getting there. Based on the ADN story, the AG directed the state troopers to conduct an independent inquiry into the entire mess. He also suspended Fellows and appointed Duncan Tish acting D.A."

"Well done, Eddie," I croaked through a scratchy throat. "I imagine Jeffries will be pissed. There nothing a judge hates more than wasting the jury's time."

"No shit. I'd better put my hip waders on for that one."

"What about Fellows' flunky, Fletcher?"

"Bet you can't say that ten times fast," he smirked. "Tish canned him, effective immediately. The police chief will have to decide what to do with him. By the time this is over, I'm betting he'll be fired—or spend what's left of his career working pawnshop detail. Wouldn't surprise me if he faced criminal charges to boot."

I studied the contented look on his face. "Chalk one up for truth and justice." I smiled weakly through the pain, feeling tired suddenly.

"Thank you, Sid. Can you imagine how excited Rudy will be when he finds out? I plan to tell him first thing in the morning." He studied me for a moment. "I'm curious. What was your part in this?"

"What do you mean?" I said drowsily.

"Don't play dumb with me. You think I don't know about you and that reporter? In this town, rumors spread faster than a grizzly lapping up warm gravy."

Through chapped lips I told him my suspicion about the missing business records, Evelyn Waters' sudden departure from Rudy's trailer, and Fletcher's part in all of it.

His chin drooped, his mouth forming a thin line. "I was a fool to dismiss your concerns about the records. About Evelyn."

"Tunnel vision," I said. "It happens to the best of us."

"Well, you're still my favorite."

"Yeah, and you're still full of shit."

He grinned and buttoned up his wool coat. "Catch you later, Sid." He paused at the door. "By the way, I called Jim Hathaway, our expert on false confessions. Told him we won't be needing his testimony after all. Thought I'd save you a phone call. Get well soon, will you?"

I raised a weary hand at his retreat and closed my eyes. Funny, I thought. Eddie was so excited about the outcome of his case, he never asked me how I ended up in the hospital. I knew Lois would keep my name out of the papers if she could. So would Mel Denton. As for Maria . . .

I melted into the pillows, but sleep eluded me. My mind flashed back to the terrible frigid blackness of the shed. I'd come pretty damn close to cashing in. My thoughts drifted to Travis. I owed that man my life. Connie had been right about him. I wondered idly where he was at that moment.

Probably Hawaii, I thought with a grin. *That's where I'd be.*

I squeezed the trigger on the morphine drip again, reached for the newspaper, and re-read Maria's story. She was a damn good reporter, although, admittedly, it wasn't her skill as a journalist that occupied my thoughts.

I sighed and browsed through the rest of the paper. A short article in the B Section caught my eye.

Body of woman recovered

A municipal snowplow operator clearing streets discovered the body of a woman buried in a snowbank along Lake Otis Parkway one mile south of Tudor Road early Saturday morning, according to the Anchorage Police Department.

The APD reported in a brief statement that Anchorage resident Connie Zwick, 26, was pronounced dead at the scene. A preliminary inquiry revealed that Zwick was walking on Lake Otis Parkway in whiteout conditions sometime early Saturday morning when she was struck by a motor vehicle. She is believed to have either died instantly or froze to death subsequent to being hit. An APD investigation is ongoing. The State Medical Examiner's Office has scheduled an autopsy for Monday.

Zwick is survived by her mother, Beatrice Phillips, of Anchorage. Services will be held at the Midnight Sun Funeral Home Tuesday at 10 a.m.

I stared dazedly at the words on the page and whispered, "They won't get away with it, Connie."

That's when I fell asleep.

Forty-three

pg 324 half way.

At 5 p.m. the nurse brought in a dinner of Salisbury steak, red potatoes, and green beans. I picked at my meal halfheartedly before pushing it aside. I was sipping from a carton of milk when Maria walked in looking tired and weary and adorable. She came to the edge of the bed and peered anxiously at my bandages.

"You're wounded," she said.

"God, I love the sound of your voice."

She bent down and our tongues danced a slow dance together. She tried to talk and kiss at the same time. "I was so worried . . . you didn't answer your phone . . . I thought you were—"

I stopped kissing her. "On vacation?"

"I thought you were dead!" She swiped at her eyes with her sleeve.

"Sorry." I reached for her hand and she let me take it. "Thanks for the worry. There were a few scary moments, but it takes more than a ruthless gang of drug dealers to do me in. As for my phone, I seem to have lost it in all the excitement last night."

She listened intently as I gave an abbreviated version of the previous night's excursions. "Thank God you're all right." She lightly touched my bandaged fingertips. "You *are* all right?"

"I've got a bit of healing to do but, yeah, I'm all right." After a pause I said, "My lobotomy was a complete success."

"Oh, shut up!" She leaned down and hugged my chest. Her long tresses gathered around my neck, smelling vaguely of apple blossoms.

I rested my right hand on her back, reveling in the fragrance of her. "It seems that while I was getting beaten unconscious, kicked, punched, and frostbitten, you were working on a Pulitzer Prize. I must say, I'm impressed."

She rose up, smiling bashfully. "Stop."

"I've never dated a reporter before," I said. "Are they all this brilliant?"

Her brown eyes danced. "Not even close."

"Do tell."

She slid her heavy wool coat off her shoulders and tossed it on a chair and sat on the edge of the bed. "You're pretty brilliant yourself. When I went to see Evelyn, it was just like you said. She was dying to talk to me—I saw it in her eyes. She told me to go away and I did, but then barely an hour later, she called and we met at Blair's in Midtown."

I pushed myself upright in bed, listening intently, feeling much better than I had that morning. With long delicate fingers she brushed strands of hair off her cheeks. They didn't stay put.

"Once I'd convinced her I would protect her identity, the floodgates opened. She was pissed at Fletcher and determined to tell her story." Maria reached for my hand and held it. "She loved Rudy, even with his addiction. She kept him focused on their business, solicited jobs for him and, best of all, kept meticulous records. She kept him from going off the rails."

"What's the saying? Behind every successful man there's a woman, or something like that."

"See? You *are* brilliant."

"Continue, *Miss* Maldonado."

"Evelyn's problem was, she couldn't keep *herself* from going off the rails. Last spring, when she and Rudy were hard up for money, they sold oxy to an undercover cop. She got off with probation, but Rudy, with his prior record, got jail time. Now this is where the fun begins."

She squeezed my hand again. "Rudy called her from jail and said he'd been arrested for the murder of Willie Olson back in January, but something didn't make sense. She remembered Rudy had been busy all that winter, getting lots of jobs, staying sober. If he'd hit anyone, she's sure he would have told her about it."

"Makes sense, I suppose."

"She checked her records for the day Olson was killed. Sure

enough, Rudy had been working all that night in Eagle River, getting one snowplow job after another. He hadn't gone anywhere near the scene of the killing. There was no way he could have killed that boy." She paused, then looked at me and sighed. "You're falling asleep. I must be boring you."

"Not at all. Please . . . keep talking. I'm . . . fine."

"I'm tired of talking."

"Okay, then kiss me."

"If you insist."

After Maria left, I drifted in and out of sleep. At some point the nurse came in with her clipboard and studied the blinking machines next to the bed, scrawling notes. As she was walking out the door, Lois Dozier walked in clutching a manila envelope under one arm.

"You look like hell," she said.

"I get that from my dad."

"You gonna live?"

"So they tell me."

She glanced around the room before settling into a chair. "That's quite a mess out there at the Cooley place. It's taking time to sort out the bodies. The EPA boys are tearing their hair out—"

"Wait a minute. What did you say?"

"The EPA boys are going nuts with all the chemicals—"

"Before that. You said bodies—plural. You meant to say *body*, right?"

"Negative, I said BODIES. We found the charred remains of three people in the rubble. Three adult males."

My mouth curled in a grin. I'd been too far gone to see it then, but now, in the warm afterglow of recovery, it was beginning to make sense. I'd assumed that when Travis and I left, Rance told Bo and Ray to collect their share of the cash and their belongings and get the hell out of there via the escape route Connie told me about. But Rance never intended to leave this world alone. Not after what his sons had done to Connie and Travis. Connie, who reminded him so much of his dead wife, and Travis, his wife's favorite. The one he'd promised to keep away from the drug trade—to protect. Kate had been the only decent thing that had ever happened to him. He did the only thing he knew to keep his promise to her.

"It's not going to be easy identifying the remains." Lois shook her head. "Talk about crispy critters." She eyed me curiously. "You're looking mighty content all of a sudden. What gives?"

"I was just thinking. Maybe I can help with the identification. Off the record, of course."

She took a notebook from her parka. "I'm listening."

"The big fellow is Rance Cooley. He's an Army vet, so there should be dental charts in his military jacket in St. Louis. The other two are, or were, his sons. Bo was the oldest. He'll be the taller of the two. The other guy is . . ." My mind flashed to something Connie had said the last time I saw her: *Promise me you won't hurt him, Sidney.*

Lois glanced up, pen poised against paper. "The other one?"

"Um, that would be Travis, Rance's youngest. From what I heard, Rance has been grooming him to take over the business."

She stopped scribbling. "Wasn't there a third son?"

"His name is Ray. He was somewhere else when the place blew. Probably long gone by now. They all lived in that big house together. The meth lab they had out there was top notch. Denton in narcotics knows all about it."

She put away her notebook and studied me closely. "The Cooley boys were operating a meth lab, all right, but that was no chemical explosion. The lab techs are still running tests, but they're thinking C-4. Pretty sophisticated setup, too. Made one helluva big hole in the ground."

I yawned. "Rance was a demolitions expert in Nam. When he and the boys operated a lab in Oklahoma and things got a little too hot down there, he blew it all up as a big fuck-you to the drug cops. I'd say he did it again."

"Except the last time he didn't blow himself up, along with his sons." She shook her head. "It doesn't make any sense. Why would he do that?"

"We'll probably never know," I said, yawning again.

She raised an eyebrow. "I don't suppose you can tell me how you know all that stuff about the Cooleys. Let me guess—attorney-client privilege, right?"

"Something like that."

"Damn you, Sid. How am I going to explain all this in my report?"

"You were one of the best CID agents I ever worked with, Lois. I'm sure you'll think of something."

"I have half a mind to subpoena you to appear at an inquest." She sighed. "But then, how would I ever get you to attend any ADA meetings?"

We stared at each other. A deathly quiet filled the room. "Lois, about the other day. I—"

"Save your strength for the grilling you're going to get from APD Homicide once they sink their teeth into Connie Zwick's death. You've still got lots of splainin' to do on that one. As for the other day, we've been friends too long to worry about shit like that."

She came and stood by the bed. "Get yourself mended so we can have lunch. Your treat." She tossed the manila envelope on my chest and walked out the door.

I undid the clasp and tipped it on end. A dozen or so sheets of white paper tumbled out.

It was Molly's autopsy report.

Forty-four

The hospital sent me home at 10 a.m. Monday morning. Rachel Saint George, the most unlikely guardian angel a P.I. ever had, loaded me into her long-in-the-tooth Chevy SUV, brought me back to the Mighty Moose, and somehow got me up the rickety stairs to my apartment without the two of us plunging to the pavement below. As soon as we got inside, I thanked her.

"You're welcome. Let me know if you need anything."

"You could bring me a mocha."

"Let me know if you need anything *important*."

"Okay."

She turned to go, then hesitated, her hand lingering on the knob. "You gave me quite a scare." Her eyes remained fixed squarely on the door. "Do you have any idea how much trouble it would be to find another renter for this place? So, you know, try to stay alive, okay?"

"I'll do my best."

The moment Rachel left, Priscilla trotted over and sniffed at my crutches before returning to the rocker. I glared at her and groused, "I missed you too."

Hearing heavy footsteps on the stairs, I turned and yanked open the door. It was Eddie Baker, looking like someone had pissed on one of his legal briefs. A chill wind swept past him.

I stared at him. "Close the damn door before I freeze to death."

He came in and looked around, his face unreadable.

I asked if I could take his coat. He ignored the question and glanced around the room. "You live here?"

"Ever since they closed the homeless shelter."

He grunted. Something was off.

I gestured toward the couch. "Why don't you take a load off."

He went over and sat down.

I limped after him. "Can I get you something?"

His eyes were two dark, lifeless orbs. "Got any whiskey?"

Something's definitely off. It must not have gone well in court.

I aimed my crutches toward the kitchen, rummaged through cabinets, and came up with a half-empty bottle of Jim Beam. I filled two glasses with ice and whiskey and called out, "You'll have to come and get it. My crutches aren't rated for the transportation of alcohol."

Eddie came into the kitchen, his usual springy step absent. I handed him the glasses and followed him to the couch.

I poured whiskey down my throat, eyeing him closely.

Eddie raised his glass and paused. "I worked my ass off for that guy."

"I know you did, Eddie."

"*You* worked your ass off for that guy."

I took another drink. It was so quiet in the room, I could hear the ice tinkling in my glass.

This doesn't feel much like a celebration.

"Hell, Sid, you babysat him through the whole fucking trial."

I decided to say something reassuring. "Criminal trials don't always turn out the way we'd like, you know that."

"Ain't it the truth."

He took his first drink, looked at me, then looked away, his glass clenched firmly in both hands. He looked at me again. "Rudy's dead."

My body stiffened. The words registered, but didn't seem real. But then, nothing seemed real anymore, as if a portion of my brain had come unmoored. Before I'd had a chance to fully process what he'd said, I asked him what happened.

Eddie closed his eyes and took a deep breath. "I was on cloud nine when I got to the courthouse this morning. Figured Tish would announce they'd dropped the charges."

He shook his head slowly. "I knew something was wrong the moment I walked in the courtroom. The judge, Tish, Banner, and several troopers were huddled together near the bench. Tish waved me over and Jeffries ordered everyone out of the room—press, family, spectators. When they were gone, Trooper Armstrong, the Court Services Officer, briefed us."

He paused to sip his drink, barely opening his eyes. Sweat pooled in my armpits. I wanted to scream at him to finish the damn story, but you can't rush Eddie Baker. No one can.

"This morning at nine-thirty, per protocol, Armstrong called AJ to have Rudy transported to the courthouse. A corrections officer went to Rudy's cell, found him lying in a pool of blood." Eddie paused again, his voice cracking a bit. "He'd made himself a damn shank, or got one from another inmate, and slashed his jugular. At least, that's the look of it."

"Jesus," I said.

"Whoever was supposed to be watching the video feed from Rudy's cell evidently dropped the fucking ball. By the time the officer got there, he'd already bled out."

Eddie emptied his glass in one long gulp and set it on the coffee table. "He'd been put in lockdown again, so he never saw yesterday's paper or heard the fucking news. He died not knowing Fellows and Fletcher had tanked his case. Not knowing Tish was about to with-draw the indictment . . . that he was going to be a free man. How's that for fucking irony?"

I gave my glass a white-knuckled squeeze. "Fuck!"

He stared at me hard. "I know what you're thinking. You're think-ing this is on you. Well, that's bullshit and you know it."

I stared at the ice in my glass and managed a stilted grin. "Is it? You know what the last thing he said to me was, Eddie? He said, 'I can't take it anymore.' I should have seen it coming. Say what you want, but I should have fucking seen it coming."

"Don't do this to yourself, Sid. You're already carrying around enough baggage to fill the Sullivan Arena. Whatever Rudy's demons were, there's nothing you or I could have done about it."

I stared at him numbly. "If you say so."

He rose to his feet. "I've gotta go. Thanks for the drink. By the way, you look like roadkill. Get yourself fixed up. I've got more work for you." He paused. "I'll let myself out."

When Eddie was gone I crutch-walked to the kitchen and poured another Jim Beam.

I spent the rest of the day watching The History Channel and popping little colored pills whenever the pain became unbearable. Mostly, though, I thought about Rudy. Priscilla camped out on my stomach much of the time, which was unusual for her, as she preferred to roost on Molly's rocker. Maybe she sensed what I was going through.

I took full advantage of my status as an invalid and ignored several calls from APD Homicide.

Mel Denton called around 2 p.m. to tell me that a search of the Cooley home had unearthed a trove of information on their drug operations, including ledgers listing distributors, amounts, and dates—"The whole shebang," as he put it. Armed with this information, the drug squad fanned out and made a series of arrests that happily included Robert Murphy, the auto shop entrepreneur formerly known as Big Tooth.

Late in the afternoon, Maria called to apologize for not coming to see me that evening. She had a ton of work to catch up on at the paper, but promised to make it up to me by cooking me dinner the next day. I was actually relieved, as I would have been lousy company.

Around 10 p.m. I popped a pain killer that had a long funny name, slid under the sheets, and fell into a deep sleep.

I felt better—or thought I did—when I eased myself out of bed Tuesday morning, so much so that I decided a walk to the Midnight Sun Funeral Home would do me good. I wrestled into my parka easily enough, but struggled mightily descending the rickety stairs with the two pieces of lumber that passed for crutches. At one point I almost lost my balance and tumbled down the stairs. By the time I arrived at the bottom rung, I was puffing like an obese marathon runner.

The three-block walk seemed more like three miles. I felt awkward and clumsy, but lumbered along as best I could and reached my destination with newfound respect for anyone dependent upon crutches. Thankfully, the painkillers seemed to work like a champ.

An usher stood just inside the door as I walked in. A look of kind indifference quickly changed to one of alarm.

"Are you all right, sir? You don't look well."

"I'm fine," I lied. I felt clammy and my head hurt. My gaze fell on several rows of folding chairs up ahead. "I just need to sit a spell."

"Can I get you a wheelchair, sir?"

"I'll manage, thank you."

I claimed a seat in the back row and glanced around. At the front of the room stood a simple gold casket, its lid closed, and a lectern. There were six rows of seats, five of them empty. A total of five mourners sat in the first row. One of them was Beatrice Phillips, looking even more frail and stooped than I remembered. A sallow, bespectacled man stood over her and they were chatting. I pegged him for the funeral director.

Leaning back in my chair, I tried to forget how much I hated funerals, a nearly impossible task given the melancholy organ music streaming from a pair of tinny black speakers mounted on the wall. The music reminded me of what happened to Rudy.

I was hot and sweaty, so I peeled open my parka. Out of the corner of my eye I saw a hooded figure in a long black coat standing alone in the far corner of the room. I gathered up my crutches and my strength and hobbled over to him. His eyes roamed nervously beneath the shadowed brow of the hood. A familiar voice whispered, "I'm surprised to see you here, Mr. Reed."

"I could say the same for you."

He sighed heavily. "I had to come."

"I know." A flash of light drew my eyes to a chain dangling below his chin. It was Connie's necklace.

He followed my gaze. "I thought she might want it back, but it's a closed casket, so . . ."

"I think she'd want *you* to have it."

He looked like he wanted to say something, but didn't.

I scanned the room. A chatter of voices rose above the organ's somber dirge. The funeral director stole glances at his watch. No one paid us any mind. I turned and peered at the dark shadow of his face. "What are your plans?"

"What Pa said. Get as far away as I can. Start a new life, or try to."

"Just remember, Travis. You can't catch a dead man."

He cocked his head. "What's that supposed to mean?"

"They tell me Travis Cooley died in the explosion. Burnt to a crisp. Unidentifiable."

There was a muted gasp. "How . . ." His body visibly slackened beneath the coat. "Oh . . . I see. Um, thank you, Mr. Reed." His eyes traveled around the room, as if expecting federal agents to burst in at any moment. "What do I do now?" It was the voice of a man at loose ends—lost.

"Become someone else."

"I don't know how."

"You're a smart guy. You'll figure it out."

I hobbled back to my seat and plopped down. Beads of sweat erupted on my forehead. I glanced over my shoulder—Travis was nowhere in sight.

The music stopped. The funeral director eyed his watch, shuffled to the lectern, and with all the sincerity of a boxing promoter, recited the eulogy, extolling the virtues of a woman he knew nothing about.

My shirt was soaked. I thought they must have jacked up the heat. The director, his voice now strangely muffled, asked if anyone had anything they'd like to share—an anecdote or remembrance, perhaps. Heads swiveled right and left. No one rose from their chair. *What the hell.*

I grabbed my crutches, grunted out of my chair, and maneuvered to the front of the room under the doleful eye of the funeral director. The room seemed to tilt as I turned my gaze to the mourners. My bandaged hands tightened their grip on the lectern. The mourners regarded me quizically; all except for Beatrice Phillips, who stared icily.

I opened my trembling lips to speak, but what came out more closely resembled random babbling than coherent speech. When I tried again the room tilted even more precariously and began to sway back and forth. Beatrice Phillips' glare morphed into alarm, as suddenly the floor opened beneath me and I felt myself tumbling through the air. Falling . . .

"What were you thinking?"

Maria stood over me, bathed in shadow, disquiet in her voice.

"I don't know. I guess I wasn't."

The previous few hours were a blur. I remembered waking up at the funeral home, being pushed along in a wheelchair, helped into Maria's car, and later, up the stairs. Now I was lying on the couch, having just swallowed a pain pill and a glass of water.

"You're supposed to be resting, not traipsing all over town."

"Sorry."

She sat beside me on the couch. "Did you get my message?"

"Message? I lost my phone, remember?"

"Oh. Well, I called last night to tell you how sorry I was about Rudy. That poor man."

"Thank you for that. And thanks for coming to get me."

She smiled faintly. "I racked up a few brownie points with my editor this week. He owes me more than a little time off."

"I should think so. You're a regular Lois Lane."

"And I suppose that makes you Superman?"

"Not the way I look in tights. You on the other hand . . ."

She leaned over and buried her head in the crook of my shoulder. "You scared me, Sidney. What possessed you to do such a thing?"

Wavy locks played across her back. I stroked them with a bandaged hand. "I wanted them to know her life meant something. I guess I didn't think it through."

"No, you didn't. Next time . . ."

She pulled back and flashed her coffee brown eyes at me. "Next time, Mr. Reed, do exactly the same thing and I might just fall in love with you."

A lump lodged in my throat. I looked away.

"Look at me, Sidney."

Our eyes met and I thought, *Molly used to look at me that way.*

"What happened to her wasn't your fault, just like what happened to Rudy wasn't your fault."

"Wasn't it? They'd be alive if—"

"Oh, fiddle fudge. If what? Damn it, we all make choices. Connie made hers, Rudy made his. Blame yourself for yours, but not theirs."

I didn't have the strength to argue. That last little white pill was kicking in something fierce and I was in no condition to resist what was coming. I watched her shadow move about the room as I drifted off to sleep.

A blast of cold air followed Maria through the door when she returned with a grocery bag and began preparing dinner. "I wanted take-out from Ristorante Giorgio," she said as she peeled off her coat, "but they were closed. I hope you don't mind my cooking."

I didn't mind at all, since I got to watch her. She'd changed into skin-tight black yoga pants and a cherry red sweater. A black scrunchie held her mahogany tresses in a ponytail that swished back and forth as she roamed the apartment, cat-like, straightening things up and getting the feel of the place.

Lois Lane had nothing on her.

At one point she paused at Molly's old rocking chair to pat Priscilla's head. She paused again to study, without comment, the framed photograph of Molly that sat atop the bookcase.

Maria turned out to be a pretty good chef. We ate spaghetti on the couch and watched a National Geographic special about whales. We both loved whales. We found we had other things in common, too.

Afterward, she insisted I lay down while she carried the dirty dishes into the kitchen and loaded the dishwasher. When she finally came back and sat down next to me, her eyes fell on the manila envelope lying on the coffee table.

"What's this?" she said, picking it up.

"If you must know, it's an autopsy report."

"Whose?" Her gaze was penetrating.

"Hey, I think there's a special on about global warming."

"Don't change the subject. Is it Molly's?"

I gave a reluctant nod.

Her fingers slid along the envelope's edge. "I guess that means it's not over for you."

"I guess not." I punched the off button on the remote. "Are you okay with that?"

She considered the question. "That depends on whether you plan to include me in whatever you intend to do."

"Figured I would, yeah."

"Really? I thought you always work alone?"

"Normally I do, but when I saw how you handled Evelyn Waters, I decided you might make a pretty good private eye after all."

She smiled. "In that case, I'm okay with it." She set the envelope on the table and lay beside me on the couch. We started making out, and though she assiduously avoided those parts of my body swathed in bandages, every so often she touched a nerve.

I didn't mind at all.

Acknowledgments

Road Kill was inspired in no small measure by the work of the Alaska Innocence Project, with which I am proud to have worked. I continue to be inspired by the work they and members of the criminal defense community do every day in support of our Constitution and the Rule of Law.

Karin Norgard, a talented writer in her own right, not only edited the book, but her keen insights on character and plot are evident throughout. I cannot thank her enough.

Larry Smith at Bottom Dog Press believed in me enough to publish the book, and provided inspiration and support every step of the way. He represents the very best of small-press publishing.

I am immensely indebted to the following for reading the manuscript and offering valuable comments and insights: Deborah Collins, Nancy Dunham, Richard Dunham, Denise Miller, Sarah Norgard, Karen O'Keeffe, Patrick O'Keeffe, Gini Stevenson, and Patty Wildman. I am grateful for their love and support.

Finally, I cannot fail to thank my friends and colleagues at the Firelands Writing Center, who continue to be an inexhaustible source of love and encouragement.

About the Author

R.J. Norgard has worked as a newspaper reporter, photographer, private investigator, and U.S. Army Intelligence officer. His debut novel, *Trophy Kill*, was the first entrée in the Sidney Reed Mystery Series. He lives in northern Ohio, where he is currently working on his third Sidney Reed novel, *Winter Kill*.

A Note to the Reader

If you enjoyed *Road Kill*, please tell others and consider posting a reader review on Goodreads, Amazon, or other sites online.
And be sure to watch for the next installment in the Sidney Reed
mysteries, *Winter Kill*. Visit the author online at www.rjnorgard.
com and on Facebook at fb.me/rjnorgard.

Other Books by Bird Dog Publishing

Lost and Found in Alaska by Joel D. Rudinger, 242 pgs. $18

Mingo Town & Memories by Larry Smith, 96 pgs. $15

Trophy Kill by R. J. Norgard, 256 pgs. $16

Symphonia Judaica: Jewish Symphony and Other Poems
by Joel D. Rudinger, 117 pgs. $16

Words Walk: Poems by Ronald M. Ruble, 168 pgs. $16

Homegoing by Michael Olin-Hitt, 180 pgs. $16

A Wonderful Stupid Man: Stories by Allen Frost, 190 pgs. $16

A Poetic Journey, Poems by Robert A. Reynolds, 86 pgs. $16

Dogs and Other Poems by Paul Piper, 80 pgs. $15

The Mermaid Translation by Allen Frost, 140 pgs. $15

Heart Murmurs: Poems by John Vanek, 120 pgs. $15

Home Recordings: Tales and Poems by Allen Frost, $14

A Life in Poems by William C. Wright, $10

Faces and Voices: Tales by Larry Smith, 136 pgs. $14

Second Story Woman: A Memoir of Second Chances
by Carole Calladine, 226 pgs. $15

256 Zones of Gray: Poems by Rob Smith, 80 pgs. $14

Another Life: Collected Poems by Allen Frost, 176 pgs. $14

Winter Apples: Poems by Paul S. Piper, 88 pgs. $14

Lake Effect: Poems by Laura Treacy Bentley, 108 pgs. $14

Depression Days on an Appalachian Farm: Poems
by Robert L. Tener, 80 pgs. $14

*120 Charles Street, The Village: Journals & Other Writings
1949-1950* by Holly Beye, 240 pgs. $15

Bird Dog Publishing
A division of Bottom Dog Press, Inc.
Order Online at:
http://smithdocs.net

CPSIA information can be obtained
at www.ICGtesting.com
Printed in the USA
JSHW022224040122
21806JS00001B/3